MICHAEL R. JOHNSTON

WHAT ROUGH BEAST

Book Three of the
Remembrance War Series

This is a **FLAME TREE PRESS** book

Text copyright © 2022 Michael R. Johnston

FLAME TREE PRESS
6 Melbray Mews, London, SW6 3NS, UK
flametreepress.com

US sales, distribution and warehouse:
Simon & Schuster
simonandschuster.biz

UK distribution and warehouse:
Marston Book Services Ltd
marston.co.uk

Publisher's Note: This is a work of fiction. Names, characters, places, and
incidents are a product of the author's imagination. Locales and public names
are sometimes used for atmospheric purposes. Any resemblance to actual
people, living or dead, or to businesses, companies, events, institutions, or
locales is completely coincidental.

Thanks to the Flame Tree Press team, including:
Taylor Bentley, Frances Bodiam, Federica Ciaravella, Don D'Auria,
Chris Herbert, Josie Karani, Mike Spender, Cat Taylor,
Nick Wells, Gillian Whitaker.

The cover is created by Flame Tree Studio with
thanks to Nik Keevil and Shutterstock.com.
The font families used are Avenir and Bembo.

Flame Tree Press is an imprint of Flame Tree Publishing Ltd

flametreepublishing.com

A copy of the CIP data for this book is available from the British Library
and the Library of Congress.

HB ISBN: 978-1-78758-653-6
PB ISBN: 978-1-78758-651-2
ebook ISBN: 978-1-78758-654-3

Printed and bound in Great Britain by Clays Ltd, Elcograf S.p.A

MICHAEL R. JOHNSTON

WHAT ROUGH BEAST

Book Three of the
Remembrance War Series

FLAME TREE PRESS
London & New York

For Dennis Troedson,
who first encouraged me to tell stories

Turning and turning in the widening gyre
The falcon cannot hear the falconer;
Things fall apart; the centre cannot hold;
Mere anarchy is loosed upon the world,
The blood-dimmed tide is loosed, and everywhere
The ceremony of innocence is drowned;
The best lack all conviction, while the worst
Are full of passionate intensity.

Surely some revelation is at hand;
Surely the Second Coming is at hand.
The Second Coming! Hardly are those words out
When a vast image out of Spiritus Mundi
Troubles my sight: somewhere in sands of the desert
A shape with lion body and the head of a man,
A gaze blank and pitiless as the sun,
Is moving its slow thighs, while all about it
Reel shadows of the indignant desert birds.
The darkness drops again; but now I know
That twenty centuries of stony sleep
Were vexed to nightmare by a rocking cradle,
And what rough beast, its hour come round at last,
Slouches towards Bethlehem to be born?

'The Second Coming'
William Butler Yeats, 1919

WHAT HAPPENED PREVIOUSLY...

I didn't set out to start a revolution.

All I wanted was to find out who killed my brother, and why. And in the process, I blew the lid off a secret eight hundred years old.

Let's back up a bit.

I'm Tajen Hunt. About eight hundred years ago, a human colony ship had a really bad day. Adrift and losing power, they were rescued by an alien race called the Zhen – nine-foot-tall lizards with nasty claws and a rigid caste system. The Zhen had no idea how to get us home, so they gave us a place in their Empire. Our ancestors traded one thousand years of service to the Empire for a home.

Fast forward eight centuries of this, and thanks to some skill – and some luck – at the Battle of Elkari, I became the first human to be given command of an entire Zhen task force. I was proud as hell when my little fleet was assigned to protect the human colony of Jiraad.

And then I lost it.

Our war with the Tabran Regency had heated up again, and a Tabran task force ambushed my ships over Jiraad, then bombed the planet with kinetic strikes. Millions of humans and aliens of the Empire died on Jiraad, among them my sister-in-law. My government was angry at my loss of the colony, and my brother was angry that I lost his wife. I was drummed out of the service and lost my family in the same week.

Anyway, fifteen years later I was minding my own business when I got a call from my brother, asking for my help. I grabbed my new crew and headed for Zhen:da, the homeworld of the Empire. When I got there, I discovered he'd been killed, leaving my seventeen-year-old niece behind. Fearing I wouldn't arrive in time, he'd left me a message, claiming to have found Earth, the lost homeworld of the human race, and implying the Zhen were after him. My crew and I set off to find Earth. And when we did, we found out that the Zhen had been lying to us since the beginning.

Earth was uninhabited; the great cities of the twenty-third century long since crumbled into dust and overgrown. There was nothing human alive on the planet. The Zhen had been worried humans would become a threat to their Empire, so they destroyed the place. Two hundred years later, they'd found our colony ship, launched long before their strike, and decided to try something different.

So we told everyone, gathered up the disaffected among the human race, and reclaimed Earth for humans again. Then the Zhen tried to take it, and we kicked their butts so hard they ran back to Zhen:da. We knew they'd return, but we'd won.

A year later, they were back. My new husband, Liam, and I were sent to the Kelvaki Assembly to ask for help for our world. While there, we got wrapped up in an internal Kelvaki political mess, and foiled an assassination attempt on my friend Dierka, heir to the office of the Ascendant, the ruler of Kelvak. And while we were gone, we lost Katherine Lawson, my co-captain and friend.

When the Zhen occupied Earth, we went home and began a guerilla war against our oppressors. This time they had some humans on their side, and the whole thing got messy. We did what we could, but every success was met with more pressure from the Zhen.

When we found out the Zhen were going to hit one of our best allies, where humans were gathering to join us, Liam and I left Earth and headed for Shoa'kor Station, where we helped the human and Kelvaki allies there escape the Zhen trap.

After the battle, my ship, an AI that had rescued me in the middle of the battle, took off for an unknown destination with me aboard. We docked with a Tabran ship, where I was greeted by a very much alive Katherine Lawson. After we'd greeted each other, she said something that rocked my entire worldview....

CHAPTER ONE

Tajen

I'd had a long day. So I couldn't have heard her right.

I'd fought my way through a space station under bombardment from Zhen forces. I'd taken down several Zhen in the process, including a Zhen:ko, the leadership caste. That fight had taken a lot out of me; he'd poisoned me and I'd barely made it to a ship. Once the ship's medical suite had given me the antidote and gotten me back on my feet, so to speak, I'd fought a space battle against overwhelming odds and barely got out with my life before being basically kidnapped by an AI – the first I'd ever met – and brought to this ship. And the first thing I'd seen when I got out was that my fellow captain and good friend Katherine Lawson, whom I had thought killed in battle months ago, was alive and well.

So when Katherine told me she'd "introduce me to the Tabrans." I was pretty sure I'd misheard her due to a combination of shock and exhaustion.

"Wait, what?" I stopped dead in my tracks. "You've met them?"

She gestured around us at the cavernous docking bay. "Duh."

"This ship's Tabran?" My hand instinctively went to my sidearm. "Where are they? Seems like there should be crew somewhere around here."

She nodded toward a corridor. "They figured it would be smarter to have me greet you. Otherwise you might have started shooting."

"I wouldn't—" I looked down at my hand, clutching the grip of my pistol. "Well. Yeah, I might have," I said, moving my hand away from my gun. "What do they want?"

"It's complicated," she said.

"What isn't?"

She led me down a corridor to a nondescript door. "Deep breaths," she said.

I gestured toward the door. "Let's just get on with it."

The door opened, and Katherine led me inside, where a human man, a Tchakk, and a Hun waited by a small table. On the table was a silver disc, over which floated what looked like liquid silver, shifting form periodically.

I glanced at them and frowned. "Where are the Tabrans?"

Katherine gestured to the two aliens. "Like I said, it's complicated." She indicated the Tchakk. "This is The Sunset After a Storm. I call her 'Sunset'." Turning to the Hun, she said, "This is Rememberer of Unpleasant Truths."

"What do you call him?"

The Hun spoke up. "You may call me 'Rememberer'," he said. His voice had a sort of metallic tinge to it – not a sound I was used to hearing from a Hun. His accent, too, was decidedly not what I was used to from his species.

I shrugged. "Beats 'Unpleasant', I suppose." I turned back to Katherine. "I thought you said you were introducing me to Tabrans."

"These are Tabrans – or, as they call themselves, the Many That Are One." I drew breath to speak, but she held up a hand. "Quick history lesson: centuries ago, the original Tabran species created a nano-weapon that was designed to wipe out the Zhen. But there was an accident; it got out, and due to a programming mistake, it wiped out the Tabrans."

"That can't be right," I said. "I've fought Tabrans in my lifetime."

"Did you ever see one?" Katherine asked.

"No, never. They don't take prisoners, so Zhen policy was to do the same and destroy all enemy ships. And we never fought ground battles. You know that."

"Right. But remember your history – there was a long period with no contact between the Zhen and Tabran sides."

"Yeah."

She gestured to the Hun and the Tchakk. "Over a few centuries, the nano-cloud released by the Tabrans gained sentience – or, well, several smaller sections of the nano-cloud did, and they either reprogrammed or assimilated the rest. The Tabrans are now sentient nanite swarms." She gestured to the silver liquid floating in the air over the table. "This is what a Tabran looks like in their truest form," she said.

My head was spinning. "That doesn't explain them," I said, gesturing to the aliens.

"The nanite swarms, on their own, lack the ability to process emotion. They operate on pure machine logic." Her face softened as she continued, "That's one of the reasons Jiraad happened."

My heart suddenly beat rapidly, and I could feel heat in my face as my blood rose. Jiraad had been a human colony world settled by the Zhen despite a warning from the Tabrans that it belonged to them. When the Zhen government refused a demand to remove the colony, the Tabrans wiped it out.

I had been there, commanding the colony's defenses in orbit. I'd witnessed the destruction of all human life on the planet, the deaths of millions of people.

Millions that included my own sister-in-law, who had been working with the colonial administration as part of her job with the colonial authority.

My failure to beat the superior Tabran forces had led to her death alongside millions of other humans, to the end of my relationship with my brother and their daughter, and to the end of my military career. I'd spent the next fifteen years on the fringes of the Empire before a message from my brother had brought me back and set me on course to lead a rebellion against the Empire. In all that time, I'd been a wreck, a broken shell of a human, pretending to give no shits about anything. Last year, I'd finally been able to put the ghosts of that experience behind me and begin to move on with my life, but healing is a long process, and I wasn't completely done yet.

"Explain," I snapped.

Katherine said, "They—"

"No," I said, holding up a hand to stop her, and turned to the aliens. "I want *you* to explain."

The one Katherine had called 'Sunset' nodded. As I watched her, I realized a couple of things I hadn't noticed before. Her eyes glowed faintly, though I noticed, as I listened to her, that they appeared to brighten when emotion flared. Her skin, too, had glowing traceries of light beneath the surface, and like the Hun, her voice was oddly inflected and tinged with something electronic. "Not everything about our origins is known," she said, "but Jiraad we remember well."

The Hun, Rememberer, leaned in. "To explain Jiraad, you must know other things. Jiraad was not our first mistake. In an attempt to end the war between the Zhen Empire and the Tabran Regency, one of us attempted to incarnate with a Zhen:ko survivor. But Keeper of Broken Promises did not understand the will of a Zhen:ko."

I held up a hand. "What do you mean, 'incarnate'?"

The human, whom I recognized as Simmons, a crewman I'd known on Earth, spoke up. "That's what they call the symbiotic joining of a swarm with a biological lifeform," he said.

I nodded and looked to Rememberer.

"The Zhen:ko was incarnated without permission. She did not volunteer. Somehow, she was able to affect the will of Keeper of Broken Promises. She killed many of our incarnates, and escaped us to return to the Empire, where she now leads."

"You've got to be kidding," I said. "Zornaav is the One, the leader of the entire Empire. And you're telling me she's a Tabran? I've never heard of her glowing like you do."

"The Empire controls the media," Katherine said. "And you know how they can edit perceptions already."

"But this? It's ridiculous."

"It is no joke," Rememberer said.

My mind reeled. It was one thing to know that Zornaav had been leading the Empire closer to war for years now. It was another to know she was – or had been – a Tabran incarnate. But I was still missing part of the story. "Okay. How does that connect to Jiraad?" I asked.

"When the Empire chose to settle humans on Jiraad, we knew they were aware of our claim to the planet. We sent a message to the Zhen Empire, requiring them to remove the settlement. We were clear that if the colony was not removed, the refusal would be seen as an act of war, and the colony would be destroyed."

"And it didn't occur to you that the humans had nothing to do with that decision?"

"We did not then understand the difference between humans and Zhen," Sunset said.

"Bullshit! You used kinetic bombardment. The math necessary to aim those damn things requires specific scans. You expect me to believe you didn't know we were a different species?"

"Tajen," Katherine said calmly. She placed a hand on my arm, gently pulling my hand away from my gun. I hadn't even realized I'd reached toward it. "He's not the enemy."

I glanced at her. "According to whom? Them? You can't trust them, Katherine. Not any more than we can trust the Zhen."

All three of Rememberer's eyestalks turned toward me. "I do not blame you for your hostility," he said. "But I did not mean we could not tell the biological difference. We knew the humans were not the same as the Zhen in physical form, but we did not realize the dynamic within the Empire between the Zhen and your race. And the message we received from the One seemed clear enough."

He gestured with the arm facing me, and a hologram of Zornaav sprang up in the center of the room. Unlike Zhen displays, which used our NeuroNets to simulate display screens, this one was directly projected from an unseen source. I started trying to figure out how it was done, but the One's face began to speak, and I focused on the voice of my former Empress. "My people on Jiraad are proud to serve, and will be proud to die, for me. But your 'Regency' will regret any move made against us. Do not tempt us to go to war with you."

"But you did," I said.

"Yes. We had delivered an ultimatum, and the Zhen refused to comply. We had told them what we would do. Having said it, it had to be done."

"It *had* to be done?" I sputtered. "You *had* to kill them all?"

"It was the will of the Corporate." Before I could speak, Rememberer raised his arm in a human gesture. "At that time, the membership of the Corporate was entirely composed of non-incarnated nanite swarms. It was thought they could rule better without interference from emotions, acting purely logically."

"So it was *logical* to kill millions."

"Yes," he said. "Logical. But…in the end, it was not the right thing to do."

I glared at him, and my voice was a study in quiet rage as I asked, "And what brought you to that point of view?"

Rememberer's eyestalks bent toward the floor. After a moment, he flicked them back to me. "When the fighting was over, we sifted through the remains of the Zhen infrastructure on Jiraad. We came upon evidence of the Jiraad government in the weeks before our attack, asking – *begging*, I believe is the correct word – for the Empire to allow them to leave. We found entries in personal journals, expressing fear and longing for Zhen:da to allow them to return. We found messages sent to Terra, asking for help relocating. We realized we had been blind."

I took a moment to get control of my breathing. "Whatever," I said, turning away from the aliens. "Why are you telling me all this? What do you want?"

Sunset spoke up. "We want your help," she said.

"Fuck you," I snapped, and strode from the room.

★   ★   ★

I was halfway to the docking bay when I realized the only ship I could use to leave was the Tabran-made ship that brought me here. And since Midnight, as the ship's AI called itself, had taken control of our course and brought me against my will by order of its Tabran makers, I wasn't sure I'd be able to convince it to take me home.

Well, worth a shot, I told myself, and kept going. I didn't get far before

I heard someone running up behind me. "Tajen!" Katherine called as she came around the corner. "Wait up."

I kept going. "You coming with me?"

She grabbed my arm and pulled, stopping me. "Tajen, they're not the enemy."

I spun to face her, jerking my arm out of her grip. "Are you fucking serious? The butchers of Jiraad aren't the enemy?"

"They're the enemy of the Zhen. They aren't *our* enemy."

I felt the heat rising in my face. "You believe their story?"

"Why wouldn't I?"

"Because it's ridiculous, Katherine!"

She folded her arms. "Is it? Think about it, Tajen. Think about the Empire before we came along. The Zhen:ko running everything, and under them the Zhen:la. And beneath *them* the Tchakk and the Tradd, doing whatever the Zhen told them to. The Hun mostly stay huddled on their world – have you ever been there?"

"No," I said.

"Why not?"

"You know why as well as I do."

"Tell me anyway," she said.

My anger faded as I began to see where she was leading me. "The Hun tried to rebel a few hundred years ago. When the rebellion failed, the Zhen imposed an occupation on them and blockaded their planet. The place is still forbidden to any but Zhen ships."

"Where do the Hun we see in the Fringe Systems come from?"

I shrugged. "I don't know. I assume some have escaped the blockade. Others...." I gestured helplessly to the bulkhead. "From out there, somewhere."

"And you never went to the Hun world because...."

"I told you – it's blockaded."

She nodded slowly, like a teacher urging me toward an answer. "And we all do what we're told to do, in the Empire – or we pay the price." She leaned against the bulkhead. "Look, I remember the visuals from Jiraad. And of course I know how much it eats at you, still. But their explanation...I believe them."

I sat on the deck, my back against the wall. "It's not that simple, for me."

Katherine slid down the wall to sit beside me. "What do you mean?" I pointed to my head and the neural computer nearly everyone in the Empire had. Last year I'd been forced to reboot mine, which had necessitated a very difficult experience facing some old trauma. "When I unlocked my NeuroNet last year, I did it in part by accepting there was nothing I could have done to save Jiraad. The Tabrans won not because I failed, but because they had the superior tech and the superior positioning. But that means I went from blaming myself for those millions of deaths to blaming *them*. And I can't let go of that easily."

"Nobody is asking you to," she said. "They accept the blame, and even your hatred, if you want to give them that. But they do need our help."

"To do what?"

It wasn't Katherine who answered, but Rememberer of Unpleasant Truths, who had walked up to us while we were talking. "To save the Zhen – and your people – from the consequences of our mistake."

"What does that mean, in terms of actual goals?"

"We wish to remove Keeper of Broken Promises from Zornaav."

"But to do that, you'd have to get to her. Which means invading the Zhen Empire." I whistled. "Even with your technological advantage, that would be a monumental task."

"Yes." After a moment, he said, "We have a plan...." He gestured back down the hall, to the conference room.

I stared at him a moment, then shook my head. "What the hell," I said. "You gotta die of something." I stood, gestured him to go before me, and followed him back in, Katherine right behind me. I looked to the Tabrans and said, "All right, I'm – conditionally – on board. What's your plan?"

Sunset After a Storm gestured to me. "You are correct, Captain Hunt, that we cannot simply invade the Empire. We would have to fight our way to Zhen:da, and even with our technological advantage, the cost in lives would be catastrophic. But there is another way." She waved her hand, and the hologram in the center of the room displayed a Zhen battleship, with information displayed around it.

I stepped closer to read the information before making a disgusted noise at myself. "I don't read Tabran."

Sunset gestured to the display, and the information seemed to disintegrate into tiny motes of light that re-coalesced into Zhen words and phrases. "English would have been nice," I muttered, but Zhen was a reasonable alternative, since, thanks to the Zhen education system, I'd been speaking it longer than I had English.

"The *Adamant*," I said. "That's the Zhen ship that abandoned the battle at Shoa'kor."

"Yes," Simmons said. "According to our monitoring, the *Adamant* exchanged communications with your fleet before jumping out of the engagement. They have not returned to Zhen:da."

"Well, no, they wouldn't," Katherine said. "They fled the battle; they'd be executed as traitors."

"But why did they leave?" I asked. "Do we know?"

"They declared themselves no longer interested in supporting the current Zhen government," Rememberer said. "But we do not know if that means they will help us. That is what we want you to find out."

"And how am I going to do that?"

Rememberer changed the display, pulling away from the *Adamant* to display a chunk of the Empire, adding in vector lines. "The logical endpoint of their jump vector is here," he said, indicating a place on the startup. "We want you to find them. If they are willing to help us, bring them into our alliance. If they are not, we want you to copy their ship's database and bring it back to us."

I blinked at him a few times. "You want me to go find one Zhen ship in the Uncharted Regions."

"Yes."

"The wildest, most lawless part of the Empire, where not even the Zhen manage to hold on to anything."

"Yes."

"The *Uncharted Regions.*"

"Yes."

"That's…that's going to be difficult."

"Yes."

I grimaced at him. "Is that all you can say?"

He made a complicated gesture with all three arms. "No. But it is the most logical thing to say."

I pointed at the map. "That's…that's hundreds of star systems, most of them not even explored by scouts. Half those systems don't even have names. Not even the Empire knows what's out there. And that's not even mentioning the natural hazards."

Simmons spoke up. "Which makes it the perfect place to hide."

"But that's the problem – it's the perfect place to hide." I gestured at the display. "The odds of finding one ship in all that – and not getting my own ship cut to pieces by a gravitic anomaly, or ambushed by gods-know-what – are utterly absurd. And that's setting aside that my little rebellion against the Empire put me at the top of their hit list."

"It is our thinking that, as one exile to another, you are the perfect person to approach them."

"Me. All by myself."

"Yes, you. However, you will have some help."

"Oh?"

"The ship we created for you is Tabran technology. This will enable you to bypass many of the known dangers of the Uncharted Regions, such as gravitic shears. The jump drive is more efficient than any the Zhen have made, and the ship is well armed and armored. The AI we created for you—"

"Wait. 'Created for' me?"

Katherine grinned. "The ship's AI was designed to fit with your personality," she said. "They told me about it – they based the AI's patterns on recorded information and psych profiles of you. Should be a match made in heaven."

"Where did they get the profiles?"

She turned to look at Simmons, who suddenly looked sheepish. Pieces fell into place, and something clicked in my head. "Ah," I said. "You were spying for them?"

He looked almost, but not quite, offended. "I prefer to think of it as 'observing,' but I suppose it could be called 'spying' as well. But I never gave them classified information that might interfere with my oath to Earth."

I took a deep breath, wondering if I should be angry. I decided there really wasn't a point to it, and turned back to Rememberer. "Go on."

"I was going to say the ship's AI will be able to hack Zhen systems, if you can get it access."

"Right, that'll do the trick," I muttered. I tried to think of any reason to avoid this, but the truth is, they were right. We needed to know what was going on with the *Adamant*, and if they would help us.

"I'm still not sure I trust you," I said. "But okay. I'll do it. I'll rendezvous with the Shoa'kor fleet, pick up my crew, and—" I stopped when I saw Katherine's expression. "What?"

"We wish you to leave directly from here," Sunset said. "We believe you – and your people's ships – will be safer if the Zhen believe they have eliminated you."

"They saw me jump out," I said. "There were fighters right on my tail. Besides, I'll just jump in, pick up Liam and my crew, and head back out."

Katherine's face tightened. "Tajen, you can't. Our information suggests there were Zhen sympathizers on Shoa'kor, reporting to the Zhen – that's how they knew when to strike. It was a trap."

"That makes sense. Their timing was a little too convenient, but I thought we'd just gotten lucky."

Rememberer said, "We have already fooled the Zhen into thinking you eliminated. This will make your job in the Uncharted Regions easier."

I thought about it. "I'm sorry, but even with that chance, I can't let Liam think I'm dead. Especially if there are Zhen spies in the fleet."

Simmons said, "If he knows you're alive, it will change his thinking, as well as his actions. If the Zhen realize you are alive, they may consider that sufficient reason to intensify their efforts against both the refugee fleet and the Earth, in an effort to draw you out."

"I'm not that important," I said.

"Did you not just point out that you are in fact at the top of the Empire's hit list?"

I opened my mouth to argue, then stopped. He was absolutely right; not only had I said it, but it was the truth. As much as I didn't want to be the Big Man of the Resistance, I very much was. "You really need to stop listening to me, Simmons."

Katherine stepped up to me and put her hands on my shoulders. "Tajen, I know you want to think you're just a part of the Resistance, but that's crap and you know it."

I considered her words. I struggled to keep my emotions from my face, my eyes and lips pulling downward. As much as I hated to admit it, they were right. Knowing I was out here would change Liam's choices, and could put the fleet in greater danger. I nodded. "Okay," I said. I looked to Katherine. "You coming with me, at least?"

"No," she said, removing her hands from me. "I've got my own mission."

I looked askance at the Tabrans and then back to her. "What impossible thing are you doing?"

"Short version? I'm headed into Marauder space."

I blinked at her for several seconds. "You're insane."

A slow smile spread across her face. "Probably," she said. "But I can handle it."

"Psh. Of course you can." I took a moment to reflect on the craziness that had become my life. "Okay, let's talk about this plan of yours."

CHAPTER TWO

Liam

I was going to kill Tajen Hunt.

Yes, he was my husband. Yes, I loved him. But I was going to kill him. Because in the middle of a battle, while I was trapped in my turret, he left our disabled ship on his own to rescue allies on Shoa'kor Station. He didn't wait for me to get free so I could go with him, and he didn't take anyone with him. He went alone, into an unknown situation, all fire and snark and oh-so-handsome derring-do.

I was going to kill him. But later.

First, I had to get our ship, the *Something Cool*, to the Kelvaki ship *Drokkha Nakar* without slamming her into the deck. It wasn't easy; we'd been hit bad in the battle and lost all systems. Kiri, my niece by marriage, had gotten us back up, but the jump drive was toast – if we didn't get aboard the Kelvaki ship, we'd be stuck in Shoa'kor with a lot of pissed-off Zhen.

I dodged some floating debris and then sucked in my breath when a comms signal intruded on my awareness. "Liam?" came my husband's voice.

My heart broke. He sounded like he was on the edge of collapse, as if he'd been fighting for days in a running battle. He sounded broken. "I'm here, Tajen. We got the ship back up. Where are you?"

"Docking bay…time to say goodbye, my love."

A shiver ran down my back as I heard the defeat in his voice. "What are you talking about?"

"The ship I was going to use is destroyed." He paused for breath. "I took the Zhen out, but the Zhen:ko bastard poisoned me. It's making it hard for me to move. I think I'm done here."

"Tajen, don't you dare give up!" I searched the plot, located Shoa'kor. "What docking bay? We'll find you."

"Can't tell. I love you, Liam."

I was suddenly angry. Angry at him for giving up – and for leaving me behind when he went to the station. No way was my husband quitting. I put all the steel of a Zhen drill sergeant into my voice. "Don't you do this, Tajen. Get on your feet, soldier!"

"Can't. Legs're numb. Kinda gettin' hard to talk."

A new voice came over the comms. "I've got his signal, and a ship in better shape," came a female voice. "I'll pick him up."

I switched to that channel. "Who is this?"

"Does it matter? I'm not with the Zhen. Tell him to get on the ship. I've got a med-bay standing by."

I switched back to Tajen. "Tajen, don't give up. There's help coming. Get on that ship, my love!"

There was no reply, but a few minutes later, the unknown pilot came back on the comms. "I have him," she said. "We'll meet you at jump Alpha."

With difficulty, I turned back toward the *Drokkha Nakar* and continued to head for that refuge, my heart hammering in my chest. Kiri somehow managed to keep her mind on her job, but I nearly slammed us into another piece of dead ship. The collision alert warning finally got through to me and I managed to only scrape part of the ship against it, but the screaming metal of that scrape brought me back to my job.

The fight was still going on. I needed to get us to the Kelvaki carrier and convince them to get me a new ship. I was just starting to formulate my argument when the antigrav generator crapped out and the *Something Cool* slammed to the deck.

"Ouch," Kiri called from behind me, at the engineering station. "Sorry, I couldn't keep it stable."

"We're landed," I said. "And any landing that doesn't kill you is a good one."

"Not sure Tajen will agree when he sees this ship."

I unstrapped and extricated myself from the pilot's chair. "Can't disagree. Her name doesn't really work anymore. Maybe we should change it to *Something That Used to Be Cool*."

She smiled at me as she unstrapped, the expression looking odd on her grease-stained face. I activated my comms implant. "Everyone, off the ship," I called.

Kiri and I made our way through the ship to the exit hatch, where we met Zekan, a Zhen defector who had joined us recently. He was standing, arms raised in the universal gesture of surrender, with a squad of Kelvaki guards holding him at gunpoint. "Whoah whoah whoah," I called, placing myself in front of him. "He's a friendly!" The guards didn't even seem to hear me, but as Injala stepped from the ship and gestured to them, the guns lowered. "This Zhen:la is under my personal protection," she said, loud enough that the Kelvaki working – and gawking – nearby could hear. "He is an ally to the humans, and at least for now, to the Kelvaki." She lowered her voice to normal levels. "Though he is to be kept away from restricted areas," she said. "My apologies, Zekan."

Zekan lowered his arms. "No apologies necessary. I would do the same, were our positions reversed."

Injala inclined her head. "I must report to the ship's captain," she said. She gestured to the commander of the guards. "Please escort my companions to the diplomatic lounge."

"At your command, *Kaar* Injala."

"Wait," I said. "Injala, it's still bad out there. I need to help."

She held her hand up in a warding gesture. "I understand, Liam. But right now there is little we can do. I will report to the captain and explain the situation. There are...forms to be obeyed. But I will return, and we will find your husband. Trust me, yes?"

I nodded. What else could I do? She turned and left us, moving quickly out of the bay. The rest of us were led to a nicely appointed room not too far from the docking bay. The guard captain showed us how to access the refreshments, then let us know there would be guards outside 'for our convenience' before leaving us alone.

When the door shut, Kiri said, "We should assume we're being watched and listened to."

"Well, yeah," I said. "But it's not like we've got anything to hide from the Kelvaki. We're not their enemies, Kiri."

"Okay, good point," she said. "Sorry. I've been working under operational security mode for a while now. Hard to let go."

"I understand," I said, taking a seat. "But Injala's right, there isn't much we can do right now."

"Should we not be helping the Kelvaki bring more of your ships aboard?" Zekan asked.

"We probably would be, Zekan, if it was just Kiri and me. But the Kelvaki aren't going to trust you just yet. I suspect Injala asked for all of us to be brought here as a safeguard for you – otherwise she might have been required to put you in the brig for now."

"I see," he rumbled. "Then I shall endeavor not to, what is the human expression? 'Overturn the boat'?"

"Close enough," I said with a grin. "Now. As fraught as things still are out there, let's sit and catch our breath. You never know when we might have to start running at full speed again."

Kiri seemed to shake herself. "Liam, how can you be so calm? Tajen is—"

"I know," I said with a transparently false cheerfulness. "But if I don't pretend things are okay, I'm going to fixate on how my husband is out there on his own, and I'm nowhere close enough to help, and then I'm going to lose my damn mind. So let me pretend, hm?"

"Understood," she said, sitting down beside me.

I put my arm over her shoulder and she tucked herself into me. "Have faith. He's going to be okay." Even I couldn't be sure whom I was trying to convince.

"Faith in what?"

I thought a moment. "Tajen's stubbornness."

She snorted despite her nervousness. "That'll work."

I tried to follow my own advice, I really did. But I was practically vibrating with my need to get back out there. My knee wouldn't stop jumping. I saw Kiri notice it, smirk at it, and decide to say nothing.

Nearly a half hour later, Injala returned. I jumped up the moment she was in the room, ignoring Kiri's yelp as her support left her. "Can we get a ship and get back out there?"

She held up a hand. "There is no need, the battle is all but over. What we need right now is help getting your people – those in ships without jump capability, as well as those we are evacuating from Shoa'kor – aboard. There are more than we expected."

"Let's go," I said.

As we walked down the corridor back toward the docking bay, Kiri stayed glued to my side. "What about Tajen?"

I took her hand and gave it a squeeze. "He can take care of himself," I said. "Provided the ship made it through the battle."

Injala said over her shoulder, "The ship made it. Tajen jumped out a few moments ago."

"Whoever that was who picked him up said they'd meet us at jump Alpha. We'll see him soon," I said.

The docking bay we'd landed in was small, and it had been busy but not overly so. This one was huge, and it was unbridled chaos. Kelvaki crew hustled back and forth, landing ships and getting them unloaded, then clearing the ships out of the way so the next could land. Kelvaki and human shuttles were coming in, dropping their passengers, and then heading back to pick up more.

I didn't wait for instructions; I could see a Kelvaki officer having trouble communicating with a group of humans. I jogged over to them. "I've got this," I said in Kelvaki. "Where should I take them?"

The Kelvaki flicked a claw at me, sending me a guidance program. "Lakala barracks. Human food and water there already."

"Thank you." I took the humans to the dorm, got them situated, and went back for a new group. As I arrived back in the docking bay, something exploded, a wave of pressure slamming me to the deck. I slowly got back to my feet and looked for the source of the blast. A human shuttle was burning; one of the engine pods was on fire. I looked around wildly and grabbed a fire extinguisher, then ran toward the shuttle. Skidding to a stop fifteen feet from the fire, I realized I didn't know how to activate the device. "Shit!" I said, hefting the canister to read the Kelvaki text. "Fuck, I'm an idiot," I muttered to myself, and triggered the extinguisher, pointing it at the flames.

As the fire-retardant foam hit the flames, they shrank but did not go out. A Kelvaki came up to me and joined with his own extinguisher as others continued to get passengers off the shuttle, some of them on stretchers.

"Fall back!" a Kelvaki voice behind me shouted. I glanced at the shuttle and realized there were no more passengers coming off. I backed up, a heavily muscled and clawed hand on my shoulder guiding me as I continued to spray the foam. My extinguisher ran out. I held on to it; one of the first rules of working on a ship is you don't just toss things away that might come back to hurt you later. Another Kelvaki came up and took it from me. "Hold here," the Kelvaki guiding me said. "They're going to push that shuttle out."

"Push it out?"

"It's blocking the bay," he said. "We have too many ships incoming to leave it there."

"Won't it just block the entrance from space?"

He gestured to the bay's entrance. "Watch."

A large ship-tractor, usually used to move unpowered ships in and out of deep storage, rolled up to the shuttle and pushed it out of the bay. Once it was floating in space, a small swarm of drones flew down from racks in the ceiling, attached themselves to the shuttle, and simultaneously fired their small engines, shoving the wreck 'down' relative to our reference. Almost as soon as it was out of the way, more shuttles flew in, landed, and began discharging humans from Shoa'kor. The drones returned a moment later and slotted themselves back into their ceiling perches.

Kiri and I leaped into action. One of the first men off the shuttle was pouring blood from a head wound. I pulled him aside into a workshop alcove and got him to sit while I checked the wound. "*Medic!*" I yelled.

A passing Kelvaki crewman thrust a human medkit to me. "No medics to spare," he said. "All engaged."

Opening the medkit, I said to my patient, "Hey, don't worry. I'm not a professional, but I've been trained in battlefield first aid. You're gonna be fine." I used some wipes to clean the wound. "This actually isn't too bad." I picked up a can of nanite-based healing foam. "This'll stop the bleeding, clean the wound, and seal it up. You won't even have a scar." Once I'd sealed it all up, I patted him on the shoulder and handed him over to a Kelvaki crewman. I turned back toward the bay and found I had a line of injured people waiting for me. "Okay then." I waved the first one forward. "Hi! I'm Liam, and I'll be your first aid provider today." The woman started to chuckle, but winced in pain, holding her left arm in place with her right. "Oh, shit," I said. "I"m sorry, you're hurt and I'm trying to be funny. Here, sit."

When I was done helping her, I moved to the next, and so on. I don't know how long it took, but it seemed like hours. When it was over, I had nine completely used-up medkits stacked beside me, a sore back, and a weary soul. I took in a deep breath, held it, and released it slowly. I didn't sit so much as collapse onto a convenient crate. "By the Nine," I said to nobody in particular. "That was hard."

"One should be careful invoking the Nine," Injala said, as she entered the alcove and sat beside me. "They do not always react kindly to those who speak of them."

"It's fine," I said. "I'm not even sure they exist." The Nine were a quasi-religious figure in the Kelvaki culture. Not gods, per se, but beings who ascended somehow to godlike power and now helped guide the universe. Originally they'd been thought to all be Kelvaki, but as the culture met new beings, the belief began to shift, and now most people thought the Nine were a mix of species – if they thought of them at all. Me, I considered them to be a neat idea, but not much more.

Her ears quivered to signal her amusement. "I hear that a lot these days," she said. "It doesn't matter. If you are ready to move, I can take you to your quarters. You will need sleep for what comes next."

"When do we jump?"

"About a minute ago."

I blinked. "Really? I totally missed the transition."

"What do you mean?"

"I get a little bit nauseous every time a ship I'm on jumps into or out of slipspace. Tajen—" At mention of my husband, I got a lump in my throat and swallowed it before continuing. "He doesn't believe me."

"Some Kelvaki experience this. Not many, but some."

"Really? I'd never heard that."

She tilted her head. "The power of machismo often crosses racial boundaries."

I laughed as I remembered the Kelvaki council member Aljek. "Yeah. So, what will I need sleep for, exactly?"

"This task force is without leaders. When we reach jump point Alpha, you and Tajen will need to take charge of the fleet."

"What about the commander of this ship?"

"Captain Tanarakh commands the Kelvaki ships in the fleet. But he cannot be seen to be in command of the fleet as a whole. This must be a human-led force. Tanarakh intends to transfer you and your team to the human flagship as soon as we reach Alpha. Tajen can meet you there, and the two of you will be in charge."

"We have a human flagship?"

"A Kelvaki-built warship – we have modified the consoles for human use. We will keep Kelvaki crew on board until your own is fully trained, but the ship must become human. Kiri is looking for humans in the fleet who have the relevant experience to shorten the learning curve." Her ears quivering, she said, "You get to name it."

"Oh joy," I said.

"Think carefully," she said. "It will be an important ship."

"Oh, don't go there," I said. "Just…let me deal with all that later. Right now I need sleep."

"Of course," she said, helping me to my feet. "Come on. It's just down the hall."

★   ★   ★

We exited slipspace at jump point Alpha two days later. Not everyone was there, but that was to be expected – no two ships travel through slipspace exactly the same, including the amount of time a jump takes. The rest of the ships would arrive soon.

I transferred to the human ship along with my team and Injala, who would help me train the human crew. Most of them were already trained but they came from various ships and most didn't have military experience; none of them were used to working together. It would be our job to forge them from a collection of half-trained space-monkeys into a team capable of working together in high-stress situations.

I was mildly irritated to find Tajen hadn't arrived yet; he'd never given me the full list of rendezvous points he'd planned, on the theory that nobody should get those until we needed them. Until he arrived, I was working at least partly in the dark. "What the hell am I doing here?" I asked myself, leaning on a viewport, looking out at open space and the fleet of ships that had fled Shoa'kor.

"Leading," a man said from behind me. "And, so far, you're blowing it."

I turned. Jeremy Quince was standing in the doorway to the observation lounge. He'd been the station administrator at Shoa'kor for the last few years, and a pain in Tajen's ass for years before that. He wasn't really a bad guy, just a moderately good guy with an abrasive attitude and a total lack of fucks given about what people thought of him.

I liked him.

He was leaning on a cane, one of his legs wrapped in a nanite cast and nanite bandages wrapped around his head. What skin I could see was heavily bruised. "Quince," I said. "You look like shit."

He eased himself into a seat, wincing in pain. "Yeah, well, I got shot to shit by the Zhen. Even nano-meds take time. They say I'll be better in a few days, but…." He paused to cough, the hacking doubling him over. He sighed as he pulled himself back up. "I'm not sure I believe them."

I leaned back against the viewport. "So, I'm blowing it?"

"A bit, yeah."

"Would you like the job?"

"Sure," he said. "But we both know I'd be terrible at it."

"I'd still rather it was someone else's job," I said.

"Alas, it's yours, and you're stuck with it. But...." He grinned, then the grin became a cough. "...as your husband recently reminded me, I have skills that can help."

"You do at that. I—"

I was interrupted by Kiri entering the lounge at speed. "Liam, we've got a problem," she said by way of greeting.

"What is it this time?" I asked.

"We've got seven ships with failed jump drives."

"You're kidding."

"Wish I was. Four of them can't be fixed, but they're smaller ships, so we can move their passengers and crews to other ships easily. Two of them can be repaired with parts they have. The last one, the *Liquid Asset*, jumped before their drive was ready. They just arrived, and their drive practically exploded. I already checked; nobody in the fleet has the parts to repair it."

"Shit."

"It gets worse. The *Liquid Asset* is big, and it's got a lot of people on board."

"How many?"

"Twenty thousand."

"*Shit*." I thought a moment, then said, "Can we move them to other ships?"

"Yes. But we have two options: do it fast, or do it right. If we do it fast, we'll end up with some overcrowded ships and have to adjust later. It'll take time to do it without causing problems."

Quince raised a hand. "I can handle that," he said. "Seems like a pretty simple logistical problem."

Kiri looked at him, then to me. I nodded. "That's Quince's problem now."

"Got it," she said.

"Anything else?"

"Not right now," she said. "I'm sure something'll come up."

"I'll be waiting when it does," I said. She left, and I turned to Quince. "So. How am I blowing it?"

He grinned. "I think you might have it figured out already," he said. "Stop trying to do everything yourself. You're the boss, but let the rest of us do what we're best at. You do what you're best at."

"And what's that?"

"The thing I'm *not* best at. Get along with people. Hold us together, make the hard calls, and then get out of our way so we can do what we need to."

"I'm only in charge until Tajen gets here to take command," I said. "I'm not looking to do this full-time."

He waited a beat before answering. "We'll see how that works out," he said. "But for now, I'd better get on resettling those civilians." He levered himself out of the chair and headed for the door. As he passed through, he said over his shoulder, "You're not Tajen. But that's not necessarily a bad thing. Your husband is a good man – but you're much more flexible in your thinking. You're going to need that to keep this fleet together."

Alone again, I thought about what he'd said. He was right, in a way. Tajen wasn't unable to change, but he was a bit – maybe more than a bit – black-and-white in his thinking. You were either a friend, or an enemy; good, or bad. People could change, but once Tajen had an opinion about someone, it was bloody hard to change it. He was a good pilot; one of the best I'd ever seen. Give him an objective and there was nobody better at getting it done, usually with a smart-ass remark along the way. But he wasn't good at setting policy. He always said that once the war was over, he intended to retire and let the politicians take it from there.

The way things had been going, I found myself really hoping he'd have the chance.

★   ★   ★

Three days later, I stood on the bridge of the newly christened Earth warship *Litvyak*, tapping my hand on the console in front of me, waiting. Beside me, Injala stood, quiet. In my peripheral vision I could see her watching me. "I know," I said. "He's coming."

Her voice gentle, she said, "He should have been here days ago."

"Maybe he got delayed by something."

"Liam, your husband is one of the best pilots I've ever seen. If he is *this* late, he's not coming."

For just a second, I held my breath. I told myself to start breathing again, forcing slow, steady breaths. "He's coming."

She began to speak, but was interrupted by the sensors officer. "Jump signature, one ship!"

"Who is it?" the captain asked.

"It's our scout ship, Captain. He's hailing us."

"Put him through."

The pilot's voice came over the bridge speakers. "*Litvyak*, this is scout vessel *Lovat* reporting in. We found Captain Hunt's ship. It looks like he jumped out of Shoa'kor on a short jump, sir."

Short jumps were a favored tactic of Tajen's whenever he couldn't get a proper line on his preferred destination. He'd line up a quick jump, just to give him breathing room, then realign and jump when he shook the pursuit.

Something in the *Lovat* commander's phrasing percolated through to me, and I felt sick. I leaned on the console for support. "Is Captain Hunt all right?"

There were a few seconds of silence. Then, "No, sir. The ship...it was in pieces, sir. We identified it from a still-functioning transponder, but there wasn't much left. It looks like the Zhen caught up to him, sir."

I tried to keep my voice steady as I asked, "Did he eject?"

The scout commander's voice was quiet. "No, sir. The escape pod was in the wreckage. It had no integrity. There was no sign of Captain Hunt."

My fist slammed into the console before I knew I was going to do it. A long string of curses followed, in English, Zhen, and Kelvaki. When it was over, I was breathing hard and leaning heavily on the console in front of me. I took several cleansing breaths before straightening up and turning to the *Litvyak*'s captain.

"Who's in charge of the fleet?"

She was about to answer when Injala spoke. "You are."

"She's right, sir," the captain said. "Tajen left word that in his or Katherine's absence, you were in charge."

"Well, that was stupid of him."

"Do not do that," Injala said. "He trusted you to lead. So *lead*."

I tried to find a way to offload this responsibility. But I couldn't. She was right – Tajen had trusted me. I couldn't let that be proven wrong; at least, not on purpose.

"Ah, crap," I said. "Captain Zhang."

"Yes, sir?"

"Signal the fleet to plot a jump to rendezvous point Beta. Send the *Drokkha Nakar* with a fighter group ahead to protect them. We'll remain to hold the rear. I'll be back by then. For now, the bridge is yours."

"Aye, sir."

I made my way back to my quarters and sagged down onto the bed. I felt wrong, and I couldn't figure out why. My husband was dead; I should be crying, at least. Raging, at worst. But other than my expletive-laden anger when I first heard, I was completely numb, and not sure why.

So I just sat and stared into space, wishing I could feel something.

CHAPTER THREE

Katherine

I turned to look out the cockpit window at Tajen's ship. Activating my comms, I said, "Good luck."

Tajen's voice came back over the channel. "Well, now you've fucked me," he said. "It was going to be easy. Now it's just gonna be a complete shitshow."

"Consider it a service," I said. "You'd be bored if everything went to plan."

"You've got me right," he said. His voice became serious as he added, "Good luck to you too. I'll see you—"

"—when I see you," I said, finishing the old spacer's farewell, and cut the link. I turned my attention back to my controls and pulled the ship onto the trajectory for Marauder space.

The Marauders were a loose conglomeration of raiders operating out of a region of space that was well outside Imperial control. They'd been around for centuries, preying on ships of the Empire, the Kelvaki, and probably even the Tabrans. Nobody knew much about them; ships had been sent into Marauder space, but few returned, and most spoke of barbaric behavior. There was some trade on the edges of their space between their raider clans and less-than-reputable traders, but mostly they survived by piracy.

As Rememberer had explained it, back when the original Tabrans had wiped themselves out in the biggest 'oops' in history, the nanite swarms had used Tabran technology to leave the homeworld and reach the colonies; their programming led them to annihilate the Tabrans with ruthless efficiency. This led to chaos throughout the Tabran Regency.

Some outposts were left entirely abandoned, and the Marauders took a few of them for their own.

One installation was the last known location of a control mechanism able to manipulate and even destroy Tabran nanites. In the aftermath of the Outbreak, the nanite swarms had deliberately destroyed and purged from Tabran computer systems all record of the device's workings, an act of desperate self-preservation as the biological Tabrans had tried to destroy them. The installation had been taken over by the Marauders, and had been in their hands for centuries.

My mission was to find that device in Marauder space and retrieve it, along with any other lost Tabran science or machinery. The hope was it was still functional; if not, the Tabrans were fairly sure they could reverse engineer it more quickly than they could create the tech from scratch.

"One thing I don't get," I said to Simmons. "They know how they work, right? The Tabrans, I mean – they know how their own nanites work."

"Of course."

"Then why can't they recreate the technology without the device?"

He pursed his lips. "Rememberer did not tell you everything," he said. "The original nanite swarms didn't just delete the reference material for the control mechanism; they also rewrote their own code to make any research into that sort of control impossible. That they are even willing to entertain using this device against the Zhen shows how desperate they are."

"But…why? Tabran tech is light-years beyond the Zhen."

"In some ways, yes. Their FTL systems are better, their communications tech is much more refined, and they have better weapons. But in other ways, there is parity between them. And the Tabrans as they are now do not innovate. Eventually, the Zhen will catch up, and they're afraid that if that happens before they fix their mistakes, it will be catastrophic for the galaxy."

"You mean the Kelvaki and Tabrans."

"No." Simmons looked at me. "They don't discuss it much, but they are aware of other civilizations out there. Some of them would be ripe for conquest if the Zhen knew where to find them. The Tabrans see part of their role as protecting everyone else from the consequences of their past actions."

"This is all *very* interesting," said a sarcastic voice from the console, "but we've been ready to jump for a while now. Can we get moving?"

I rolled my eyes at the AI. Dagger in the Dark was, like Tajen's AI, supposedly designed to meld nicely with my personality. I wasn't sure what made the Tabrans think I needed a sarcastic, snippy AI, but that's what I had. I did appreciate his baritone voice and Terran accent, though. It reminded me of my childhood.

"I saw that," the ship said, voice dripping with disdain. "Such a rude gesture. It's a wonder you were never taught better."

"Sorry, Dagger."

"I suppose I'll forgive you," he said. "This time."

"You're too kind."

"I have been thinking that very thing," he said, deadpan.

I suppressed any reaction and took us to slipspace.

★   ★   ★

Three weeks later, we dropped out of slipspace. I swung the ship around, lining up the vector for our next jump. The space around us appeared empty, the far-off sun of this system little more than a bright point of light no bigger than my fingernail. "Tajen was right," I said.

"I beg your pardon?" Simmons said.

"He said once that space is big and boring, with occasional pockets of 'fucking scary'." I gestured out the viewport. "Welcome to big and boring."

"I guess we should hope that we do not run into anything fucking scary."

I grinned at such language spoken in Simmons's habitually measured tone. "I think the likelihood of that is pretty slim. We'll find something awful out here, I guarantee it. Just a matter of how long it takes."

Seconds after I said it, alarms started blaring. Dagger spoke, his voice cutting through the alarms. "Multiple contacts closing in."

"That was faster than I expected. What the hell are they?" I asked.

Simmons's hands fluttered and flew over his console. "Confirmed," he said. "Trying to lock on."

The ship shuddered as something – or several somethings – exploded against the shields. I fought to control the ship. "They're mines," I said. I reversed thrust, moving the ship away from the mines' detectors. "Dagger, can you do anything here?"

"Point-defense cannons activated," Dagger said. "Scanning for more."

A few small explosions shook the ship, but the damage was absorbed by the shields. "How many of those things can we take?" I asked Simmons.

"Not many," he said. "I counted eleven detonations, and our shields are down to sixty percent of capacity. There are many more mines left in the field."

An image took form in the navplot. Dagger said, "The minefield is globular in form. Standard Marauder mine types, according to my records."

"Can we take them out?"

"Yes – and no. The outer layer of mines is made up of homing mines, designed to find and attack ships entering the area. After that, the layers alternate between turret mines, missile mines, and more homing mines. The turrets and missile launchers won't move to attack, but they will fire on any ship in their detection range."

I frowned. "Any idea what it is they're protecting?"

"There is a structure at the center of the sphere." A hologram of the object appeared in the space between me and Simmons, along with measurements.

"Looks like a station," I said. "A big one. And it looks Tabran."

"It is also heavily damaged," Dagger said. The hologram focused in on a section of the station where a hole had been blasted into the structure big enough to pass our ship through. "Unfortunately, I cannot focus on the debris inside at this range."

"Guess we'll need to get closer," I said.

"Are you sure that's wise?" Simmons asked.

"Of course it isn't," I said. "But it's part of our mission. So find me a way through the minefield."

Simmons considered the situation. "Will our stealth system hide us from the mines?"

Dagger's reply was icy in its precision. "Even if the stealth system hides our heat signature and EM emissions, the gravitic sensors will detect something nearby and attack it. No system can hide our effect on spacetime at that close range."

"Let's use that against them," I said.

"How?"

"Dagger, how many drones are we carrying?"

"We have thirty repair drones and twenty sensor drones in storage," the ship said. "In our active magazines, there are ten drones of each type."

"Okay. What will the homing mines do if we fire on them with our plasma weapons?"

Dagger answered, "They will explode."

I tried not to laugh at his aggrieved tone. "But others won't come looking for the source?"

"I cannot say for certain," he said. "But it's not a usual program for mines, as you are no doubt aware."

"Just checking to see if your advanced systems know more than my meat-based brain," I said.

"Now you're just trying to flatter me," he said, his deadpan voice dripping with feigned offense. "Keep it up," he added in a brighter tone. "I quite like it."

I turned to Simmons. "We'll take out the first layers with the plasma beams. Once we've burned through the ones we're in range of, I want you to launch drones loaded with ECM toward the turret and launcher mines. Get them in close. If you can get them to buzz the remaining homing mines on the way in, so much the better."

"Confirmed," Simmons said. "Prepping the drones now."

"Dagger, ready?"

"First mines targeted," he said.

"Fire." The bright white of plasma fire stabbed out into space. Dagger's systems fired, switched targets, and fired again, far faster than I could have on my own. Tajen almost always prefers to control his weapons on his own, and he loves to talk about how good he is at dogfighting. That sort of thing works pretty well in close-quarters ship-to-ship combat, but at the distances involved here, not even he could hit anything. The precision of the computer and its targeting and fire-control systems is far better than any living being at targeting long-range fire.

"Reading explosions," Dagger said. The viewport showed only a few small flashes at this distance, but the scans showed mines blipping out of existence. After several minutes of sustained fire, the guns went silent. "No more targets in range," Dagger reported.

"Launching drones," Simmons said. "First wave away."

We watched the drones approach the field on the tactical plot. Hopefully, the drones would cause the mines to attack each other, forcing the minefield to clear more of itself for us. I wasn't sure it would work – the Zhen doctrine for minefields was to send in waves of specialized drones designed to explode them. But we didn't have any on board, and the Tabrans hadn't given us anything specifically for minefields. "Dagger, I should have asked. What's the usual Tabran doctrine on dealing with minefields?"

There was a moment's silence, and Dagger said, "There isn't one. In the time since the emergence of the new Tabrans, they simply haven't been a factor."

"Isn't there anything from before that?"

"Not in my databanks. We have created a gap in the field large enough to get inside. However, the mines will adjust their position within an hour. We'll be surrounded again when we try to leave."

I took a deep breath. "We'll figure something out."

"Should we not figure it out before we enter the station?"

"Probably," I said. "But humans are like that. You're the hyper-intelligent spaceship, you figure it out."

His voice dripped with derision. "As you command, Captain."

In truth, I wasn't worried about it. I knew that most Marauder minefields required a central computer to control them, and I didn't see any reason for this one to be any different. All we had to do was find that central computer and deal with the problem there. But it had already become clear that Dagger had an inflated opinion of himself, and I couldn't resist the temptation to show him he didn't know everything about the galaxy.

As we came closer to the station's docks, I said, "Dagger, any life readings?"

"I'm reading no life signs on the station," he replied.

The station was weird-looking. Most human and Zhen stations are either cylinders or stacked rings, and Kelvaki stations tend to be spheres with extensions at the poles. Tabran stations I'd seen before were diamond-shaped.

This thing was.... Well, it looked like an illustration from a child's book I'd read a lot when I was little, about Earth's animals. It looked like a giant squid. There was an elongated diamond shape at one end, with eight large arms emerging from the other end. They looked articulated, and some of them were in seemingly odd positions relative to the others. They were big – my ship could easily fit inside one of them and still not scrape the sides. "What are those?" I asked Dagger.

"According to records, stations like this serviced ships too large for the docking bay. They would attach to those arms to transfer cargo and personnel."

"I'm seeing multiple hull breaches," Simmons said.

The beams of our lights found the edge of one of those breaches. It was at least thirty feet across. "Whatever hit this station, it was powerful," I said.

"I am still not sure what it— Oh." Simmons flicked his hand and highlighted something in the interior of the structure. "Give me light there, please."

Dagger adjusted the beams to light up the area Simmons had indicated. Among the wreckage, a body was hanging, one limb caught in a junction of machinery.

"What is that?"

"It is a Tabran," he said. "One of the original biological Tabrans."

"Dagger, can you confirm that?"

"Confirmed. It appears your desire to explore this station may have been the right call."

"Such effusive praise," I said. "The question we have to ask, though, is why the Marauders bothered to protect a place with no life signs."

"There must be something aboard worth protecting," Simmons said.

"So let's go find it."

*   *   *

Once we'd landed the ship and battened her down, we headed for the equipment room, just inside the main airlock. Simmons reached out to me as if to give me something curled in his fist. I held out my own hand, and he dropped a small object into it.

"What's this?"

"Your spacesuit."

"Seriously?" Zhen spacesuits came in two varieties – the basic type you climbed into, which I'd used for years, or, if you had the money and the connections, the nanite-based suits like Tajen used. Unlike those nanite-based suits, which in their inert form resembled large gray bricks you held to your chest and activated, this was a small black ring with a tiny blue gem in the center of the band. Simmons held his left hand up; he was wearing one just like it, the ring's gem facing outward.

"You're kidding," I said.

"Not at all. It's also your link to Dagger – it will interface with your neural implant when you slip it on." He turned away, then quickly looked back and said, "There will be a slight prickling – don't let it alarm you."

I looked over the ring. "Is it nanite-based?"

"No, it's a quantum fabricator/storage device. Once you put it on, it will figure out your personal dimensions and create the suit perfectly sized for you. When you command it, the suit will be released from its subspace storage."

I looked at the ring a moment. "They are far more advanced than they've let on, aren't they?"

Simmons shrugged. "In some ways they are thousands of years ahead of us. In others, less."

I slipped the ring onto my finger. As it slid down, I could feel it adjust size to match my finger width. A second after I put it on, a line of white-hot pain fired from the ring, up my arm, and into my head. I reached out to the nearest bulkhead for support. "Shit!"

"I did warn you."

I glared at him. "You said 'a slight prickling', not 'a dagger through your brain'."

"Sorry," he said. "It's been my experience that nobody ever feels it the same way."

"Uh-huh." I looked at the ring again. "It changed size when I put it on. Will it resize if I move it to a different finger?"

"Of course."

"Neat."

Dagger's voice came over the comms. "Just don't ask me to explain the math," he said. "I have a feeling my central core would explode at the strain."

"Don't be an asshole," I said.

"Are we ready?" Simmons asked.

"Yeah, let's go."

"The ring has integrated with your NeuroNet," he said. "Just visualize it activating, and it will. Make sure you gather your hair first or you'll end up irritated." He handed me a hair tie.

"You do know I've been doing this kind of thing for decades," I said, gathering my hair into a tight bun. That done, I visualized the suit surrounding me, and tried not to flinch as it seemed to flow like fast-moving liquid from the ring, quickly enveloping me. It was similar to the way the Zhen nanite-based suits worked, but it was different in an odd way I couldn't put into words. "That's...really weird."

"You'll get used to it, I'm sure," Dagger said.

"Interesting." I gestured to the outer doors of the lock. "Shall we?"

The docking bay looked a lot like the one aboard the *Sudden but Deep Understanding That Comes upon You When Least Expected*, the Tabran ship where I'd met Sunset and Rememberer. But where the *Sudden but Deep* was bright and relatively clean as docking bays went, this one was dark, with only some emergency lighting on the far bulkhead. "Looks like the bulkhead is closed," I said.

"On Tabran stations of this age, that will likely be an airlock," Dagger said. I could hear him through my neural implant, as clear as if I were still aboard.

We crossed the bay. Dagger helpfully translated the Tabran writing for me, layering the translations over the Tabran symbols through my NeuroNet. "Here we go," I said, and slapped the command to open the airlock. When nothing happened, I hit it again. "Ideas?"

"Try hitting it again," Dagger drawled. "I'm certain that always works."

"Are we going to have a problem?" I asked him.

"Nobody appreciates humor," he said. "Very well. I'm connected to the airlock's controls. Attempting to create access."

While he worked, I set some drones to disperse through the bay and light the place up. The space was big, but empty – there were no ships left, no wreckage, just bare deck and equipment bays that looked locked down. I frowned. "This place isn't abandoned," I said.

"We read no life signs on the station," Simmons reminded me.

"I'm not saying anyone is here. I'm saying they haven't abandoned it. Not only is there a minefield protecting the place, but there's no debris in here. This place is locked down and cleaned. That implies it's still in use."

"Interesting. A backup base?"

"Could be. We'll have a better idea when we get inside."

The airlock door opened. "Be careful," Dagger said. "I'd hate to have to go back to the Tabrans empty."

"Aww, you'd miss us?"

"No, I'd just be bored. It took weeks to get here."

Simmons and I traded amused looks. We entered the airlock and cycled it. As the inner doors opened, the lights came up, revealing a corridor that looked slightly less lived-in than the docking bay had.

We made our way down the corridor, checking each room as we passed. The fact there wasn't anything alive on-station didn't mean there weren't automatic defenses, so we were careful. But after three levels and several dozen rooms, most of them living quarters that looked as if they'd been untouched for years, I was pretty sure we were safe.

"This is a bolt-hole," I said.

"How do you mean?"

I glanced at Simmons. "Everything is untouched, but set up for immediate occupancy. The station is defended, but there are no personnel aboard. It's a hiding place, a redoubt if they need it."

"Remarkable that nobody else has found it," Simmons said.

"Not really," Dagger said. "Space is big, and most ships wouldn't come this far out, especially not into Marauder space."

"This was Tabran space when the bio-Tabrans were alive," I said. "Why didn't the nano-Tabrans ever reclaim it?"

"It seemed a waste of resources in the early days," Simmons replied, "and by the time they'd come to terms with their existence, the station was already claimed by Marauders." A beat later, he said, "'Nano-Tabrans'?"

I shrugged. "We need a way to differentiate between the living Tabrans of the past and the Tabrans of today." He nodded in understanding but didn't reply.

Eventually we found a computer terminal, completely locked down. "Dagger, can you get in?"

"I'm already in the station's systems," he said. "I have been for some time."

I closed my eyes and counted to ten. "Why didn't you say so? And do not say, 'You didn't ask.'"

Dagger didn't say anything. I took a deep breath in, held it for several seconds, and let it out slowly.

"Your breathing seems altered," he said. "Is there a problem?"

I could not deal with this AI. "Dagger."

He must have heard something in my voice that caused him to relent. "My apologies, Captain."

"Find anything of use?"

"As a matter of fact, yes," he said. "I have a list of Marauder bases and docking codes for each." He waited a beat, then said, "One of them is named 'Dakcha'."

There was a note of triumph in his voice, but I didn't understand. "I'm not familiar with that word."

"It's from an archaic form of Hun," he said. "The closest translation into your language would be 'homefires', a holdover word from the Hun's time as nomadic wanderers that usually means the world of the Hun itself. But the coordinates do not lead to Huna."

"What's the system name?"

"Unknown. But judging by the schematics of the system's defenses, it is an important place to the Marauders. There is an access code algorithm attached. When signaled by the in-system servers at Dakcha, it should give us a working entry code."

My eyebrows climbed toward my hairline. "I've heard legends that claim the first Marauders were Hun. Are you saying that's true?"

"No, I am simply saying that a base is named in the Hun language. However, it is a good place to start looking."

He wasn't wrong. Any place called 'homefires' was probably important, even if what we were seeking wasn't there. It could cut the mission time down considerably in any case.

"All right," I said. "We're done here. Start calculating a jump to Dakcha."

CHAPTER FOUR

Tajen

Slipspace is convenient, but spending days or weeks in a communications cutoff is never exactly what I'd call 'fun'. After spending fifteen years on my own, I'd begun to take having a crew again for granted. Now that I was without them, I was starting to lose my cool.

"Hey, Midnight," I said from my spot lounging on the bunk.

"Yes?"

"Got any entertainment programs in your memory?"

"As a matter of fact, I do." A list of programs blossomed into my visual field. "These are the dramas. I also have comedies," she said, her voice dripping with disdain as she said the word 'comedies'.

"What's wrong with comedies?"

"Nothing, I suppose. But in my survey of human entertainments, drama was superior at illuminating a species' strengths and weaknesses."

"You're not watching the right comedies," I said. "Bring up that list." I perused it, deleting some that I'd hated from the menu. "Some of these are pretty recent," I said. "How'd you get them?"

"We regularly sample Zhen slipnet activity, including news and entertainment channels, to keep an eye on the races of the Empire. I downloaded the most recent data store before we left the *Sudden but Deep Understanding That Comes upon You When Least Expected*."

"Tabran names are too long. Can we shorten that?"

"One could just as easily claim human names are too short. But yes, in practice we often use shorter names when speaking with slower lifeforms."

"'Slower'?"

"Relatively, in terms of input/output, yes. If I was speaking to a Tabran I could hold an entire conversation in less time than you use to take a breath."

"That must be interesting."

"Indeed."

A thought struck me. "Did Rememberer and Sunset speak to each other in that mode during my conversation with them?"

"I wasn't there, but I would not be surprised if they did."

"Huh." I found a video program and selected it. "Here, let's watch this." It was a comedy, supposedly based on a pre-space Earth story, about twins separated after their ship crashes. One disguises herself as a boy to infiltrate a patriarchal society, and sets off a chain of mistaken identities and plots.

When it was over, Midnight was silent for all of thirty seconds before saying, "All right. I stand corrected."

"I was wondering. Do Tabrans tell stories?" I asked.

"The original Tabrans did," she said. "The nanite-based Tabrans didn't, but now that incarnates are becoming a larger part of Tabran society, they are reintroducing fiction. By the way, we're dropping out of slipspace in fifteen seconds for a course change. Do you wish to oversee the navigation plot?"

"You handle it," I said. "Should be interesting to see how their stories evolve."

"I think that—" She stopped abruptly. "I'm picking up a distress call," she said.

"Out here?"

"No, back in Zhen space," she snapped. My eyebrows rose; while Midnight had been a bit playfully acerbic when we first met, she hadn't been quite so snippy. "It's about twenty light-minutes out, a few degrees off our intended course. Shall we check it out?" She added, a moment later, "It seems to be human."

My eyebrows rose even farther; with no known human settlements out this far, I had no idea why a human ship would be out here. "Yes," I said. "But be careful. Much as I hate to admit it, not all humans are on our side."

She set the course and we engaged the chain drive. Unlike slipspace, which is great for interstellar jumps but crap for local travel, the chain drive makes slogging through normal space much easier. It does something with physics I've had explained to me hundreds of times, and all I can ever remember is that it tricks the universe into thinking the ship is going at speeds approaching that of light.

When we dropped out of chain drive, our displays flickered off for a moment. It's not common, but it can happen when ships exit chain drive too close to another ship with active scanners. When the sensor distortions cleared up, we saw a few small human ships near a drifting hulk. The ship was completely unfamiliar to me, an enormous, bulbous ship twice the size of the largest Zhen battleship. "Midnight, you recognize that thing?"

"Negative. It doesn't match anything in my data stores."

"Give me comms."

The comms logo showed up in my visual field. "Unknown ships, this is the *Clear Skies*, answering your distress signal."

A window opened in my view, a disheveled man's face and shoulders showing. "*Clear Skies*, we've got— Hey, you look familiar. You're...." He blinked, trying to place my face. "*Shaak!* You're Tajen Hunt!"

"Yes," I said.

"*Shaak*," he repeated. "Tajen *karking* Hunt."

"Yeah," I said. I cocked my head. "You've heard of me, I guess?"

He blinked at the camera. "You're pretty much the most famous human in history," he said. "I've seen your broadcasts announcing the Zhen's attacks on Earth, and the reports from Earth after that."

I spend so much time convinced I'm not nearly as important or known as people insist I am that I forget my self-perception isn't reality. "Right, of course." I shook my head. "Your emergency?"

"Emergency? Oh!" He looked sheepish. "I'm Jim. We're refugees from Earth. We barely got out before the Zhen took the planet back. We found this old ship and decided to explore it, but...." He looked directly at his video pickup, as if meeting my eyes. "One of our people is lost in there. We know where she is, but something she did caused a problem. Now she's not responding to hails, and we can't get to her. It's too hot."

"Hot?"

"Radiation," he said. "Nothing we've got can handle the rads, even for a short time. She's shielded where she is, but the areas surrounding her are saturated."

"Can you send me your scan data?"

"Yeah. Sending now."

Another window opened, and the scan data appeared. "Midnight, are you seeing this?"

"Of course. It's well within the tolerance levels of your suit."

"What suit?"

A drawer opened in the console to my right, containing a small black ring with a blue gem in the center of the band. "Put it on," Midnight said.

I picked it up and slipped it on my finger.

And then my world went white with pain.

★ ★ ★

"You could have warned me," I said.

Once Midnight had explained the ring's function to me, I'd had no trouble controlling it, but I was still pissed about the pain when it first connected with my implants.

"I'm sorry," she said. "I don't have that issue. I didn't realize it would hurt so much."

That brought a question to mind. "Do you feel anything when you're hit by weapons fire?"

"I feel feedback through my systems. I'm not sure if it's what you'd call pain, but I don't like it."

"That stands to reason," I said. "Nobody likes getting bits of themselves shot off."

"Exactly."

I made my way to the airlock and got suited up. As the outer doors slid open, the two suited figures waiting for me waved in the 'spacer's hello', their right hands rising to their helmets and back down. "Captain Hunt," the one on the right said. "Thank you so much for coming."

"Hi," I said. "Can you lead me to the high-rad zone?"

"Of course," he said. "Follow us."

They led me to the hot zone. "She's in there," he said. "Her name is Pamela." He offered me a handheld scanner, but I waved him off.

"I've got a scanner built into my HUD," I said. "I just copied the data to it."

"Already?"

"Yep."

"Wow," his partner said. "That's some good tech. The stories are true about you."

"Some of them," I said. "Listen, I'd love to talk, but your friend needs help. Anything I need to know about this hulk? Strange layout, weird controls, messages written on the walls in blood?"

"What? No," she said. "We don't know where it came from, but the controls seem pretty intuitive, and the corridors seem pretty standard. Well, for unknown alien ships. And nothing written on the walls."

"Understood," I said. "I'll be as quick as I can." I turned and walked into the high-radiation zone quickly. As I moved, I switched to a private channel. "Midnight, you there?"

"Affirmative," she said, a slight distortion in the signal.

"That distortion caused by the radiation, or range?" I asked.

"Radiation," she said. "Shouldn't get much worse, though."

The walls were odd, no matter what the humans had said. Most species build their corridors either in rectangular cross sections or, in the case of Kelvaki, as hexagonal cross sections.

These were hemispherical in shape, and where the corridors of Zhen and Kelvaki ships were often gray and black metal, the deck of this ship appeared to be black stone, and the walls were covered in what looked like scales of a deep, burnished bronze color. I touched one of the walls and felt a faint vibration within. "Midnight, is this thing powered?"

"The power core is still functional – that's where the radiation is coming from," she said. "But it isn't powering anything else in the ship. And I'm not sure it could – the reactor's shielding is shot. It appears to me that the human who caused the problem tried to restart this ship's engine."

"Before checking the shielding?"

"It could have been an accident," she said. "It's not like they can read the controls. Regardless, the result was an increasing overload in the engine. Radiation levels are higher than they were in the original readings, though well within the safety margin for your suit."

"Question is, what were they trying to do?"

"Do we care?"

I thought about it. "Not really. But the idea of a bunch of random humans experimentally pushing buttons on an unknown alien ship gives me the willies."

"The what?"

"It's a human expression, denoting fear or reservation about something."

"I see." A few moments later, she said, "We are approaching the human crew member."

We found her in the middle of a large empty room. She was unconscious. I crouched over her. "I heard you needed rescue," I said. There was no response. I grabbed her left arm and checked her vitals; they were all within acceptable parameters. "Shit," I muttered.

I looked around the empty space. It was hexagonal, the walls rising a good thirty meters above us to a vaulted ceiling. That was unheard of on a space vessel, where space, if you'll forgive the unintentional pun, was always at a premium.

Above the downed woman, a panel was set into the wall at my eye level. I glanced back at the doorway, which was only slightly taller than a human would build it. Zhen also built panels a bit high for human convenience, but they were much taller than us, on average. These aliens, whoever they had been, didn't seem to be taller; they just liked their panels higher on the wall, apparently.

I frowned at the symbols on the panel. There were no switches, but the graphics seemed to hover just within the surface, as if they were fish swimming in a tank. "Midnight, any idea what these mean?"

"Unfortunately, no, Captain. That language does not appear in my records."

I reached out with my NeuroNet to the human's suit computer. The systems linked up easily, thanks to standardization of comms protocols in the Empire. I accessed her suit camera's log and ran the feed back to before she was knocked out. As I'd suspected, she'd been messing with the console.

I ran it back even further, to when she first walked into the room, and watched what she'd done with the panel. "That's…weird," I said.

"How so?"

I shook my head. "It's just the controls work differently than I'd expect. It's all gestural." I reached out with my right hand and made a grabbing motion over a symbol, which enlarged and changed color. I pulled, as if pulling the symbol out of the console, and it dissolved, another symbol appearing from behind it. I moved that one left, then pushed it back in, and the original symbol replaced it.

I did a series of similar moves, reversing the changes the woman on the floor had made. When I placed the last one, a synthesized voice sounded in the chamber, speaking in an alien language I'd never heard before.

"She's waking up," Midnight said.

I turned toward the woman and waved. "Heya," I said.

Her eyes rose slowly. When she saw me, she backpedaled, her heels slipping on the floor as she pressed herself to the wall. "Who are you?!"

"Hey, relax!" I said. "Pamela, right? Jim sent me to get you. Can you stand?" I took a closer look at her. "You look familiar. Have we met?"

"Um, I don't think so?" She gathered her legs beneath her and stood. She was shaky at first, but managed to support herself fairly well. "Who are you?" she asked again.

"Tajen Hunt," I said. "What happened to you?"

"Tajen Hunt?" she asked, in a tone that suggested she didn't believe me. "*The* Tajen Hunt?"

I blinked a couple of times as I tried to marshal my response. "I'm not aware of another one, so yes?"

"*Kark,*" she said. "You're...you're shorter than I'd expect."

"I get that a lot," I said. "Wait. I'm of perfectly normal height."

"Aren't heroes supposed to be taller than normal?"

"Sorry to disappoint," I said. "So. Again, what happened to you?"

She looked embarrassed. "I was trying to bring the engines back online. Something I did caused some sort of energy surge. Knocked me right out."

"Any idea what it was?"

"No idea. But it picked me up and slammed me against the wall. That's the last thing I remember."

"Lucky it didn't do the same when I reversed your changes."

Midnight spoke up again. "I'm reading a change in the engines. The radiation appears to be falling."

"Great. Can we take her back through yet?"

"Who are you talking to?" Pamela asked.

"My ship. Midnight? Broadcast to Pamela as well, please."

"I'm afraid it will be some time," Midnight said. "I estimate two hours before it will be safe to move her through the corridors."

"Why isn't it safe?" Pamela asked.

"Whatever you did flooded the areas surrounding this room with radiation levels too high for your suit," I said.

"But not for yours?"

I shook my head.

"Huh," she said. "I thought I had the best anti-radiation shielding in the Empire in this thing."

"Mine isn't made in the Empire," I said.

"Oh."

I sighed and looked over the room. "This room makes no sense."

"What do you mean?"

I gestured around us. "Why is there an engine control panel in a giant room with no other instruments? There's no signage except the panel."

"Switch your suit to infrared," Midnight said.

I did so, and whistled at the result. The room was covered in symbols, running from the ceiling to the floor in vertical lines. The script was alien, angular. "That's...interesting," I said. "But what does it mean?"

"Still don't know," Midnight said.

Pamela added, "I don't either."

"And yet you used controls you can't read."

"I'm smart," she said. "I never claimed to be wise."

Something about that phrase tickled my mind, but I couldn't figure out what it was. This woman was familiar, though. "Are you sure we never met?"

"Pretty sure, yeah."

I let it go and gestured back toward the panel. "What were you hoping to gain?"

"I thought, maybe if I could make the engines work, we could use this ship. Or at least restore enough power to work in it without suits."

"But you've no idea what atmosphere the beings who owned it used, or why they abandoned it."

She nodded. "Again, smart but not wise."

I shook my head at the foolishness. "Well, we may never see this again," I said. "Let's give future xenolinguists some fun." I detached a drone from my suit and sent it up the walls, recording the glyphs. When the probe returned to me, I reattached it to the suit and turned to the door.

It wasn't there.

I glanced around the room, and finding nothing but walls covered in the alien script and no doorways, said, "Well, *shrak.*"

"Technological intrusion," Midnight said. "Activating countermeasures."

"Can you keep it out?"

It was a good fifteen seconds before I got a reply. "Apparently not.

Something on that ship connected to my data core, ransacked my files, and withdrew."

"Any idea what it was?"

"Not with any real confidence," she said. "But if I had to guess, I'd say that ship has an AI far more advanced than I am."

"Any idea how I get out of this room?"

"No, I—" The transmission cut off.

"Midnight? Midnight, come in!" I called. "Midnight!"

"That's such a cliché," Pamela said. "Why does everyone do that?"

I shot her a look that said 'Don't start with me' and turned to the control panel. As I did so, both Pamela and I were pushed back against the wall hard enough to rattle my teeth. I struggled to move, but couldn't – I was pinned to the wall as if fastened there by gravity itself, but I felt none of the strain of a high-G field.

I used my NeuroNet to activate my suit's gravity nodes, thinking I could use them to counteract whatever was keeping me pressed against the wall, but they failed to activate.

In the center of the room, an image took form. It was abstract, swirling motes of blue, red, and green light, suggesting, but not perfectly delineating, a bipedal shape. It had the symmetrical limbs of a human, but the shape was slightly taller, with longer torso and arms than any species I'd met. The figure of light leaned in, and a voice came from it, speaking English. "Why are you here?"

"You speak my language?" That seemed unlikely.

"I have accessed your files. Learned your tongues." The voice switched to Zhen. "Do you prefer this one?" And then, in Kelvaki, "Or this one?"

"The first one is fine. And to answer your question, I came to rescue her," I said, my eyes darting to Pamela, off to my right somewhere.

"Why?"

"What do you mean, why?"

"Why did you come? This is a dangerous place. Death is always possible. Why risk it for her?"

I cocked my head. "Why wouldn't I?"

The figure moved closer, the swirling energies of its...well, let's call it a head...so close I couldn't focus on them. "Self-preservation. Expedience. Misanthropy. Selfishness. Fear. Any of these might lead one to refuse help when it is needed. Why didn't you?"

"She's a human being. She needed help. I help people."

"If she were not human, you would not have?"

I opened my mouth to answer, then hesitated. I'd been about to make a joke about thinking twice if it was a Zhen in trouble, but apparently I was learning to control my mouth. "No, I still would have helped."

"And if she were Kinj?"

Wait a minute.

The Kinj were an ancient race who had conquered the Zhen about twenty thousand years ago. They'd tried to mold the Zhen to be more like them, but the Zhen had chafed under their rule, and in the end they'd spent a hundred years wiping out the entire Kinj civilization in one of the bloodiest wars in history. There was probably more to it – I'd gotten the 'simplified version' of the history from a contact, as the history had been suppressed in favor of the Zhen myth of 'bootstrapping' themselves into the space age. They used the myth to assert their superiority to other species and justify their half-assed 'uplift' – what anyone else would call 'enslavement' – of less advanced races.

"I don't know anything about the Kinj," I lied.

"So you would not help those you do not know?" It sounded disappointed.

"I'm not saying that. I probably *would* help. Provided the Kinj wasn't actively trying to harm me, I would see no reason not to."

The figure moved back, as if satisfied. "I am Kinj. I need help."

I cocked my head. "You've a funny way of asking," I said.

"I needed to be sure," it said. "Many have come. Zhen. Some others. None have helped. Some tried to harm me, steal my data."

"What are you, exactly?"

"I am the Intelligence."

"Care to unpack that a bit?"

"The Kinj created me to run the ship. I am its mind, its guiding force."

"Do you have a crew?"

"Once," it said. "All gone now."

"The entire race, or just your crew?"

It seemed to consider this. "Unknown. I have not seen a living Kinj in many thousands of years. I believe they are all dead."

I had the feeling this ship might not know the whole story about the Kinj and how they died. "How long have you been trapped here?"

"In your terms, according to stellar readings, I have been here for twenty-five millennia."

Shrakking hell. That meant this ship had been out here since my people were still fighting among themselves back on Earth, before we even got out of our gravity well. Hell, we hadn't even formed our first civilization. The Kinj had been in space when my people had been barely scraping together a civilization. Given that, I wasn't going to worry about whether they'd been good or bad. I just needed to do what I had to do in order to get out of here.

"I'm not sure how much help I can be to you, but I'll help you," I said.

"Excellent." The pressure keeping me against the wall suddenly released, and I steadied myself on the wall for a moment. "You okay?" I asked Pamela.

Or, rather, I asked the blank spot where she'd been. "Where'd she go?" I demanded of the AI.

"She did not exist."

I sighed. "Is this one of those 'she was an illusion created to test me' scenarios?"

"Correct. I created her from your memory."

"That's why I thought I knew her," I said. And then it snapped home. "For Siharen's sake," I said. "Pamela. She was my babysitter when I was little. I don't remember her being that pretty, though."

"Memory is unreliable."

"What if I'd recognized her immediately?"

"Steps were taken to prevent that possibility. Even so, it was worth the risk to find someone who would help."

"And her friends in the other ships? On this ship?"

"Also created. Some from your memory. Some from my last encounter with your kind. It...did not go well."

"What happened?"

"They tried to steal my data. My ship. Kinj protocols engaged."

"Did any of them get away?"

"One ship," it said.

"Ever seen a Zhen ship called the *Adamant*?" I brought up my scans of the ship from Shoa'kor.

"The ship you are seeking has been here. It did not come close enough for me to test them."

"How do you know what I'm seeking?"

"I read the files your ship AI carries."

"She's not going to like that."

"I interrupted her runtime cycles. She is not aware."

"Any idea where they went?"

"Yes."

"I'll help you – but I want that information."

"This is an acceptable trade."

I looked around the room. "You have excellent VR capabilities. Did I even board your ship?"

The AI cocked its 'head' at me. "You are neither as stupid nor as craven as those who came before you."

And with that, I was back in my ship. Midnight immediately said, "Welcome back."

"What's going on?" I asked, checking the controls as I spoke.

"Oh, nothing much," she said. "But nothing works – that ship's AI took over your NeuroNet feed as soon as we got close, the illusory human ships disappeared, and my systems all shut down. I've been aware, but unable to do anything. They locked me out of my systems."

The Kinj AI appeared in my cockpit, and I nearly jumped out of my skin. "Destroy these nodes," it said. "Once they are destroyed, I will be free to leave this place." A schematic of the system came up, with several locations highlighted.

"What are those?" I asked.

"Traps left in this system."

"By whom?"

"Unknown."

"Great. Today I learned there were *two* ancient space empires when my people were digging in the dirt looking for food. Why can't you take care of them?"

"It took me centuries to locate them. I have no weaponry that is able to attack from these distances, and the ship is immobilized by the energies of the nodes."

"But they won't harm us?"

"They are not designed to operate on anything as primitive as your ship. Our engines and propulsion systems are nothing like yours. They were designed specifically to stop Kinj vessels."

I'd known the Zhen 'bootstrap' was in reality a takeover of the Kinj technology, but I realized now that there had to have been a gap between the end of the Kinj and the rise of the Empire. While Zhen technology was based on the Kinj, there had clearly been some tech loss.

"Were the Kinj the aggressors in their war with these other species?"

"Like all species, the Kinj had positive and negative attributes. I am not equipped to judge them beyond that. If I knew who laid these traps I might be able to judge who was the aggressor, but I do not."

"Fair enough. What will you do when you're free to go?"

"I will seek surviving Kinj. I suspect there are none, but I must discover the truth."

"Where is the Kinj home system?"

"It is very far from here, well outside your ship's jump range. You could not reach it in your lifetime."

I had no way to know if it was lying, but at the end of the day, I needed that information, and this seemed like a problem for another day. "Okay," I said. "Midnight, fire up the engines."

It didn't take us long to find and destroy the nodes. The Kinj AI was right, they weren't designed to counter us. It was a classic case of 'primitive' overcoming 'civilized' technology.

When it was over, the Kinj AI appeared again. "Thank you," it said. "Here are the coordinates you seek." A stream of numbers appeared in the air before me.

Midnight said, "Coordinates captured. Plotting the jump now."

There was a flash of light, and a small device appeared on my console. "It will take our engines some time to fully charge," the AI said, "but when they do, we owe you more than coordinates. I believe you will have need of help yourself, and soon. When you have need, use the device, and I will come. But do not wait too long – I must return to Kinj spaces."

"Thank you," I said. "I—"

But it was gone.

"The Kinj could be a powerful ally in our war," Midnight said.

"I'm sure she could," I said. "But there was an edge of hatred in her voice when she mentioned the Zhen."

"Isn't that a good thing?"

"I don't know," I said. "The Zhen are my enemy, but I don't hate them as people. If I did, I'd be willing to do things I can't even stand thinking about. That kind of hate, over that kind of timescale? What would she do if she faced them? I'm not sure I want to know the answer to that."

I sighed and turned back to the controls. I turned the ship toward the outer system, and got us on course for the jump limit at standard acceleration. "Got that jump plotted yet?" I asked Midnight.

"Affirmative," she said.

"Good. Take us into slipspace as soon as we pass the limit. Let's go find us a warship."

CHAPTER FIVE

Liam

The jump to rendezvous point Beta ran smooth as silk from our end. The *Drokkha Nakar* and her fighters went first. We waited a few hours to give them time to set up their perimeter, then started sending ships through.

One of the problems with slipspace travel, as Tajen is so very fond of telling me, is that journeys don't always take the same amount of time. One ship can do a jump in a week, but for the next ship, it takes a few more days, or even a few less. The factors that control it range from ships' drives to the number of times a given route is used in a given time period, but the truth is, nobody really knows for sure; we can only project possible travel times with a margin of error of a few days. Our ships would stagger in, but they'd arrive within a few hours or days of each other.

I hoped.

We waited in-system while all the smaller ships jumped out, then recalled our fighters and jumped. The *Litvyak*, named for a war hero I'd found in an old historical text, made the jump in six days, which was actually a day less than our projected travel time.

When a ship exits slipspace, the energies of that other dimension cling to the ship for a few moments, blinding the ship's sensors and making it difficult to see out the viewports. I was about to order my comms officer to check to see if everyone had arrived when the other-dimensional energies cleared. The blood drained from my face as I saw what we'd arrived into.

Zhen ships had arrived before us, and they were attacking the fleet. It was a small task force, only one capital ship with several wings of fighters, but that was more than enough to cause our mostly civilian fleet a lot of damage. The *Drokkha Nakar* had launched fighters and was slugging it out with the Zhen destroyer, but it looked like we were in trouble. "Launch fighters!" I yelled, and only then realized that someone had already given the command and hit the alert. I could hear the ship's public address announcing the alert and sending crew to battle stations.

I strode to the combat plot and took a moment to take in the tactical situation. I'm more of a long-term strategy guy than a battle-tactics guy like my husband, but I could see what was needed. "Helm!" I snapped. "Bring us to heading two eight zero mark six. Starboard batteries, fire on that destroyer! Port batteries, weapons free."

As the helm started to follow my orders, I could see Zhen ships moving to intercept us. I reached out with my NeuroNet and selected a channel. "Alpha flight leader, intercept Zhen fighter wings *Zeta* and *Iota*. Blow them straight to hell for me."

"Ackknowledged," came Alpha leader's voice. "We'll light 'em up for you." She seemed to be enjoying herself, and I shook my head. I was no stranger to that emotional ride. Tajen and I both enjoyed a good fight, even – or maybe especially – when we were outnumbered, but my appreciation for a good shitstorm had been worn down by the struggles on Earth and the battle at Shoa'kor.

Something caught my eye at the edge of the engagement, and I focused on it with the tank controls, trying to make sense of the swirling icons. My eyes widened as I realized one of the human ships had just arrived, having taken longer to travel through slipspace than anyone else, and had come under immediate attack by a Zhen squadron. "*Skalk*," I said, mentally 'reaching' for another comms channel even as I searched the plot for the nearest ships in range. "Beta flight, break off your attack run and head for the *Sparrow*. Get those Zhen off her."

I held my breath a moment as I watched the ships change course. I pulled up the *Sparrow*'s information and my heart sank. She was a slow ship, a small cargo runner, today carrying a hundred and fifty refugees from Shoa'kor and twenty crew.

And the Zhen had taken out one of her engines.

She was still moving, but Beta flight wasn't close enough. I got on the comms. "Beta flight, they're running out of time!"

"We're moving as fast as we can, command!" Beta leader replied. "They're too far out."

He wasn't wrong. The *Sparrow* had not only taken longer than the rest of us in slipspace, but she'd arrived well outside the expected arrival zone.

"Commander Kincaid to *Sparrow*. Captain, help is on the way. Hold on, you're well outside the margins."

"Our astrogator *karked* it up, sir," the reply came, the captain's voice backed by the sounds of his crew calling to each other. It didn't sound good. "We're doing what we can, but the Zhen are all over us. We're not going to make it."

Beta flight was still ten seconds out when the Zhen cracked the *Sparrow* like an egg, secondary explosions throughout the ship's structure finishing the job. I was thankful that the plot only showed the ship had broken up, and didn't show me in detail the bodies and debris floating in the void. My mind was good enough at that to make me sick; I didn't need the reality. I watched Beta wing take their revenge on the fighters that had destroyed the *Sparrow*, but the action gave me no satisfaction.

"We can't win here," I said. "All ships, make a break for jump point Gamma-twelve. Standard evacuation protocol." I realized I was chewing my lip and stopped. Bad enough I was presiding over another bug-out; I didn't need my nervousness to show.

Our fleet began to jump. Unlike point Alpha, point Beta had been set in the interstellar void to prevent being trapped in a system unable to make for the jump limit. That small bit of foresight was all that saved us.

Most of the smaller ships were able to jump quickly, and the *Drokkha Nakar* had been here longer than the rest of us, so their drives were charged up and ready. I could see on the plot that they were recalling fighters and preparing to jump. I turned to Captain Zhang. "Xiao Ming, how long until we can jump?" I asked.

"We can jump in five," she said. "I'm holding off on recalling all fighters until most of the others are away."

It was a tense five minutes, watching as our ships jumped out. When the last had left local space, Captain Zhang ordered her fighters back. We kept the Zhen at bay with long-range weapons, but we took quite a few hits in the process. Fortunately our shields held, but it was close. When the last of our fighters were aboard, we jumped immediately.

Once safely in slipspace, Captain Zhang turned to me. "Not to be picky," she said, "but I hope we're in the clear on the other side of the jump, because after that it's going to take us a couple of hours to charge the drives enough to jump safely."

"We should be." I turned to the plot again. "Once we arrive, coordinate with the *Drokkha Nakar*'s flight ops to keep patrols active." I turned to Injala, who had been waiting nearby. "How long can we count on the *Nakar*'s aid?"

"My lord Dierka pledged the ship to your cause until Earth is safe."

"So, at least another hundred years, then."

Her ears quivered slightly in amusement. "I would not expect *that* long," she said. "That said, I received a data update from the *Drokkha Nakar*. The situation back home is interesting, Lord Aljek is making noise in the Assembly High Council about the expense of protecting you. But the Ascendant feels he owes you and Tajen a debt, and Dierka's position gives him a great deal of leeway. I would not worry, in your place. You may count on the *Drokkha Nakar*'s presence for quite some time."

"Good." I thought for a moment, but I had nothing left. "I need sleep. We should have, what, about a week in slipspace?"

Captain Zhang checked the plot from her navigator. "More or less," she said.

"All right, I'm headed for my quarters. Hopefully I'll have some ideas later. Captain, let's meet in the morning."

"Aye, sir."

My cabin was a deck below the bridge, in the first block of cabins. Though we kept the bridge and other duty stations at full brightness always, the lights in the residential corridors were lowered at night. Tonight they seemed a bit darker than usual, but I was so tired I didn't think about it.

I entered my cabin and stood there, in the room that was supposed to be mine and Tajen's. The room he'd never see. I didn't bother to turn on the room's lights; the tiny night-lights against the bulkheads were plenty. The viewscreen on the outer bulkhead showed me the view of slipspace out the window. I turned it off and went to bed. Sleep, often elusive, came quickly this time.

★   ★   ★

Almost every culture has a concept that describes the hours between deep night and dawn, when the demons that haunt us are at their strongest, sleep has deserted us, and all we can do is suffer. The Zhen call it 'Sleeping in the Enemy's Jaws', the Kelvaki know it as 'the Hours of Second Thoughts', and some humans call it 'the Hour of the Wolf'.

I call it a complete pain in the ass.

I'd slept fitfully, and awoken at 0200. Unable to get back to sleep, I'd lain in bed fuming until, finally, I threw off the covers, dressed, and left my quarters. I wandered the deserted corridors of the *Litvyak*, thinking – and also trying not to think.

The battle at rendezvous point Beta had been a hard one. Even though we'd only lost the one ship, it had been a heavy blow. That ship had held nearly two hundred people on board. We'd been planning to transfer most of them over to another ship at RPB, but the Zhen attack had made that impossible.

"Tajen would have saved them," I said to no one. At that thought, I stopped in the middle of the corridor and leaned on the wall, holding back a sob.

I missed my husband. The pain of losing him was a dull ache, one I knew I'd carry forever, but I'd cried my way through the worst of it and was trying to do the 'survival' part. It was still hard.

I turned into a corridor I hadn't been in before. It was one of the residential sections, a mix of ship's crew and refugee passengers from Shoa'kor. Every single cabin was occupied, even though the *Litvyak* hadn't been fully crewed when we began.

In a small section set up as a common area, a lone human sat with a cup of fragrant tea. As I drew close, he turned to look at me and waved a hand at the couch next to him. "There's more in the pot. Non-stim," he said. "Have a seat."

I grabbed a cup and filled it from the pot. I sat on the couch next to his chair and inhaled deeply, breathing in the scent of the tea. "Thanks. I'm Liam Kincaid."

His mouth quirked in a half smile. "I know, Admiral."

I waved that off. "Ugh, don't call me that. Right now I'm just Liam."

"Hi, Liam," he said. "I'm Alex. What's keeping *you* up? You want to talk, I'll listen." He gestured to the viewscreen on the wall, which showed the wild shifting colors of slipspace. "You'd certainly be more interesting than the viewscreen."

I regarded him a moment. It was tempting to respond with sarcasm, but I tended to save my sarcasm for Tajen. At that thought, tears welled up, and I took a moment to gather my words. I looked into Alex's eyes. He was a surprisingly handsome man, and I felt a rush of intense attraction, which I quickly suppressed. I wasn't ready for that. But – I could certainly use someone to talk to.

"Ever since I realized we lost my husband, I've been trying to do his job," I said. "He was supposed to be the leader of this fleet, not me. But every time I try to do things the way he would, I fail."

He sat with that for a moment, then said, "I guess the question is, would he have succeeded?"

"Probably," I said. "He's a better pilot, and better at battle tactics. I'm getting people killed."

"From what I heard, the Zhen were at the jump point and attacking the fleet before the *Litvyak* even got there," he said. "I don't think even Tajen Hunt would have been able to save the *Sparrow*, even if he'd been out there during the battle."

"You never saw him fly," I said.

"Oh, I did."

I looked up at him. "Really?"

He nodded. "I worked Shoa'kor for a long time. He came through every once in a while, and I've seen him do his thing. He was a good pilot, but he wasn't a god, if you'll forgive me."

"He'd agree with you," I said.

"So maybe it's time to do things *your* way," he said. "Stop trying to be Tajen Hunt, and just be Liam Kincaid. From where I sit, that should be enough."

"Maybe."

"Well, I mean, there's not really an option, is there?"

"No," I said. "Either I figure this out, or more people die."

He cocked his head. "Don't hear me wrong, Liam, but I think it's more that you'll figure this out, *and* more people will die." He held up a hand to forestall me speaking. "It's not that you won't be any good, but the reality of our situation is that unless you can manage to totally evade the Zhen, they're going to get more of us. There's nothing you can do about that except escape them. And…well, I'm sorry, but that seems pretty unlikely right now."

"Why do you say that?"

"Well, they've hit us twice, and I know the jumps were randomly chosen — oh, I should have mentioned, I was the astrogator on the *Burgundy* until they found their original astrogator on another ship and got her sent over. I got transferred here for training."

"Well, welcome aboard," I said. "Why didn't the *Burgundy* keep you as backup?"

He looked embarrassed. "Well, ah…there was some concern that the astrogator wouldn't like that. I'd, uh…I'd been sleeping in her bunk."

"So? They could find you another."

"It's also the captain's bunk."

A wave of something like warmth passed through me, and I felt my face reddening. "Ah," I said.

He smiled salaciously at me, as if he knew what I was thinking. His lips parted as he looked me up and down. "My current bunk's in a crowded room," he said. "Maybe you know somewhere else I could sleep tonight?"

I'd be lying if I said I wasn't tempted. But as attractive as he was, as lonely as I was, it still hadn't been long enough. And the awareness of that was like a splash of cold mountain water across my soul. "I, uh. I'm sorry, but are you kidding me? My husband *just died*," I said. "I'm not ready for that."

"It doesn't have to be permanent," he said. "I just thought—"

"Yeah, I get it," I snapped. "Not okay."

"I'm sorry," he said. "I – yeah, I was wrong." He grimaced and rubbed at his face. "But can I say – I didn't just mean to seduce you. I find you interesting, and for some reason I'm drawn to you in a way I can't explain."

I understood what he meant. It was exactly how I'd felt when I met Tajen. I couldn't tell him that, of course. That would be tacky. "I get it," I said. "But now is not the time."

"No, of course not. But maybe someday there will be a better time, and – I'll be here, if and when you're ready for that."

I wasn't sure what to say about that. Several options flitted through my head, most of them rude. But I could admit it to myself: it felt good. In fact, it felt good enough that I was suddenly not sure I wanted to say goodnight. So I did the only thing I could: I fled. "I'm…wow, I'm tired," I said, aware I was fooling nobody, and determined to proceed anyway. "I'll, uh…I'll see you around, I guess. Good night."

"Good night, Liam," he called, his voice pitched low and silky.

I returned to my quarters, suddenly as tired as I'd been horny a few minutes ago. "What the hell?" I asked myself, and climbed into bed. I'm pretty sure I was asleep before I even closed my eyes.

CHAPTER SIX

Katherine

The jump to Dakcha took about a month. Slipspace travel times are never the same, even between two systems. The math is way over my head, but travel time depends on a lot of factors – heavily traveled routes tend to have shorter transit times, almost like the trip is being 'burned in' to the fabric of spacetime. If a route isn't traveled often, times can get longer, as the jump drive has to work harder to burrow through. Looking at the coordinates, the system we were aiming for wasn't all that far from where we'd begun, which told me this route hadn't been traveled in a long time.

We came out of jump well outside the jump limit. "Nothing on scanners," Simmons said. "The computer just received a code request and sent the required key."

"Excellent. Dagger, is the chain drive ready?"

"'Chain drive'. What a ridiculously human term for a quantum displacement system."

"How so? The quantum displacements are chained together to create the effect of near-luminal speeds. Hence, 'chain drive'."

"Human language is an absurd construction."

"True," I said, "but we got the term from the Zhen. Besides, most of us just call it C-drive."

"Perhaps I ought to amend my position. Biological language is an absurd construction."

"No argument there. But can you answer my question?"

"Chain drive is available, Captain."

I put the ship into motion and shook my head. I had a feeling the Tabrans had made Dagger a smart-ass because I was used to traveling with Tajen, but Tajen wasn't quite so supercilious. "You've got a lot of attitude for someone who basically lives in a computer core," I said.

"Yes."

Before I could add anything, Simmons abruptly raised his hand in a cutoff gesture. "I've got six ships incoming," he said. "Looks like they scrambled at full burn from the inner system."

"How far out are they?"

"Five minutes, at present speeds," he said. A moment later, he added, "I am reading targeting locks from several nearby defense systems."

"Let's not do anything stupid," I said. I switched on my broadband comms. "This is the *Dagger in the Dark* to approaching ships. Please identify."

The reply came shortly, but not over the comms. "Incoming missiles!" Simmons snapped. "Four sources!"

"Point defense system initiated," Dagger said.

I threw the ship into a series of evasive maneuvers, trying to put more distance between us and the incoming missiles. This wasn't my best skill, though, and several of them impacted on our shields. I glanced at the shield status and saw we were only down by a few percentage points. I saw Simmons rerouting power priorities to charge the shields up, so I focused on flying and trying to evade any more fire.

I pulled the ship back to a heading for the inner system and activated the chain drive. We leaped forward, the ship's display changing to indicate our greater speed, drawing vector markers on the incoming ships' trajectories to help me locate them.

The Marauder ships adjusted to our changed speed by looping around, coming onto our vector. Most weapons were pretty useless at our current speeds, so they couldn't fire, but they could easily match our course and wait us out. Some came in close on our six, others stayed farther out, on parallel courses. I was getting worried. "*Skalk*," I said. "We're being her—"

The ship bucked and dropped out of chain drive. Even with the inertial dampers on, we were thrown against our harnesses. "*Skalk!*"

"Inhibitor mine," Simmons said. Inhibitor mines are nasty; they temporarily flood a region of space with a quantum particle that makes it impossible for the C-drives to operate until the field density drops.

"Obviously," I snapped. "Guess we fight, then."

The six ships chasing dropped into space around us. They'd known this trap was here, which explained why some of them had set themselves up to be there when I got yanked into normal Newtonian space.

"Missiles incoming," Simmons said, his voice dropping into his usual mid-fight calm. "Point defense is not working optimally."

"Yeah, we're maneuvering a bit more than they'd like," I said. "But, you know, there are six ships firing on us, so the PDCs can fucking deal."

"They're not sentient," Simmons said.

"Then *you* can fucking deal!" I snapped. "This is not my—" The ship slammed down, and the straps holding me in my chair cut into my shoulders hard enough that I was pretty sure there'd be some bruising. "What the hell was that?"

"A missile detonated on the upper shields," Dagger said. "Shield collapsed. Rerouting power to recharge."

Another hit shook us. The ship didn't buck as badly, but there was a large *boom* from the back of the ship, and the bulkhead between the cockpit and rest of the ship slid closed. "Hull breach," Dagger said.

"You gonna make it?"

"It's relatively minor," he said. "I've sent auto-repair drones to seal the breach. But the shield generator is now offline."

"Dagger, tell me the truth, can we win this fight?"

"I am one of the most advanced ships in known space," he said.

"Is that a yes?"

"No. Despite my advances, we are outnumbered and outgunned."

"All right," I said. "Time for Plan B." I switched comms back on and called into the void, "Attention Marauder vessels. We are ready to heave to and surrender. Stop firing!"

A man's head appeared in my vision, courtesy of my comms implant. "We do not accept your surrender. The Makara Tribe was declared anathema twenty years ago! I don't know how you've lived this long, but your time is done."

"What the hell are you talking about?" I stopped talking while I cut thrust, hauled back on the stick to change my heading, then slammed into full thrust again. "We're not Makara! We don't even know what they are! We're from Earth!"

"You lie! You used the Makara codes to enter the system! You are Makara!"

"We stole those codes from a deserted space station!" I cried. It must have worked, because they stopped firing.

"Heave to and prepare for boarding," the Marauder snarled, and the comms cut out.

"Captain, I object to this plan," Dagger said.

"I get that," I said. "I really do. But you said we can't win. So shut up." I cut thrust and brought the ship down to a stop, the other ships keeping pace. When we'd reached full stop, I powered down the weapons and shields and hoped the Marauders didn't decide to just end us immediately.

It wasn't entirely a fool's bet; Dagger might have been outnumbered and outgunned, but he wasn't wrong when he said the ship was more advanced than anything the Marauders had. If we'd been up against a smaller number of ships, or worse pilots, we'd have had a chance. "Dagger, I want you in full passive mode."

"Captain, I—"

"That's an order," I said. "You're going to be my ace in the hole. If the Marauders start trying to take you apart, you can defend yourself. Otherwise just hide and keep them from figuring out what you are. We'll do our best to get through this, and we need you when we're ready to go."

"Yes, Captain."

The lead ship came in for docking; the universal airlock design in use throughout known space allowed them to dock easily. Simmons and I met them at the airlock.

I wasn't sure what I expected to see when the doors opened. Turns out I didn't see anything – as soon as they opened wide enough, the Marauders fired a stun charge through the gap. The shooter was either good or lucky; the charge hit me right in the neck. As the electricity locked up my muscles, I had just enough time to think, *Shit, that hurts*, before I dropped to the deck and slid into unconsciousness.

★　　★　　★

I was signing back into work after a particularly unrestful 'rest period' when I heard motion behind me, as well as a gasp. I didn't think; I just stepped to my right, and the doubled fists that had been aimed at the back of my neck hit the table instead. The fists belonged to Deacon, a man I'd already dealt with when I'd first awoken in the work camp four days before.

I was already pretty sick of his crap, so I lifted a leg and, placing my foot on his hip, gave him a good shove. "We done?" I asked the clerk at the table.

"We are," she said, and looked at Deacon, who was climbing to his feet and glowering at me. "I don't think you two are, though."

I turned to Deacon and gave him my best *don't fuck with me* look. "This is stupid," I said. "Let's just get back to work before—"

He interrupted me with a yell and a charge. I sidestepped him easily. Just as I was starting to tell myself this was going to be easy, he pivoted. The charge had been a feint, I realized too late, and he managed to grab my left wrist and pull me off balance, his right hand coming around to grab me by the back of the neck.

I windmilled my left arm, turning into him, to break his grip. Just as I managed to break free, my entire body was seized by pain. My back arched as the muscles contracted involuntarily, my command of my own body interrupted by the pulses being sent through my system by my NeuroNet.

I fell backward, hitting the deck hard. The fall itself didn't hurt, but I'd landed on something small and pointy just under my left shoulder blade, and *that* was excruciating.

The 'boss' of my workgroup, Rosco, stepped into view. "Fighting is off-ticket during work time! You two shitbrains want to play grabass, do it on your own time. Not mine!" he yelled. He waved his hand, and the pain stopped. "That's ten debits to both of you," he snarled.

I climbed gingerly to my feet and faced him. "Come on, boss. It wasn't my choice to fight," I said. "I—"

Rosco stopped me. "You sign in?"

"Yes."

"Then *get back to work*! You can whine at me on your own time!"

As he stalked away, another member of my workgroup stepped up beside me. "You shouldn't antagonize Rosco," she said. "He hasn't got a sense of humor." She gestured to the area we'd been assigned. "Let's get moving."

It had been four days since Simmons and I were captured. There'd been no contact from Dagger, which told me he was either still hiding from the Marauder techs, or he'd been found and dealt with. Hopefully the former. I'd woken in what looked like a prison, and assigned to Rosco's workgroup. I'd worked out that we were underground, but not where. Judging by the slight angle at which dropped things fell, it was either a very small planet or an asteroid. We were set to work nearly all day clearing debris, and had a few hours at night to ourselves, but we couldn't leave – there were guard posts at every tunnel entrance.

In the four days I'd been here, not one member of my workgroup had talked to me until now. I stared at her a moment, then shrugged to myself and followed her. "Yeah, I was beginning to realize that," I said to her back. "How much power does he have, anyway?"

She bent to pick up several large pieces of debris and tossed them, one by one, into the waiting antigrav sled. "Enough that nobody will care if you wind up dead," she said. She grinned at me. "I'm Andra."

"Katherine."

"Yeah. Heard you when you got here."

"Your bunk's right next to mine. But you haven't said shit to me until now. What changed?"

She shrugged. "I like to watch new people before I decide if they're worth talking to."

"And I am?"

She eyed me, her expression saying she wasn't quite sure yet. "You'll do. Where'd you come from?"

I eyed her warily, trying to decide how much I could say. I decided to hell with it. "I was captured when I came looking for the Marauder home base," I said.

She cocked her head at me. "You move like a soldier. But you don't seem like a *Zhen* soldier."

I helped her lift a large chunk of metal onto the sled. "I was, once." I shook my head. "I'm not anymore. Haven't been for years."

"So who do you fight for?"

"I fight for Earth."

"Earth!" she barked. "Don't give me that. Earth's been lost for centuries."

"Well, yeah," I said. "But we found it. We laid claim to it. We were living there for a year before the Zhen took it back."

She stared at me for a moment, standing still as everyone moved around us. Rosco, leaning on a wall a few meters away, cleared his throat meaningfully. She got back to work. "I heard you might be Makara," she said.

I heaved a chunk of metal into the cart's bin, but didn't answer her.

We kept working for hours, clearing debris from tunnel floors. It seemed as if these tunnels had been dug recently, but when I'd asked about it, I'd been told to mind my own job and not ask questions.

Finally, Rosco yelled, "That's the day! Get to your bunks!" We filed back toward the bunkrooms in near silence. I sat on my bunk, my back against the wall. Andra took a seat on her bunk, right next to mine, and faced me. "So. Are you?" I gave her a quizzical look, and she said, "Makara."

"I don't even know what that means." She didn't look like she believed me. "Look," I said. "I don't know who or what Makara are, but I'm Katherine Lawson. I come from Terra."

"So you *are* a Zhen pet."

"No," I snapped. I turned to face her, my cheeks hot. "I grew up in the Empire, yeah. I believed all their bullshit for years. And then I joined up with Tajen Hunt and we found the truth and started the war. My brother, and some of my friends, *died* so Earth and humanity could be free of the Zhen. I am not their *pet*. Don't *ever* call me that."

She looked confused. "What war?"

"What do you mean, 'what war'? Do you people not pay attention to what's out there?"

"I'm in prison, remember?" She shook her head. "Not that we got much news from outside even before I got put in here." She looked up, to the bunk above hers, where a Hun sat reading from a slate. "Hey, Fraz!" she said. "This one here says there's a war on, over Earth. Heard anything?"

"Yeah."

She waited a moment, then reached up and smacked his leg.

He braced himself with two of his arms and peered over the bed, his head upside down to us. "You didn't ask for details."

She took a deep breath – seemed like this was a common conversation. "I'm asking. Now," she said. Something in her voice changed as she said it, and I started to wonder why she was in here. She didn't seem like a woman who belonged in a work gang.

The Hun, for his part, flipped himself over, landing perfectly on all three feet. "Human captain Tajen Hunt discovered the Lost Earth nearly two years ago," he said. "He discovered the Zhen betrayal and their role in the destruction of Earth and disseminated this information to humans throughout the Empire. A coalition of human and Kelvaki ships destroyed the Zhen garrison and began colonizing Earth."

"And then?"

"A year later," I interrupted, "the Zhen came back and occupied Earth again. They fought a war, but it wasn't enough. Zhen are still on Earth, and there's a human fleet out there on the run from them."

Andra looked hard at me. "Why didn't you fight with them?"

I shrugged. "My ship was hit. I got rescued, but didn't go back. I will, once my mission's over."

She turned to Fraz. "And you! Why didn't you tell the queen about this?" she hissed.

"I did," he said. "I was put in here ten minutes later."

"Why didn't you tell *me*?"

His head waggled back and forth a bit. "Didn't seem like it would do any good."

She closed her eyes for a moment. I started to speak, but she held up her hand in a 'shut it' gesture. I looked to Fraz; he shook his head.

After an uncomfortably long silence, Andra shifted across the space to my bunk and lowered her voice. "What is your mission? Why did you come looking for the Marauder base?"

"Why should I tell you?"

"Why tell me any of this?"

"Nothing I've said is secret," I said. "It's on all the news channels in the Empire."

Fraz nodded.

Andra frowned and turned back to him. "Why wasn't it shown here?"

"Nikara ordered it removed from the feeds."

"Things are worse than I thought," she muttered. She forestalled another interruption and sat beside me, clearly thinking through something.

"Okay?"

"No, it's not okay," she spat. "How much do you know about the Marauders?"

"Nobody knows much about them," I said. "They occupy a territory on the edges of the Empire, they raid Zhen and other settlements and ships whenever they can...they're made up of lots of different species." I shrugged. "That's about it, other than that they're vicious as hell. They don't take prisoners."

"Well, good to see our image is still holding up."

"I thought you might be one of 'em."

"Yeah, I thought you had me figured out."

"Wasn't really that hard," I said. "I'm not an idiot, and like I said, the Marauders don't take prisoners."

"Oh, we do," she said with a grin. "Just mostly from our own ranks. This place is a punishment detail. We put people in here when they fuck up."

"So you were planted here to see what I know?"

"No," she said, shaking her head. She chuckled. "I thought you were smart. I've been in here a while now. No, I'm in here because I fucked up."

"What did you do?"

"I told the truth." At my confused look, she said, "Where do you think the Marauders originally started?"

"Most people seem to think the Huns began it, when the Zhen fucked up their homeworld. Then disaffected humans and other races from the Empire joined up."

"More or less, that's true. The first Marauders were Huns, but they were joined by humans later. Some of them had found out the truth about the Zhen, and got exiled. Others just found themselves among us. It's not entirely true, the idea that we don't take prisoners. Sometimes we do – if a crew surrenders and we think they have potential."

"And if they don't?"

She shrugged. "Then we do what we have to."

"You don't have to kill—"

"I'm not going to argue with you about how we do things," she said. "We don't have time. We don't even have time for me to give you the full story, so shut up and listen." She took a breath. "The Hun started the clans, but over time, the humans began to outnumber them – we breed faster and live longer, after all – and things started to change."

"Change how?"

Her lips pursed and she glared at me.

"Sorry," I said. "Continue."

"Over time, certain customs became codified law. The Marauders are led by a single ruler. When one dies, there's a contest to choose the next one."

"What kind of contest?"

"A battle. Everyone who wants the job goes into a fight. Whoever comes out the victor is the new ruler."

"Brutal."

"Yeah. Again, it wasn't always like that, but it's been the case for generations, now. Once the monarch takes over, they have full control of the Marauders. Their word is law. And that's the problem." She leaned in closer. "When Nikara took the throne, she had every intention of making the Marauders better than that. She'd studied our history, knew our ways had devolved from the original intent."

"Which was what?"

She was clearly annoyed at my inquisitiveness, but indulged me. "The first Marauders just wanted to be free, to live apart from the Empire and its authority. The rules were strict, but they weren't brutal. But over time, things changed – the monarch didn't have absolute power in the beginning. The first ten Marauder kings and queens were decent people. Then, human nature being what it was, shit started to go bad. Nikara wanted to reverse as much of that as she could. Then the Makara turned on her."

I raised a finger to stop her. "How do you know all this? Who are you?"

"I told you, my name is Andra. I used to be Nikara's friend. Hell, I was her *amaya*."

"That's Hun for 'hand', right?"

"Yes. It means I was her closest advisor and aide."

"So how'd you end up in here?"

"I told her the truth – that her orders made no sense, and she was losing the trust of the clans."

"Is that what Makara are?"

"Yes," she said. "There are several clans. They all have their own leadership, but they all answer to the current ruler. About twenty years ago, a Makara ship turned on the queen over a matter of honor and fired on her ship. Her husband and son were killed."

"She didn't take that well, I imagine."

"She ordered the Makara clan exterminated, down to the last child." She closed her eyes for a moment. "I argued against it, but she gave the order anyway. The entire clan was destroyed. All we could find were killed."

"Then why did you think I was one of them?"

"I said 'all we could find'. The Makara Clan is effectively dead, but no massacre is complete. Some of them escaped. Every few years one of them tries for revenge. We figured you for another one."

"I'm not."

She took a breath, then said, "I believe you."

We sat silently for a moment, and then I said, "Did you join the fight against them?"

She looked pained. "Of course I did," she whispered. In a stronger voice, she said, "It was an order from my queen, and may my bones rot for obeying it, but I did it." She sighed. "Afterward, I tried to get her to declare mercy on the survivors, but she declared them anathema, to be shot on sight. Over the years, as her orders became more and more unusual, I tried to mitigate her excesses. Then one day she ordered me to kill an entire family because one of them displeased her. I refused. I expected to die, but she needs me too much. So I've been here for two years now."

"What happened to the family?"

"Oh, they're still alive. Once a month an emissary from the queen comes and asks if I'll carry out her order. If I were to say yes, they'd let me out, I'd go kill them all, and then I'd be welcome at her side again."

"That's insane."

"Yep."

"Why not say yes, then go kill her?"

She grinned. "I thought about it," she said. "But I can't – she's too well guarded, and Marauder law won't let me challenge her. I've been cast out. I'm not technically a Marauder anymore."

"Challenge?"

"The only way to replace the monarch, short of natural death, is to challenge them to ship combat. The winner becomes the new monarch. The loser becomes space debris."

I sat up straighter. "How do I challenge her?"

She waved me back. "You can't. You're not a Marauder. And before you ask, becoming one takes some solid neutronium naughty bits and a willingness to get your hands dirty." She narrowed her eyes at me. "What are you after, anyway? Cards on the table."

I frowned as I considered her. Odds were she was full of shit, and just telling me whatever made it easier to get what she wanted out of me. But somehow I didn't think that was what was going on. "I'm after an ancient piece of Tabran tech," I said. "It's supposed to be somewhere in Marauder space. I started with that Makara station where I got the codes, then came here."

"What's the tech?"

I cupped my hand and used my NeuroNet to show her the machine the Tabrans had sent me for. "This is what it should look like," I said. "I can't tell you what it does."

She grinned. "I've seen that," she said. "We don't know what it does either. You're unlucky. It's here – but it's in the queen's treasury. There's no way you're getting to it even if you get out of here."

I leaned forward and looked into her eyes. "One step at a time," I said. "First – how do I become a Marauder?"

★   ★   ★

The next morning, at the beginning of the shift, I walked straight up to Rosco. I reached out, grabbed his shoulder, and spun him around, my other hand coming up and pressing a very sharp shiv against his throat. "You even consider using my 'Net against me, and I'm shoving this into your throat," I said.

He snarled something, but I didn't even bother to listen.

I marched him to the security station and, as the guard rose, I shoved Rosco forward into him. As the two men tried to untangle themselves from one another, I tossed the shiv onto the security desk.

"I am no prisoner," I said, as if it was an obvious fact. "By conquest I demand my rights. By blood and sweat I am purified. Test me, and find in me a Marauder."

Rosco stood and regarded me for a moment before saying, "If you fail, you better hope you die in the attempt."

I smiled sweetly at him. "I never fail," I said. "Not when it matters."

CHAPTER SEVEN

Tajen

We came out of slipspace for the third time since leaving the Kinj ship. The first two systems had been empty. I was hoping this time would be different.

Hope was rewarded when the sensor sweep came back with evidence of ships out there. "Are they Zhen?" I asked Midnight.

"Analyzing their emissions," she said. A moment later, "Zhen vessels confirmed. I'm reading one battleship, as well as several smaller ships."

"What are the smaller ones doing?"

"They appear to be sentries," she said. "Incoming transmission."

The air before me filled with motes of light that resolved into the face of a Zhen. "Unknown vessel, identify yourself or be destroyed."

"If I identify myself," I said, "you'll probably want to destroy me anyway. This is Tajen Hunt of Earth."

"'Of Earth'? Don't be ridiculous," he said. "Right now, Tajen Hunt, you are a man without a planet."

"True enough, Captain…."

He drew himself up. "I am Commander Jinasek, commanding the Imperial…" He paused a moment, as if tasting the words for the first time. He seemed to realize that, having deserted the Empire, he had no right to declare himself commander of an Imperial ship. He finished, "…commander of the *Adamant*."

"I'm not here to fight, Commander."

"Which is well, considering that your little ship is no match for the full firepower of this battleship."

"True. May I start by asking a question?"

"Go ahead."

"Why did you leave the battlefield at Shoa'kor?"

He looked uncomfortable. "Perhaps you should come aboard," he said.

"How do I know you won't arrest me immediately?" I said.

"You do not," he said. "Though if I wanted to kill you, I would already have fired at your vessel."

"Point taken," I said. Without speaking, I goosed the controls, moving position and changing my vector to throw off any incoming weapons.

The commander's crest quivered with his amusement. "Come, Captain Hunt. I give you my word, one warrior to another – no harm shall come to you, or your craft, while you are under a Seal of Truce."

I regarded him as I considered my options. Strictly speaking, I was no longer a recognized warrior of the Empire, and thus the Seal of Truce didn't apply to me. But in my experience, there was what the Empire said, and then where was what those in 'the trenches' actually did and believed. I knew Jinasek by reputation; if he was offering the Seal, he meant it.

"All right, Commander. I will come aboard, under a Seal of Truce."

"The Seal is recognized. My comms officer will assign you a berth," he said, and logged off.

The comms officer came on after a few seconds and gave me instructions on where to dock.

When I shut down the comms, Midnight spoke up. "Just so you know, I will defend myself if they try anything."

"Good," I said. "What do you do if I die?"

"I blow up."

"Seriously?"

"Yes. The explosion should cripple the ship, if not destroy it."

I was speechless for several moments. "I guess I'll try not to die, then."

"See that you don't," she said primly.

Docking went fairly smoothly. When I left the ship, I looked at the four guards and an officer waiting on the deck. "Wow, all for me? Kind of overkill, five Zhen for one human."

"The guards are necessary," the officer said.

"I'm that dangerous? Really?"

"You misunderstand," he said. "These guards are for your protection. Not all of the crew will be pleased to see you among us. You have killed many of our kind."

"Ah," I said. "Only in battle, and only when I had no choice."

"As you say." His tone did nothing to reassure me. He gestured, and I walked with him to the corridor.

I'd served on a ship of the *Adamant*'s class, so I had a pretty good idea of where I was being taken, though there'd been a few changes in the layout. We weren't going anywhere near the bridge, and I began to get nervous. We passed many Zhen soldiers, some of them glancing my way, others studiously avoiding looking at the human.

We stopped beside a door in what should be officer territory. I could hear the snarling, vicious sounds of two Zhen arguing inside, but not well enough to make out the words. The door opened, and I heard, "You are compounding your error, Commander. You are only being allowed leniency due to your family line. If you do not correct your course immediately, your execution is certain."

A Zhen:ko stormed from the room. When he noticed me, he snarled in Zhen and lunged for me. I tried real hard not to react, but I totally failed to stop myself from leaping backward. Fortunately, I managed not to piss myself. I'll give this to the guards – they moved fast, restraining the red-skinned Zhen. I admired their willingness to act; the Zhen:ko are the ruling caste of the Empire, and it had to be scary for these men to act against one who could order their deaths later.

"Release me," he roared, "or I am your death!"

Yeah. Like that.

The Zhen, for their parts, grimaced but didn't release him. The commander stepped from the room, surveyed the scene calmly. "Captain Hunt. Welcome aboard." His eyes slid over the straining *:ko* and the guards, and he said, smooth and as calm as a mountain sunrise, "Place him in the brig." He looked back to me and gestured into his office.

As he followed me in, he waved the door shut and sighed, a rumbling sound from deep in his chest. "That was Andark, our 'political officer'." He gestured me to a seat, and took one opposite me, a small table between us. "I've never liked him, but he's become even worse since we deserted. I suppose I cannot blame him, his purpose is to represent the One, and I have seemingly turned against her Empire."

"Seemingly?"

He gestured *complicated truth.* "I have not truly abandoned the Empire, but I am not proud of what it is becoming. I will not allow my command to be used to kill innocents who want only to be allowed to choose their own destiny."

"And your crew?"

His crest flattened. "Most agreed with me, and volunteered to join me, despite the personal cost. A few did not agree, but stood down and were released when we reached safety."

"Why didn't Andark leave?"

"He believes it is his duty to remain and convince me to rejoin the Empire." His eyes narrowed. "He is a fool to believe I am not aware that, even with my relatives in the Talnera, once I return, I will be forgiven – moments before I am executed."

"That would be a tragedy, to waste such a being as yourself."

"Flattery is not useful to you, Tajen Hunt."

"I'm not flattering you, sir. The exploits of Commander Jinasek were required reading when I went through training. Your performance in the Fourteenth Tabran Campaign is foundational to modern strategic thinking."

"It was what was needed at the time," he said. "Please, allow me to cut to the chase. Why are you here, Tajen Hunt?"

"I want you to come work with us."

"Work with the humans?"

"And others."

"Such as?"

"The Kelvaki. The Tabrans. Maybe more."

His crest rose to its full height, and my combat overlay showed me his arms and legs were priming for motion. "The Tabrans? You ask much, human."

"They are not the enemy you once fought. Not anymore." Before he could reply, I threw the data I'd prepared on the Tabrans into the air between us.

He read it over. From time to time he got the look of someone consulting his NeuroNet. Finally, he sat back and stared at me for several long moments before asking, "How can I know this is all true?"

I gestured toward his head. "You already checked everything you can. What did that tell you?"

"I will need time to consider this, Captain Hunt. I must not only make my own decision, but decide how to present it to the crew."

"Shall I return to my ship while you consider your options?"

"That is a good idea," he said. "The guards outside will escort you."

I rose and went to the door. Before I touched the door's control, I turned back to him. "If it helps…the Alliance I'm putting together isn't interested in destroying the Empire. We just want to fix the problem with Zornaav. The Tabrans think that if we neutralize the Tabran nanites, it will revert her to her base state."

Jinasek rumbled deep in his chest. "I will consider this." It was a clear dismissal, so I turned back to the door and opened it. As I stepped into the hallway, I said to the guards, "To my ship, please."

One led the way while the others fell in around me. Despite knowing any of these Zhen could easily kill me, I didn't feel endangered. A tiny part of me, one I wasn't completely happy about, felt right about being surrounded by Zhen. I guess it made sense; after all, the Empire hadn't been my enemy forever, and most of my life had been spent among these beings.

My sense of belonging faded when I realized we weren't going to the docking bay. I got on the comms immediately through my NeuroNet. "Midnight, can you hear me?" I hoped the Zhen didn't notice my lips moving as I subvocalized; I'd never gotten the hang of communicating entirely silently.

"I hear you, Tajen."

"I'm supposed to be returning to you, but I don't think that's where I'm going."

"Confirmed. You are moving toward the brig."

"Can you get me a path back to you?"

"Easily."

"All right, let me figure out how to break free of my escort here. Maybe I—" I stopped when the soldiers stopped beside a cell.

"His Excellency Andark requested a conversation before we return you to your ship," one of the guards said, gesturing to the forcefield that shuttered the cell.

"Uh-huh," I muttered. I stepped to the faint shimmer in the air that marked the forcefield's presence. "Hey, Andark. How's your tail hanging?"

He cocked his head at me. "I have read your file. Let us not indulge in your usual games, Hunt. Let us speak as soldiers."

"Fine. What do you want?"

"You know you cannot beat me. Why do you persist?"

"I'm not against you, Andark. Just your leader."

"It is the same thing," he said. "But we have seen our mistake. Your species is a heartbeat from extinction. It's a pity. There will be so much work to do when you are gone." His crest rose to its full height. "But we have other servant races. The Empire will live on, and your species will be nothing but a bad memory."

The blood was roaring in my ears, and my anger made me stupid. I knew I should just leave, not talk any more, but I couldn't stop myself. "Fuck you. You and your kind have killed enough of us. Your time has come and gone. You want to come for us now? Go ahead. Come after me and I'll kill you stone-cold dead, you ugly son of a bitch."

He flung himself into the field and bounced back, sparks flying. I couldn't even hear his words as the guards hustled me out of the room.

★   ★   ★

The next morning I rose from my bunk to a signal from the bridge.
"Captain Hunt," Midnight said, "the Zhen are asking to speak to you."

"Put them through."

"You misunderstand. Commander Jinasek is asking you to join him.
There are guards waiting to escort you."

"Ugh, fine. Give me a minute to get ready."

I dressed and left the ship, unprepared for the number of guards
waiting. As I stood in the hatch, Midnight spoke to me. "I'm reading an
elevated heartbeat in the Zhen lieutenant," she said.

"You could have warned me."

"That's not normal?"

"No, that's not normal." I cut the channel and stepped down. "Is
there a problem?"

"You will come with me," the lieutenant in charge said. He spun
on his heel and led the way. I didn't really see an option other than
following him, so I did.

I compared our route with my journeys through the ship yesterday,
and my heart sank. "Midnight, things look to be going south," I
subvocalized. "Be ready."

"For what?"

"Anything."

We arrived in the brig, where the commander stood, looking into
Andark's cell. He didn't look at me. "How did you do it?" he asked.

I gave the lieutenant a confused look, and he gestured, directing me
forward. I stepped up to Jinasek's side and looked into the cell. "By the
Nine," I said, genuflecting.

Jinasek's voice rumbled with promised violence. "Your gods cannot
save you if you did this."

"What?" I looked up at him, incredulous. "I've been in my ship all
night. Even if I wasn't, how in the hells would I be able to do *that* to a
Zhen:ko?"

Andark – one presumed, based on the color of his scales – lay in the middle of the cell, facedown and clearly dead, his body faded to a dull orange.

"I do not know," he said. "But according to our records, you were the last person to see him alive."

"That was hours ago," I said. "Nobody checked on him since?"

"The brig is an automated system," he said. "Nobody entered the brig after you left."

"I had four guards with me."

"Yes," he said. He gestured, and an image appeared in the air before me. Four Zhen lay dead in a compartment, their blood covering the floor.

"Those were the guards? Shit."

"As you say...shit." He turned to me, and his eyes met mine. "Do not mistake me, Tajen Hunt. I have questions, and those questions have not been answered. If you did this, then you have dishonored my command and I will have no choice but to kill you."

I stared him in the eyes, and I knew – he didn't believe I did this. But by the rules of Zhen society, he had no choices here. If he didn't kill me, he'd lose status and authority in the eyes of his men. He would, in a very real way, be inviting an attack.

Such things weren't common on Zhen vessels, but they weren't unknown. They'd been much more common during the *Ashrati* period, long before humans had come on the scene, but centuries of the dominant philosophy of the Empire, the *Zhen:saak:arl*, with its insistence on regimented class distinctions and adherence to the command structure, had made instances of cowardice rare, giving fewer opportunities for challenging one's way to high rank by ridding the empire of craven officers.

Had Jinasek been younger, he might even have welcomed a challenge, but he was getting older, and a successful challenge to his authority now would cost him his rank, his life, and probably his family their status as well. He didn't want to risk it.

So he was giving me a signal – *Save yourself, because I can't.*

I stood as tall as I could. "I invoke the Right of Defense, Commander."

He nodded, and I knew the nod was both agreement and acknowledgement I had read him correctly. "You have that right," he said. He reached out with his left hand and pointed at one of his officers. "Sub-captain Shirenas will assist you. I assume you will give him no trouble." He met my eyes, and I knew from the way his eyes narrowed that he was helping me with that choice. "You will have two days to gather evidence in your defense."

"Sir." I gave him the human equivalent to the Zhen sign of deference – something we're not anatomically equipped for – and turned to Shirenas.

He said nothing, but gestured *patience,* with a significant look at the rest of the room's occupants. I waited as Jinasek gathered his guards and departed. When we were alone, he looked from me to the mess in the cell, and his crest practically wilted. "I know you've a reputation for being a bit of a smart-ass. I hope you realize this is quite serious."

"Yeah," I said, regarding what was left of Andark's body. "Our lives – both of them – depend on getting this right. I'm sorry you got forced into this."

"I volunteered," he said.

My eyes snapped back to him. "Why in the hells would you do that?"

"I believe you are innocent," he said.

"Of course I'm innocent! But that's not the same thing as being able to *prove* I'm innocent!"

"True. But your people have been given the pointed end of the weapon for a long time. I thought maybe it would be a good thing to help you."

"That may get you killed, Shirenas."

He gestured *acceptance.* "It may. Let us do our best to prevent that outcome." He gestured to the body. "The science team has already gotten all they need. We are free to act."

I nodded and activated comms. "Midnight, how good are your scanners?"

"Not good enough to scan the remains from here," she said. "But I don't have to. I've connected your implants to my system. I see what you see, hear what you hear – and through your combat and medical implants, I can scan what you need."

I silently held my hand up in an ancient human rude gesture, pointed back at my face.

"Very funny. Can you get any closer?"

I stepped up to the cell and palmed the forcefield off. Without the field sterilizing the air coming in and out of the cell, the stench of Andark's remains hit me. Like humans, Zhen tend to void their waste when they die, and I know I'm probably not being fair, but Zhen shit is the worst smell in the universe.

"Gods, that's awful."

"Breathe through your mouth, then," Midnight said.

"Hells no, I don't want to *taste* it." I used my NeuroNet to dial my sense of smell down quite low, until the scent was bearable.

"I believe I see your point." A targeting reticule appeared in my vision, settling on a particular bit of former Zhen:ko. "Can you get me a better view of that?"

"Not without touching it," I said.

"Then prepare to get your hands dirty," she said. "Because I have some theories that need testing. Unless, of course, you'd prefer to die."

I reached out and turned the body over. I wasn't particularly grossed out – I'd seen bodies before – but I didn't usually have to touch them. I'd never gotten used to the feel of a body, the stiffening tissues, the weight and inertia of something that had once been vital robbed of its life. It gave me a sick feeling that had nothing to do with the physical grossness of the body and everything to do with the metaphysical horror of death. I prefer space battles partly because they're fun, gods help me, but mostly because in space, nobody has to handle the bodies. We commit them to the stars and that's that. This was…. It made me confront my mortality like nothing else. It was horrifying.

On the other hand, it could have been worse. "There's no blood," I said. "Shouldn't there be some?" I searched the body. "I don't see any obvious wounds."

"The medical scan done before you arrived said that the damage was all internal," Shirenas said. "Apparently there was massive trauma that destroyed his brain."

"How deep a scan did they do?"

"Down to the cellular level, I believe," he said.

"Confirmed," Midnight said. "I've got the scan now."

"All right. Shirenas, lead me to our workspace. Let's get to it."

CHAPTER EIGHT

Liam

Tajen and I stood on the shores of a lake, looking out over the peaceful beauty of the calm waters. He took my hand in his and said, "Think we should build here?"

I knew it was a dream. Some part of my mind knew that the house he was suggesting building had been completed a year ago, in this very spot. It was probably lost to the Zhen Occupation forces, who had to have found it by now. But here, in this dream, we hadn't built it yet. So I squeezed his hand, looking at the greenery that was somehow more vibrant and alive than any green I'd ever seen, on any world, and said, "Yeah. I like this place. What'll we call it?"

"Well, the records say the lake was called Loch Lomond."

"Loch?"

He shrugged. "It's an old word for *lake*, from the language of the people who lived here. Kiri even found me a song about it in the Archives." He began to sing, and his voice was richer and more practiced than I remembered it from life. Tajen could sing, but he wasn't trained like this.

By yon bonnie banks and by yon bonnie braes
Where the sun shines bright on Loch Lomond
Where we two have passed so many blithesome days
On the bonnie, bonnie banks of Loch Lomond

O ye'll take the high road and I'll take the low road
And I'll be in Scotland afore ye

But me and my true love will never meet again
On the bonnie bonnie banks of Loch Lomond

When he finished, he turned and smiled at me.

"That seems sad," I said.

"It's about two soldiers. One lives, one dies."

"I don't like the thought of that."

He pulled me to him. "Don't worry, my love. I won't leave you behind."

I felt tears welling up, and the part of me that was awake and monitoring the dream was angry. "But you did," I said, the words harsh in the cool air. "You're gone, and I have to keep muddling through this without you. I was doing fine, and then you came along and changed my whole life around, and then you left me. And now I have to pick up the pieces alone."

He turned me toward the lake and, standing behind me, put his arm around me, holding my back against his chest. "I didn't do it on purpose," he said.

"But you did it."

"Don't worry. You'll join me soon."

That didn't sound like something my husband would say, and the dream-monitor within me pulled back from the dream. "Wait, what?"

His arm rose, until it draped around my neck. And then it tightened. And suddenly I realized this wasn't part of the dream.

I snapped awake, and found myself facedown on my bed. Someone was straddling my back, his arms tightening on the belt wrapped around my throat, cutting off my air.

I tried to activate my comms implant and call for help, but found nothing but dead air. Apparently the assassin wasn't stupid; there were comms jammers in the area.

I struggled, but I couldn't get enough purchase with my arms to do anything about the man on my back strangling me. I tried to rear back and put him off balance, then I tried to roll to the side and get him off me, but he expertly shifted his weight and slammed me back to the bed, his elbows on my shoulders, pressing me down.

My lungs were burning, my face hot. I struggled to get any air at all, but it was a losing battle. The pressure on my throat wouldn't let up, and I couldn't dislodge my assailant. I could feel my consciousness fading, and I knew I wasn't long for the world. I hoped those I left behind found this bastard and made him pay for my death.

There was a loud sound. I couldn't, in my half-conscious state, recognize it, but I felt a wash of heat and then nothing.

I came to a few moments later, on my back, and heard Zekan's voice. "Medical team to Admiral Kincaid's office, immediately," he said. "The admiral has been attacked." I felt claws lightly touch my face, and opened my eyes to see Zekan. "Do not try to talk," he said.

"Is he dead?" I asked, my voice rasping.

As I grasped my throat, my eyes bulged in pain, and Zekan gestured *disdain*. "Did I not say 'Do not try to talk'? Your throat is badly damaged. I applied a nanite pack, but it will take some time to work. But yes. He is dead." He glanced to my side, and I pushed myself up and looked.

On the floor next to my bed was a human male, maybe in his thirties. He was average in every way, and dressed in normal civilian clothing. There wasn't any blood, but he was clearly dead. Instead of trying to talk again, I switched to my comms implant. "No blood. Did you snap his neck?" I asked.

"I did not," he said out loud. "My intention was to take him alive. But as soon as I grabbed him to pull him from you, something happened. He died."

"'Something happened'? You can't be more precise?"

He shrugged. "I have never seen the like."

The medical team arrived, and while they began to work on me, I connected to the doctor via comms and concentrated so I could communicate without subvocalizing. "How bad is it?"

"Not too bad," she said. "It'll take some time, but luckily we can repair everything. I'll need you to come to the med-bay."

"Fine. I need you to figure out what killed him," I sent, gesturing to the would-be assassin.

She nodded. "We'll get right on it, Admiral."

★   ★   ★

"You need a security detail," Kiri said.

"Don't be ridiculous," I replied. I'd been given the once-over in med-bay, including several hours of nano-surgery to repair my throat, and then released. Kiri had met me there and then returned to my cabin with me. I was very tired, but we had things to discuss.

"How are you holding up?" I asked, in an obvious attempt to change the subject.

She knew what I was doing, but she let me get away with it this time. "I'm fine," she said. A beat, then: "That's bullshit. I'm a mess."

"I know."

"Oh, thanks for that."

"Not what I meant." I sighed and sat on the low couch built into the inner wall and stared across to the viewscreen. "But let's not pretend either of us is okay."

She sat beside me and leaned into me, her head on my shoulder. "Yeah." We sat in silence for a few minutes, then she said, "I just can't make sense of it. How can he be gone already? I just got him back."

"I feel like I just met him," I said. "Two years with him, and now I have to muddle on without him."

"How can we?"

I sighed. "We don't have a choice. Tajen left us with work to do."

"So we have to do it to honor him?"

"Well, yes," I said. "But also, we have to do it because if we don't, we're dead. And a lot more people besides."

She laughed through her nose; it was so much like Tajen's habitual reaction that I felt a pang in my heart and my eyes welled up.

"I don't know how to do this," I said.

"Lead the fleet, or go on without him?"

"Yes." She didn't say anything. "I'm trying to hold it together, but all I want to do is sit here and gnash my teeth in despair."

"Not very Liam-like."

"Well, that's just it," I said. "Everyone has this idea of who I am, what I can do, that's based on my just surviving. Everything I've done, I did because Tajen was beside me. Without him I don't think I can manage it."

"Liam, I love you, but that's crap."

I stood and went to the viewscreen. It did an excellent job of looking like a window, and we got a great view of the stars. I stood before it, gazing out across the system. I could feel her eyes on me. I waited for her to speak.

"You were a soldier long before you met Tajen. You joined with Katherine and worked your way across the Empire before you met him."

"That was different. I was an employee doing a job."

I felt her hand on my shoulder. I glanced at her as she stepped up beside me. "Don't try to sell me that *skalk*. I talked with Takeshi a lot before he died, and I've spent a lot of time with Ben since then. You were Katherine's second, and you know as well as I how many times you stepped up when she needed you to. You've done the same so many times since you met me, I can't tell you. I know it sucks, Liam, but you *can* do this. You were doing it long before you met us."

I regarded her for a moment. Kiri'd done a lot of growing over the last couple of years. Since the day Tajen and the rest of us had come to Zhen:da, and taken her from her life there – by her choice, as much as her late father's – and started on the path that had led us here. She'd been a newly minted adult back then, still full of fear, but now she was truly coming into her own.

"You're right," I said.

"Of course I am," she said, her voice dripping with the same 'I know everything' air that Tajen always put on when he was secretly relieved something he tried had worked.

I pushed the sudden knot in my throat down, and looked at the clock. It had been a few hours since the attack, but neither of us had slept, and it was now very early in the ship's day. "Let's get some sleep," I said. "You want to use the couch?"

"Hell no," she said with a grimace. "My quarters are just down the hall, why the hell would I stay here?"

I blinked. "Not sure, really," I said. "I guess I figured you'd be wanting to stay and guard me or something, in case there was another attempt."

"Ah," she said. "No." She walked over to the door, grabbing her computer as she passed the low table on which she'd left it. As the door opened, she gestured grandly to the corridor.

I peeked out and saw Zekan standing there, armed to the teeth and armored up with a full Zhen nano-armor suit. "Oh," I said. "You're guarding me?"

"Yes," he said, his voice resonating down the corridor.

"How long is this going to last?" I asked him.

"Until we are certain there are no other Zhen agents on the ship," he said.

"You're technically a Zhen agent," I said. "I mean, you're a Zhen, and as a security officer, you're an agent of your government. Right?"

He cocked his head at me and used the Zhen gestures that meant *tolerant amusement.* "Not anymore," he said. "If that is the definition you are using, then I am now a *human* agent."

I grinned at him, and he shook his head. Even with the relatively non-expressive features of the Zhen, I could tell he was both amused and irritated at me. "All right, Zekan. Thank you," I said. I kissed Kiri on the forehead. "You too."

"Don't mention it." She nodded to Zekan and went down the corridor to her own quarters. I noticed she, too, had a guard stationed outside. I waved to him and went back into my quarters.

Kiri had had the right of it. I could do this. I *would* do this.

The alternative was unthinkable.

*   *   *

"Admiral, I've finished my examination of the assassin."

I held up a hand to stop her and looked to Injala, who was running a scan for listening devices. "Are we secure?"

Injala sat. "There are no foreign listening devices in this room."

Kiri added, "And I've shut down all the built-in links."

"Can't someone else hack them?" I asked.

"Nope." She looked impressed with herself. "I installed hardlink cutoffs. Even if someone had the hacking skill, the systems in this room are actually separated from the ship's systems until I hook them back together again. The only way to listen in now is to hack our NeuroNets." She gestured out the viewport at the shifting colors of slipspace. "Unless someone's out there with a way to listen, I guess."

"Let's not borrow more trouble than we have to," I said. "But hacking our NeuroNets – can it be done?" The Zhen had done it before.

"Not if you've installed the patches we sent out."

"All right, we're good, then." I looked around the table at Injala, Kiri, and across the table from them Zekan and Captain Zhang. "This meeting is called to order," I said. I looked to the doctor. "So what killed him?"

"Not to put too fine a point on it," Dr. Astarte said, "but his own implants did it."

"You're kidding," I said. "I was saved by an accident?"

"No. It was no accident. And it wasn't his NeuroNet. He had other implants throughout his body – not just the usual kinds we see, but something I've never seen before, spread through his brain and spinal cord."

"Do you have extensive experience with implant systems, Doctor?" Injala asked.

"I've specialized in them for most of my career, yes."

"And you cannot identify these devices?"

Dr. Astarte pursed her lips in annoyance, and when she spoke, she sounded like a teacher tired of stating the obvious. "The implants were fried. If I had to hazard a guess, they were probably intended to do just that."

"They were CYAs," I said.

"CYA?"

"Cover Your Ass," I said. "They were probably intended to take out the assassin after he killed me. Instead, they took him out for failing – probably a secondary set of directives."

"Or someone in the fleet was monitoring, and triggered them," Injala said.

I looked at Dr. Astarte. "Thank you, Zahira. If you come up with anything else, let me know?" She nodded and left.

When she'd gone, I sighed. "We had one traitor on board, it stands to reason we might have more. We need to find them."

"No shit," Kiri said. "I'm not sure how much more of this chase the fleet can take."

"We've jumped three times, and every time the Zhen show up within a day. Have we intercepted any transmissions?"

Captain Zhang looked up. "No," she said, "but frankly there's so much communications traffic both before and after a jump it's hard to track them all."

Injala spoke. "Your fleet has a standard procedure of checking in with each other after every jump. It is possible that the transmissions being sent to the Zhen are hidden within this signal traffic."

"True," I said, "but we've been jumping to systems with no slipnet relay. How are they getting the word to the Zhen?"

"Your ships also disseminate the new jump coordinates via comms before every jump."

"Yeah, but those are secured—" Injala was shaking her head. "What's wrong?" I asked.

"There is no such thing as truly 'secured' transmissions. Even with your encryption, even with tightly focused comms, there are too many failure points. How do we know that nobody has a slipnet relay tucked away in a ship's hold? How do we know that all of the ships are exactly what they claim to be, for that matter?"

Kiri said, "She's right. We've looked for transmissions, but we can't catch everything. Our attention can only be split so many ways."

"Wonderful," I said. "So how do we find them?"

"Trap them," Zekan said. "It will be difficult, but it can be done."

"How?"

He began to sketch in the air, his NeuroNet sending the information to my own, showing me what he was doing. My blood ran cold and I looked to Kiri. "Could they be using Zekan's NeuroNet?"

"No," she said. "I wrote a new patch for his that blocked the Zhen out. He can use his just like us, but if he ever goes back to Zhen:da, he's going to need an update."

I accepted her explanation and turned to Zekan again. He sketched out a small representation of the fleet. "Send different coordinates to each ship," he said, "using tightbeamed comms. Send a single small ship to each jump destination. If the Zhen appear at one of them, we know which ships to focus on. Give each captain sealed orders to be opened once they realize they are clear – these will give them a rendezvous to rejoin the fleet."

"What if more than one shows up?"

"It still narrows our search down."

"That's still a lot of people to risk."

"Yes," Injala said. "But it narrows the field."

I nodded. "Do it. Anything else we need to deal with?"

Captain Zhang said, "Probably, but we're supposed to revert to realspace in about two minutes. I need to get to the bridge."

"I'll join you," I said.

As Zhang and I headed for the bridge, Zekan shadowing me as always since the attack, Zhang glanced over at me. "You're doing well," she said.

"I don't feel like it."

"Well, that's command for you. It never feels like you're doing the right thing."

We reached the bridge, where I traded an awkward nod with Alex, who was sitting beside the astrogator on duty. He nodded politely, but I saw a twinkle in his eye I chose to ignore.

We approached the command station, where the XO was standing watch. "Reversion to normal space in fifteen seconds," he said.

"All hands, ready," Captain Zhang's voice rang out.

Moments after we burst into normal space, every ship trailing the liquid light of slipspace for a few seconds, I heard the ship's flight officer granting Injala's Kelvaki pilots permission to launch.

The first time we'd exited slipspace, the Zhen had been only seconds behind us. When they didn't jump in this time, I began to breathe again.

Until I saw several ships start flashing emergency transponders in the tactical plot. "What the hell?"

"Six ships reporting explosions!" called a member of the bridge crew. "Internal! All are losing integrity. *Serenissima* reports most passengers safe, but the ship has lost atmosphere. They've sealed off the passenger quarters, but they've only got a couple of hours of air."

"*Earthborn* reporting in," another comms officer said. "Captain is reporting—" He paled and said into his comms, "*Earthborn*, *Litvyak*. Confirm your last transmission." He turned to Captain Zhang and me, and his voice had lost its strength. "The captain is reporting the explosion was caused by multiple suicide bombs in the civilian holds. The blasts opened the holds to space. They lost everyone in the hold."

All over the bridge, the men and women of our crew looked either at the command station, or out the viewports toward where *Earthborn* was. We couldn't see the ship from here, but it didn't stop anyone from trying.

Zhang glanced around the bridge. "There are civilians out there who need our help. Work now, fall apart later!" She turned to comms. "Get the other ships on the line. Find out how badly they're damaged. If they can't be repaired quickly, get shuttles over there to offload their passengers. Bring them here for now. *Move!*" She dropped her voice and said to me, "We'll be able to manage them here for a time, but we'll need to get them redistributed around the fleet pretty quickly, or we'll lose fighting effectiveness."

I nodded. "Get Quince on it. He handled the— What?"

Zhang's face was stricken. "Quince was on *Earthborn*, checking on the refugees' situation."

"Oh, shit," I breathed. "I'll be on the first shuttle to *Earthborn*," I said. "I need to see this."

"Admiral, I don't recommend—" She met my eyes and stopped talking. "Very well, sir."

★   ★   ★

I stood in the *Earthborn*'s hold, Zekan beside me, both of us suited in full combat-ready spacesuits. "Gods above and below," I said. "Why would they do this?" I looked to Zekan. "What in the *zhen:saak:arl* allows for this?"

I couldn't see his crest, but his voice made his feelings clear. "There is nothing in the Struggle that allows for this," he said. "Killing innocents is an act of dishonor."

"But that applies only to Zhen."

"A Zhen almost certainly gave the order," he said. "Liam, even if I had not already joined your cause, this act would have made me do so. We must send word of this into the slipnet."

"We do that, we'll give away where we are," I said.

"Send it with one of Injala's spies," he said. "They can transmit it from a system far from us."

"Makes sense." I walked to the edge of the biggest hole, where the bomb had blown through both the ship's inner and outer hulls. "They knew just where to put the bombs," I said. "They wanted as many dead as they could get."

"Yes."

"Quince was here?"

"Yes. His death is confirmed."

"Damn it," I said. "I was beginning to like him."

We returned to the shuttle. Neither of us spoke again as we removed our suits and returned the nanite blocks to the shuttle's racks for charging. We took our seats, across from each other. The *Earthborn*'s survivors – four of them, out of a crew of thirty and over a hundred passengers – kept to themselves at the other end of the shuttle. Their captain was staring at nothing, his eyes unfocused. He looked broken, his soul in pieces.

I stared out the viewport, trying not to turn away from the sight of bodies, each spinning away from the wreckage in its own direction. We'd considered recovering them, but we'd decided it was better to get out of here while we could, to maximize the people we could save. Besides, no ship had room to store so many bodies. *Earthborn* had been the worst hit, but all five of the ships had lost most of their passengers, and one had lost the entire ship.

I took a breath and said what I was afraid to even think. "Zekan, in the beginning this was about control. I don't think it is anymore."

"No. The One does not wish to control humans any longer – at least, not those here, in open revolt." He met my eyes, and his crest flattened to his scalp. "She means to destroy you."

I was silent for a few moments, and then asked, "Will the Talnera help? Can they?"

"I wish I could say yes. But…the power of the Talnera is minimal. When claw comes to flesh, it is the Twenty and the One, Zornaav and her Council, who have the real power. The Talnera are merely supplicants who handle the 'unimportant' work of running the infrastructure of the Empire. They are glorified bureaucrats given a modicum of power to pacify the masses. When it comes to policy decisions, only the Twenty can help – and they will not even consider it."

I blinked. "That's the most you've ever said to me at one time."

"Yes."

"You're much more erudite than you pretend."

He looked uncomfortable. "Yes."

"Why?"

His hands rose from his sides, then fell back – a human gesture he was clearly using very deliberately, since it had never really transferred to the Zhen. "We do not speak of it often," he said, "but the Zhen:la are not entirely our own masters either. And sometimes, appearing *too* intelligent can get you…noticed, I suppose is the right word."

"By the Zhen:ko."

"Or by Imperial Intelligence."

"Is that dangerous? You were a cop."

"I'm sure you've heard of Zhen who were killed mysteriously, or 'accidentally', just as there are humans. I believe that the reason so many Zhen mistreat humans and our other clients so much is that it helps them forget that they, too, are subjects of an uncaring oligarchy concerned mainly with remaining in power."

I turned back to the viewport, deep in thought. We needed to find any remaining Zhen agents among the humans of the fleet. But then what?

I opened comms. "Injala."

"Yes, Liam?"

"When are your scouts due to report in?"

"Sometime in the next few hours," she said.

"I want to hear their report immediately."

"Did you truly believe I needed to be told this?"

"Just making sure."

"Humans," she said with a sigh. "I'll alert you as soon as I receive the report."

★   ★   ★

Later that afternoon I got a message from Alex. "You could probably use a short distraction," he said. "Since we're in slipspace, there's not much for you to do, right? So come hang out, have some food, some drink, and unload a bit." A room code was attached.

I decided to accept the invitation. Dinner would be nice, a change of pace from sitting in my cabin replaying the explosions over and over in my mind.

Alex answered the door with a glass in hand. "Come in," he said, handing it to me.

I took it and sniffed at it. It had the slightly sweet scent of whiskey. "Where'd you get this?" I asked, taking a sip.

"One of the refugees on the *Burgundy* had a few bottles in his bags," he said. "I did him a favor in exchange for one."

"How'd you know I like it?"

He winked. "Oh, I have my sources," he said.

I narrowed my eyes as I followed him into the room. It was about half the size of my own, with a couch that converted to a bed at one end, and a small galley at the other, and a doorway into a tiny refresher closet. "I thought you said your current bunk was in a crowded room," I said.

"It was. But I signed up as permanent crew. Based on my prior experience, they made me a lieutenant, so I get a room. Luckily there was one still available." He looked around. "It's fucking tiny, but it's heaven compared to where they've got the refugees quartered. I even have my own 'fresher, and it only cost me two years of my life."

"Is that the going rate now?"

He shrugged. "Way I see it, in two years this war we've found ourselves in will be over one way or another. But tonight is not supposed to be about that, so sit, try to relax, and I'll get dinner ready."

I sat as he moved to the little galley at the other end of the small cabin. "I hope you're not expecting a feast," he said. "All I could get out of the mess was standard meal trays." He popped one into the small cooker and set it to going. "It's not good food, but it's food, and at least the company's interesting, I hope?"

"Well, we'll see," I said.

"Ouch," he teased. "A hit!" He brought the trays over and placed one before me as he took his seat. "Don't stand on ceremony, eat." He picked up his fork. "Mmm, reconstituted protein seventeen," he said with false gusto. He popped a bite into his mouth, chewed with a thoughtful expression, and swallowed. "Huh. It's not as bad as I expected."

The rest of the meal passed in companionable silence. Standard rations are designed to be filling, but they aren't big, and it didn't take long to finish. We moved to the couch, and Alex poured me another whiskey. "How's command?" he asked.

"You serve on the bridge, you know what it's like," I replied.

"Sure, but I'm just a jump operator," he said. "I'm not privy to all the cool insider info."

"Afraid I can't help you there," I said. "You probably know as much as I could tell you already. Everything above that's classified to command staff only."

"I'm wounded," he said, hand over his heart. "Utterly wounded." He sighed dramatically, and moved his hand to his brow in the ancient gesture of woe. "Well, maybe a little less important a topic, then. How'd you meet Injala?"

"She's attached to the Kelvaki Assembly's court," I said. "Tajen and I met her there. When we left, she was assigned to help us."

"Seems a bit shifty, doesn't it?"

"How do you mean?"

"Well, she's a Kelvaki agent, clearly. And yet she's here, helping humans in an open insurrection against what, to the Kelvaki, is an enemy power. How do they justify that?"

"I'm not sure they have to," I said. Of course, Injala's presence had more to do with Tajen being friends with the heir to the Kelvaki throne, but I wasn't going to admit that. If we managed to survive all this, I didn't want the helpfulness of the Kelvaki reduced to cronyism in the inevitable holo-dramas. "Of course they have their own agenda, but helping us fits with that. I'm not going to refuse that help when we so clearly need it."

"Don't blame you," he said. "But I can't lie, she scares me a little bit. It's her eyes. She always looks like she can see right through you."

"She can," I said. "Kelvaki can see into the X-ray spectrum."

He stared at me for several seconds before grinning. "Bullshit."

I kept my face straight as long as I could, but in the end I laughed. "Yeah, but I had you going there for a minute."

"Not even close," he said with a laugh. He reached out to punch my shoulder playfully. I fended off the 'attack', and we quickly descended into horseplay for a few moments.

And then I came back to myself, and stood up. "Thanks for dinner," I said, "but I need to go."

He pointedly looked at my crotch and said, his eyes twinkling, "You sure? Doesn't look like you really want to."

And that was the splash of metaphorical cold water I needed. "Yeah, I need to," I said, a smile on my face. "No offense, I like you – more and more, I do. But it's just not time, not yet." I didn't wait for a response, but quickly left.

I managed to hold myself together as I collected my bodyguard in the corridor and all but fled back to my own quarters. I waved the guard back as I entered and sat on the couch, breathing deeply and holding my arms tightly around myself.

The truth was, I'd been tempted. Of course I had been. My husband was dead. I was lonely, and Alex was definitely attractive and interested. So why was I so hesitant? It had been months since Shoa'kor, and I'd dealt with my grief. At least, I thought I had.

So why was I still waiting for Tajen to come home?

I sent Kiri an invite to a virtual conference. She appeared on the couch next to me. "What's up, Liam?"

"Kiri, I wondered what you'd think of me...well, I—"

"Yes, you should ask Alex out."

"How did you know about—"

"Oh, please. You're the admiral, and my only remaining relative. Do you really think there's anything about you I don't know? On *this* ship?"

"But Tajen—"

"Is gone. I hate it, and I wish you two had been given more time. But the universe is what it is." She leaned toward me. "You miss him, I know. You always will."

"He was the love of my life, and probably always will be."

Thanks to the visual fidelity of our systems, I could see the tears well in her eyes. "Tajen would have loved that. He was always a little bit arrogant about that kind of thing. Don't get me wrong, he was a good man, but I've done some digging. He left a string of broken hearts behind him and he loved it." She laughed exactly like Tajen would have, and my heart cracked anew. "But because he was a good man, he wouldn't want you to be lonely. Especially given the job you're doing. He'd want you to be happy."

"I'm not sure Alex is the man to replace him," I said.

"So what? Who said he has to be? Have some fun, enjoy him for as long as it makes sense. If it's forever, great. I'll love you being happy too. If not, I'll console you when you break his heart."

"Hey, he might break mine."

She gave me the Hunt Deathstare. "We both know that's not gonna happen. Do what makes you happy. Don't worry about me, or Tajen. He's beyond it, and I want you to be my wonderful Uncle Liam, and not a weeping widower to the end of your days."

"You're a very wise woman," I said.

Her voice took on a haughty tone. "I am what my father and my uncles made me," she said, then dropped her tone to a deadpan, accusatory tone. "So it's your bloody fault."

She signed off, and I sat in the dark for a little while, then said to myself, "Time to move on."

★   ★   ★

Injala scanned the conference room as Kiri disengaged the room from the rest of the ship's systems. Scan done, she turned to me. "We have a problem," she said.

"Your scouts returned?"

"Yes." She tossed the report into the air, where it unfolded into a visual. Kiri looked up, and her gasp echoed my own.

"By the Nine," Zhang whispered.

The central admin building was still standing. Originally built by the Zhen during the long years they'd been running the place as an outpost for their military, we'd taken it over and made it our colonial administration center.

The city had grown outward from there, in the year between our retaking of Earth and the beginning of this war, from a central administration building and a landing field to a full-sized city of a hundred thousand people. It had a sports arena, homes, and parks. A performing arts center was being built. People were making lives there.

It was all gone.

Except for the central building, the city was a mess of rubble, with a few buildings barely hanging on, their sides blasted from the metal and plascrete skeletons, once-thriving homes and centers of industry now open to the weather. It looked like the Zhen had just flattened it.

The camera's angle shifted, and a Kelvaki woman's voice said, "This is the city now. Some humans escaped into the outlying areas, but many died in the destruction."

The camera settled on a young man, huddled in a blind. "Lieutenant Ryan Hitchens reporting. We got as many people as we could out of the city. Some of the settlements were spared, if they submitted to Zhen rule, but others are deserted and destroyed now, their people in hiding. We're doing what we can to keep as many alive as possible, but we need help. We—" He broke off as the sounds of a Zhen aircraft began to build. "We need to get out of here! Follow me!"

The camera view shifted to pure data – numbers of dead, locations of Resistance hiding places, comms codes to reach them. When the report ended, Injala looked to me.

"Can we send them any help?" I asked.

"We have already begun the process of humanitarian aid," she said, "but the Zhen government has rebuffed our requests to offer that aid openly, so we're having to filter it in clandestinely. But getting more than a handful of people off-planet is simply impossible."

"Can we—"

"Retake the planet?" she asked. "Yes, I thought you might ask that. But no. The Assembly High Council is still not willing to attack openly. We simply don't have the strength to do so effectively, and they will not commit when the most likely outcome is a war where we are not guaranteed survival."

I couldn't really blame them. The Zhen don't do peace; either you have to be able to hammer them back, or you have to avoid the fight until you can. "We can't go back to Earth," I said. "And we can't keep running forever." I looked at Captain Zhang, a question in my eyes. She nodded in agreement, as did Kiri. I turned to Injala. "I would like to request formal asylum in the Kelvaki Empire for my fleet."

"I have already been instructed to grant it if asked. But first we need to find our remaining traitors."

"Of course. Are your preparations ready?"

"Yes."

"Very well. Captain Zhang." I handed her a slip of actual paper on which I'd written several systems, all chosen at random from a curated list of systems. "Send these destinations to the ships listed for each. Do not tell them there are any variances. As far as the ships are concerned, we're all jumping to the same place. Give them sealed orders, set to open once they've been clear for two days, instructing them to wait for a courier." I grinned. "We're going low-tech on this one."

"Yes, sir."

I looked back to Injala. "Let's hope this works," I said.

CHAPTER NINE

Katherine

I was taken to a lift, which rose for a few minutes, then released me into a short corridor. I could hear the rumbling sounds of a crowd echoing down the passage. "Go," my escort said, giving me a shove.

I followed the corridor; it led into an octagonal chamber. The level I was on was small, only about ten meters across, but it rose in tiers above us, opening into a huge chamber. Each tier was full of Marauders; as I entered the space, the crowd went silent and turned to face the center of the room.

A man stood there, bald and gray-bearded, wearing ornate robes of cloth with metal panels sewn in various places. Painted geometric patterns covered his face and scalp. He gestured to the space before him, inviting me to enter it.

He raised his eyes to the room as I did so. "A penitent has come to us," he said. "She asks that we allow her to become a Marauder – a member of our tribe." He looked down to me, and his voice lowered in volume, but only just. "Is this so?"

"No," I said.

He feigned shock. "No?"

"I *ask* nothing," I said. "I *demand* the right to prove that I am *already* a Marauder, forged by the universe, tempered by pain and honed by struggle."

"And at whose throat are you pointed?" he asked.

"I am aimed at the Zhen," I said. "At the Twenty and the One."

He looked a little surprised at my answer – or perhaps just at the second part, which I had added myself to the ritual words Andra had taught me. He gazed into my eyes for several long moments, then nodded. "So be it," he said. He gestured to a pile of clothing on the table beside him. "Change into these clothes, for the ritual."

I looked around for a changing area, but saw none. In response to my questioning look, he said, "A Marauder has no secrets from the tribe."

That was clearly propaganda, but being nude in front of others wasn't something I particularly cared about, so I simply ditched my clothes and placed them into the box he provided. They'd already taken what gear I'd had on me when I'd been captured, or I'd have been instructed to place it in the box with my clothes.

When I stood before him again, he indicated I should kneel. "You understand the rules?" he asked.

"Yes," I said, trying very hard not to show my annoyance. "I'm to find and steal cargo valued at a minimum of half a million *dekka* and bring it back here – without pursuit."

"A *ship* with cargo valued at five hundred thousand *dekka*," he said.

"Right. A ship with cargo. And I'm to do all that without any help?"

"A Marauder finds a way," he intoned.

I'd been warned; that meant the conversation was over. "A Marauder finds a way," I repeated.

And then I felt a sharp pain in the back of my skull, and—

★　　★　　★

I woke in darkness, pressed in on all sides by – I wasn't sure what, actually. *What the hell?* I wondered. I activated my implant's low-light mode.

At least, I tried to. Nothing happened, and the room was still dark.

I tried to activate a diagnostic, but there was no response. In fact, none of the functions of my NeuroNet were responding.

Calm down, I told myself, and began to take stock. I was in an equipment locker, and it was on a starship – I could feel the vibration of the engines through the deck plates, and I could hear, at the edge of my awareness, the subsonic rumble of starship engines.

And I was naked.

My brow furrowed at that, and then I realized the Marauders hadn't been kidding when they said I'd be sent out with 'nothing'. But they were wrong, of course. I might not have had clothing or gear, but I was in an equipment locker, and that meant I could maybe find some.

I opened the locker door a tiny bit, made sure there was nobody outside, and worked my way out of the cramped locker. It opened into a small equipment room, with lockers and equipment racks lining the walls. The lights were harsh and bright, but I acclimated quickly, and turned to see if there were any supplies in the locker I'd been stashed in.

There wasn't much there, so I moved on to another locker. There I found a crew shipsuit. The shapeless garment was a bit too big, but I managed to cinch it with the belt so I wouldn't look too out of place on first glance. I also found an arc-thrower, which I tucked into my belt.

Now. Where the hell was I? There was a terminal in the room, inset into the wall over the workbench. But without a NeuroNet, I couldn't access it easily. NeuroNet failures are almost unheard of, and while there are redundant controls on most ship systems, computer terminals don't typically include built-in physical input devices.

I opened the drawers of the workbench. In the first two, I found a few small useful things and shoved them into my pockets. In the third, I found what I needed – a computer interface. I pulled it out and extended the cable, plugging it into the computer terminal's UI port.

If Kiri had been here, I could have had her hack directly into the crew information system. But that kind of thing was beyond my ability. The public system, though, wasn't protected. I discovered I was on the transport vessel *Alakaar*, headed for Karada Station, where we'd dock in three days.

"Shit," I breathed. Karada Station was a Zhen transport hub, deep in the Empire. To get me here, I must have been kept unconscious for weeks, but I wasn't hungry, so I'd been nourished somehow. I must have been put in the locker recently, but had been in transit longer. This situation gave me a whole set of problems to solve beyond what I'd expected. "Let's see," I muttered to myself, "I've got to get on board the station without getting caught, find a ship with the right kind of cargo, and somehow manage to steal that ship and get it back to Dakcha, by myself, with nobody to help me, no weapons, and no NeuroNet. Somebody really wants me dead."

Andra had warned me I'd be sent out with little, but she'd said nothing about my NeuroNet being disabled. So either she hadn't known, or it wasn't standard procedure in these initiations – if they had anything like a 'standard procedure' in the first place. "Well, it's supposed to test my ability," I said. "I guess it will at that."

We still had three days in transit before we arrived at Karada. It was pretty unlikely I'd be able to bluff my way through meeting anyone else in the crew, so the first thing I needed to do was find a place to hide. But moving about the ship was going to be much, much harder without a working—

Oh. I had an idea.

I downloaded a map of the ship's passenger sections to the keyboard's onboard memory storage and slipped out of the docking bay, making my way toward the passenger areas. Whenever I could I kept to the engineering spaces in between the inner and outer hull. I was able to avoid a couple of human crew members, and eventually found myself in the first-class section.

I made my way to a cabin and, using the electronics skills I'd spent decades honing, got the door open. I quickly made sure nobody was in the cabin and went to the wardrobe. Sadly, nothing in it was anywhere near my size, so I moved on. In the next cabin, I found civilian clothing. As I slipped into it, I noticed the cabin's owner staring at me from the bed.

"Shit!" I exclaimed. "Please don't call for help."

She didn't say anything, and a moment later I realized her eyes were open, but she wasn't seeing me. I crept closer, and realized she was gone. I turned her head to the side, suspicious, and sure enough, there was an em-chip plugged into a neural interface port behind her ear.

Em-chips had begun as 'emotion stimulators', hence the name, but the newer ones did more. Many created altered states in the brain, giving the user anything from a vague high to full-on hallucinations. And sometimes, rarely, but it happened, they could interact with problems in the user's NeuroNet and fry the user's brain completely.

I pulled the em-chip from the socket and plugged my interface into the port. Her NeuroNet's system information told me that her name was Peri McDonald, and according to the datashunt, she was traveling alone. "Not a great day for you, Peri," I said, "but Earth thanks you for your sacrifice. Even if it wasn't your choice."

I quickly copied the data keys from Peri's NeuroNet and stored it in the interface's onboard storage, then moved to the room's computer. I used the terminal and Peri's keys to hack into the system and change her portrait to mine. Once that was done, I wrapped Peri's body in her sheets.

The room, like all first-class cabins, had a stasis capsule for use in emergencies. Big enough to hold one person, it was for unplanned drive failures that left the ship years from rescue. The crew and lower class passengers would have the common shelters, but first class got their own. I placed Peri's body into the capsule, then disabled the system's ability to tell the ship's computer it had been activated, and turned it on.

I finished dressing in the poor woman's clothes, then headed for sick bay, acting as if I belonged. When I entered, a human medic approached me. "Can I help you?" he said.

"I hope so," I answered. I tapped my head. "For some reason, my NeuroNet's stopped working."

He cocked his head at me. "That's not normal," he said, looking concerned. "We don't have any neuro-specialists, but maybe it's just a software issue. Hop on up." He gestured to a medbench.

I laid myself down on the bench, and he placed the sensor net over my head and flipped some switches. "That's really weird," he said.

I played myself like the wealthy tourist I was supposed to be. "What?"

"Well, I was right – it's a software issue. Your system has been shut down," he said. "Completely."

"What?" I said. "How could that happen?"

He frowned for a moment, then shook his head. "It's not unknown," he said. "Sometimes criminals will lock down someone's NeuroNet before assaulting them – to keep them from calling for help." He peered closer at his screen. "But it's not usually done this well. Normally it's a masking program, brute-forced into the victim's implants. It keeps them from doing anything with their 'Net, but it's not shut off like this." He frowned. "This would require someone to be *really* close to you. It's not something you can do with a handheld device. Did you go to anyone's cabin recently?"

"Well," I said, giving him a flirty look, "a girl hates to kiss and tell."

"Did you lose any time recently? Wake up feeling more fuzzy-headed than usual?"

"Yes," I said, acting like I was suddenly worried, and then sliding back into party girl mode, "but no more than the usual party favor headaches."

"You need to be more careful," he said, not rising to my charms. "Here, I can reset your 'Net." He flicked another switch, and my system sprang into life. "Is there anything else I can do for you?"

"No, that was all I was worried about," I said, and left before he could ask any more questions. I'd been lucky – thank the Nine for full-service cruises – but I didn't want to push my luck.

I returned to Peri's – or my, now, I supposed – cabin. As I entered the cabin, I caught a hint of motion on the edge of my vision. I had just enough time to raise an arm in defense. I managed to block the strike, but my assailant was good. He grabbed my arm and swung me around and into the wall. His weight pressed into me, and he maneuvered my arm around and up near my shoulder blades. "Who the fuck are you?" he asked.

"I'm Peri— *Ow*," I said, as he twisted my arm up farther.

"I want your real name," he growled. "And don't even fucking lie to me."

In the stress of the moment, I didn't do what I should and give him a fake name. "Katherine," I said.

His face came around to peer at mine. "Oh shit," he said, and backed up, releasing me. Confused, I turned so my back was to the wall, and just looked at him, my arms still raised defensively.

"'The best lack all conviction'," he said, waiting for me to say more.

I relaxed, relief flooding through me. "'While the worst are filled with passionate intensity'," I said, and relaxed. It was a code phrase, a way for agents of the Earth resistance to ID each other.

He touched his right brow and said, "I'm Dax Ng'ang'a."

"You're Resistance. What are you doing here?"

He looked sheepish. "I got into some trouble on Terra. I was told to lay low for a while, so I took this job to get off-planet. You're Katherine Lawson, right?"

"Yes."

"I thought you looked familiar," he said, "and when you said your name, I thought – well. Maybe it's her. What do those lines mean, anyway?"

I shrugged. "Beats me. Tajen Hunt chose them. He's got a thing for some Old Earth poet."

"Okay," he said. "That explains…well, nothing. But okay. Katherine Lawson, in the flesh." He looked to the stasis chamber. "Did you have to kill her?"

"I didn't. I came here to steal some clothes and found her dead."

He groaned. "She fried herself with an em-chip, didn't she?"

I nodded, and he shook his head. "Well, shit. Dammit."

"She a friend?" I asked.

"Worse," he said. "I was hired by her dad to keep her safe. But she wouldn't listen to me about the em-chips. She's been using them for a while now." He looked at the unit again. "I guess I can say goodbye to the bonus."

"I'm sorry," I said.

"Well, what're you gonna do?" he said. "Not your fault. So. I take it you needed her clothes for a reason?"

I nodded. "I'm on a mission. Got sapped and put here. I need to get off at Karada to continue my mission." It was close to the truth. He didn't need to know the full details, but he could help me.

"Okay," he said. "I can help you get off. Need me to stick with you at Karada? I don't have anything to go back to now. Soon as I report in, her dad'll just cut me loose, I'm pretty sure."

"I'd love the help," I said, "but I can't take you with me. Wish I could."

"I understand," he said. "I'll help you as long as I can, then. For now, we've got to get through three more days on this ship. Might as well keep up the pretense – if you stay close to quarters, nobody will notice 'Peri' has changed."

"She doesn't interact with the crew? Other passengers?"

He snorted with amusement. "The crew are – were – beneath her notice. The other passengers are mostly older than her, so – *also* – beneath her notice." He sighed. "She wasn't my favorite client. Still, she didn't deserve that."

"Seems like she chose it for herself," I said.

"I guess so," he said. He looked toward the stasis unit. "I saw that you disconnected the alarm circuit, but when we get off this ship and she's found, it's going to send red flags up."

"Were you transferring at Karada?"

"No," he said. "We're bound for Kintar." At my expression, he said, "Peri was into slumming it with the fringe elements. She wanted to experience life on the fringe before she went to work in Daddy's company."

"Are you going to have trouble when you report in?"

"Probably," he said, "but only a little. My contract didn't specify protecting her from her own vices, and it's not like I gave her the chips."

I thought about it, and something occurred to me. "Crap," I said. "I changed the information on this ship's database, but that's not going to fool the authorities at Karada. Not only will the information on the slipnet not match with the ship's database, but Peri wasn't scheduled to leave the ship." I frowned. "And my face is probably all over the Zhen feeds – I'm on the most-wanted list."

"So if you show your face, you'll be under arrest immediately."

"No, I'm pretty sure they'll just shoot me on sight. So we need to get me through security without them seeing me to get a visual."

"A visual isn't the only problem – though you getting shot is definitely something we need to prevent," he said, his eyes twinkling. "If you use your NeuroNet you'll set off every alarm in the place once the system recognizes you. And then we're back to you getting shot."

"Got that covered," I said, tapping myself on the temple. "I've got an overlay in my system – it disguises who I am."

He cocked his head at me. "Why didn't you use it to pretend to be a passenger on this ship, instead of telling the computer you were Peri?"

I shrugged. "My 'Net wasn't working at first. But then once it was reactivated, I needed to pretend to be a passenger. It wouldn't do for a person who hadn't been on the ship manifest to suddenly show up."

"Good point. Okay, so the problem now is how do we get you past security. I have an idea," he said. "Once we jump out of slipspace, we put you in the stasis unit, then I get you off the ship and turn it back on once we're away from the Zhen."

"One small problem," I said. "Setting aside whether or not I want to trust you to get me through – please understand, I don't doubt your intent, but I'm not sure about your ability – if they find her body in here, that'll send up alerts on Karada once they see 'she' has left the ship there. That'll make my mission eleven kinds of difficult I'd rather not have to deal with."

He looked thoughtful. "I've got it," he said. "Be right back."

He was gone for only a couple of minutes. "Solved it," he said, and hefted a small cylinder. "We use these on Terra to avoid leaving evidence. It's a nanite colony. Pour it on a body, it eats the body, then turns on itself – dissipates and shuts down."

I stood slowly. "Nanotech like that is heavily regulated," I said. "Where did you get it?"

"My quarters?"

"Dax, I'm from Terra, and I know how hard that kind of tech is to come by there. How did the Resistance get it?"

"I don't know," he said. "We made contact with someone from off-world. They've been supplying us with weapons. These came in a few shipments before I left." He held the vial out to me.

I took it and examined the casing. It didn't seem Zhen. But it did remind me of the architecture of the Tabran ship. Were they helping the Resistance now?

I handed the vial back to Dax and said, "I think this is our best chance. But if I wake up from stasis in Zhen custody, you'd better be dead."

He looked offended, then shook his head ruefully. "You're Katherine bloody Lawson," he said. "If the Zhen get you, I will definitely already be dead. They won't have a chance otherwise."

"Okay. Let's do it."

CHAPTER TEN

Tajen

Shirenas and I were standing in a 'virtuality workspace', a room more or less empty of anything but a couple of chairs, a refresher closet with fittings for both our species, and a few scientific instruments we might need.

Of course, that was just the physical space. What we saw, though, was far more. The room held Andark's body in the center of the room, currently appearing to float at chest height.

Virtualities were in common use throughout the Empire, but Midnight's capabilities as an AI were not. The Zhen didn't like AI, and in fact the use of AI was forbidden under Zhen law. "Shirenas, there's something we need to discuss. You see, my ship has an AI."

He turned to glance at me, his crest quivering with amusement. "I am aware," he said.

"What? How?"

"She introduced herself when we were still in the cell," he said.

"Oh. Um."

He waved at me. "Relax. I am not in favor of the Zhen law against AI. Besides which, you are already a rebel and a wanted criminal in the eyes of the Empire – why worry about this law when so many others are being ignored?" He gestured *amusement*. "But it is probably best that we tell nobody else unless we have no choice."

My anxiety deflated, just for a moment. "All right, let's zoom in on the brain," I said.

The graphic of Andark's body seemed to expand, his now-dulled red skin fading away as Midnight's processors peeled away the outer layers of skin and skull to show us the Zhen's central nervous system. The brain matter was in the skull, just like in humans.

There were several areas in the brain, as well as in the secondary structures, that appeared to have suffered injury. I placed my hands around one of them and pulled them apart, enlarging the image to many times its true size. "What does that look like to you?" I asked Shirenas.

"It appears that the major cause of death was severe brain trauma," he said.

"Well, sure. His NeuroNet was fried, for one thing – the shocks caused by that probably did some of the work. But here, and here," I said, indicating specific zones, which Midnight highlighted for me. "That looks to me like something ate him."

"Inside his brain?" Shirenas said, doubtful. He looked closer, and ran a new scan. "You are correct. Something attacked the tissue in these specific regions."

I noticed his crest was repeatedly flexing, a sign of agitation in a Zhen. "What is it?" I asked warily.

"These are not new injuries," he said. "This was done some time ago. But that doesn't make sense."

"Why not?"

"These specific zones are believed to regulate the Zhen sense of individual self," he said. "With damage like this, it is possible – even probable – that Andark would have had nearly no conception of himself as an individual being. He would have been nearly dormant."

"But I talked to him," I said. "Believe me, he knew who he was."

"Did he?" Midnight asked.

"What do you mean? Of course he did."

The hologram of the brain shifted to one side of the room and shrank. In its place, a recording from my 'Net's view of my last conversation with him took form.

"I'm not against you, Andark. Just your leader."

"It is the same thing."

I paused the playback. "Yeah, okay, I remember the conversation," I said. "What's your point?"

Midnight emulated a long-suffering sigh, and I spared a moment to promise retribution on her programmers. "Try to focus, Captain. What is heard is sometimes not recognized."

The holo of Andark continued. As Andark's last words were repeated, I watched his body. I didn't get it. "Play it again," I said.

"But we have seen our mistake." Something about his voice, not the sound of it...not the accent, but the cadence, the rhythm of his speech, was familiar to me. It was something I'd heard in my nightmares for months, that I'd heard in the Sol System.

And then it came to me, and I tried as hard as I could to reject it. "Andark is related to the One," I said.

Shirenas accessed his files. "Not according to Imperial records," he said. "They are both *:ko*, but they are not of the same clan."

"Then why do they sound so similar?" I asked. "It's not just their caste. There's more to it. But come on, there's no way." I accessed my 'Net's recordings on my own and flung one to the center of the room. The One, Zornaav herself, appeared there.

"Molding your race more directly will slow our expansion plans, but in the end, we will have human soldiers who will fight and die at our word." The cadences were exactly the same.

"He was never Andark," I said.

"That fits with what I'm seeing," Midnight said.

"Impossible," Shirenas growled. "It makes no sense."

"Look here," Midnight said, and the holos returned to Andark's brain. Labels and markers appeared. "The regions of his brain that made him an individual were destroyed, but if you look closely, the scar tissue is old – years old, if I am not mistaken, and I doubt I am."

Shirenas looked closer, and ran some data. "Confirmed," he said, his tone betraying his nervousness.

"And secondly, the NeuroNet, even damaged as it is by the power discharged during the execution, is identifiable. While it is of Zhen manufacture, it has been modified."

"How so?"

"It uses Tabran technology."

*   *   *

"He was definitely killed by his NeuroNet, which received an instruction to kill him through an overload," I said to Commander Jinasek.

Shirenas and I had used up most of a day running more tests. We'd worked late, but eventually we'd had to sleep. Now we were on our second and last day, and though we'd figured out *how* Andark had died, we were no closer to discovering who had initiated the command to his NeuroNet.

Jinasek regarded me for several uncomfortable moments. Finally, he said, "How were these Tabran nanites introduced to his systems?"

Midnight spoke to me, and I relayed her words to him. "They've been part of his system for a long time," I said. "Probably for years now."

"Years."

"Yes."

"How do we know that?"

"The nanites recovered from the tissue samples contain logs," I said. "They have a record of minor fixes and comms activity going back months. And they aren't a new Tabran design."

"How do you know that?"

"Date codes in the logs," I said. It was a true statement, but not a completely truthful one.

"We have no record of where this command came from?"

"Not specifically – they attacked him because of a command from outside this ship, routed through a slipnet relay."

Jinasek grunted and flicked his hands toward a comms display. "Communications officer," he said.

A Zhen officer appeared. "Yes, Commander?"

"Check the communications logs between the time index I am sending you," he said. "Did we receive any transmissions through the slipnet relay?"

A few moments passed, then, "No, Commander. No transmissions during that period."

"Could the instructions have been programmed earlier?" Shirenas asked me.

"No, the log is very clear that the transmission came in from outside the ship."

"But there's no such transmission in the ship's logs. Could the command have overridden the logs?"

"It's possible," I said. "But that would still leave anomalies in the log files. There aren't any. There must be another slipspace relay on board." At Jinasek's and Shirenas's dubious looks, I spread my hands wide. "It's the only thing that makes sense. A transmission came in, there's no evidence of tampering, and it has to have come in last night."

"Slipnet relays are not small," Shirenas said. "Where would it—"

"Lizard-boy's thought of something," Midnight said.

I did my best to show no reaction to that, but I failed, and choked down a laugh.

Jinasek's eyes narrowed at me. "What is it?"

"It would take too long to explain," I said. I looked to Shirenas. "You thought of something?"

"Andark's personal vessel in the hangar bay," he said. "Nobody on this ship is allowed to access it. And it is large enough to contain a slipnet relay."

I stood. "Let's check it out." I looked to the Commander. "With your permission?"

He waved us off, and Shirenas and I headed for the docking bay.

Tabran science being fairly advanced compared to— well, everyone else's, it didn't take long for Midnight to break the encryption on the ship's lock. Once in, it was relatively easy to prove there was a subspace relay on board.

"Well, that tells us how the command got to his system," I said.

"But not why, or from whom."

"I just hope it's enough to save our butts."

★   ★   ★

"So," Commander Jinasek said, "we have an explanation of *how* he died, but nothing about why."

"That's…accurate," I said.

"Well. You've saved your life, Tajen Hunt, and Shirenas's as well. But I am still not satisfied."

"Captain Hunt," Midnight said.

I ignored her. "I wish I could answer all your questions," I said. "But some things are just not findable."

"Captain Hunt, I can answer his question," Midnight said. She quickly told me how, and my eyes widened. I turned to the commander.

"Commander Jinasek, there is in fact a way to answer your question. But it's dangerous, and more than that, just telling you about it is a danger to me."

"Explain," he growled.

"First, I need an assurance," I said. "No matter what I tell you, you won't use it against me now."

"Captain Hunt, you may have forgotten that you are a leader of a rebel faction, and a wanted terrorist in the eyes of Zhen law, but I have not. I remind you that I myself am now as wanted by Zhen Imperial Security as you are. I am hardly going to change my mind about you now. What new charge are you adding to your list of crimes?"

"Well, when you put it like that…I have an AI on my ship."

"A *full* artificial mind?"

"Yes," I said.

"Interesting. I did not realize humans had developed such technology."

"Well, no, we haven't. Like my ship, she's of Tabran design."

He shot to his feet, and for a moment I thought I was a dead man. Then his mouth dropped open in that terrifying Zhen smile. "Show me."

I led Jinasek to Midnight, Shirenas trailing behind. When we got to her, I signaled her to open. Jinasek ignored the open hatch and walked slowly around the ship. "I fought in the last war against the Tabrans," he said. "I recognize elements of this ship's design, but it has human design elements as well." He turned back to me. "You have allied yourself with them?"

I thought about lying, but what was the point? "More or less," I said. "It's a bit of a long story, and I'd love to fill you in, but now is not the time. We need to work quickly if we want answers about Andark."

"Explain."

I led him up the boarding ramp. "First, allow me to introduce *Clear Skies at Midnight on a Night with No Moon*. And yes, all Tabrans have names like that, ships and people both. I call her 'Midnight'."

"She approves?"

Midnight's voice came from the open hatch. "She tolerates," she said.

He bowed as Zhen do to honored enemies. "May I enter?" he asked. "I offer amnesty and truce."

"I accept your truce," she said. "You may enter."

Jinasek looked around the ship's interior. "This does not seem much different than our own ships," he said.

"Appearances can be deceiving," Midnight said. "This ship was designed for human use, so the interfaces were made to be similar to those the Empire uses. Tabran ships use substantially different control interfaces. You'll forgive me for not being more specific."

"Of course. Are you a fully sapient AI system?"

"Yes."

"You feel emotion?"

"Of course," Midnight said. "And if you're going to argue that my emotional responses are only simulated by my software, let me remind you that your own emotions are also derived from software running on meat processors."

Jinasek's crest quivered with his amusement. "I would never presume to make such a claim."

"Good."

I cleared my throat. "If you two are done appreciating each other's senses of humor, we do have some work to do."

"As you say, Captain," Jinasek said.

"The rest of this conversation should remain private," I said to the commander. "May I seal the door?" He gestured *permission granted*, and the hatch slid shut. I gestured both Zhen to seats.

"Midnight tells me that some of the nanites recovered from Andark's remains were placed in stasis and are still operational," I said. "She can use them to bridge the gap between this ship and whoever sent the command to kill Andark."

"Whom you believe to be the One," Jinasek said.

"I...yes," I said. "I know that sounds far-fetched, but—"

He raised a clawed hand to stop me. "It does not," he said. "I know we have not spoken much about why I deserted the field at Shoa'kor, but let us just say that things have been smelling foul in the Empire for a long time now. The revelations you released last year did not rock me as much as they did some. They confirmed suspicions I had long held. The One is not sound. And your claim only confirms what I suspected – there is something rotten in the heart of the Empire." He leaned toward me, and even a lifetime among the Zhen didn't make it less than terrifying. "I must know what it is."

"As near as I can tell," Midnight said, "the nanites from Andark are in a constant state of communication through his ship's slipnet relay with a closed network piggybacked on the main Imperial slipnet. I can use the nanites to link you to that closed network."

"Without detection?" Shirenas asked.

"I can't mask your intrusion forever, but I should be able to mask your presence for a time," Midnight said. "But I can only send two of you."

The commander said, "Captain Hunt and myself will go. Sub-Captain Shirenas will stay and record the feed from my 'Net as an Imperial witness."

"You think that will matter?" I asked.

"One never knows," he said. "But it may be useful to have the information later."

"Of course. Midnight, how soon can we begin?"

"I am ready now," she said.

"Commander?"

"Ready," Jinasek affirmed.

I sat back in my seat. "Then let's—"

The rest of my statement was lost in the static of a virtuality building itself around me. I was suddenly standing in what appeared to be the Imperial Palace on Zhen:da. It looked like crap – like the place hadn't been cleaned in decades. The walls and floor were covered by a thin film. It appeared to be crawling with motes of light. "What is that?" I asked Jinasek.

"It looks like a *shgadan's* web," he said, leaning closer to it. "But it is technological in nature." He reached out toward it, lights coalescing under his fingers.

I grabbed his wrist before he could touch it. "Maybe don't touch the creepy web," I said.

Jinasek bristled at my presumption, but nodded and moved back. "You're probably right," he said. "What is this place?"

"If Midnight did her job right, it's the data store of that closed network she mentioned. And if my upgrades are still working, then I should be able to find what we need." I cupped my hand, creating a data probe. The tiny mote of blue light pulsed as I fed it what I was looking for, and then began flying off down the corridor. "This way," I said, following it.

The mote led us on a short journey through twisting corridors, all of them connected by the techno-web. We ended up in a huge circular room, filled with ranks of statues, all of them of Zhen:ko, and all of them covered in the webs. The mote stopped in front of one of the statues, hovering. "Holy shit," I said. It was Andark.

I looked around the room, taking in all the statues. Most of them were bright red, but a significant minority were, like the Andark statue, the dull color of a dead Zhen:ko. Others were in various stages of decay, with those in the most advanced stages appearing as little more than a pedestal with a small pile of rubble, overgrown by the web. "Commander," I said, "how many Zhen:ko are there in the Empire?"

"There is no official number published," Jinasek said. "The numbers are classified."

"Damn. I was hoping it was one of those things humans weren't told but you were. Why would the Empire control that information?"

"The most obvious answer," he said, "is that they don't want us to know how precarious their position is."

I looked around the room, letting my implants calculate the distances and numbers. "I see a little more than five hundred statues," I said. "Twenty in the innermost ring, and then in ranks around that, with the one in the center. No bets on who that is."

"It's Zornaav," he confirmed.

I turned back to the statue of Andark. The webs covering the body seemed different from those on the statues to either side. As I studied them, I realized the difference – those on the brighter statues were teeming with tiny motes of light, all moving back and forth, following the threads from the statues to the one in the center of the chamber. Those on Andark were sluggish, barely moving, and none coming toward the statue – all were moving away.

I was familiar enough with the conventions of virtuality environments to realize the lights were data. "The speed of the lights is relative to their priority," I said. "Has to be – Andark's dead. All the information is moving away from him, none to him."

"What information is still with him?" he asked.

"Those must represent the nanites that are still active," I said. "They still have data, but the network doesn't want that information. And some of it's us, basically."

I reached toward the webs on the Andark statue. Jinasek cocked his head. "*Now* you want to touch it?"

I sighed. "No other way. Let's hope Midnight's stealth protocols keep us hidden." I reached for the web again. Motes of light began to gather under my fingers. I held out my hand to Jinasek, who took it. "Here we go," I said, and touched the lights.

Information flooded into me. I was in Andark's cell, sitting on the hard bunk. The One stood over me, displeased. "I did not dedicate resource cycles to your individuality for this, Andark. You were tasked with bringing the *Adamant* back into the fold. And not only did you fail at that, but they have made contact with Tajen Hunt. You have failed the Collective."

"I did what I could, Zornaav. The commander of this ship is one of the old guard. I warned you he should be replaced!"

The One's calm tone was more frightening than any scream of anger. "How dare you question me. You, who have failed me time and again." She flicked a claw at him. "It isn't your fault, I suppose. Your line has always been weak, too eager to curry favor and not eager enough to wet your claws in your enemy's blood. Very well. Andark of the Clan Toraak, I accept your failure. But I repudiate you and all your remaining line." She faded out, and a moment later there was a searing pain, and the vision cut out.

"What was that?" Jinasek asked.

"His last moments, I guess." I frowned at the webs nearby. Before I could stop myself with some logical thinking, I touched one of the larger threads, one linking the cluster we were standing in with the central statue.

Images flooded through me. I was standing on Zhen:da, watching the sun rise, and I was standing in a docking bay overseeing a deployment of troops to Earth. I was on Earth, looking out over Landing. I was on Jiraad, and Elkari, and Imiri. Kieli. Muljat. I was standing on a ship overlooking the ruins of Shoa'kor Station, and eating lunch at Korta's, and a thousand other places.

And at the center of it all, I was also in the throne room of Zhen:da's palace, the *shgadan* in its web, aware of and part of them all. I felt a niggling from a dormant and ignored part of myself, and turned my focus upon it. A human, of all things, in my web? How is— Ah. Of course. *I am coming for you, Tajen Hunt. Enjoy your last moments.*

I pulled my hand away from the web with a shock, and yelled, "Midnight, cut the feed!" I came to in my chair aboard my ship, Jinasek across from me, shaking his head as if to clear it.

Shirenas looked surprised. "You're back sooner than expected," he said.

"We're under attack," I said.

"No, we're not," he said, his crest rising.

"We will be soon," Jinasek said. "Captain Hunt, I must return to the bridge."

I unsealed the door, and he stormed out, calling orders as he went. I followed, ignored by basically everyone. As I did, Midnight asked, "What did you find?"

"First," I said, "isolate and log the data, then cut those nanites off from the rest of their network. Do not allow them to connect to anything – *anything*."

"Done," she said. "Data is logged, and the stasis field has been reactivated. What did you find?"

"The Zhen:ko are a hivemind," I said. "Individuals, but linked through their nanites. Zornaav has infected them all."

"What about the ego centers of Andark's brain? They were nearly totally gone."

"My guess is she takes away their sense of individuality, but not their identity as such. She mentioned having dedicated resources to his individuality. But she seems to be all Zhen:ko, or connected to them, all the time."

"That's going to make things more difficult."

"You think?"

We reached the bridge just as the battle began. "Where the hell did they come from?"

"Doesn't matter," Jinasek said. "Comms, open channel Zeta-twelve."

"Open, sir."

The commander stepped up to his command post. "This is Commander Jinasek," he said on comms. "Sending target coordinates. Execute."

"What was that?" I asked him.

"A little surprise I planned in case of hostiles," he said. "They should arrive…now."

On cue, four battlecruisers, each accompanied by a small task group, dropped out of chain drive behind the attacking loyalist ships and opened fire. I watched Jinasek and his staff run the battle. At first I was ready to run to Midnight and launch myself into the void, but as I watched, the tide quickly turned.

Half an hour later, the enemy ships were dead or crippled. Rebel casualties were light – the *Adamant* had lost some fighters, but most had returned to the fold battered but whole.

As the fighters returned, I stepped up beside Jinasek. "Now what?"

"Return to your ship, Tajen Hunt. I will meet with the other commanders of my task group. I will urge them to join you. When we have made our decision, I will let you know."

Well, there wasn't much to say to that, so I did as he asked. I had a meal and tried to remember what I'd seen in my brief foray into the hivemind, sketching out the details on the worktable. As a particular impression in the torrent of memories popped into my brain, my blood ran cold. I focused in on it, trying to see the details clearly.

A Zhen:ko and several Zhen stood over a map table, the map floating in the air between them. I noted the coordinates – a backwater system; nothing interesting.

"They will die here, Commander," the Zhen:ko said. "Do you understand?"

The Zhen:la looked at the :ko, his crest flattening to his scalp. "All of them, High One?"

"All of them!" the Zhen:ko snapped. "Every ship. Every being on those ships. Do not leave a single escape pod floating in the void. Burn. Them. All. Am I understood?"

His fist slammed to his chest. "Understood," he said. "For the Empire." Around the table, the rest of the Zhen:la echoed him.

I snapped out of the vision. "Midnight, get me Commander Jinasek."

"No need, Captain. He is asking permission to enter."

"Open up." I jumped up and met him at the hatch. "My fleet is under attack by a Zhen task force," I said. "Or it will be soon."

"How fortunate, then, that we have decided to join you," he said. "Do you know where we can find them?"

"System Shim-7439X," I said. "It's a nowhere system near the edge of the Empire."

"How long have we got?"

"If I'm right about the timing, the Zhen attack fleet will arrive in two days. If we jump within the next three hours, we'll get there soon after the attack begins. After that, we'll probably be too late."

I gave Jinasek the coordinates. His eyes went unfocused for a moment, and then I heard the klaxons outside my ship announcing imminent jump. I met his eyes and said, "Thank you."

"Let us go save your people, Tajen," he said. "Then we can discuss how to save mine."

CHAPTER ELEVEN

Katherine

I woke up in the pod. I had Dax's backup pistol in my hand, just in case. As the pod's canopy lifted, I readied the pistol. When I saw the very human legs of Dax Ng'ang'a outside the pod, I relaxed, and handed him the gun as I sat up. "Where are we?" I asked.

"Corridor near the med-center," he said. "What's our next move?"

"Well, I go back to the docks and steal a ship," I said. "You keep moving. Report to your boss, then make contact with the Resistance and get new orders."

"I can help you," he said.

"I'm sure you could, but once I've got the ship, I have to go back to Marauder space. I can't take you with me."

"Come on," he said. "You can't seriously go into Marauder space alone."

"I *have* to," I said. "Trust me, I'd much rather have your help and take you with me, but it'll just get you killed."

"All right," he said. "But I'll be on-station for a few days at least. If you need me, call me." He sent his comms-code.

"I will," I said. I saluted him, then turned away. A few meters down the corridor, I said over my shoulder, "Thank you. I'll make it up to you someday."

"I'm gonna hold you to that."

I gave him a wave and went on my way.

The merchant docks weren't far, and I was able to use my own NeuroNet capabilities to find and avoid sensor platforms. Using the identity overlay in my 'Net, I bought a carryall bag in a gift shop, some clothing to put in it, and a coffee, then sat down at a table. To anyone looking my way, I was a passenger reading the news on her 'Net. In reality I was checking the station's dock listings. They didn't give a lot of information – just the ship's name, classification, and slip number. *Shit*, I said to myself. I was supposed to steal a ship worth at least 500,000 *dekka* on the open market. Cargo worth that much required space – and there was nothing in dock big enough to carry that much of anything.

The moment I thought that, I came across an entry on the station list that made me stop and close my eyes in embarrassment at my own stupidity. The actual instructions said 'a ship with cargo worth 500,000 *dekka*'. If the ship was worth a lot, maybe the cargo didn't have to be. And a smaller ship would be easier to steal.

I scanned the docks for small personal ships. There were a few, all belonging to independent traders like I used to be, but most of the ships were old and outdated, or too small to carry much of anything.

Then I found her – a small *Sakan*-class pleasure yacht. It was called the *Terakasha*, and was registered to a Zhen named Shka Tikarna, a minor member of the Shka clan. According to the station's records, he was traveling alone. And a man like that? Even the lesser son of a clan should have enough crap on his ship to meet my requirements.

But even better, the Shka clan was known to the Resistance to be supplying weapons and gear to the Empire's Occupation forces on Earth. Causing them some grief would be a bonus to my mission, and hopefully do a lot more than I'd set out to do in the first place.

An innocent enough request for information from the station's computers told me Shka Tikarna was currently in a meeting in the station's commercial zone, and was expected to remain occupied by additional meetings for the next several hours. When the system asked if I wanted to relay a message, I demurred, hung up, and got to work.

Pulling what I needed from the Resistance dead drops wasn't too hard; we'd stashed information in highly encrypted files that propagated throughout the slipnet. Putting that information into the security subsystems files without setting off their intrusion countermeasures was much harder.

After an hour of nerve-wracking work, I engaged the comms protocols developed by Kiri and her hacker friend Aleph, then connected my 'Net to the station's systems. I routed a call between several dozen subsystems just in case they tried to trace it, and then let it connect.

"Station security," came a Zhen voice.

"Shka Tikarna is funneling money and matériel to the human resistance," I said. "I've left evidence in your files."

"Who is this?"

I disconnected the call.

With any luck, the files the Resistance had ginned up would work. But it was possible security would see through them; they'd been created to be as generic as possible, and my work in tailoring them to tell the story I wanted to tell was probably several levels below what Kiri or one of her data-wranglers could have done. I'd have to move fast, and get off the station before security decided to search the *Terakasha* for more evidence.

I made my way to the slip where the *Terakasha* was berthed. With Kiri's electronic lock-picking subroutines in my 'Net's memory, it only took me twenty-seven tries to get past the locked gate into the berth. Fortunately, Shka Tikarna hadn't updated his ship's security, and the spike ripped right through it. The door slid open. I entered and closed it behind me, then quickly worked to change the lock code using one of Kiri's algorithms. She'd assured me it would take a standard computer years to break the encryption by brute-force methods.

I made sure the ship was empty of people. A quick glance at the cargo bay showed it was full, but I didn't have time to look at whatever was in the crates. Hopefully it would be worth enough.

I headed to the cockpit and took stock. The controls were pretty standard, though of course they were sized for a Zhen. I accessed the controls with my 'Net, then paused, considered my next moves, and started the engines.

As the sublight drives spun up, my implants notified me the ship was getting a call over comms. *Here we go.* I opened the call but said nothing.

"Freighter *Terakasha*, you are not cleared for departure," the comms said.

"I am aware of that," I said. "Nevertheless, I'm leaving. Either release the clamps or deal with the consequences."

"Negative. Disengage your engines."

"Negative," I said, mocking his tones exactly. "Disengage your docking clamps before I rip them off." Docking clamps are designed to break free of the station to minimize damage if a ship goes rogue. But 'minimize damage' is not the same thing as 'negate damage', and if they didn't release the clamps it was going to cause them a lot of time and money to fix the dock. To make my point, I goosed the maneuvering jets, pulling against the clamps for a moment.

When that didn't get results, I checked the scopes. Sure enough, control was trying to keep me in place long enough for security to get ships into position to interdict me. Well. That wasn't going to happen.

I slammed the thrusters to full, pulling against the docking clamps. The engines screamed, and the sound of stressed metal echoed through the ship. I called to control, over the comms, "Come on, you assholes. Let me go or you'll have a hell of a repair job."

There was no reply, so I did what I had to do, and maxed out the thrust. With a scream of tortured metal, my ship tore the docking clamps off the station as I broke free. I hauled the ship around to face away from the station and slammed the thrust to maximum.

I was lucky I'd been sent to a transfer point. Unlike in-system bases, transfer points are often built in deep space, using their own engines to maintain position relative to nearby bodies. This means that one doesn't have to aim for a specific lagrange-based jump point, but can engage their jump drives as soon as they get far enough away from the station itself to allow for jump.

On the other hand, I hadn't yet worked out my first jump solution, let alone the series of jumps I'd have to make to get back to Dakcha. And without anyone else in the ship with me to do the math, I was going to have a hell of a time working out a solution while also flying the ship. And there was nowhere in the system to hide.

"Fine," I said. I turned to the navplotter and began to work out the math, keeping an eye on the sensors and flight controls. Plotting a jump wasn't actually that hard, but in order to do it I had to know where I was relative to where I was going. I didn't have time to work it out for Dakcha, so I called up a list of nearby systems and scanned their characteristics quickly. *Ah*, I thought.

The Cochran System had a couple of mining operations in the larger asteroids and gas giants, but little else, and there was no military presence to speak of. Best of all, it was on the same jump vector as several other systems that would be much more attractive to a thief looking to sell a hot spaceship. With luck, the Zhen would begin their searches there. I set my coordinates for that system, working to solve the equations quickly while also trying to keep the pursuing ships off my butt and out of range. I took a few hits in the process, which didn't exactly help my concentration. But eventually, I had a working – I hoped – jump solution. My hands were shaking as I fed it into the computer.

The security ships were just coming into range when I finished, and I changed my vector to line up with my jump even as they opened fire. I took several hits on the rear shields before I was able to activate the jump drive and leap away from Kadara.

"Well done, me," I said.

The journey from Kadara to Cochran only took two days. I spent the time working out my jump solution to get back to Dakcha, sleeping, and exploring the ship. I was especially pleased with the cargo. Most of it was crap – the odds and ends of a traveler mixed with a few crates of pedestrian trade goods. But the last crate held five warp diamonds, each about four centimeters across.

Warp diamonds are incredibly rare jewels. They don't refract light like most cut gemstones; they have their own luminescence that shifts constantly. Nobody's exactly sure where they come from – so they're incredibly valuable. Cutting them into gem shapes ruins them, so their value is often dependent on shape. These were all either nearly perfect spheres or oblongs. They'd clearly been polished and prepared for setting, but not one of them had a flaw. The collection was easily worth ten times what I'd been told to find.

As the ship broke free of slipspace on the outskirts of the lonely mining system, I was smiling.

And then the ship went dark.

I was drifting in space with no engines, no lights, no gravity, and no life support. Shit.

I climbed out of the pilot's chair and activated my 'Net's sensor net. It fed a more or less normal view of my surroundings into my visual feed, allowing me to move around as well as if the lights were full on.

I made my way back to the engine room. Since the power had been the thing to cut out, I began there. I discovered that the power plant itself was still working, but the power wasn't getting anywhere.

I began laboriously tracing power conduits. I found the first cutoff after only twenty minutes, but disabling it only restored power to the engine room. Clearly there was a series of such cutoffs. I sighed and inched myself along the floor where I was jammed underneath the console, beginning the trace to the next—

I stopped, and laughed at myself. Here I was thinking like an engineer, instead of the Zhen who owned this tub. Tikarna flew the ship alone, no servants to do his work for him. Even if he knew the location of every single cutoff switch, he wasn't going to want to spend his time manually resetting each one. There had to be a way to reset them all automatically.

I went back to the first and re-enabled it, then scanned with my 'Net for any signal sources in the ship. When I found none, I frowned a moment, then set my 'Net to look for passive connections and walked slowly around the ship, beginning at the main airlock and then doing a slow circuit. Passive connections were rare, because you had to know exactly where the receiver was located, and you had to get really close to it to activate it.

I found the receiver in the back of a supply locker tucked away in the ship's galley. Once I'd locked on to it, it was a relatively simple task to decrypt the code and trip the switch, bringing the power back on.

If only.

In truth it took three days.

I'd like to spin an exciting yarn about how I was running out of air by the end of the first day and spent the next two in a pressure suit, but come on. I was one woman in a freighter – it might have been a smallish one, but it was still large enough to hold enough air that I could have stayed like that for months, if I'd had enough food and water. Let's not get melodramatic.

Anyway, three very boring days later I got the code, entered it, and the ship came back to life. My jump solution was still in my 'Net's files, of course, so I entered it and got underway. Nobody in Cochran ever even realized I was there.

The trip to Dakcha took another couple of weeks, and I made my plans using the information Andra and Fraz had given me.

When I arrived in Dakcha, I set my transponder to the frequency I'd been given, to mark the ship as spoils, and not to be destroyed. I picked up an escort almost immediately. They rode beside me all the way into the station itself.

I landed the ship and, as I shut her down, looked out the viewport at the assembled crowd. The bald graybeard from before stood at their front, waiting.

I stepped off the ship with a small box. In it I'd placed four of the warp diamonds; the rest I'd hidden throughout the ship and would retrieve later, if I was successful today.

"You return sooner than anticipated," he said as I walked toward him, "and your success is not assured by it. This ship does not look like much."

I stopped just outside his personal space. "Looks can be deceiving," I said. "She's top of the line."

"And the cargo?"

"There's plenty. But the important part is right here," I said, and handed him the box.

His skeptical look vanished when he opened it. "You have done well," he said.

"Thank you."

"What is your name?"

"Katherine Lawson."

He shook his head. "Who you were before is irrelevant. You are to be a Marauder now. You must take a new name to be used among us."

I looked him in the eye and leaked steel into my voice. "I have lived through fire and hell to arrive at this spot in this moment. None of it is irrelevant, not to me. I am not abandoning all I was. I. Am. Katherine. Lawson."

He nodded, the corners of his lips lifting. "Andra was right about you," he said, his voice pitched for my ears alone. He turned to the crowd to shout, "Welcome this Marauder back home from her trials! Her name is Katherine! Her soul is iron! Her heart is fire!"

The crowd responded in unison, "Her name is Katherine! Her soul is iron! Her heart is fire! She is a Marauder!"

Have you ever heard your name shouted by hundreds of people at once? It's disconcerting. The voices mix and echo in such a way that sounds like the universe itself is calling your name. It's a cool sound – and a terrifying one.

The man gestured for me to walk with him, and we began making our way through the crowd. Many patted me on the back or shoulder, welcoming me, but most faded away pretty quickly. As we walked, he said, "My name is Verdna, by the way. You know what happens next?"

"Andra told me I get presented to the queen."

"Yes. Normally the ceremony is short. Queen Nikara welcomes you, and calls you to her to receive her blessing. She gives it, you go away and get assigned to a position in the Marauder fleet." He glanced at me sideways. "I am given to understand it will be different today."

I kept my voice neutral, even bland. "I don't know what you're talking about."

He smiled tightly, turning to meet my eyes. I noticed his were wary. He was worried. "As you say," he said.

When we arrived in the throne room, the crowd was even bigger than the one in the docking bay had been. My pulse quickened.

While she wore no finery, no obvious badge of office, the air of command the queen gave off was palpable; even if she hadn't been seated on an obvious throne, I'd have known her for what she was. What I hadn't expected was her age.

Nikara wasn't much older than me, and in better shape than I'd assumed. Based on the descriptions, I'd created a mental image of the woman that was at odds with the reality. Where I'd been led to expect a clearly crazed despot, I found instead a woman whose eyes followed everything, who knew exactly where everyone in the room was and tracked them constantly.

This was no mental burnout randomly making decisions for entertainment. This woman was an apex predator who'd lost her way, but not her mettle. That just made her more dangerous.

Right now, her eyes followed me across the floor, but there was no madness in them. She just looked bored.

Well, I'd soon fix that.

I stepped forward as Verdna instructed. He approached closer to the queen, kneeling before her and holding the opened box up to her. "Your Majesty, this new Marauder has brought you a gift, and seeks your blessing," he said.

"Oh yes?" She reached into the box and picked up one of the warp diamonds. "A worthy gift, indeed," she said, her teeth bared in a predatory grin as her eyes moved slowly to me. "What is your name, girl?"

"Katherine," I said.

"Come forward, Katherine, and receive my blessings."

I squared my feet, planting them firmly, and even before I spoke, her eyes narrowed and her mouth widened in a rictus grin. "No."

"A challenge?" she asked, anticipating me. As I opened my mouth to speak the words, she raised her hand, palm out. She rose and approached me, moving with a liquid grace. "You seem capable enough, but are you ready to do what must be done?"

I looked into her eyes, and yes, I saw the predator there, but I also saw something I hadn't expected to see.

My brother was killed by a Zhen right in front of me. It had sent me into a spiral of despair that had left me useless to my friends – my family. I'd been lucky; I had Tajen and Liam to pull me out of my despair and remind me who I was. Who had Nikara had?

This wasn't a woman who'd lost her mind. She had lost her faith – in herself, in her people, and in a universe that made sense. She'd done terrible things in the wake of her tragedy, and every despicable act altered her self-image even further. The idealist she'd been had been replaced by a woman who was trying desperately to forget what she'd done and who she was.

I could have been her. If I hadn't had Tajen and Liam, and Ben and Kiri, I could easily have thrown myself into an embittered battle. I'd be dead today if I hadn't had people who were there for me even though I didn't want them to be.

Something had gone wrong for Nikara, and the people around her didn't know how to pull her back. They were too hampered by her position, her authority, and too afraid of her madness to reach into it and stop her descent.

But I wasn't afraid.

I'd been there. I'd seen what grief could do, and I wasn't afraid to reach in there. So I looked her in the eyes and softened my expression. "I'm sorry for your loss," I said.

She was taken aback. "What?"

"Your husband," I said. "Your son."

"That was a long time ago," she said, each word no more inflected than the last. "I don't think about them anymore."

I shook my head slowly. "It doesn't work like that," I said, my voice gentle. "I lost my brother a little more than a year ago, my parents many years before that. It never leaves you. Not really. It gets easier over time – and it's been a long while for you – but it never leaves. How old was he?"

"Who?"

"Your son," I said.

She recoiled as if I'd slapped her. Turning away from me, she shouted, "Clear the room!" As the crowd made for the exits, I made sure the nanites that formed the bracers I was wearing were ready to deploy if I needed them. "Dagger," I subvocalized, "be ready."

"For what?" his voice came immediately. "All systems are ready, but what's going on?"

I restored his access to my NeuroNet, giving him the ability to see and hear through me again. "Oh, shit," he said.

"Stand by," I sent, returning my attention to Queen Nikara, still struggling to control her reaction.

She took a deep breath, her shoulders rising and falling, then turned back to me. "How dare you?" She was shaking, and I knew I was on dangerous ground here. I could relent, beg apology, and find another way to get what I wanted. Or I could challenge her here and now – kill her and take her throne. It would be easier. Even if it was a hard fight, I knew I could win.

But that would be the easy thing to do. And I have never been one to take the easy road.

"I could challenge you," I said. "We could fight. But I'd much rather talk to you. One survivor to another. How old was he?"

"He was five," she whispered. "A tiny, perfect little man."

I lowered my voice and spoke calmly. "In your grief, you did some terrible things."

Something changed in her eyes, and I knew she was remembering the terrible order she'd given that day. "Yes," she said.

"You've been running from that ever since."

"What do you know about it?" she snarled.

"When my brother was killed, I wanted to burn the Empire down," I said. "I wanted to kill every single one of them. I wanted to throw my life away trying to make them pay for that one life."

"You were too weak to do it," she said.

"No," I said. "I had friends who knew how to keep me from losing myself."

"I had friends," she said, her voice still and deadly.

I conceded that point with a nod. "But they were also your subjects.

And they were too afraid to force you to look in the mirror. I'm not."
I gestured to an empty space on the floor and sent a command through
my 'Net to Dagger, who used the room's holoprojectors to create an
image of Nikara's little boy playing with his toys.

"How did you—"

"I have many strengths," I said. Another command, and a holo of
her husband appeared beside her son, laughing and ruffling the boy's
hair. "This is your most-watched memory of them," I said. "But have
you ever wondered, as you watch them play, what they would think of
you now?" I gestured, and a visual of her as she looked now appeared,
next to a version of her from her youth. "How would they react to this
change?"

Her hand moved faster than I thought possible, and a dagger was at
my throat. "I will kill you for this impudence!" she snapped. Her face
was a mask of rage, but in her eyes I saw fear.

"They wouldn't hate you," I said. "They never could. But they
would weep for what you've become. Stop this. Reclaim who you
were, before you're lost forever and the Marauders become a hated
memory." I flicked my eyes to my right hand, where a dagger that had,
a short moment ago, been a bracer, was pointed at her heart. "Or tell me
now that you can't, and I'll send you to join them and fix what you've
broken."

"You would do such a thing?"

"Sure," I said, "if you don't give me a choice. But it would be much
easier for you to fix the Marauders than for me."

She slowly removed her dagger from my throat. "It's been a long
time since anyone dared to speak to me like this."

I shrugged at her. "That's kinda what happens when you keep
putting them in prison for it."

She actually laughed, and the dagger disappeared into her sleeve as
she stepped back from me. I didn't let down my guard, though – I'm
good, but there's no way to fix twenty years of madness in a few minutes.
"Guards!" she snapped, and the doors opened to admit two guards, their
rifles in ready position. "Bring me the prisoner Andra," she said.

As the guards departed, one of them casting a wary glance at my dagger before leaving, Nikara returned to her throne and sat delicately. "You've given me much to think about," she said. "But you know it isn't this easy."

"Of course not," I said. The dagger in my hand dissolved, the mass of nanites crawling up my hand like a cool liquid, reshaping themselves once more into a wide bracer on my forearm. "This is going to be with you for a long time, and you're going to have to find people you can talk to."

"Not you?" she asked.

"For a time, perhaps, if you need me," I said. "But I have a war to return to."

"Then why become a Marauder? Why come to challenge me?"

I sighed. In all the excitement, and my need to help her, I had almost forgotten what brought me here in the first place. "Honestly? There's something in your vault I need for the war against the Zhen. An ancient device that my allies need to have returned."

Her eyes turned flinty. "So you became a Marauder just to take something from us."

Inwardly, I flinched. "Yes. But it wasn't my favorite plan."

"Despite myself, I like you, Katherine Lawson. I think—" She was interrupted by the doors opening. The guards entered, with Andra between them. They forced her to her knees at Nikara's feet. As she glared, first at Nikara, and then at me, the queen rose from her seat and walked over to Andra. She knelt before her old friend and took her hands. "I'm sorry," she said. "I have been a fool."

Andra looked at her, then me. "Don't look at *me*," I said. "I'm not the one apologizing."

Nikara rose, pulling Andra to her feet. Her voice rang out so loudly the people in the corridor outside would easily hear her. "Andra's imprisonment is at an end. Andra of the Clan Dare, I offer you your position as my *amaya*, and ask you to return to that office in which you served so well."

Andra stared at her a moment and said, "I still won't kill them."

Nikara bowed her head a moment. "Nor should you. My sentence against the Indiri family is vacated. They are free of my regard, and restitution shall be made to them for their persecution over the last two years."

Andra was clearly having trouble believing all this. She looked at me, a question in her eyes.

"I found a better way," I said. "It's not over, but you can take it from here."

Andra turned back to the queen. "And the policy on the Makara survivors?"

Nikara looked pained, and her eyes clouded. "We will...discuss that," she said. "Openly, and with honesty between us. It is a larger problem than the Indiri." She turned to me. "Is there anything we can do for you besides the device you came for?"

"I have a friend still in the work camps," I said. "His name is Simmons."

"Ah yes. We'll release him immediately," she said. "And then let's have a discussion about this war you're fighting."

CHAPTER TWELVE

Liam

When I entered the bridge the morning we were due to leave slipspace, I went straight to Alex's station. "Hey," I said.

He smiled warmly at me. "Good morning, Admiral."

"Everything according to plan, Lieutenant?"

"Yes, sir."

"Good." I stood there like an idiot for a minute, then said, "When we get another breather…let's have dinner again. My cabin, this time." I met and held his eyes, lowering my voice. "Bring an overnight bag."

He grinned at me, and I at him, and I have to admit – it felt good. But right now I had work to do, so I turned back to the command post and got my mind back on my job.

We'd split the fleet among several systems, each group having a small fighting force with it. All of the systems should be a short jump away from the others. The hope was that the fighters they had would be able to keep them alive long enough for the rest of us to get there.

What none of us wanted to face was the question we hadn't been able to answer: what happened if the Zhen came for all of us at once? It didn't bear thinking about. But in the darkness of my cabin, a few minutes before we dropped out of the jump, I'd spent a long time imagining just that.

When we came out of slipspace, I was primed for action. It was almost disappointing when nothing happened. "We're not out of the woods yet," I said to Captain Zhang, who was standing beside me in command.

"Yes, sir. Injala's couriers have launched and are standing by." Each group had a set of couriers whose job was to immediately jump to the other groups and report which was under attack.

Six hours later, I was beginning to get antsy. "Anything?" I asked the sensor operator.

"No, sir," she said.

"Nothing on comms either," Captain Zhang murmured, coming up beside me.

"Just because they aren't here yet, doesn't mean they aren't coming," I said. "Maintain readiness, but rotate the patrols to keep the pilots fresh."

"Sir." She moved off to give instructions to the commander of the ship's fighter wings.

The next day, we were still alone. There were no couriers, no Zhen, nothing. Everyone was on edge. We'd become so used to being attacked that every minute an attack didn't come was a minute spent getting more and more nervous.

The next day, we were still waiting. By the middle of the ship's day, I decided it had been long enough for the Zhen to show up. "Captain."

"Yes, sir?"

My voice rang across the suddenly silent bridge. "Send the couriers," I said. "Call all the ships back. Prepare a jump solution for our next jump." We'd agreed on our new destination previously – a system much closer to Kelvaki space, on the outer edges of our jump range. We'd recharge our drives and jump from there deep into the Assembly's territory.

"Yes, sir," Zhang replied.

A few minutes later, Injala appeared to be communicating with someone. She met my eyes and motioned I should wait. A few seconds later, a message arrived: *There was a coded transmission sent into deep space moments after your order. It came from this ship. We are decrypting it now.*

Oh, hell. I sent back: *Do we know where on the ship?*

Negative. It was a prepared burst, too quick to locate the origin to that level of detail. It must be someone on the bridge, but we cannot learn who until we locate the transmission. My ships are realigning themselves. If there is another, we will be able to narrow it down.

I met her eyes again and nodded.

Over the next two days, the other groups arrived. Moments after the last group, Injala walked swiftly to me. "We found it," she murmured. "The transmission was long enough to track."

"Who sent it?"

She sent me an image, and I opened it.

By the Nine. Of all the godsbedamned—

It was Alex.

I turned and walked over to his console, as if nothing had happened. As I reached him, he raised his eyebrows as if asking what I needed; as I stood before him for a moment, silent, his brows lowered and his lips compressed into a line. "Ah," he said.

"Ah," I said, in the same tone.

"Well, I'd hoped I'd— Fuck it." He leaped back from his console, his arm jerking free.

I surged forward, slapping the gun out of his hand and sending it skittering across the deck. "I trusted you," I said. "I was beginning to *feel* something for you. And you were *playing* me?"

"It wasn't difficult," he snarled. "So wrapped up in your dead husband you can't even see what's in front of you clearly. If you're the best your people can do, no wonder you've lost."

"We haven't lost yet," I said, and whipped my foot up into his face, knocking him against the bulkhead beside him. "In case you didn't read my file, I was a ground-pounder long before I started working in space. You know what we're really good at?" I slammed my knee into the small of his back. He grunted with the impact. "We fight dirty."

He fell to one knee, then lunged, not at me, but to the side. He reached out, and then his arm whipped back toward me. I had just enough time to realize he'd grabbed his weapon before a long blade tore through his arm. His hand and weapon fell to the deck as he fell back clutching the stump and cursing.

Zekan swept in, kicking the hand and weapon aside and grabbing

Alex by the front of his shirt. He lifted him and looked to me, his short sword ready.

In that moment I could not honestly say if it was from fear, adrenaline, or anger, but I was shaking. "Get him off the bridge," I said, voice tight.

"You are all going to die," Alex said. "My forces are already on the way, and you don't have time to run again."

Something was wrong. He seemed calmer than he should be, even allowing for nanite pain management. But he also was speaking in a pattern that didn't sound like himself. "Your forces? What are you—"

"Sir!" called the tactical officer. "Zhen ships exiting slipspace!"

"There they are," Alex said. "Your death approaches."

Zekan yanked him close and growled in his face, "You will die with us, scum."

Something changed in Alex's eyes. "I die for the Empire," he said. "And my death will bring their victory even sooner." A moment later he looked at me. "What did you do?"

I shook my head. "I honestly don't know what you're talking about."

Injala stepped beside me. "Admiral, you have a battle to run. I'll explain this fool's inability to explode himself later."

I nodded and turned, crossing to Captain Zhang, who was busily launching the ship's fighters. "We're boxed in. Unless we can beat these ships, we're not leaving here."

"Shit." I glanced over the tactical plot. "Send Blue group to attack this target," I said, tapping a Zhen cruiser. "If we can take it out, we'll create a hole in that vector. Keep Red and Gold on defense – they'll screen our ships and take out bombers and any torpedoes launched. All other fighter groups are to act as a fighter screen and be ready to deploy to specific objectives."

"Sir." She began relaying orders and I turned to Injala.

"Explanation. Now, please."

Her ears quivering, she said, "I didn't want to say so earlier, but I suspected him – as well as some others aboard. So I made arrangements."

"Such as?"

"I had my agent slip a nanite colony seed we've developed into the food of all suspects. The moment he was revealed, I activated it – and it ate *his* nanites and disabled his NeuroNet. Fortunately, you kept him talking long enough for the seed to do its work."

"So he's cut off from his transmitter?"

"Yes," she said. "The memory core of his NeuroNet will be intact, if you want to try to drag some information from it, but he has no access to or control of it."

"Nice," I said. A flicker in the tactical plot caught my eye, and I turned my full attention to it. I activated my comms. "They're moving on the *Taj Mahal*. Blue group, break off your target and intercept enemy group designate *Claw*."

My entire universe shrank to the tactical plot and the assets I had to direct. The Zhen had one objective – to wipe us out utterly. Mine was to bring as many of the fleet through as I could and try to find an escape.

The pilots of Blue group threw themselves between the Zhen and a defenseless freighter and were lost, every ship dying in a hail of plasma fire and missile strikes. The freighter *Taj Mahal* didn't last more than a minute longer.

Red and Gold groups were thrown into disarray by a salvo of missiles equipped with chain drives. Half of them were lost or drifting, and there wasn't anyone close enough to help them.

My focus on directing the battle strategy, I didn't take time to think about any of it, but somewhere in the back of my mind I knew that in the unlikely event I lived through this, I'd be thinking of nothing else.

"Sir, we've got more ships incoming!" one of the operators cried out. "Oh my god."

"What is it?" I snapped.

"They're Marauders, sir! Dozens of them!"

I looked back at the plot. "Oh hell," I said. The Marauder ships already in the system outnumbered both the Zhen and our own fleet. And there were still ships arriving in-system, the colorful trails of slipspace energies marking their arrivals. I shook my head, disbelieving. "Either they're in league with the Zhen now, or we've got a multi-front battle on our hands. Either way, we're dead."

"Marauders are launching ships. They're on an intercept course with us."

I felt someone at my side. I looked and saw Kiri standing there. "Can we win?" she asked.

"I don't see how," I said. "I didn't think we could *before* the Marauders arrived. I'm sorry." I enfolded her in my arms for a moment. "I'm not gonna stop trying, though." I released her and got back to the plot. "Wait, what...."

The Marauders had bypassed us entirely, their ships flashing past at full speed – and opening fire on the Zhen.

"They're on our side...." I breathed. "How is that possible?" In the hundreds of years of human existence in the Empire, nobody had ever reported Marauders doing anything to help anyone. If they'd opened fire on us all, it would have made sense, but attacking the Zhen alone just didn't fit with historical facts.

"Sir, we're getting a hail from the Marauders," comms said.

"Put it here," I said, gesturing toward the holo-tank.

The image of a middle-aged woman appeared in the plot. "Human ships, I am Queen Nikara of the Marauder Clans. We are here to help, but do not get in our way. My pilots are not used to playing well with others." Her voice softened. "That's something we'll work on in future." The transmission ended.

Kiri and I looked at each other. "What..."

"...the fuck?" Kiri finished.

★   ★   ★

The Marauders fought hard. They lost a lot of ships, but they just kept coming. I think they knew they weren't going to win, not entirely, but where the Zhen's goal was the destruction of the human fleet, the Marauders just wanted to make us a hole through which we could escape.

I was about to order the human ships to retreat when an alarm sounded from a nearby console. My head whipped around to the console and the operator there. She looked at me, her eyes brimming with tears, and all the hope drained right out of me. "More Zhen," she said.

"How many?"

She shuddered, then visibly pulled herself back together and turned back to her console. "Five battlecruisers and their task groups," she said. She frowned, and then I saw something one rarely gets to see – the return of hope, dawning bright and beautiful. "Captain, Admiral – the new ships are firing on the Zhen!"

"What?" Zhang said.

The officer was right. The new ships had opened fire on the others. I zoomed the tactical plot in on the lead ship of the new forces. "It's the *Adamant*," I said.

Zhang turned to me. "The ship that fled from Shoa'kor?"

I nodded. "And she brought friends," I said.

"Message from the *Adamant*," one of the comms operators called. "Message reads: *We are on your side. Do not target our ships.*" Her eyes widened. "Sir, they're transmitting a Resistance clearance code."

"Seriously?"

The comms operator nodded. Zhang crossed to her and placed a hand briefly on her shoulder. "Carry on," she said softly.

The *Adamant* and her friends, along with the Marauders, made short work of the Empire's forces. Some were crippled, and the *Adamant* and her fellows began to systematically fire killing shots into each of their engines.

"What are they doing?" Kiri asked.

Zhang answered. "They're making sure none of those ships can get back to the Empire. Looks like they're taking out long-range comms too."

"Sirs, the *Adamant* is hailing."

Zhang looked at me questioningly. I nodded. "Put it through."

The form of a large Zhen took center stage in the command center. "I am Commander Jinasek, late of the Zhen military forces, now leader of the Zhen Forces in Exile. We wish to send an emissary to negotiate our joining the human resistance against Zornaav. I give my personal assurance of peaceful conduct."

Zhang looked to me, deferring the question. "Stand by, *Adamant*," I said, and gestured to mute the transmission. I turned to Injala. "Do we know anything about Jinasek?"

"He is known to the Kelvaki Assembly to be an honorable foe," she said. "If he gives his word, he will keep it."

I took a deep breath, held it for a moment, and then let it go. I gestured to the comms officer to resume transmission. "Commander Jinasek, we will welcome your emissary," I said.

"I look forward to meeting you," he replied, and cut his transmission.

"Sir, the Zhen are signaling their shuttle is away."

"Send them to docking bay one," I said. "I'll meet them there. Injala, with me." I gestured to the nearest guards and Zekan to follow us. "Trust," I said to Injala, "but always be cautious."

"It appears you may actually be learning. As your people say, wonders never cease."

I led Injala and my guards to the main docking bay. On the way, I got a call from Zhang. "Liam, the Marauders have also sent an emissary. They didn't ask – just informed me their 'ambassador' is on the way."

I couldn't help but laugh. "Zhen joining the human resistance and the Marauders having an ambassador. What is this universe coming to?"

"Hopefully something better than it has been in the past."

"May the Nine grant it."

As we arrived in the docking bay, the Marauder shuttle was already touching down. "They sure burned hard," I said. "Even with gravitic drives, that must have been rough."

"Perhaps they are very eager to see you," Injala joked. "An offer of a royal wedding, maybe?"

"Don't even joke," I said. As the shuttle's hatch began to open, I stood a little straighter – and damned near fell over as the ambassador stepped out. "You're alive," I said.

Katherine Lawson, one of my oldest friends, and someone I'd thought killed nearly a year ago, said, "What, you thought the Zhen could take me out?" She shook her head sadly. "Liam Kincaid, I thought you knew me better than that." We stared at each other for a moment, and then we flew into each other's arms.

I held her tight, my eyes filling with tears. Tears of joy, sure, but also sadness. "I want to hear all about what happened to you," I said. "But first—"

"We need to talk about the Marauders," she said, nodding.

"Well, yeah. But even before that…. Katherine, Tajen's gone."

She pulled back from me. "No, he's not."

"Well, we never found a body, but we found his ship in pieces."

"He's not dead."

"You don't know—"

"Yes, I do. I can even tell you where he is."

Something halfway between hope and joy passed through me, and I grabbed at her. "Where?"

She grinned. "This is why we wanted to get here first – I didn't want to miss this moment."

She took me by the shoulders and turned me around.

CHAPTER THIRTEEN

Tajen

We shot out of slipspace straight into a nightmare of ships fighting.

Zhen ships were hammering the humans, and Marauders were everywhere. I stood beside Jinasek and studied the tactical tank, trying to suss out the situation. It quickly became apparent that the Marauders weren't attacking the humans, and in fact were defending them. "What the hells?" I muttered.

"The Marauders have allied with the humans," Jinasek said. He turned to his adjutant. "Relay to all ships: the Marauders are not targets." Turning back to me, he gestured *amusement*. "It seems your alliance has grown."

I nodded. "Katherine was headed into their space. Looks like she was more successful than expected."

"Comms, open a channel to the Zhen command ship," Jinasek said. The comms officer looked momentarily confused, then realized he meant the *other* side's ship, and signaled the channel was open and broadcasting.

"Attention Zhen forces," Jinasek said. He sounded confident, but years of analyzing Zhen body language told me he was worried. I glanced over the tactical plot and wondered why – our forces were superior to the Zhen's in every way. "I am Commander Jinasek of the Imperial cruiser *Adamant*. I assume I have been called a deserter, but that is not the truth.

"There is a cancer in our Empire, and I have evidence to prove it. Stand down, and I will transmit the proof. Once you have seen it, I know you will stand down. Our fight is not with the humans, but with the forces destroying us from within."

An audio channel opened, and a Zhen voice rang out. "You *are* the forces destroying us from within! You and the humans! We will destroy you all and erase the stain of your desertion today!"

Jinasek's crest completely flattened to his scalp, a sign of sadness and disappointment. "I had hoped you, of all people, would listen, Kallenn."

"I have listened to our leaders, Jinasek, not the *grelkin* you have become."

Jinasek stood silent for a moment. "Then we are at war." He signaled to comms to close the channel, turned to flight ops, and said, "Launch fighters."

"Who was that?" I asked quietly.

He regarded me silently for a moment that seemed like forever. "My brother," he said at last.

"I'm sorry," I said, though the words seemed inadequate.

His voice was sad. "I doubt we are the only family who will find themselves on opposite sides in this struggle," he said. He seemed to shake himself before speaking again. "I realize you would probably rather be out there, but I need you here. Please take command of *Shir* group."

It wasn't unusual for Zhen commanders to give tactical authority over a smaller unit to an individual officer. It was usually seen as either a chance at glory and proving oneself, or a demonstration of trust. Jinasek, I could see, was giving me and his crew both – showing them how much he trusted me, and allowing me to prove to them I was as skilled as they'd been told.

I hoped I wouldn't fuck it up.

"Honored to, Commander." I turned back to the plot. "*Shir* group, this is Captain Hunt. I have the command."

"So we have been informed, Captain," a Zhen voice came back to me. "How may we serve?"

I scanned the plot. "Launch and head for relative coordinate zero-zero-seven. The *Newton Was an Asshole* needs help." Gods help me, I had to stop a moment to keep myself from laughing at that ship's name. "Get the...*enemies* off their sterns."

"Acknowledged," the *Shir* commander sent.

I watched the icons representing my ship head out to follow my instructions, but I was also keeping an eye on the battle at hand. My eye was drawn to the ship at the center of the human fleet. The *Litvyak* – *nice name, my love*, I thought – was well-protected, at least for now.

I wanted to reach out through the comms and talk to Liam, let him know I was here. But the last thing a commander needs is his presumed-dead husband calling him up in the middle of a battle.

My fingers itched with the need to be on ship controls, piloting my own ship through the chaos outside. I remembered this feeling from when I commanded the task force over Jiraad so many years ago – I was good at command, but not as good as I was at piloting. In many ways, being promoted had been removing me from my intended place in the universe. I wasn't a commander, not really. I was a pilot, and I lived for flying.

My navel-gazing was interrupted by the tactical system informing me that *Shir* group had accomplished their objective. The Zhen loyalists attacking the *Newton* had been dealt with. "*Shir* leader, be advised that the loyalist cruiser *Savage Claw* is beginning an attack maneuver on civilian freighter *Steers Like a Yak*. I'd like you to focus fire on this section," I said, sending him a technical readout.

A few seconds later, he replied, "*Shir* command, please confirm – there's nothing valuable at that target."

"Target is confirmed," I said. "Trust me, I used to command that class of ship. Do as much damage as you can. I promise it'll be worth it."

"Understood."

The ships of *Shir* group scrambled around and through the chaos of the battle, headed for the *Savage Claw*. I indulged myself, dropping into the individual feeds of several pilots, seeing the battle more or less through their eyes – cameras in their cockpits recorded the battle for later debrief, and I was able to access those at will. When the pilot I was observing went into a mad spiral maneuver, I lost my sense of balance and grabbed at the console. "That's some fancy flying, *Shir* twelve," I said. "I'm impressed."

"That? That was nothing," she said. "I was doing maneuvers like that before I'd left the creche. Did I make you dizzy, command?"

Despite the tenseness of battle, I smiled. "A bit," I admitted.

"Then I am a good pilot today." Her ship fired a missile that slammed into a Loyalist ship, the blast taking out the enemy's shields. She fired several plasma blasts into the ship, then as she passed it, flipped her ship around and continued firing while traveling backward – the 'bonehead maneuver' I'd used many times in my own career. As the Loyalist ship exploded, she completed her ship's flip and, back on the original vector, increased her thrust, catching up to her squadron just as they reached the *Claw.*

Shir group's fighters madly scrambled around the *Savage Claw,* whittling down the shields and slamming the armor. Half the squadron concentrated fire where I'd told them, while the rest harassed the ship and kept its gunners focused on their ships.

One of the ships was slammed by a defensive gunnery emplacement. The readings on the ship didn't make sense, so I slipped my consciousness into the ship's feed. "*Shir* twelve," I said, "your engines are reading as damaged."

"Confirmed," the reply came. "I cannot disengage thrust."

I scanned the plot. "*Shir* twelve, follow the vector I'm sending. Get out of the fight. We'll pick you up when it's over."

There was silence for a few seconds, and then, "Negative, command. *Zhen:ka ne'kal sharak.*" Zhen never stop fighting. A central tenet of the *Zhen:saak:arl,* the Story of the Struggle, that governed nearly all Zhen existence, the closest thing to religion in the Empire. "I give my life to your people, and to my own. See it is not wasted." A moment later, her voice returned. "Tell my clan I fought well."

I nodded, though of course she couldn't see it. "They will be told of your valor," I said, the ritual words as automatic – and as honest – as they had ever been.

Her ship traveled away from the *Savage Claw* for several seconds, then flipped over, the thrust from her engines slowing her, then pushing her back toward the enemy ship. She maximized her thrust and hit the boosters, bringing her ship quickly back to maximum velocity, firing the entire time at that one spot on the *Claw*'s dorsal surface I'd told the squad to attack.

The rest of the ships scrambled out of the way as the ship slammed into the target, exploding as her fusion reactor's containment failed. Like a small star, her ship flared and was gone.

In its place, the armor had been obliterated, and under it the ship's main engine coolant feed was shattered. The coolant boiled into space, and the engine flared. As my pilots continued to pick off the *Claw*'s guns, its engines failed, leaving it a more or less harmless brick floating in space.

Jinasek growled with approval. "An interesting choice of target," he said.

"It's not a well-known vulnerability," I said. "But I'm sorry it cost a pilot."

He gestured *rueful necessity*. "War is war," he said, a Zhen aphorism I had grown to hate – partly because it held too much truth in it. "But that is Kallenn's ship, so thank you for not destroying it. My brother is a fool, but I would rather not have his blood on my claws."

When we had disabled or destroyed most of the Loyalist forces, Jinasek turned to his comms officer. "Open a channel to the Zhen forces." When he got the confirmation the channel was open, he took a deep breath and began speaking, his voice ringing in the bridge. "Attention Zhen vessels. I am transmitting a record of my investigations into the events overtaking our Empire, along with my conclusions. Read them. Make your own decision. You will have time." He turned to flight ops. "Hole the drives and long-range comms systems of all Loyalist ships. We'll leave them alive, but unable to report back."

"Sir."

"Comms, open a channel to the human ship *Litvyak*," he said. "It's time to meet with their commander."

★　★　★

"You seem nervous," Jinasek said as our shuttle prepared to dock with the *Litvyak*.

"I am, a bit," I said. "I never told Liam I was still alive."

"You had good reason."

"Sure."

"So he will forgive you."

I looked at him. "You ever been married?"

"You know our family relations are not like yours." While Zhen formed family relationships among siblings and parents, the major center of Zhen society was the clan, large groups of families who banded together for support and defense, sharing child-rearing duties and other responsibilities among the clan's adults. There was nothing like human marriage customs in their culture. One mated within the clan, avoiding family members. Occasionally adults would bond long term, but it was rare.

"Let's just say he'll forgive me, but he'll make it hurt for a while."

Jinasek gave me an amused glance. "You probably deserve it."

He was probably right.

The shuttle set down in the *Litvyak*'s docking bay. I looked out the viewscreen and saw Katherine and Liam hugging. Almost vibrating with anticipation, I opened the hatch and walked up behind Liam. At the edges of my vision, I could see several of the guards react to my presence with gasps. Injala, standing near Liam but facing me, merely tilted her head, her ears positively vibrating with her amusement and happiness.

As I stopped, Katherine reached out, took Liam by the shoulders, and turned him around to face me. We couldn't have done it better if we'd planned it.

"Hi," I said.

He stared at me for several long moments, silent, his breathing hard. Finally, he said, "Taj?"

I stepped closer. "I'm sorry," I said. "I couldn't tell anyone I was okay without endangering—" I was cut off as Liam rushed forward, wrapping me in his arms.

My own wrapped around him, and a moment later I was sobbing, and he was sobbing, and the two of us were the most undignified couple of humans that had ever existed. Then Liam let go with one arm, reached behind him, and beckoned Katherine forward. She joined us, in both the hug and the sobbing.

And then Kiri arrived, shrieked, and came running up, slamming into the three of us. We folded her into the hug, laughing and crying at the same time.

There was still a war on, and it was going to be hard and painful. But at least one thing was right and perfect in the universe.

The moment was ruined when a woman's voice huffed, "This is all very sweet, but there *is* actually work to be done."

We reluctantly let go of the now-ridiculous hug, but Liam grabbed my hand and wouldn't let go. I was inclined to agree with that.

Katherine turned to the woman who'd spoken. "Your Majesty, may I present Liam Kincaid and Tajen Hunt."

The woman was dressed in a standard ship's jumpsuit, but made of the finest materials. She stepped toward me and looked me up and down. "You're the one who began this whole mess, aren't you?"

I inclined my head. "I suppose you could say that," I said, "though personally I think Zornaav did the real work."

"Thank you," she said. "The Marauders are with you."

"Wait, seriously?"

She looked amused. "I know we've fostered an idea of barbaric warriors in the cold of space, and there is some truth in that...but we're also human." She shrugged. "And Tradd, and Hun, and even a few others. But we know what Earth means, and...." She glanced at Katherine, and the woman still standing in the Marauder shuttle's hatchway. "Well, I've made some mistakes in the past couple of decades. I'd like to get started on fixing them. Step one is this fight."

I nodded. "We're glad to have you, then." I gestured toward Jinasek. "Please, allow me to introduce Commander Jinasek, late of the Zhen Star Force and now the leader of the Zhen:la Rebellion." Jinasek looked startled at the name I'd given to his nascent movement, but he didn't argue with it.

The Marauder queen nodded her head to Jinasek. "I am unaccustomed to working with Zhen," she said, "and it may prove difficult for my people. We have spent too many years hating you and your empire. But I welcome the experience. It has recently been proven to me that we were perhaps aiming our hate too broadly."

"Hate has done much to lessen both the Empire and our relations with others," Jinasek said. "Perhaps this war will put an end to such things. I, too, have learned much recently that has changed my views."

"Such as?"

I interrupted them. "It has been a long day already," I said. "While we can certainly talk now, perhaps I can convince you to give Liam and me a short time to talk? I need to find out what's happened while I was away. Then we can share everything we know and decide on our next steps."

"Actually," Liam said, "we should leave this system. The Zhen know we're here. We can't guarantee they won't send another force to check on the one we've disabled – and if any of them get their guns back up…." He left that unsaid. "We can rendezvous elsewhere and hold our conference then."

"A sound strategy," Jinasek said. "Where shall we rendezvous?"

Liam looked to Injala. She nodded. "We have established listening posts in several systems at the edges of our space. We can rejoin each other at this one." She waved her hand, and an illusory mote of light flew from her fingers to each of us. "The jump should take only a few days. I trust that will be long enough for your purposes?"

I blushed. "I suppose it'll do," I said. Liam elbowed me. I said to Jinasek, "Before we jump out, I'd appreciate if you'd send Midnight back."

He gestured toward the docking bay's main entrance. I saw Midnight entering through the atmosphere shield. "I made the request a while ago," he said. "I will join you all at the coordinates." He slammed his fist to his chest, then appeared slightly troubled at the Zhen salute's appropriateness. He returned to his shuttle.

As it lifted off the deck a few minutes later, the queen turned to Katherine. "Will you be returning with us, or will you stay here?"

"We came in my ship," Katherine said. "I'll fly you back, but I'd like to return here before jump."

"Of course." She indicated the other woman. "Andra and I have much more to discuss. We could use the time."

Katherine hugged Liam and me, then Kiri, and then poked both Liam and me in the shoulder. "Don't you dare spend the entire jump in your quarters. I want some time with my brothers."

My eyes welled up and my throat developed a lump at that. "We won't," I promised.

"Damn right you won't," growled Kiri, who still hadn't left my side.

Katherine returned to her ship, and a moment later, her ship rose from the deck. As it left the bay, the three of us turned and moved as one toward the corridor.

To Kiri, Liam said, "I know he's your uncle, but he's my husband. Can we have a minute?"

She grinned at us. "I'll give you *two*," she said magnanimously.

I narrowed my eyes at her. "You'll regret that joke."

She looked at me, all wide-eyed innocence. "What joke?" She glanced to the side. "One minute fifty."

Laughing, Liam and I left her behind and went to 'get reacquainted'.

CHAPTER FOURTEEN

Liam

I hadn't seen my husband in months. Our reunion was energetic, frantic, and involved a lot of moaning, grunting, and moving.

Afterward, unable – or maybe just unwilling – to let go of each other, we lay with my forehead pressed to his, our limbs entangled and the sheets in what my mother would have called 'a sorry state'. I said, not for the first time, "You could have told me you were alive, you know."

"I wanted to," he said, "but I was convinced that the best and safest thing was to leave you in the dark."

I prickled at that, and backed away from him. "Who was it supposed to be safer for? I thought you were dead. What if I'd met someone?"

"Did you?"

I paused, and he saw it and knew what it meant. To his credit, he didn't waste time with stupid questions. "Is he important?" he asked. "I mean, I'm a bit of the jealous type, but maybe I could—"

"No!" I said, interrupting him. "First, give unto me a break – we're insufferable as it is. If we added another man to this perfection, Katherine and Kiri would band together to murder us before we could say, 'Meet our new husband.' Second, it didn't get that far before he turned out to be a Zhen spy." I shrugged. "You'll meet him later. He's in the brig."

"He didn't suicide?"

"Injala took out his NeuroNet and his nanite clusters with some kind of Kelvaki poison."

"Ah," he said. "The *kalantiik*. I didn't know they'd perfected it."

"You know about it?"

He rolled onto his back. "They were testing it when I met Dierka. Didn't work back then. I'm glad they got the kinks worked out."

"You should be – if they hadn't, you would have come home to a dead husband."

"I'm sorry. Thing is, if I'd told you I was alive, it would have changed things. The Zhen would have known."

"I could have kept it to myself." I got out of bed and crossed to the kitchen to pour myself a glass of water.

He sat up and gave me a long look. "Could you have?" he asked. "Watching Kiri weeping over her uncle, could you have stopped yourself from telling her?"

I thought about it. "I want to say yes, but probably not."

"And even if you were that heartless," he said, "it would have changed how you handled everything. And if the Zhen were able to deduce I was out there somewhere, it might have given them a reason to intensify their efforts. I might have come back and found a ship's graveyard with my last remaining family floating in it."

"Katherine would have been alive," I said peevishly.

"Katherine is like a sister to me, my love," he said. He rose and walked over to me, wrapped his arms around me, and nuzzled my neck for a moment. "But she's not my husband," he murmured, "and she couldn't replace you even if she wanted to."

I felt myself responding, and as much as I ached for another go, I pushed him back. "No, love. Plenty of time for that later."

"Aw, c'mon. It's been so long, husband mine," he growled, his voice dropping a register and taking on the brogue of ancient Scotland he had, like me, learned from old movies. "Would ye deny your husband so soon?"

"Yes, I would," I said, enunciating each line carefully. "Look around, Tajen."

He looked around the cabin. The space reflected my state of mind before today – there were empty plates, cups and ration packs on every table and counter, and there were clothes disgarded everywhere. "So it's messy," he said. "We'll get it later."

"No, we'll get it now. The family is coming in" – I glanced at the chrono – "twenty minutes."

His head tilted adorably. "I can go that fast."

I felt a laugh bubbling up. I tried very hard to hold it in. "And that's a good thing?"

He held up both hands, as if weighing something. "Well, if I go fast, and if I can get *you* to go fast, then we'll still have ten minutes to clean." He shifted to the side as I reached for something, and ended up behind me, nuzzling my neck. "Please?"

"And dress, and—" I yelped as he pushed me back toward the bed. I fell to the mattress, and he fell upon me, licking and biting at my earlobe. "Okay, okay!" I laughed. "You win!"

"I do?" He paused for a second. "I usually do."

Neither of us said much after that.

★   ★   ★

After some frantic cleaning, showering, and dressing, Kiri and Katherine arrived together.

I glanced up and down the corridor. "No Injala?"

"She said she'd come later," Kiri said. "She wanted to give us time first."

"Ah," I said. "By which you mean she plans to sour the mood with business."

"Probably," she said. "In the meantime, here – an offering from the tech department." In her hands was a large package of Terran pastries.

"Where the hell did those come from?"

"One of our guys knew a shopkeeper on Shoa'kor," she said. "He asked me to give these to you."

"Let him know we appreciate it," I said. "Tajen loves these." I dropped my voice and leaned in, stage-whispering, "Maybe we should hide half of them."

"Maybe you should find a divorce lawyer," Tajen quipped, taking the package from me. He hugged Kiri and pulled her farther into the cabin. "Sit, sit," he said. "Tell me what you've been up to."

"Well," she said as she sat at one end of the couch, "remember when you made me an ensign in the Earth Navy? I've been promoted to lieutenant and placed in charge of signals intelligence."

"And what do they do?" he asked, as if he didn't know.

As Kiri took the bait and started explaining her job and the current state of intelligence, Katherine followed me to the kitchen. "Let's give them a bit," she said softly.

"Glad to." I grabbed some glasses and poured us each a drink. "How are you, really?" I asked. "I know you said you were fine, but it sounds like you've had a hell of an adventure."

"You have no idea," she said.

"So what are the Tabrans like?"

"Weird," she said. "Deeply weird."

"What do you mean?"

She sipped her drink and seemed surprised at the taste, savoring another sip before answering. "The one I work most closely with is mostly human," she said. "His name's Simmons – he was on my staff when I was running Earth's defense force.

"Anyway, he's been working for the Tabrans as an observer for years, reporting back on human/Zhen relations, what we were trying to do on Earth, pretty much everything. He's a nice guy, but he's so precisely spoken, so exact, that he comes off as a robot. But he's flesh and blood, and not at all an incarnate."

"I'm not familiar with that word," I said.

"The original Tabrans – the ones the Zhen have been fighting for so long – wiped themselves out a few hundred years ago," she said. "The Tabrans today aren't the same at all. They're nanite-based."

"Wait, you mean they're all nanites?"

"No, not so much. Some of them are sentient nanite swarms, but that didn't work out well for them – those were the Tabrans behind the decision to wipe out Jiraad. A lot of them choose to join with people from other species. The swarms – and the whole race, kind of – are called the Many That Are One. The ones who join with living beings are called incarnates. The joining gives them an understanding of us emotional beings."

"And what do the people who join get out of it?"

"Long lifespans, I guess. Maybe something else."

"Huh. Okay, that's that. What else happened to you?"

"Hey," Tajen called. "Come tell us too."

I poured two more drinks and we joined Tajen and Kiri. "It wasn't that fun," Katherine said. "I was captured, I had to steal a ship to prove I was Marauder material, and then I was supposed to duel the queen for the leadership."

"Supposed to?" Kiri asked.

Katherine shrugged. "It was the plan. But when I came face to face with her, things changed."

As she explained, I found myself smiling. Back when Katherine's brother, Takeshi, had been killed by a Zhen while we were escaping Earth the first time, she'd suffered a crisis of confidence. When she came out of it, she was almost her old self, but not quite. She was as competent as she'd always been, but she didn't seem to realize it, and she second-guessed herself a lot. As she told the story of her meeting with Queen Nikara, I saw the old Katherine, the one who'd led us on the *Maggie's Pride*, and who'd been co-captain with Tajen on the *Dream of Earth* up until Takeshi's death, come out from behind her grief. She'd found herself again. "I'd planned to kill her. But I found a better way," she finished.

"That sounds like you," Tajen said. "But did you get the device?"

Katherine nodded.

"The device?" Kiri asked.

"The Tabrans sent me into Marauder space to get a piece of tech from the pre-Disaster era. They think it will help when we move to deal with Zornaav."

The door annunciator chimed. "That'll be Injala," I said, and opened the door.

As if summoned by mention of our enemy, Injala stood in the doorway. "I trust you've dealt with all the mammalian body snuggling?"

Tajen waved her in. "Yes, the monkeys have finished grooming each other," he said. "Come on in."

She crossed to us and sat, somewhat daintily, on a small bench Tajen moved into place for her. "I have finished cross-referencing my agents' reports with the information we got from your prisoner," she said.

"You got him to talk?" I asked her.

"With some encouragement," she said.

Kiri looked alarmed, and Tajen waved her down. "The Kelvaki don't use torture," he said.

"Of course not," Injala said, primly. She turned to Kiri. "We use drugs."

"Is that really any better?"

Injala indicated uncertainty. "Perhaps not, but when the survival of your people and another is at stake," she said pointedly, "then it is sometimes necessary." She turned to me. "In any case, the prisoner knows little of value to us. All he really had was that there are no more Zhen agents in the fleet. He was the last one."

"You're sure he told the truth? He's not holding out?"

"Yes."

Tajen nodded. "Now what do we do with him?"

Kiri said, "We can put him on trial, lock him up in the brig."

"*Kark* that," I said. "Space him."

"Without a trial?" Katherine said.

"We don't need one," I said. "He pulled a gun on me on the bridge, in full view of everyone."

"Even in Zhen law, a trial is guaranteed."

"And most of them aren't fair," I said.

"We're supposed to be better than that," Kiri said. "Earth's charter guarantees a trial for anyone accused of a crime. This qualifies."

"We're not on Earth," I snapped. "The charter doesn't apply."

Tajen said gently, "Why are you so sure he needs to die, Liam?"

I surged to my feet, suddenly irrationally angry. "They killed *hundreds* of us, Tajen!"

"Who?"

"Him! Him and all the other Zhen agents they got aboard the fleet from Shoa'kor."

"Wait, what happened? I haven't gotten the reports yet."

I stopped long enough to take several deep breaths. "A few weeks ago, six ships were hit by suicide bombs. Most ships had one, a freighter called *Earthborn* had more. We're not exactly sure how many. Between all six ships, we lost four hundred and twenty-three people, near as we can tell. Records aren't entirely sure.

"The bombers were all in league with Alex. I think he's their leader."

"What makes you think that?"

"He's the only one who didn't suicide, and he manipulated me, Tajen. He made me feel something, gave me hope I'd live on without you and find something worth— And it was all bullshit and I fell for it!" I stopped, turning away from them all, my face red with both shame and anger.

I felt Tajen come up behind me. He wrapped his arms around me. "I'm sorry," he said. "I was so happy to be home with you I didn't think about what you'd gone through while I was gone."

"It's not your fault," I said. "You had to do what you did. But there was a cost. I paid part of it here. You're going to have to pay part of it waiting for me to let go of my anger."

I could feel him nodding. "I understand. I'm sorry."

I turned, hugged him for a moment, and then pushed him back. "I don't need you to be sorry," I said. "I just need time to process it all, and I need you to be patient."

"Patient as a tortoise."

"What the hell is a tortoise?" I asked him.

He looked confused. "I...don't actually know," he said. "My mom used to say it."

"The tortoise was an animal on Old Earth. Reptilian, with a hard shell around its vulnerable body," Injala said. "There are likely still some on Earth. They are very long-lived."

Both Tajen and I turned to her. "Thanks, I think," I said. I returned to my seat. "Okay, so maybe we shouldn't just space the bastard. But if he's tried and sentenced to space, then I'm pushing the button."

Tajen waited a beat, then said, "Seems fair. Katherine, you got the device, you said?"

"Yes. It's on my ship."

"Any idea what it does?"

"Rememberer said it can control or destroy Tabran nanites."

"And they couldn't build that on their own?" Kiri asked.

Katherine shrugged. "You're our expert on that. They said something about having destroyed all the relevant data and not having the time to work it all out again. Does that sound right?"

"It could be," Kiri said, "or they could be lying. No real way to tell." She looked between Katherine and Tajen. "Do we trust them?"

"Yes," Katherine said.

"No," Tajen said at the same moment.

The two of them looked at each other. Katherine spoke first. "I trust them – at least so far as I don't believe they mean us harm."

"I can agree with that," Tajen said. "But I'm not sure if I trust them much farther than that – everyone always has their own agenda." Katherine raised her glass to him.

"All of which is beside the point," I said, each syllable deliberate. "This is supposed to be a welcome home, not a strategy meeting. That's tomorrow."

Tajen smiled at me. "Hear, hear."

For the rest of the night, we talked. Katherine, Tajen, and I told our versions of what had gone on while we were split up, with Kiri and Injala interrupting from time to time with questions or comments. We talked deep into the night, sharing our stories, remembering and renewing our connections to each other, our shared pasts and intertwined futures. We reminded ourselves what it was we were fighting for, on Earth and everywhere else in known space.

Families. Everyone's, of course, but if I was being honest? I was fighting for my family more than anything. After all, it had taken me thirty-seven years to put them together; there was no way in hell I was letting it fall apart now.

CHAPTER FIFTEEN

Tajen

Bright and early in ship's morning, Liam called the captains of each ship to a meeting via NeuroNet. The virtuality looked like the docking bay of the *Litvyak*, but cleared of all the ships and personnel that would normally be working. As he and I entered the virtual environment, the captains were standing in groups, talking amongst themselves. It was possible for them to talk from across a room without raising their voices, but humans had a hard time with virtual spaces that differed too much from normal reality, so we tended to behave in them just like we did in the real world. Liam had set up this virtuality so that everyone in it looked just as they did in reality – any change of position, any expression, was set up to mirror their meat bodies.

"Thank you for coming," he said, and the chatter faded, each captain turning to look at him. "We've come through a difficult time, and I'm proud to have served you all – but now it's time for me to step down."

I was as surprised as the others. Liam hadn't said anything to me about this. I looked to Katherine; she was clearly as surprised as I was.

"Admiral, what are you talking about?" asked one of the captains. She was shocked, but also afraid. "You've brought us this far."

Liam thought a moment before answering. "I did, Ellen, but the reality is that I've been running at the very edge of my ability here. I'm a groundpounder at heart. What I'm good at is leading soldiers on the ground with clear objectives. I'm not made for this job." He raised his hands over other objections. "Hear me out!" As they settled, he continued. "My decisions nearly got the fleet destroyed – if it hadn't been for the intervention of the Marauders and the Zhen rebels, we'd have been wiped out. I honestly don't believe this is the job for me – remember, I only did it because Tajen was missing. I'm a fair pilot, but only fair – I don't have the skills needed to command a space battle. I want to step back and take on the job I was originally assigned to do – lead our ground forces."

"We don't have any," one captain said.

"We have a few – I need to train more. We're going to need them if we plan to retake Earth," Liam said. "But don't worry – I have just the officer for you."

"Tajen Hunt!" one of the captains cried.

I drew breath to speak, but Liam waved me to silence. "No," he said, "as much as I love my husband, and believe he could do that job, I don't think it's what *he's* good at, which is leading our attack wings." He looked over his shoulder and winked at me. "I want to keep him where he does the most good, and Tajen's better at small-unit tactics than he is at large-scale fleet battles."

I wondered who he had in mind. I glanced at Katherine and saw her cringe at the idea it might be her, but Liam gestured, and a new figure emerged from behind me. When I saw who it was, I nodded in agreement.

Liam turned and beckoned Captain Xiao Ming Zhang to his side. "Captain Zhang has been the *Litvyak*'s captain since we began," he said, "and almost every good decision I've made was with her help. She's the best choice to lead this fleet."

Heads nodded. "Who will lead the *Litvyak*?" one captain asked.

Captain Zhang stepped forward. "Day-to-day operations of the *Litvyak* will continue to be handled by the current XO. If I need to leave the ship, he will be in command. But for now, I will command both this ship and the fleet as a whole."

One young captain looked to me. "Do you agree with this, Captain Hunt?"

"Absolutely," I said. "Captain – *Admiral* – Zhang has my full confidence, and I won't hesitate to follow her commands myself."

"If there are no objections?" Liam asked the room.

Every captain signaled assent to his plan. "Very well," he said. "Admiral Zhang, the command is yours."

"You are relieved, sir," she said. As the captains left the virtual environment, she said, "I'll try to do as well as you did."

"Oh gods," he said. "Do better, please."

"Do my best. In the meantime, you go talk to your ground forces." Her attention switched to me. "Captain Hunt, we lost our CAG and his XO in that last fight. I'd like to make you CAG." When I nodded my assent, she turned to Katherine. "Will you accept the XO position?"

"With pleasure," Katherine said.

"Excellent. Why don't you check in with your new command – but be in briefing room one at second *ahn* for the strategy meeting."

We both snapped a perfect salute. "Sir," I said, and dropped out of the virtuality.

Across from me on the couch was Liam, grinning. I shook my head at him. "You could have warned me."

"You might have tried to talk me out of it."

"I probably would have," I said. "But it would have been wrong of me."

"Don't get me wrong," he said. "I know I could have done the job, but…I've been thinking Zhang is a better choice since day one. I just needed *her* to realize it."

"Well, look at you," I said. "You went and became a leader while I was gone."

He looked offended. "Screw you," he said. "I've always been a leader."

A comms signal came in. "Hey, Tajen," Katherine's voice said in my ears. "You plan on joining me?"

"Just putting my husband in his place," I said, waggling my eyebrows at Liam. "I'm on my way now."

*　　*　　*

Katherine and I swept into the briefing room late. As we entered, Jinasek paused as everyone glanced at us, then continued what he'd been saying. "We left the Empire because we did not trust the Twenty or the One any longer. I will do much for the Empire, but slaughtering humans who committed no crime is not something I will do."

"We appreciate that," Zhang said. She was sitting at the head of the table, with Liam to her left. Beside him was Injala, then Kiri. On the other side of the table, Jinasek and one of his advisors sat beside Nikara and the woman who'd been with her earlier. Katherine and I took the seats between the Marauder woman and Kiri.

"Sorry we're late," I said.

Injala raised a finger, and Zhang gestured for her to begin. "Now that Tajen is here," she said pointedly, "I have important news. I received an intelligence packet from home this morning, and I must inform you that the situation with my government has changed." She paused and looked around the room. "A week ago, the Zhen openly fired upon a Kelvaki merchant convoy passing through Imperial space."

Jinasek's crest rose to its full height. "Did they give a justification?"

"They claim the convoy was carrying weapons for the human resistance."

"Was it?" I asked.

"No, as it happens. It *was* carrying food and supplies to Earth, but no weapons."

"Even under Imperial law," Jinasek said, "that is legal. There is no justification for such an attack."

"And yet it happened," Injala said. "And consequently, as of two days ago, the Kelvaki Assembly has declared war on the Zhen Empire." She looked around the room. "I am instructed to inform you that the Assembly wishes to ally with your cause. We are with you, in full, as of now." She looked to me. "A Kelvaki force is on its way to meet us here."

I looked at Jinasek. "Does this change anything for you?" I asked.

"No," he said. "I do not in any way like the idea of fighting and killing my own people, but the truth is that even if I went straight to

Zhen:da and declared us returned to service, we would be immediately killed." He gestured *uncomfortable*. "My Empire has committed illegal actions and given up all honor. My ship commanders have agreed that our honor as warriors and as Zhen is on the line, and we are with you until the Empire is brought back to itself."

I nodded. "I, for one, am glad to have you."

Zhang glanced at me, but directed her next words to the queen. "You said earlier you also wished to join us. May I ask why the Marauders decided now was the time to come out of hiding?"

Queen Nikara bristled, but the woman beside her laid a hand on her arm, causing her to stop, take a breath, and let it out. She gave her advisor a grateful glance, then turned back to the table. "We weren't hiding from you. But the Empire has had a 'kill on sight' order against us for several hundred years. We've maintained a policy of non-engagement, other than raids, for some time out of self-preservation. When I took the throne, I had intended to change that – I wanted to face the Empire openly again. But I got sidetracked from that desire." She paused, sipping from the cup of tea in front of her. She looked haunted, as if facing something unpleasant within, and there were a few seconds of silence until the other woman spoke.

"You have to understand, when the Marauders began, the savagery was a mask, something we pretended to be when dealing with the Empire. At home, we were much like anyone else. Over the centuries, though, the facade became more and more a match for our inner selves, until there was not much difference between the masks we showed the world and our true selves. Nikara and I had seen the problem and planned to change it, but...." She stopped speaking, looking to Nikara.

"I fell into a dark place for a time," Nikara said. "Some of my reforms stuck – such as our ending of the killing – but my goals were abandoned, until Katherine brought me out of it. She reminded me of my desire to engage with the galaxy again, to reform my people from the savages we'd become."

"Uh...." I said, trying to remember the name she'd given us.

Katherine gave me an exasperated look. "Andra," she stage-whispered to me. Around the table, the humans chuckled.

"Thank you. Andra, when Katherine and I first joined up, it was because I had rescued her from an attack by Marauders. If you had begun a policy of not engaging with the rest of us, why were they attacking?"

"Where did this take place?"

"Kintar System," I said.

"Ah. That would be the Shimo Clan. They have been slow to change, and are to be arrested on sight within our spaces."

"I see. One more question, then. My understanding is that the Hun began the Marauder clans, and that humans joined later, as they fled the Zhen sphere of influence. But when we boarded that Shimo ship after the battle, there was a map of the Sol System, and around Earth there were words: *The Great Lie*. How did you know?"

Nikara smiled. "It is true that many of our human members came from the Zhen Empire," she said. "But the first humans to join the Marauders didn't."

"What?"

Andra said, "It's true. I'm descended from a Group Captain Elizabeth Padgett. She was the commanding officer of a ship in the Royal Air Force."

Kiri leaned forward. "When did they join with the Marauders?"

"Oh, very early on," Nikara said. "The HMS *Typhoon* was discovered by a Marauder clan about fifty years after the destruction of Earth."

"When we showed up later, and the Zhen took us in – why didn't the Marauders tell us the truth?"

Andra said, "According to our records, they tried. But every ship they sent into Zhen space to make contact failed to return. Eventually, they decided the humans of the Empire had fallen for the Zhen's lies." She shrugged. "It took a long time for us to realize what was going on in the Empire, and by then things had changed. When Marauder ships found humans, they gave them the choice. Some joined up, some didn't."

Nikara added, "Our information is that many who made it back to Zhen space tried to tell the rest of you, but were discovered and shut down by the Zhen. And by 'shut down' I mean killed, of course. Eventually, we stopped sending anyone."

"All right," I said. "So now here we are – the Marauders, the Zhen:la Rebellion, and the Human Rebellion, along with our friends the Kelvaki. Now what?"

"We—" Zhang stopped cold, her eyes widening.

At the same moment, alarms began blaring. As we all jumped to our feet, my comms system automatically accepted a message from the bridge. "Unknown vessel has just arrived!" the sensor operator sounded, his voice slightly panicked.

"Visual!" snapped both Zhang and I.

In my vision, a large ship appeared. It took less than a second for me to recognize it. I looked to Zhang. "Friends," I said.

"Stand down alarm," she said. To me: "Who are they?"

"Tabrans," I said. "Specifically, that's the *Sudden but Deep Understanding That Comes upon You When Least Expected*. And yes, they're all named like that. People *and* ships." I grinned at Katherine. "I guess they want to join up, too."

Zhang took a moment to recover. "Well," she said. "Let's not keep them waiting."

★　　★　　★

"We are sorry that our arrival caused such consternation," The Sunset After a Storm said as she walked between Zhang and me. Behind us, Rememberer of Unpleasant Truths spoke softly with Katherine.

"Think nothing of it," Zhang said with a bit of false bravado. "We are grateful you come as friends."

"It is our hope to be more," Sunset said.

"Oh?"

"It is best we speak to you all at once," she said.

"Of course. Here we are," Zhang said. I slipped into the briefing room just before Sunset, motioning the others to relax. When they saw her, their confusion was evident.

"We never got the chance to bring most of you up to speed on the Tabrans," I said. "Let's fix that now."

We spent a good thirty minutes rehashing the history of the current Tabrans, the Many That Are One, who had begun their existence as an anti-Zhen weapon that got out of control and wiped out the original, biological species called the Tabrans. After a few centuries of pondering what the hell they'd done, the sentient nanite swarms had begun creating more of themselves, trying their best to live more or less as their creators had.

When the Zhen, having not known their ancient enemies were gone, had reached into Tabran space once more with conquest on their minds, the nanite Tabrans had reacted exactly as their creators had – with vicious, efficient violence.

Eventually, they'd figured out that bonding with biological life gave them a more complete experience of living, and the Tabrans had spent the last few years rebuilding their world and searching for a way to fix their biggest mistake – the bonding of a sentient nanite swarm with Zornaav, the Zhen:ko who had become the leader of the entire Empire.

"You really think you can free Zornaav from the nanites infecting her? Is it really that simple?" asked Jinasek.

"Simplicity is unlikely," Rememberer said. "The Many That Are One should be able to leave their host at any time. That the swarm within Zornaav has not done so indicates there may be a problem."

"Such as?" Zhang asked.

Rememberer looked to Sunset, his Hun stature forcing him to look up. The Tchakk looked to Zhang. "I wish we knew," she said. "We have made many attempts to discern the trouble, but the nanites do not any longer connect to our gestalt. The Corporate believes that Zornaav somehow dominated the nanite swarm and, rather than join with it, forced it to submit to her will."

"That's possible?"

"We did not believe so," Rememberer said. "But it seems the most likely explanation."

"She's done more than force it to submit to her," I said. I flicked my hand, sending the information Jinasek and I had discovered to the center of the table, where it was disseminated to everyone else's NeuroNets and displayed for them. "She's created her own gestalt." I gestured to Jinasek, who continued.

"She has joined the entirety of the Zhen:ko caste to her by using Tabran-created nanites," he said. "Every member of the Zhen:ko is connected to their network. She can see through their eyes, talk through them...kill them."

"Monstrous," Sunset said. "To use the Many That Are One in such a way is an abomination. It is a betrayal of everything we wished to bring to the galaxy through our joining." She stood straighter, looking at each of us in turn. "The Tabran Regency wishes to join your alliance. We wish to help undo what we have done."

Everyone looked to Zhang, and she turned to me with a questioning expression. "What?" I asked.

She seemed exasperated. "We're not going to have that whole argument about you being the leader of the rebellion, are we? Again?"

I blinked at her a few times, then smiled. "No, I'm just being difficult," I said.

"That's my husband," Liam said, mock-proud.

I frowned at him. "Sarcasm is the last resort of the fool," I said.

"What's worse, the fool, or the guy who married him?"

"Gentlemen!" Injala said. "Are you quite finished?"

Both Liam and I were fighting to withhold laughter. I took a deep breath and turned back to Zhang. "I was effectively the leader of the human resistance on Earth," I said, "and I'll gladly remain so. But this alliance is something new." I gestured around the room at our gathered allies. "The Tabran Regency wishes to join the Human Resistance, the Kelvaki Assembly, the Marauder Clans, and the Zhen:la Rebellion in an alliance to end the threat of Zornaav," I said.

Sunset raised one spindly arm. "Correction: the Tabran Regency is what our creators called themselves, and though we are not offended by that name, we wish it known that we represent the Tabran Corporate."

"So corrected," I said. "Under any name, the Human Resistance accepts them."

"The Zhen concur," Jinasek said.

"The Marauder Clans accept the Tabrans as allies," Nikaru said.

"As does the Kelvaki Assembly," Injala said.

I turned back to Sunset. "Welcome to the Alliance," I said. "Now we just have to fix the Empire. No big deal."

"How do we neutralize the Zhen:ko gestalt?" Liam asked.

"That we do not know. We must study the technology Katherine and Nikara brought back, if the queen will permit."

"It's yours," Nikara said. "Do with it whatever you wish."

"All right," I said. "Injala, how long until your forces arrive?"

"My best guess is a day or two," she said.

"Sunset, why don't your people examine the artifact. When the Kelvaki get here, hopefully you'll have some ideas on how to make it work for us."

"We will do our best," she said.

*　　*　　*

Two days later, the Kelvaki Assembly task force jumped into the system with us. Injala informed me that her 'replacement' was on the way and, having a good idea who that might be, I decided to meet the shuttle.

When the shuttle door opened, an eight-foot-tall and nearly four-foot-wide mass of reptilian muscle stood filling the hatch, dressed in the robes of a noble of the Assembly. My old friend Dierka's voice boomed out, "*Draka!* I am delighted to see you!"

I tried not to run as nearly a thousand pounds of muscle bore down on me. He raised a four-fingered fist and thumped me soundly on the shoulder as he reached me. Despite years of asking him not to, he did this every time we met, so I was prepared for the hit and managed to keep from falling over. "How many times?" I asked him, rubbing my shoulder.

"Until the end of you," he said, beaming. "Actually…perhaps, when you are old and feeble, I'll stop. I would not want to be the one who kills you, after all." He laughed in that horrible way Kelvaki men do, and the sound of a thousand puppies being stomped on echoed throughout the cavern.

"Kelvaki humor is unique in the galaxy for one thing," I said.

"Yes? What is that?"

"Not being funny."

He laughed again, the horrible sound punctuated by the sound of his fist thumping me on the shoulder again. This time I wasn't prepared, and staggered back. "Ow," I said, straightening. "Are you ready to meet the rest of the Alliance, or are you not done pummeling me yet? The others are waiting."

"Lead on, Tajen, and on the way you can tell me of your life since last we met."

I led him from the bay and down the corridor, glancing sidelong at him. "I'm sure you've been given a full accounting by your spy."

"Spy?" He seemed confused. "I have no spy among you."

"Oh, so Injala was just here for *my* benefit? How unlike the ruler of a civilization."

"*Heir* to a civilization's throne. I rule nothing yet."

"How is your uncle?"

His hand moved in the Kelvaki equivalent of a shrug. "His death comes closer," he said, "but he is still himself. It is our hope that this war will be won before I must take the throne."

Kelvaki were in some ways less militant and violent than the Zhen, but they were still alien, with alien ways that seemed odd even to humans raised in the Zhen Empire. The Assembly was largely ruled by twelve Great Houses, the heads of which were the closest advisors to the Ascendant, their ruler. His word was law, but he had to work within the constantly changing loyalties and schemes of the Houses if he wished to hold his throne. I'd been caught up in some of their maneuverings last year, and I still didn't understand exactly how I'd been used. "You're hoping the war gives you enough social credit to override the Houses," I said.

"For a time, yes," he said. "Eventually I'll get them in line, but winning this war would go a long way to solidifying my hold on the throne before I am called to sit on it."

"Well then," I said, "we'll do our best to win it quickly for you."

His ears quivered in amusement as we entered the conference room.

Dierka stopped cold when he saw Jinasek. In Kelvak, he growled to me, "What is that *thing* doing here?"

I started to speak, but Injala spoke first, also in Kelvak. "Stop it," she said. "You were informed that Zhen had joined us, and who the Zhen representative was, *and* you *already* informed me you would behave. This posturing does not become you."

Dierka stared at her, and I worried for a moment. Under Kelvaki law, Dierka had power of life and death over his vassals, and Injala was one of them. I'd never known a Kelvaki to use that right – it was largely ceremonial and had been for centuries – but after working with Kelvaki for as long as I had, I was adept at reading their expressions, and Dierka's promised murder. I didn't really blame him – as much as I had internally cheered Injala's reprimand, Jinasek almost certainly had understood the exchange in Kelvak, though he was doing a good job pretending he hadn't.

After several long moments in which nobody moved, he relaxed. "Fine," he said in English.

"Commander Jinasek and his subordinate commanders have joined us," I said, "as have Queen Nikara and the Marauder Clans, as well as Rememberer of Unpleasant Truths and The Sunset After a Storm, who are here representing the Tabran Corporate."

Dierka glanced at them. "Fascinating," he said. "Injala briefed me, of course, but it's still fascinating to see you in the flesh, as it were." He sat in the rather large chair that had been provided for him and gave Zhang a measuring glance. "Who is this?"

"Allow me to introduce Admiral Xiao Ming Zhang," I said. "She's the captain of the *Litvyak* and the commander of the human fleet."

"Not you?"

"No," I said. "I command the fleet's fighter wings, but not the fleet itself."

He turned that measuring look on me for a moment, his nostrils flaring and his ears quivering. "*Tcho'ka* no more," he said to Injala.

Zhang cleared her throat. "Sunset has a report for us, I believe."

"Yes," the Tchakk said. "We have analyzed the device recovered from Dakcha, and it is what we had hoped." She gestured, and a readout appeared in front of me and, assumedly, everyone else. "The device has two functions. The first is to measure and affect the communication field of a nanite swarm, and the second is to control it."

Katherine frowned. "The Tabrans were destroyed by the accidental release of the first swarm. If they had this device, why didn't they use it?"

Rememberer answered. "Surviving records indicate that the device was created in response to our release. We believe they intended to bring it to Tabra to destroy us, but things moved too quickly. There simply wasn't time to put the device into play before all Tabran life on the planet was gone."

"What happened to the Tabrans on Dakcha?" Kiri asked. "They didn't just die, did they?"

Andra spoke up. "They were long gone when the Hun refugees found Dakcha and made it their home. We have no idea what happened to them."

"A mystery for another day," I said. "Right now, we've all got our own work to do."

Injala nodded. "I have an intelligence update to examine. I will let you know if there is anything important." She saluted Dierka, then left the room. The others followed, and I led Dierka to my quarters. "What did you mean, "*Tcho'ka* no more?"

He looked at me for a long moment. "You remember that *tcho'ka* means 'hunter of life'."

"Yes."

"As I told you before, it was a joke based on your name, Hunt."

"But that's not all. You told me I was looking for my life. So how am I no longer the 'hunter of life'?"

He stopped in the corridor and gestured widely, turning in a circle.

"You have married. You have Kiri to care for – a child not of your flesh, but of your clan, and thus your child as much as if you'd sired her. And you have figured out where you are best placed and made sure you are there to serve." He leaned close to me, and put one four-fingered hand against my chest. "It seems to me, brave *draka*, that you have finally *found* your life."

My vision blurred slightly as my eyes filled with tears. It had cost me my brother and my illusions, not to mention two years of constant war and terror, but he was right. I had a life. More importantly, I had a family.

Now I just needed to protect it.

CHAPTER SIXTEEN

Liam

Admiral Zhang called us to order. "We had planned a series of hit and fade attacks to draw out our enemies and whittle down their forces," she said. "However, we have received word that will require us to accelerate our plans." She gestured to Injala.

The Kelvaki woman stood and flicked a visual into the space over the table.

"What. The hells. Is that?" I said. I reached out and pulled a copy of the visual to myself. It was a brutal brick of a ship, aggressive in its form.

"You are looking at the Empire's newest dreadnought, the *Deathclaw*."

Tajen grinned. "Well, nice to see the Zhen are still dedicated to the whole 'aggressive naming scheme' thing." A few people seemed to appreciate the joke, but most were intently studying the ship.

Jinasek said, "I had heard rumors of this ship. It is supposedly being built in a secret shipyard known only to the One. You've found it?"

"Unfortunately, no," Injala said. "But we have learned it will be operational soon. We'll need to remove the One before that ship can be launched."

I zoomed in on the ship. It was bristling with weapon emplacements and had four docking bays. It looked enormous, but without anything else to establish a comparison, it was hard to tell how big it really was. I asked Injala, "How big is that thing?"

In answer, she flicked another image into place. "This is the *Adamant* at the same scale."

"My gods," Tajen said. I just nodded.

"Impossible," Jinasek breathed. "The *Adamant* is one of the most powerful ships in the Imperial fleet. This monstrosity dwarfs it in size *and* firepower. How have they built this ship so quickly?"

"They didn't," Injala said. "They've been building it for years now." She shook her head. "That it took so long for me to find out about it is a monumental failure." She looked to Dierka. "I will resign my position when you have found another to replace me."

Dierka's eyes narrowed and his teeth showed. "Say anything that stupid again, Injala, and I give you the most ridiculous ceremonial role in the Assembly – *in addition* to your duties as spymaster."

"Understood, *Kaar* Dierka."

"None of that either, *mon'kala.*"

I shot Tajen a look; his wide eyes told me I wasn't the only one who'd finally realized what Injala and Dierka were to each other.

Injala inclined her head to Dierka and continued from before the digression. "If the *Deathclaw* is launched on schedule, it will give the Zhen an incredible advantage in the war." Her face looked grim. "And they have another one coming online in a month. We must remove the One from power before this ship launches, or it *will* be used against us."

"So we need to deal with her now," Tajen said. "Well, we've got the nanite control device." He looked to the Tabrans. "Can it be used from orbit?"

"No," Sunset said. "The device's useful range is quite short."

I felt irritated at the nonspecific answer. "Define 'short' for me."

Rememberer's eyes swiveled toward me on their stalks. "No more than ten of your meters," he said.

I had the sensation of hope fading. "Shit," I said, drawing the word out. I turned to my husband. "We're going to need to land a ground force."

"That won't be easy," he said. "Even if it's just the Home Fleet guarding Zhen:da, that's a lot of ships to fight our way through. Odds of making it to the surface would be pretty much nil."

"We could draw them off," Katherine said. "Attack somewhere else, somewhere vital to their war effort."

"That's our job," Nikara interjected. "The Marauders are quite good at hit and fade tactics. We can attack and draw the Home Fleet out far enough to let your landers through."

Tajen thought about it. "We'd need a lot of ships to draw off the fleet."

Nikara bared her teeth like a wolf sighting prey. "We have the ships. We just need time to call them to action."

"Okay," he said. "That brings up another problem. We need a staging area. Slipspace is too varied to time things unless we all begin from the same place."

Dierka flicked a readout to the center of the table. "We can use this place. I've spies holding there. They tell me the Zhen have no idea they are there."

"What's the probability they're wrong?" Kiri asked. "The Zhen could be watching."

"My agents on Zhen:da have uncovered no evidence of it," Injala said. "I find it unlikely."

Tajen took a deep breath and nodded in approval. "We gather our forces there. That gives us a place to launch our mission and minimal time in slipspace. Timing is going to be incredibly important." He turned to Injala. "Do we have any intelligence on security over Zhen:da?"

Before she could speak, Jinasek said, "Zhen:da has not increased their security presence since this began. At least, not according to the last reports we received."

"How old are the reports?"

"A month."

Tajen whistled. "Not good enough, I'm afraid. Injala?"

"I have nothing more recent than the commander's report," she said. With a gesture toward Jinasek, she continued, "I will let you know if better intelligence comes in, but for now I would take Jinasek's report as true. It is unlikely anything has changed much in the time since that report was sent out."

Jinasek acknowledged her. "Let's hope not," he said. "The usual is quite bad enough."

"All right," Tajen said. "The Marauders attack a Zhen target near enough to Zhen:da that Home Fleet must respond. Any suggestions?"

"The shipyards at Karateia are vital to the Zhen war effort," Jinasek said. Tajen glanced at Injala, who gave him a very slight nod.

"Karateia it is, then. Nikara's forces attack with a fleet big enough that Home Fleet is forced to send at least some of their ships to bolster the defense of the shipyard. How do we communicate?"

"I can detail a ship to hack the slipnet relays," Kiri said. "It shouldn't—"

"That will not be necessary," Sunset interrupted. "We will provide you all with Tabran communications gear."

"How's that helpful?" I asked.

"If you integrate it into your systems, it will give you real-time communication no matter where you are."

"Wait," I said. "You can communicate across interstellar distances in real time?"

"Yes," she said. "We also have encryption algorithms that have not been broken by the Zhen."

I whistled. "I like it."

Tajen continued, "Once Home Fleet sends fighters to protect Karateia, we'll send our landers in with the ground team and escorts to engage the remaining forces."

"It's going to be rough," I said, "but we'll get it done."

Tajen glanced at me, and I saw in his face that he wanted to keep me with him. We'd been separated in the last big battle of this war, and he'd nearly died. Neither of us wanted to face that again. But I shook my head, just enough that he saw the motion. "Liam will lead the ground forces," he said firmly, as if it had been his idea all along. "Once the Zhen give us an opening, the landers go in. Once the team hits the surface, they'll have to fight their way to the One. That's not going to be easy."

"I'll go with them," Injala said. "I have information that may be of use on the ground."

I held my hand up to stop Tajen and get Injala's attention. "Once we get on the ground, what are we likely to face?" I asked.

"Lots of large Zhen with guns, claws, and teeth," she said, "all wanting to kill us."

"So, the usual."

Her ears quivered, but she made no reply.

"Then what?" Katherine asked. "What if things get too hairy over Zhen:da?"

"I have an ace up my sleeve I can call on," Tajen said. At our expressions, he said, "Better if I don't say what it is right now."

Tajen looked to me, and I took over. "Once the ground team gets access to the One, we use the nanite control device. Rememberer, Sunset – is that something we can do, or do you need to come with us?"

"We are creating new devices based on the original," Rememberer said. "These will be made to your own specifications. All you will need to is activate the device and hold the target lock on Keeper of Broken Promises."

"Who?"

Sunset held her hand up. "That is the name of the nanite swarm within Zornaav," she said. "It is our hope that, if successful, the device will separate them and allow Keeper to communicate with us."

"How do you estimate the chances of success?"

"We estimate a ninety-seven percent chance of total success," Rememberer said. "There is a slightly less probable result of just destroying the ability of the nanites to function as a swarm. This would have nearly the same effect as removal, except that it would kill Keeper of Broken Promises."

"Let's hope that isn't where we end up," Tajen said.

"Once this is over," Jinasek said, "there will be much work to do in cleaning up Zhen:da and the Empire. Can we count on the humans?"

Tajen sighed. "Jinasek, you'll have our support in theory, but I'm fairly sure the citizens of Earth will agree with me when I say we don't plan to go back to the Empire. We'll help you – but from a distance."

"I suppose I can accept that. What of the Kelvaki?" he said, looking to Dierka. "Will you pursue your war once Zornaav is removed?"

Dierka took a moment before answering. "We did not want this war," he said. "Zornaav's ambition and the beating of her war drums is what has brought us to this place again. Once the threat to our people is ended, we will gladly agree to peace with the Empire. If you tell me that removing Zornaav will end the war on your side, then I am willing to accept that."

Jinasek rose from his seat. "I do not know who will lead the Empire when this is over," he said. "But I will do all in my power to make sure the Empire's war ends with Zornaav's reign."

"For now," Dierka said, "that is enough for me."

We batted some more ideas back and forth for a while, breaking into smaller groups to figure out our plans. When it was over, people filtered out, until only Tajen and I were in the briefing room.

"I know you don't want me down there," I said. "But I'll have Injala and a few others with me. I'll put together a good team. I'll be okay."

"I trust you," Tajen said. "But I can't help but be afraid." After a moment, he said, "I can go with you – I'll put Katherine in command of the wings."

"Bullshit," I said. "I'm best on the ground, and you're best in the air."

"There's no air in space."

"Thank you, Captain Pedant," I said. "You know what I mean – you're the best man to run the battle up here, and I'm the best one to lead my team. Tajen, one of the things I have loved about you from the very beginning is that you've never tried to stop me being who I am." I shook my head at him. "It would be a shame if you started now."

"I won't," he said. "It's just that there's a shortage in this galaxy of incredibly attractive men who are competent *and* willing to put up with my shit. I'd hate to lose you."

I rose and walked to him and bent to give him a kiss. "I love you too. Now – it's been a long day, and I need some rest." I moved to the door and stopped as it opened to look at him over my shoulder. I dropped my voice to the lowest register and said with a wink, "You coming?"

CHAPTER SEVENTEEN

Katherine

When we were nearing our reversion point, I strapped into the pilot's couch and made sure my battle harness was in place. I glanced at Simmons, who was once more in my copilot's seat. "Glad to have you back," I said.

"I am glad as well," he said. "While the Marauders were not as barbaric as I'd expected, I did not enjoy my time on Dakcha."

"I'm sorry. I got you out of the work camp as soon as I could."

"I understand. It's of no consequence. The mission was far more important than my personal comfort."

Dagger spoke up. "Don't expect me to be glad either of you is back."

"Wouldn't dream of it, Dagger," I said, sharing an amused look with Simmons. "Ready for war?"

"I am the *Dagger in the Dark*," he said. "I am always ready for war."

Simmons finished his checks. "All systems read operational. Ready for reversion to realspace."

"Reversion in thirty seconds," I said. I stared out the viewscreen at the bizarre colors of slipspace. "It's pretty. I forget that, sometimes."

Simmons said, "Sad that so often we leave this beauty behind to engage in violence."

I shrugged. "It is what it is," I said. "Reverting."

The colors flashed and faded, slipping back along the hull as we shot out of slipspace and into reality. Dead ahead, the ocean world of Karateia was overshadowed by the jewel of the shipyards, the solar collection panels and flitting construction pods glittering in the dark. It was beautiful, really.

"Shame we have to destroy it," I murmured.

"We could always change our minds," Simmons said. I glanced at him and realized he was joking. I switched to comms. "All ships, attack the shipyard." Alarms blared as our computer registered targeting beams trying to lock on to us. "That was fast. Dagger, give me targets."

Target priorities began popping up in my visual feeds. Normally when we went into battle, we gave our enemies a chance to disengage and leave the field. This time, we couldn't do that. Our entire purpose was to overwhelm these ships and get them to call for help from Home Fleet. "All ships! Open fire!"

I locked on to several small ships headed our way and began pouring plasma fire at them while Simmons ran the electronic warfare board, trying to defeat their weapon locks and keep our shields charged. The Zhen pilots were good, and they managed to avoid most of my plasma shots. I was beginning to get frustrated when I saw a solution. I quickly programmed a firing pattern into the computer and then hit the stud to use it.

This time, for every shot aimed to actually hit the target, the ship fired four blasts designed to herd the target into position for the next shot. Not all of them hit, but enough did that it caused the Zhen to break ranks and scatter. I picked one at random and stuck on him. "Shock two, take the other one!" I said, trying to keep on the Zhen's tail. My missile locked on him, so I cut throttle for a bit, creating more distance between us. As soon as we were far enough away, I fired the missile. As it raced toward the Zhen, I continued to pour plasma blasts into the rear shields, wearing them down. The missile impacted on the shield, but did enough damage it took the system down. "Lock on to his thrusters!" I snapped.

"Thrusters targeted," Dagger said.

I fired, concentrating the plasma on the unprotected thrusters and sending damage ricocheting up through the system. There was an explosion within the ship – not enough to destroy it, but it began tumbling uselessly.

As I came around to find a new target, I caught a glimpse of the Marauder fleet in action. "Holy shit," I said. I'd seen the fleet before we left, but it was one thing to see a fleet preparing for a jump, and another to see it in battle.

The Marauder ships I'd seen in the past were largely collections of substandard parts held together with shitty welds and hope. But I'd learned those were the outliers, the ships they allowed us to see.

The ships in this fleet were old, but they were in excellent condition, and their crews had learned to work together in a way very few ever managed.

As the battle went on, I realized that while we were doing damage, it wasn't enough. "Lawson to Marauder Prime," I said. "We need to hit harder than this."

"I know," Nikara's voice came. "We're in position. All ships, clear the firing field for the Death Lance." A graphic came up delineating a firing pattern, and I saw we were out of the dangerous area.

"'Death Lance'?" I asked Simmons.

"One of their pilots told me it would be used," he said. "But he would not tell me more than that I should get my ship out of the firing area if I was caught within it."

Seconds after the comms message, the Marauder flagship and three other large ships of its class each fired a massive plasma beam at the largest defending ship. The *Red Claw*'s shields held at first, but the beams just kept coming without pause.

Most plasma bolt weapons divert small amounts of plasma from the engines and send them across the void. The range is limited, as the plasma disperses over time – magnetic fields keep it confined at first, but they only extend a short ways out from the weapon. Over the centuries, range had increased, but only to a point.

These beams were coherent, held in place by forcefields that stretched all the way from the firing ships to the target, across thousands of meters.

I said, "Where the hell did they get those, and can I have one?"

"They are unlike any tech I have ever seen," Simmons said.

"Obviously," sniffed Dagger. "The weapon signature resembles those of the Tabran Regency. They must have scavenged them from

Dakcha and reverse engineered them. Such weapons are now forbidden within the Tabran Corporate."

The shields of the *Red Claw* buckled and dispersed with a flash. The plasma beams slammed into the unprotected hull of the ship and almost immediately out the other side. Once they pierced the ship, they shut off. I hauled my ship around to avoid incoming fire, and busied myself with the fight. When I next could look at the *Red Claw*, the leftover plasma had dispersed, and the ship was obviously crippled.

"Reading a transmission from the station," Dagger said. "Playing."

"Zhen:da command, this is Karateia shipyard," the call came. "They've taken out the *Red Claw*. We are requesting immediate aid. Remaining forces are not enough to protect the station."

I switched my comms to Tajen's frequency. "Tajen, this is Katherine. We just caught the transmission from Karateia to Zhen:da asking for help. Should hit their slipnet relays shortly. You're on deck. We'll keep going here as long as we can."

"If we flee when the Zhen arrive, they will simply return to Zhen:da," Simmons said.

"We've got something in mind for that," I said. "Tajen's doing the same thing over Zhen:da. That man's got a delicious sense of irony."

CHAPTER EIGHTEEN

Tajen

"Tajen!" came from behind me. I stopped on Midnight's loading ramp and turned. Liam was running up to me, weighed down by his gear, a small troop of soldiers following behind. Farther back, Injala leisurely crossed the docking bay, looking like her own gear weighed nothing at all.

Liam came up the boarding ramp, leading his team. "Glad you're flying."

"No argument?" I asked.

"Hell no. When Zhang told me you were going to be the pilot putting us on the ground, I knew we'd make it down alive." He grinned. "Oh! Look what I found!" He reached to the soldier beside him and snatched the man's helmet from his head, revealing a shock of red hair.

My smile was instantaneous and involuntary. "Ensign Hitchens. Glad to see you, kid."

"Thank you, sir," he said, "but, uh...." He pointed to his shoulder, where bright new rank bars shone.

"I stand corrected, *Lieutenant* Hitchens. Where'd you come from?"

"I've been on Earth, working for the Resistance. When we heard this attack was prepping, a bunch of us volunteered to join the operation."

I looked to Liam, and he nodded. Both of us had developed a soft spot for this kid back when he'd been assigned to us on Earth last year, and we'd tried to keep him out of danger. But he'd proven himself several times over, and I wasn't going to be the one to say no this time. "Welcome aboard," I said.

The smile he flashed me was bright. This kid wasn't stupid; he'd known what the looks between Liam and me meant.

As the ground team stowed their gear, a message came in from Katherine. I acknowledged it and said to Liam, "Show's about to begin."

"Is the package ready?"

I grabbed a support beam and checked via my NeuroNet. "It's about to leave slipspace," I said. "I better get strapped in."

He followed me to the cockpit, where I strapped myself in and glanced to the copilot's seat beside me. "Everything ready?"

Kiri welcomed Liam, who sat in the spare seat behind me. "Yep, she's coming up now," she said, flicking a control node toward me. It slid to a stop on my board, and I placed my palm on it, activating the link.

My vision blossomed into a view from the drone we'd sent ahead. It was small enough that its exit from slipspace shouldn't trip any alarms; it would be barely the size of Zhen:da's slipnet relays, which constantly bobbed in and out of slipspace every few minutes. With luck, anyone who happened to be looking in its direction would assume it was only one of those. There was no sense in relying on that, though, so I goosed the reaction drives and sent the little drone away from the relays.

"Stealth field appears to be holding," Kiri said. "Keep her slow, though, so nobody—"

"I know what I'm doing," I said. I moved the drone, getting well out of the way of a passing patrol. "Nearly there."

When we were in position, I said, "Let tactical know we are in position. Waiting on the Zhen."

"Tactical says to proceed on your initiative."

It only took a few minutes for a good portion of Home Fleet to break away from the rest. The ships jumped into chain drive, and then our sensors picked up the telltale flares of jump drives activating.

"We're go," I said.

Seventeen years ago, I'd been in command of a defense fleet at Jiraad. The Zhen had surprised us with an attack that wiped out the colony. It began with the detonation of a device that flooded the area with a peculiar kind of radiation that interfered with both jump drives and chain drives.

Unable to get in position to defend the planet, many of my ships had been destroyed en masse. And those were the lucky ones; the rest of us were forced to stand by and watch as the colony was bombarded from orbit, killing millions.

I'd been haunted by that for fifteen years, but a couple of years back I'd realized the Zhen had maneuvered humanity into that massacre as an excuse to move against the Tabrans. It was only dumb luck that the Tabrans – or rather, the nanites that were now all that was left of the original Regency – had been surprised by the reaction and had sued for peace.

Now I was going to use that same weapon to save my people.

As soon as all the Zhen ships had jumped, I hit the device's detonator and, just before it blew, released my hold on the drone's systems. I snapped back to myself. "All ships – jump!"

While the fleet's attack ships were in slipspace, I powered up our engines. The moment we broke free into Zhen:da's orbit, I shot out of the landing bay. "All wings, on me!" I said over TacComm. "Alpha wing, Beta wing – you're on defense. Keep the Zhen off our capital ships."

I saw the *Drokkha Nakar* and the *Litvyak* angling for the flagship of the Home Fleet, the *Claws of Zhen:da*. The *Adamant* was engaging the defense control platform, a heavily defended station. Jinasek would engage Zhen ships once that was done, but it was a priority target and the *Adamant* was better equipped than most to deal with it.

My first job was to get the ground team to the surface. I wasn't the only ship carrying members of the ground assault. Four troop carriers were following me in. But I held the command team. "Midnight, ready for dive?"

"Ready," she said. "Though in point of fact, it doesn't really matter, does it? Even if I'm not, you'll go when you've decided to."

"You're not wrong. Where'd the fatalistic streak come from?"

"I'm piloted by Tajen Hunt. A fatalistic streak is a good idea. You have a track record of losing your ships."

"Not planning on dying today," I said.

"That's good, but not particularly reassuring. Your record is for surviving while your ship is destroyed."

I couldn't help but chuckle even as I yanked the controls, rolling the ship to avoid incoming fire. I returned fire at the ship that had nearly hit me, scoring some hits but not doing much damage. "Don't worry," I said. "You're a better ship than any of the others – I'll keep you alive."

"You'd better – there's no such thing as an AI backup."

"Now or never. Midnight, get me the drop ships."

"You're on."

"Landing team, we are go for dive. Let's go!" I pushed the stick forward, taking Midnight into a steep dive. We passed through a storm of ships, juking constantly to avoid collisions. Even I had to admit it was a miracle none of us got hit.

As we burst through the last layer of defenders, my comms chirped. "We've got Zhen on our tail!" one of the other pilots in my group called out. "Can't shake 'em! Gunners are trying, but they can't hit 'em!"

"Maintain your dive," I sent back. "I'll take care of 'em." I glanced over my shoulder. "Hang on back there!"

Liam said, "Hope nobody back there ate too much this morning!"

I hauled back on the flight controls, flipping my ship so we were headed backward. I fired on the pursuers and increased thrust, slowing my dive. The other ships flashed past me, and I cut thrust, flipped the ship back to the original heading, and slammed the throttle to full once more. Now I was behind the rest of my ships – and the attackers.

"Missiles locked," Kiri said.

I fired the missiles, then began pouring plasma fire into the rear shields of the closest Zhen ship. We were beginning to hit the outer edges of the atmosphere. Normally ships hit atmosphere at carefully calculated angles of attack to minimize heat, but we were on an attack run, which meant all the ships in this dive needed our shields to take more of the strain than usual. This helped me, as the pursuing ships had their shields mostly forward, and shaped to minimize atmospheric drag that would make insertion too difficult for our bodies to take even with the inertial dampers at full.

Even with the shields giving us a more streamlined shape, the drag was knocking us about, making it difficult for the firing computers to hit the Zhen ships. I managed enough hits to take out one pursuer before we reached equilibrium and the shaking stopped.

It was a different game now. In space, the lack of friction and atmosphere means you maneuver quite differently than in atmosphere, where even ships with gravitic drive systems have to contend with air resistance and wind. I managed to land several hits on another Zhen ship, but they'd already returned their shields to full coverage. "Find me a weak spot!" I called to Kiri.

She worked her board, analyzing the sensor profile of the Zhen ship's shields. "Here," she said, flicking her fingers, and a spot on the shields changed color. "Hit 'em there!"

I quickly targeted the indicated spot and fired on it. Moments later, the shields collapsed, and my fire began slamming into the bare armor of the ship. I stayed on their tail as they tried to maneuver out of my firing arc, and watched their armor sizzle and burn under the punishing fire. The Zhen pilot panicked and, in trying to get away, slammed into one of his own squadron, taking both ships out in a massive explosion.

"Shit!" I cried out. The shockwave of two fusion drives going out in atmosphere sent Midnight tumbling, and I fought to get control. The other ships in my flight were having the same problem, as were the pursuers.

Eventually I managed to get the ship righted, and looked wildly around to see if the others had as well. "All ships, report in – by the numbers!"

"Drop two, we're good."

"Drop three, five by five."

Nothing more came, and I started searching the air. "Come on, four," I said.

Kiri scanned her board. "We lost drop four," she said.

"What happened?"

"Looks like they got hit by debris. They hit the last Zhen on the way down – didn't blow, but they ruined their flight ability. Both ships are spiraling out of control."

"Can you get drop four on comms?"

She tried, then looked at me and shook her head.

Liam said, "I've lost their telemetry feeds too. They're gone, Tajen."

"Dammit." I shook myself and said to Kiri, "How's our course?"

"We're nearly where we should be. One hundred fifty klicks to the capital."

There was no way we'd be able to get into the city itself, let alone near the palace, if we came in high. The defense turrets would see to that.

"Get as low as you can," I reminded the remaining drop ships. "We need to stay below the sensor floor."

For one hundred kilometers, we flew barely one hundred and fifty meters over the ground. It was exhilarating for me, but whenever I glanced at Kiri, I saw her sweating as she looked between the viewscreen that showed the world zipping past beneath us, and the sensor board, looking for signs of another attack.

Fifty kilometers outside the city I said, "Look lively, it's going to get harder from here." The straight-line paths we'd been flying were impossible now, as buildings rose ahead of us, and the flight became a slalom course around skyscrapers.

Kiri jerked forward in her seat. "Incoming! Five Zhen Security Service interceptors inbound, bearing one hundred thirty degrees."

"Bastards got behind us," I said. "So much for surprise."

Liam spoke up. "Never thought we'd surprise 'em," he said.

"All ships, Zhen incoming," I said. "Scatter and meet at the LZ." I glanced at the scope and took a more or less random heading. "Incoming Imperial ships," I broadcast. "Welcome to your last fight! I'm Tajen Hunt, I'll be your death today!"

"What the hell are you doing?" Liam asked.

"I'm pulling as many of them on us as I can," I said. "The other drop ships aren't quite as maneuverable or well-armed. This should give them a better chance."

"Oh, give *them* a better chance. I see," Liam said.

"I knew it," Midnight interjected. "I'm going to die on this planet."

"Quit bellyaching," I said.

The Zhen came in hot, firing their plasma blasts in a steady stream of fire. "Looks like they're angry," I said.

"Can't really blame 'em, I guess," Liam ground out as I took us into a corkscrew maneuver to avoid incoming fire. The Zhen were firing indiscriminately, not caring if their shots hit civilian buildings around or below us. Liam's voice sounded slightly strained as he said, "I love you, Tajen, but I kind of hate you a little bit right now."

"No, you don't." I noticed a Zhen close behind me and pulled up on the stick while hitting the air brakes and retro thrusters both. When the Zhen flashed past me, I opened up the throttle once more. Now I had three more behind me, but one ahead of me, and I fired steadily at him as I juked the ship back and forth to avoid the fire from those behind. "Come on, you sonofabitch," I growled, "just let me hit you."

"That ever work?" Kiri asked as she was buffeted by a blast on our shields.

"Not in my experience," Midnight said. As if to punctuate her words, a series of hits shook us.

I fought to maintain control. "I'm getting tired of these guys," I said. "Midnight, ready for maneuver twenty-seven."

"Oh gods below," she said. "Ready."

I flew steadily on, allowing the Zhen to get closer. When they were in position, I snapped, "Go!" and hauled back on the stick.

The ship bounced upward as Midnight fired the antigrav systems briefly. I flipped the ship backward, completing a backward somersault while still hurtling less than two hundred meters above the ground. As the nose of the ship came in line with the Zhen, Midnight began firing both plasma weapons and missiles, her computerized targeting algorithms finding the precise angles of attack. One of the Zhen was destroyed outright, another was pushed into the buildings below by the force of the hits on his upper shields, which shattered the ship and buildings both, and the third avoided Midnight's shots but ended up in front of us as the somersault completed.

We chased him around buildings, flying over and under bridges and avoiding civilian traffic. Finally, I managed to whittle his shields to nothing and fire a missile that took the ship out.

"Tajen, I've been monitoring Zhen comms. More ships are incoming," Kiri said.

"Aw, *kark*," I said. "How are the other ships doing?"

"All three are still alive," Kiri said. "No pursuers at this moment."

"Drop zone ahead. Ready to deploy?"

Liam glanced back at his men. "Ready," he said.

I brought Midnight in low and fast, slowing dramatically over our planned drop point, pulling the ship's nose up and firing the belly thrusters to shed velocity. As the ship settled back to the horizontal, I said, "Open up." Midnight, hovering only feet above a park, opened the rear door.

"Everybody out!" Liam called. He glanced at me. "I'd love a proper goodbye, but there's no time," he said. "See you for dinner, honey."

"Be safe out there," I said.

"Do my best," he said, and left the cockpit. A few seconds later, he said over comms, "We're down. Get out of here. Good luck!"

I pulled the ship around and moved out, avoiding the other drop ships, who were all disgorging their squads and heading back out. "Burn for orbit," I said, pointing us outward at a steep angle and burning full throttle.

"You okay?" Kiri asked.

"Not really," I said. "I just dropped my husband into a shitstorm and I've got another one to deal with up there."

"We'll make it," she said. "So will he."

"I know," I said. I'm not sure I convinced her. I know I didn't convince myself.

As we climbed back into orbit, I spent a few moments wishing Liam and his team luck. War has always been messy and terrible, and the glory of a warrior's death, in Old Earth stories and Zhen *Ashrati* plays alike, has always been a lie. The Nine weren't my gods, and even Liam barely paid them any mind except in the oaths he'd grown up saying, but I spared a moment to ask them for his life, and his team's lives, just this once. I didn't know if they'd answer. So far as I knew, they didn't tend to.

The sound of our engines and the buffeting of the atmosphere faded to a dull throbbing through the deck plates as we left it behind, and I turned my mind back to battle.

I had work to do.

CHAPTER NINETEEN

Liam

As I watched Tajen and Kiri climb back into the sky, I hoped the Nine would protect them. I switched on comms. "Team leads, on me," I said.

The three team leads rushed to me as the teams formed a defensive wall around us. The first to reach me was a tall woman, Izibele Ma'Bhayi, followed by James Dillon and Aliyah Burhan. Each of them commanded a platoon three times the size of my seven-person command team. They were the best ground soldiers I'd found, all of them with experience in multiple campaigns in the Zhen forces.

"Any problems?" I asked them.

Ma'Bhayi cocked her head. "Aside from the fact we're on a hostile planet run by a psychopathic Zhen:ko and her hiveminded caste? No problems on my end." The other two signaled agreement.

"I have one," Injala said. "My agents are not responding. I believe they may have been discovered."

"Injala, they're our way into the palace. Are you telling me they're not going to be here?"

She looked grim. "It appears so."

I cursed. We'd been depending on Injala's spies to get us into the palace quietly. Now they were off the table, we had to find our own way in. "It's going to have to be a frontal assault," I said. "Not on the planet ten minutes, and shit's already going pear-shaped. Seems like an average day. Let's get busy. Ma'Bhayi, Dillon, you'll take routes B and C. We'll rejoin at the palace. Keep your comms open to the command staff – let us know if anything goes wrong." I frowned. "Anything *else*?"

"We'll cover it," Dillon said.

"I have no doubt." Dillon was a veteran of the ground war on Earth, and before that ground campaigns on a dozen Imperial worlds. His team was made up of people with just as much skill. They'd do their job.

Burhan looked to me expectantly. "You and yours are with my team," I said. "Remember, all of you – we're down a platoon, which means we've got no more redundancies. We're all essential. Keep your people sharp, and keep this front and center in your minds – this world may be hostile right now, but it used to be our homeworld."

"Not mine," Ma'Bhayi said with a grin. "I was born on Terra."

"I was born in space," Burhan said.

I realized they were blowing off steam, so I reined in my impatience. "Point taken. *My* point is, the civvies are not our enemies. Do not fire on them unless you've no other choice."

They all signaled understanding. "All right," I said. "We've got a lot of ground to cover, and the more of it we can do before they find us, the better. Let's move out."

As the platoons began moving out on their planned routes, my command team formed on me. We'd landed in a park relatively near the palace – as close as we could get without getting hit by the anti-air-missile installations on the walls of the Palace of the One. But we had several kilometers of capital city between us and the palace, and getting there in one piece was going to be a challenge.

Hitchens, walking beside me, gestured to the city as a whole. "Do you think we're likely to meet resistance?"

"We are definitely going to meet resistance," I said. "Just a matter of when."

Seeker said, "Shouldn't we commandeer some buses or something? We'd move much quicker; get off the streets."

I glanced at her. Seeker had grown up on Shoa'kor Station, the niece of a crime lord who ran the place. We'd helped her take over his operation a while back, and then rescued her when the Zhen destroyed the station a few months ago. She was a good fighter and an amazing hacker, but her 'street smarts' were largely station-based, and she wasn't used to operating on a planet. "And we'd have a higher chance of all getting taken out at once," I said. "We need to be able to move quickly and change up our options when necessary. Can't do that if we're trapped on the streets."

"We could get flyers."

"For nearly seventy-five operatives?"

"Oh. Right. Got it." She looked up at me. "Liam, I was flattered you asked me to be on your team, but I have to ask – why? I'm a fighter, but I'm not experienced at this kind of fighting."

"I know, but I needed a hacker, and Kiri says you're almost as good as she is."

"Probably true."

"Your first order: I want you hacking every camera you can find – either shut 'em down, or make them look elsewhere. Snarl traffic if you can – make it harder for civilian authorities to move on us."

"What about the military?"

I glanced at Injala, walking beside Hitchens and clearly already at work. "That's her job," I said.

Injala didn't look at me, but she gestured toward me as she spoke. "Zhen command is trying to scramble the second Shak:ta battalion to intercept us. I am blocking the routing of the orders, but it is only a matter of time before they work around my hacks and send them."

I looked around at the skyscrapers surrounding the park. Once we got into those canyons, it was a crapshoot what we'd be up against, and the second Shak:ta was likely to be the least of our worries. Any of those windows could conceal a hero ready and willing to prove his loyalty to the Empire, either by reporting our presence or firing on us themselves.

"Let's move quickly, then. We're on borrowed time here."

*　　*　　*

We'd made good time, and had only minimal contact with Zhen forces that we'd easily routed or evaded. As we approached the Intari Plaza, a wide-open space that surrounded the palace grounds, we'd been rejoined by the other two platoons. Ma'Bhayi and Dillon had joined my command staff to finalize our assault strategy when Hitchens tackled me, dragging me down behind a low wall.

Seconds after he knocked me over, the space where I'd been standing was hit by several plasma rounds. A moment later, we were being fired upon by numerous emplacements.

"Damn, I hate being right," I groused.

"I am not particularly fond of it myself," Injala grunted beside me. She rose and fired a couple of shots at a Zhen trying to get closer, then dropped down again. "Maybe you could stop?"

"'Fraid not," I said. I grabbed a small drone off my harness and activated it. As the little device rose swiftly, I connected to its feed, giving me a bird's-eye view of the battlefield. "Well, shit."

We'd allowed ourselves to think we were moving quickly enough, but it was fast becoming obvious that we'd been outmaneuvered. To get into the palace we'd need to breach the walls, and the places we'd carefully chosen to do that turned out to be traps, every one of them laid deliberately to look like a weak point even though they were actually reinforced. I was just starting to map out the positions of the defenders when my drone was shot out of the sky.

Worse, I could hear aircraft incoming. In moments we'd be dealing with air-to-surface attacks.

"Pull back!" I shouted into comms. "Airstrikes incoming!"

We began to pull back into the shadows of the buildings, finding ourselves hunkering down in a park between two of the towers at the edge of the plaza. There were plascrete planters and benches scattered, as well as plinths on which sat monuments to various Imperial victories.

As we rushed through the park, Zhen soldiers ahead of us – on the side of the park away from the palace – began firing, forcing us back.

The good news, such as it was, was that the park was actually quite defensible, thanks to the design, which featured high walls built to resemble a fortress, several short mazelike passages on either end.

The bad news, of course, was that we were trapped here. And I couldn't shake the feeling that the Zhen wouldn't have let us get in the park if they didn't have a plan to get us out of it.

As I crouched behind a planter holding a giant *yorsha* tree, I sent another drone around it to check the position of the enemy. Something landed at my feet with a solid *thunk*. I looked, and in a moment of panic I picked it up and threw it back over the wall. A moment later, I heard the explosion.

My drone showed me a wall of Zhen, but among them one in particular concerned me. A Zhen stood with a harness full of grenades and a launcher carried in the crook of one arm. He was loading the launcher as I watched.

I marked the target, then shunted the feed to Seeker. "Seeker, can you do anything? Mess with his targeting or something?"

"Got him," she said. "I've got an idea – hang on!"

A few moments later, there was the sound of multiple explosions. I checked the feed again. The grenadier was nowhere to be seen, and there was a circle of dead or hurt Zhen where he'd been. I whistled. "What did you do?"

"Hacked his grenades," she said. "Blew 'em all."

"Impressive," Injala murmured.

A growing whine started to build, familiar to me from years of service. I looked at Injala, crouching beside me, and her expression was as grim as my own. "Gunship's coming. We need a way out of this," I said.

"I'm working on it," she said as she tapped her temple. "Having difficulty getting through to my agents thanks to Zhen emergency firewalls. I may need Seeker's help to hack them."

"Seeker, see if you can help her."

"On it, boss-man."

The gunship came into view between the two towers, presenting its broadsides, and the two railguns mounted there, to us. It began to fire, tiny metal pellets accelerated by magnetic coils taking chunks out of the plascrete, the buildings, and my soldiers.

I heard Dillon on the comms. "Rogers, take out that gunship!"

Seconds later, a series of small projectiles fired from the ground to the gunship. The first few impacted on the armored sides of the aircraft and knocked it out of position, but the third and fourth hit the gravitic nodes on that side of the aircraft. The remaining nodes were no longer enough to keep the gunship in the air, and it fell to the street just outside the walls.

"Secure that wreck!" Several of my soldiers rushed forward, threading the maze to check the gunship's crew.

"All dead, sir."

I turned to Seeker, but realized she was busy. "Burhan, get your hacker on that gunship," I said. "See if there's anything we can do with it."

"On it, sir," Burhan replied.

"Hitchens, get our people set up to defend," I said. "We need to make sure they don't get in here. Set up some shields to keep grenades out too."

"I'll get it done, sir." He turned and pointed to several soldiers in turn. "You, you…you! Get overhead shields set up. You – get your fireteams in position at the south entrance. You, at the north!"

Burhan reported in. "We've taken a look at the gunship's insides, sir. It's not going to fly again, and the guns facing this side are smashed up. But the ones on the other side still seem operational."

"Can you use them against the Zhen?"

"We're prepping now. They won't last forever, but there's enough ammo in them to do some damage. I have another idea too. We can use the remaining gravitic nodes to create a shield – won't be perfect, but it'll give some cover. But it'll shield them too. It's not possible to make it one-way."

"Keep that in reserve in case we need the cover later," I said. I turned my attention to the drone and saw the gunship's remaining guns begin firing on the Zhen. Seeker wasn't spraying bullets at them, but firing carefully, with measured shots aiming for specific targets. It was helping, but it wasn't going to get us out of this.

I turned the drone to get a better image of our situation. Our defenders on the north and south walls were doing a great job of keeping the Zhen out, with some assistance from the gunship's guns on the south side.

On the other hand, we were pretty effectively trapped, with no way to get the roughly seventy soldiers under my command out of this.

Hitchens met my eyes. "Doesn't look good, does it, sir?"

I shrugged. "We've gotten through worse."

He gave me a look that suggested I was full of shit.

"No, really," I said. But then I relented. "I've gotten through worse – but that doesn't mean I can find a way out of this. If Injala's agents don't get us some help, I think we're done."

He grinned. "Sir, you're forgetting the one thing the Zhen taught us that's actually worth more than the tech they gave us."

"Yeah, what's that?"

He cleared his throat and said, "*Ne'kal sharak*. Never stop fighting."

"Not sure that applies to humans," I said.

"If you'll pardon me, sir, that's some defeatist bullshit. If it didn't, I'd have died in Landing during the siege, or in Hotty when they came for us later." He looked intense, almost angry. "Doesn't matter what they do to us, we don't quit."

I regarded him silently for several moments, then said, "You're not wrong, Hitchens. Thanks." I glanced at the north wall for a moment. "Collins has been on that post for a while. Maybe give her a chance to rest."

"Yes, sir." He rose and rushed to Collins and tapped her on the shoulder, taking her place on the firing line.

Something caught my attention, and my head whipped around to the east, to the residential tower that formed one of the walls of the park. I couldn't figure out what it was, but—

The wall exploded outward, a chunk of masonry hitting a young soldier, shearing his head right off. His body slumped over, blood pouring from the wound, and I stared, shocked, almost unaware of anything else. I felt an alien hand grab me and pull me down, and realized it was Injala pulling me to a safer position.

The Zhen were firing plasma bolts at soldiers who hadn't expected them to come from the side. Soldiers scrambled to find cover as Zhen began to come through the hole they'd made into the park itself.

"Incoming!" shouted Hitchens. He rose from behind the barricade and pulled his rifle to his shoulder, aiming carefully, ignoring the impacts around him.

"Cover him!" I shouted.

As the rest of us tried to keep the attention of the enemy on ourselves, Hitchens sighted in on the Zhen stalking toward us. He fired with an uncanny precision, each shot taking down a Zhen soldier. Several were taken out by the rest of us, but none of us hit anywhere near as many as he did.

When the attack was broken and we'd all ducked back down to brace for the next group, I got on comms. "Secure that hole," I snapped. "Put a forcefield over it."

A team of engineers scrambled to follow my instructions. I connected my comms to Hitchens's. "Nice shooting, kid," I said.

"Thank you, sir," he replied, methodically reloading his rifle's power pack and checking to make sure he hadn't overheated the barrel.

"But don't get yourself killed," I said.

He flashed me a grin. "Promise, sir."

And then he went down as a plasma bolt hit him in the chest.

CHAPTER TWENTY

Katherine

I yanked the ship to the side just enough to dodge the incoming wreckage. "Anything?"

"I will let you know the moment I see them on— Ah. They are arriving," Simmons said.

"Excellent. Get me Andra."

"On comms."

"Andra, is it in position?"

"In position and armed."

"Blow it, then."

An energy signature blossomed in the space near the shipyard, quickly bathing the entire system with radiation tuned to make both chain drives and jump drives useless.

When the Tabrans had used this thing over Jiraad seventeen years ago, it only lasted a little while. Tajen was able to jump just a few minutes later. But in the time since, the Tabrans had refined it. The effective period, Rememberer assured us, would be measured in days. But we still had to get our own ships away, so we had a ride coming. "All ships, withdraw," I sent over TacComm. "Our chariot will be here shortly."

"Incoming transmission from out-system," Simmons said. "Coming over the Tabran comms bands."

"Don't tell me they're going to be late."

"No," he said, looking confused. "The transmission is from Terra." He suddenly looked at me, stricken. "Perhaps you should hear this yourself." He flicked the channel toward the center of the console.

"—this is Terra, calling any human ships! We are under attack by Zhen forces. Send help! Repeat, send help! The defense system has been deactivated by the Zhen! We're dying and we—" The transmission screeched and then went silent.

"Can we verify that?" I asked.

"Working on it," Simmons replied. A few moments later, he said, "Tabran observation satellites in the Obrina System confirm Zhen attack on the planet Terra. It appears the Zhen elements were already in orbit before they were ordered to destroy the planet's population centers."

"That's insane, there's billions of people on Terra."

"Yet that is their aim."

I opened the Tabran comms equipment. "Tajen, the Zhen are attacking Terra – the orbital garrison was ordered to destroy the cities."

"Not just the cities—" Simmons began before I waved him to be silent.

Tajen's voice sounded as horrified as I was. "We should have seen that coming," he said. "Stand by."

I dodged several incoming volleys and took down a few missiles headed our way before Tajen came back. "Katherine, the Tabrans are headed your way. When they get there, get your ships close to them."

"Why send them here? We blew the inhibitor. We don't have jump here! Just send them to Terra!"

"They're going to Terra next – their jump drives are immune to the inhibitor. They're taking you with them. Save Terra, Katherine."

Moments later, reality rippled like a pond with a rock dropped in it, and the *Sudden but Deep Understanding That Comes upon You When Least Expected* simply appeared. I immediately got on TacComm. "All ships, get as close to the *Sudden but Deep* as you can. We're headed out."

There was confusion in some of the replies, but Simmons and I confirmed the order. As soon as the ships were tucked in to the huge Tabran ship, all of reality rippled again, and we were in orbit over Terra.

Below us, the Zhen motherships fired on the cities and defended themselves from the tiny Terran Defense Force Fleet, the token force the Empire had allowed the Terran government to build.

"All ships – weapons free!" I called.

Our force numbered in the hundreds, from small one-man ships to larger Marauder battleships. We bore down on the Zhen, burning for their position to get within missile range.

Once in range, thousands of missiles leaped into the void in both directions, their tiny chain drives activating moments after launch, sending them flying across the millions of miles between us at ridiculous speed.

"Point defense cannons online," Simmons said calmly.

Dagger added, "Taking control of PDC system. Acquiring targets."

Bright flashes on our shields heralded the fragments of missiles destroyed as they came close. A few missiles got through, shaking us as they detonated against our shields. And, yes, we lost some ships in the charge.

As we closed to what Tajen calls 'the fun stuff', the missiles stopped and the PBCs and plasma cannons began firing. Our shields flashed every time a PBC shot hit them. I dove farther in, to a range so close it made it harder for their PBCs and plasma cannons to lock on to us. Of course, it also made it hard for our weapons to lock on to them. "Dagger, give me a lead indicator."

"Done," he said. In my vision, every ship I targeted had a small indicator that told me roughly where the ship would be when my shots reached their distance, and it changed based on the target's speed and heading. It didn't guarantee a hit like a full lock-on would, but it made it easier to hit them than it would be without Dagger constantly doing the math for me.

And of course, when I was going up against the bigger ships, that was less of a problem. I wasn't aiming at those so much as pointing my weapons at them and firing everything.

"Flight two needs help," Simmons said. "They have a fighter wing stuck on their six." He flicked their position up toward the viewport, and a marker indicating their position appeared.

"Flight one, on me," I said on comms, and hauled the ship around to head toward flight two. I poured on the speed, dodging around a capital ship and taking several hits in the process. The rest of my flight took the initiative and fired on the cap-ship's cannons, knocking several of them out as we passed.

As we cleared the large ship, I saw that flight two had been whittled down to just over half its original size. I shook my head and locked on to a Zhen ship, opening fire with everything I had.

I didn't do much damage, but I got it to try to shake my fire instead of firing on its own target. I stayed on his tail, firing into his shields, while the rest of flight one chose their own targets.

My target whipped around and headed for the cruiser we'd passed, trying to take cover under its guns. "That's not going to work," I said, and followed him.

"The cruiser's guns are still eighty-six percent operational," Dagger informed me. "I suggest caution."

"Noted." I hauled the ship back and forth as I chased the Zhen, avoiding incoming fire where I could and letting the shields take the hit when I couldn't.

"This is not caution," Dagger said peevishly.

"Caution isn't always possible," I said.

"Of course it is," he argued. "You're just choosing not to use it."

"You got me." This Zhen pilot was good – whoever he or she was, they were expert at avoiding my hits. As he headed for the far side of the cruiser, I realized his plan was to slip under the ship, where the operational cannons were more numerous. "Can't let him do that," I murmured.

"He is attempting to call for help," Simmons said. "I am jamming him."

"Good work. Now let's finish it – Dagger, use the PDCs to add to my fire. Don't worry about aiming, just fire on a wide arc and fill space with shrapnel."

"I cannot recommend—"

"Do it!" I snapped.

"As you wish."

I fired at the Zhen, and the solid metal rounds of the PDCs added to my plasma bolts, filling the space ahead of my ship, making it impossible to avoid any fire. It was incredibly wasteful – the PDCs only held so much ammo – but it helped whittle the Zhen's shields to nothing. "I just need one…more…shot," I said, firing as I said the last word.

The Zhen fighter disintegrated, the bits flashing off our own shields as we passed through the debris. I increased thrust, getting us away from the cruiser, setting up a burn to bring us back around to the battle proper.

"Incoming transmission," Simmons said.

"Let's hear it."

"Captain Lawson, this is Sunset on the *Sudden but Deep*."

"Go ahead, Sunset."

"We are reading several Zhen ships in the atmosphere. They are strafing civilian targets."

I felt suddenly cold. Terra was my homeworld, more important to me than Zhen:da and more intimate to me than Earth. Billions of humans lived on Terra, with only a few Zhen and other races of the Empire. Terra had been the first off-world colony granted to the humans, a few years after the Big Lie, and over eight hundred years we'd made it our own. It was a beautiful world, a veritable gem, and we'd taken good care of it, always conscious of how our ancestors had come so close, on Old Earth, to destruction even before the Zhen had found them.

"How the hell did they get down there through the Tabran shield?"

"They were already below it when the Tabrans began shielding the planet."

I opened comms to the Marauder flagship, currently going toe-to-toe with the Zhen command ship. "Your Majesty, I need a favor."

"Now?"

"Zhen are attacking the surface. I need atmosphere-capable ships to join me in stopping them."

"Done," she said. "Now, I'm quite busy, so—" The transmission cut off.

Moments later, a flight of ships converged on me, dropping into formation. "*Dagger* actual, this is Andra. Knife flight is yours. Lead on."

Where Earth forces divided our combat elements into 'squadrons', the Marauders used 'flights', a holdover from the Hun founders.

"Knife flight, dive for the surface." I glanced at Simmons. "Make sure they open the shield for us."

"They are creating a hole for you," he confirmed.

"Good. Let's go save us some Terrans."

★   ★   ★

In peacetime, it's simple to get into a planet's atmosphere. Unlike the ancient days, we don't need to worry about angles of attack and reentry heat so much – gravitic drives and shields take care of all of that. But in combat dives, the grav-nodes can't spare the energy to protect the ship, and the shields have to do all the work. We weren't in danger of exploding from the heat, but it did pretty much blind our sensors for the minute and a half it took us to get through the worst of it.

As the sensor blindness cleared, Simmons began looking for our targets. We'd entered atmosphere more or less above them, but they'd had a couple of minutes to move. "Found them," he said, and flicked a marker to me. "Jamming their scanners. They should not see us coming."

"That'll only work once," I said.

"Then we had best work quickly," he said.

I set an intercept course and fed full power to the engines. "We might shatter some windows today," I said over comms, "but let's try to leave Terra more or less intact. Check your fire and do not fire if civilians are likely to be hit by stray shots. Assigning targets now." To Dagger, I said, "Allocate targeting priorities according to best hit chance. Adjust as necessary."

"Yes, Captain. Allocating targets now."

Andra's voice came back over comms. "Knife two, you're on knife leader. Knife three, you're with me. Knife four, stick with six."

I glanced at Simmons. "Wonder what happened to knife five?"

Dagger answered. "Knife five was destroyed in the first engagement," he said. "She did not make the jump to Terra."

The other pilots acknowledged the commands. As we dove, I spotted our targets and locked my firing systems on to the target Dagger had chosen for us. As soon as we entered range, I fired two missiles. The first was taken out by the enemy's point defense system, but the second impacted on his shields.

"Minor damage," Dagger said. "Their shield is still fifty-seven percent operational."

"Well, let's whittle that down, then," I said. The other ship's pilot knew we were here now, and split from their flight to run a twisting course.

"Target is headed for the downtown area of Galileo," Dagger said.

"Buildings are thicker there, makes flying – and firing – harder," I said. "They're good."

My intercept course kept changing as the target's position changed. They dodged around one building, then cut across their flight path to swing around another, then went farther still off their path to swing around another. "The buildings are *karking* with my lock," I said. "Where the hell are they now?" I got on comms to my wingman. "Knife two, go high," I said. "Be my spotter."

"Acknowledged. Climbing now."

We broke through the airspace over a large plaza, and flew right into plasma fire coming from the starboard side. The Zhen had looped around and come at us from the side. "Shit!" I cursed, yanking my controls to roll the ship and place our stronger shields in the path of the incoming shots. As we hit the cover of the next building, I rolled back to level flight.

"Knife lead, he's on your tail!" shouted my wingman.

"Well, of course he is," I muttered. "Simmons, anything in the rear launchers we can use?"

"Not without destroying a great deal of the structures around us," he said.

"I was afraid of that."

Now the hunted, I began slaloming between buildings, trying to shake my tail. "Knife two, can you get this *kffar* off me?"

"Doing my best, leader." A seeming lifetime of white-knuckled flight later, I heard, "I can't get a bead on him, leader!"

"*Kark* this," I said, and pulled back on my flight stick, dropping throttle to half as I did. My ship's nose climbed for the sky, then came down back toward the ground as I executed a backward somersault. It's an easy maneuver in space, but in atmosphere, wind forces and gravity make fancy maneuvers much harder. Not to mention the scenery is more dizzying as it flashes by; the black of space is much easier on the eyes, and the inertial dampers work better in space when they don't have to fight the planet's gravity as well as…well, inertia.

As the nose of my ship came level with the ground again, I re-engaged thrust, and we were once again on the Zhen's tail, but he – she? – it? – was much farther ahead of us than earlier. I slammed the throttle to maximum, catching up and firing plasma into their shields as soon as I was within range. I grimaced; too many of my shots were going wide. "Dagger, take over firing control," I said.

"Finally," the AI replied, and the guns kept firing as I released the trigger. With Dagger's more precise control over the guns, wide shots were greatly reduced, and a higher percentage of my shots impacted the shield. An idea occurred to me, and I filed it away for use when this was all over. If I made it that far.

The shields of my target collapsed, and all four plasma guns fired simultaneously, converging on the ship's main thruster array. The feedback caused a series of small explosions within the ship, sending it out of control and blowing it up. Fortunately, the fusion core's fuel feed had already been interrupted by the internal explosions, causing the fusion reaction to cease before the ship blew apart. Still, the residents of Galileo were going to have metal raining down for a bit. Hopefully they'd all been smart enough to seek shelter when the attack began.

I came back around and looked for a new target. As I did, I said on comms, "Knife flight, report status."

"Knife one, we're chasing down one more. Almost— Got him! Knife one and three, green board."

"Knife two, green."

A frantic voice said, "Knife four! I've got three Zhen *Sik* bombers headed for Archimedes Tower, accompanied by six *Kamakkar* fighters! They took out knife six! They're all over me!"

I suddenly felt cold. Archimedes Tower is the single biggest building in Galileo. It houses the local offices of the colonial government, shopping and entertainment, and residences for over 150,000 people. It's the crown jewel of Terra, and destroying it would harm the Terran psyche for decades, if not longer, even though the number of people who live there is a tiny portion of the planetary population.

"Hang on, six. All fighters, head for six. Take out the fighters if you can, but the bombers are the priority. Do not let them hit that tower!" I hauled the ship up, clearing the buildings, and turned to face the tower looming over the center of Galileo. Archimedes Tower hadn't been the first thing built in the city; it had been built to replace the original municipal center, destroyed in a Marauder attack several centuries back. Even as I raced toward the bombers approaching it, I could appreciate the irony that it was about to be saved by Marauders.

As I closed the difference, I saw that knife four had managed to take out one of the Zhen fighters. Dagger got a lock on one of the fighters still harassing her and launched two missiles at it. Each had an onboard electronic warfare suite that managed to fool the enemy's sensors long enough to make escape impossible. The missiles impacted on the ship's shields, seriously depleting them and knocking the Zhen vessel off course. As we zeroed in, knife one swept in and fired plasma cannons, taking out the shields and destroying the ship.

"Nice work, Andra," I said. "Now let's save some civilians."

"Seems like a plan," she replied.

"You're with me on the bombers. The rest of you, pick a fighter and take 'em out."

Each of the remaining four fighters showed as targeted on my scope. I picked the closest bomber and began an attack run, doing my best to overload the shields. Simmons said, "Switching shields to full forward."

"Good idea," I said, as the bomber's turrets began firing at us. The intensity of the firepower on my shields caused them to fluoresce so much it made visibility nearly nothing. "Dagger, switch me to virtual imaging," I said.

My vision switched from normal to an enhanced image provided through my NeuroNet, filtering out the light distortions caused by plasma impacting on the shields. I kept firing into the bomber, Andra's ship doing the same, until we flashed over and past it. Our rear turret, controlled by Dagger, began firing as soon as the bomber was in its firing arc.

We looped around, coming at the bomber again. The pilot tried to evade, but *Sik*-class bombers are notorious among military pilots. They have truly terrifying destructive capability, and they certainly look intimidating, both on the ground and in the air, but in an atmosphere they steer like shit.

On our second pass, in the middle of our attack run, we started getting hits on our rear quarter. "Adjusting shields," Simmons said, at the same moment that Dagger announced we had a fighter on our tail and began firing the rear turret.

"Andra!" I snapped, and her ship vanished from my peripheral vision as she braked hard and banked to get into a firing position on my attacker. I stayed on the bomber, keeping one eye on the shield indicator. Just as I was about to flash past him again, the shields collapsed. On instinct, I triggered a weapon release, ejecting a small mine out the back of the ship. It locked on to the bomber immediately, using a small gravitic node to attach itself, and blew moments later, tearing the bomber apart and raining metal onto the city below.

I checked scopes as I looped around to the next bomber. Andra had dealt with our attacker, but we'd lost knife three. I took a moment to ask the Nine to protect her, then got on comms. "All ships, focus fire and take these bastards out." All four of us concentrated plasma weapons and missiles on the bombers. With no more fighters to guard against, we made short work of the less agile bombers.

When it was over, I sagged back in my seat. "Anything else on scopes?" I asked.

Dagger responded. "Nothing in the atmosphere," he said. "There is of course still a major battle going on in orbit. I am monitoring the situation. The Terran government is attempting to get the orbital defense system back online, but the orbital garrison is blocking their ability."

"Well, plot us a course to get back to orbit," I said. "And give me a technical readout on the orbital garrison."

I looked over the readout, turning the hologram over and zooming in and out, searching for weaknesses. I spotted one. "It can't be that easy," I said. I checked the garrison's public information, then rechecked the schematics. "Dagger, can you confirm the accuracy of this?"

"It is based on the readings from the *Sudden but Deep*'s sensors," he said. "Confirmed to be accurate."

I turned to Simmons. "I have a plan."

Simmons was worried. "Why does that make me afraid?"

I tilted my head a moment. "I'd say it means you're getting to know me." I got back on the flight's secure comms. "Okay, everyone. Here's what we're going to do."

When I finished my explanation, Andra was the first to speak. "That's insane," she said. "We'll never make it."

"You may be right," I said. "It's dangerous and maybe even insane. But look at this way – if we succeed, we've won the day, and if we fail, they'll be singing songs about how glorious our deaths were for centuries."

There was a moment of silence, then, "What the hell. Nobody lives forever, anyway."

"That's the spirit," I said. "Now, as Tajen likes to say, 'Let's kick some ass.'"

And with that, we climbed toward orbit and whatever it had in store for us.

CHAPTER TWENTY-ONE

Tajen

"What do you mean, it isn't possible?" I snapped. "All the Zhen's tactical comms are routed through orbital command on Shrakan Station. We need to cut them off."

"I mean, we can't get close enough," Midnight said. "The station's defenses are simply too powerful. Even my shields aren't robust enough."

"Could the *Sudden but Deep* do it?"

"Possibly, but there are two problems with that idea: the first is that the *Sudden but Deep* is not a warship and has minimal weapons. The second is that the ship is busy at Terra, defending the planet. They cannot be spared to help us here."

"Can we call in another ship?" Kiri asked.

"The Corporate only has the one at this time," Midnight said.

"What? The Tabrans had lots of ships at Jiraad."

"In their grief at what they did there, the Tabrans destroyed those vessels," Midnight said. "In the years since, all resources were put toward development of the *Sudden but Deep*."

"Well, that was stupid," I growled.

"I am beginning to agree with you."

"Shit," I said. Even with a significant portion of Home Fleet sent to help Karateia and trapped there, Zhen:da was still protected incredibly well. We'd managed to get our ground forces landed, but we still needed to take the highport in order to control the system, and that wasn't going so well.

Kiri brought up an image of Shrakan Station, highlighting the ribbon that connected the ancient space elevator to the ground. "We could blow the ribbon."

"Have you lost your mind?" I asked. "No way."

"It would send the orbital out of position," she said. "That would soften it up."

"And the ribbon would land on the planet," I said. "Those things only look delicate. That'd drop hundreds of tons of cable on innocents."

"I didn't say it's a *good* idea," she clarified. "Just giving you options."

"I get it," I said. "But that's a *bad* option."

"You said this thing's purpose is to bring help," she said, pointing at the device the Kinj ship had installed on my console. "Maybe it's time?"

"I don't know," I said. "The Kinj ship wants vengeance, not justice. I'm not sure that's the kind of thing we should be asking for."

"Way I hear it, the Zhen kind of deserve it."

I dodged an incoming shot. "Hold that thought," I said, bringing the ship about and locking on to a Zhen ship. "Midnight, target their power system."

"At this range, that kind of precision is not easy," she said. "I'll lock on, but I cannot guarantee your shots will hit the precise spot you're aiming for. There's too many variables to calculate."

"I get it," I said. "Just do it." I increased power to the engines, closing the distance between the Zhen and myself. As soon as I hit optimum range I fired, the computer taking my priorities and turning them into action. The bright flares of plasma fire lashed against the Zhen's shield, and the PBC cannons fired a shot each before cycling down to recharge. I didn't get through the armor to their reactor, but I did manage to take a chunk out of the ship, and the pilot spiraled away in a complicated escape maneuver.

I locked in our next target and said to Kiri, "The Kinj were awful according to the Zhen history, but my experience with them calls that into question. The Zhen wanted their masters dead, sure, but were the Kinj any worse than the Zhen? If it was up to you, would you kill all the Zhen?"

"The ones who killed Earth? Sure."

"Okay," I said, dodging another ship, "but what about the ones alive today, a thousand years later? Is it their fault their ancestors were assholes?"

"No, but they're still benefiting from what those assholes set in motion."

"I'm not arguing that they don't need to change," I said. "Shit, hold on!" I took the ship into a ridiculously complicated maneuver that not only avoided three incoming missiles, but changed our heading and speed. "I'm just saying we need to avoid collateral damage as much as we can."

"I get that," she said. "Incoming on our six."

"Well, that's gonna have to change," I said. I quickly hauled the ship's nose up ninety degrees, letting the ship's belly thrusters slow our continued movement in our previous direction as the main thrusters propelled us along our new vector.

Midnight began firing the rear turret, but the Zhen on our tail was good; he avoided the worst of our fire and let his shields absorb the rest. I tried all my usual tricks, but could not shake the guy or get a good firing angle. "I may have met my equal," I said. Even to myself, I almost sounded admiring.

"That's not a good thing," Kiri said.

"Oh, come on. I can't be the *only* pilot this good. And it's nice to have equals."

"Tajen, he *is trying to kill us.*"

"Yeah, you're right," I said. I shook my head and headed for an area with more Alliance ships, getting on the tactical communications channel. "This is Tajen Hunt," I said. "I've got a Zhen on my tail I can't scrape off. Can I get some help?"

A Kelvaki voice answered, "Captain Hunt, come to bearing two-nine-eight mark forty." A marker appeared on my navplot, marked *navpoint Delta*. "*Kaltai* squadron, converge on navpoint Delta and help the captain."

"On our way," came the response.

"Maintaining ECM," Kiri answered. Her tone was calm, but there was a waver in it.

"Don't worry," I said. "We'll make it."

I didn't just fly straight to the navpoint – that would have been foolish. I flew a constantly changing course, flying for a few seconds on a relative vector, then changing it whenever it felt right. Even as I flew a vector, I was constantly adjusting position with the directional thrusters, avoiding fire by never being in the same place for more than a few seconds. "Midnight, how can you not be hitting him?" I asked peevishly.

"For your information, Captain, my accuracy is impeccable. Perhaps if you weren't jerking the ship all over the sky, I could hit more."

I glanced sidelong at Kiri, who was trying not to laugh despite her worry. "Everyone's a critic," I grumbled.

We shot through navpoint Delta, and Kiri said with satisfaction, "*Kaltai* squadron is on his six."

At the same moment, a Kelvaki voice said, "Captain Hunt, break right!"

I yanked the stick over, rolling Midnight up onto her right side and firing the ventral thrusters. We shot to the side, clearing the space we'd been in, allowing the Kelvaki ships to begin firing. Six ships firing in unison burned through the Zhen's shields, and the ship blew up in short order.

My sense of triumph died as soon as I saw what was happening to our forces. The *Litvyak* and the *Liberator*, the *Shalakash* and the *Drokkha Nakar* were all getting hammered by Zhen forces, and our fighter forces were getting slammed by both the Zhen ships and the automated defense platforms. "*Litvyak*, come in. What's your status?"

Captain Zhang appeared in a window to the side. "We're getting beat all to hell, Hunt. All the forces we sent to Karateia are busy at Terra and the Kelvaki reinforcements are—" Her comms went silent.

"Admiral?" I asked. "Are you still there?" I jerked the ship around toward the *Litvyak*'s position. We were too far out for visual, but the computer painted the Earth ship where it should be. "Midnight, did they lose comms?"

Before the AI could answer, Zhang came back. "Hunt! Something big is coming out of slipspace! It's—"

I lost the rest of what she said as alarms began going off on my own ship. I didn't waste time with conscious thought; I flicked a direction away from the worst of the fighting and pushed the throttle as high as I could.

For just a moment, the sky was lit by the multicolored streams of light from slipspace. As the massive object resolved, the light bled toward the rear, revealing the fully operational Imperial vessel *Deathclaw*.

"Oh shit," Kiri said. "We're too late." A moment later, "Admiral Zhang is ordering all ships to attack the *Deathclaw*." She was trying to be brave, but the shaking in her voice betrayed her fear.

"Acknowledge the order," I said. "Alpha squad, on me." I reached out and touched Kiri's arm. "Stay with me, kiddo," I said. "I need you."

"I'll keep up," she said.

"Hey. I don't mean I need you on the board. I mean, yeah, I do. But I need *you*, Kiri. You're my family, and I can't get through this mess unless you're with me."

"Literally, in fact," she said with a smirk. "Since if I let up on this ECM dance, we're going to get hit by something, and *you* need to focus on the flying. So maybe let's get through this, and save the mushy stuff for another time?"

"Oh, I like this one," Midnight said.

"Of course you do," Kiri said, her hands still roving across her board. "I'm amazing. Now, can we get on with shooting that son of a bitch out of space?"

"Yes, we can," I said. "Alpha, let's show the *Deathclaw* who's the boss around here. I want a standard skindance formation, take out all the turrets you can, and above all, do *not* get hit."

The six ships under my command acknowledged the order and, as one, we swept down toward the *Deathclaw*'s dorsal surface. "I haven't done this since the Battle of Shoa'kor," I said. A thought occurred to me and I grinned. "When I did this at Elkari, I got named a Hero of the Empire. Guess this'll cancel that out."

Kiri grinned at me. "Maybe this time Earth will name you prime minister, or something."

"Oh hells, anything but that."

The *Deathclaw*'s firepower was intense, and I switched my shields to full forward. The shields flashed as the Zhen vessel's shots hit. I increased speed, trying to get within their firing envelope as fast as possible. At the last second, I pulled out of the dive, skimming only meters above the ship.

I fired at a turret, then flinched the ship away from the resulting explosion. My shields flashed, and I frowned. "That's a lot of debris," I said.

Kiri's frown matched my own. "That wasn't debris," she said. "That was a turret shot."

"That's not possible," I said. "We're well below the firing arcs of the turrets."

Midnight spoke, a hologram backing up her words. "The *Deathclaw* appears to have deployed a set of secondary turrets designed to attack ships using this maneuver," she said.

"Stands to reason," I said, "The Zhen taught me how to do it. They'd know more than anyone how damaging it can be." I switched to comms. "All ships, this beast has secondary turrets designed to defend against skindancing. Be on your guard."

"Bit late on that warning, Alpha leader!"

"Yeah, took me by surprise too, Landen. Be careful."

"Always."

Once the secondary turrets were deployed, it became much harder to hit our targets. Most of my energy was spent trying to avoid the turrets firing at me. "Midnight, take over firing control," I said. "If you get a bead on any target, fire."

"Understood."

I rolled the ship across the firing arcs of two turrets. "This is a nightmare," I said. "Can you get me a status check on the others?"

Kiri's hands flew across her console. "We just lost Alpha two. Incoming comms."

"Let's hear it."

"Alpha leader, this is three. These turrets are easy pickings, but there are too many of them. We can't—" The signal cut off.

"We lost her," Kiri said.

"All ships, break off!" I sent over comms. I yanked the ship away from the *Deathclaw*'s surface, putting my shields full aft and burning as hard as I could. On my way out, I dropped my entire stock of homing mines behind – at least maybe they'd do some damage.

Once we'd reached a safe distance, I asked Kiri, "Did they make it?"

"Checking." A few moments later, she said, "Tajen...we still had one, five, and six with us when we aborted the attack. They're all off the scan now." She turned to me. "We lost them."

"Aw, hells." I pulled around, letting the shields regenerate as I pointed the ship back toward the battle just in time to see the *Deathclaw* open fire on every Alliance ship it could reach.

The fighters still in range of its guns died with minimal hits, obliterated in the hail of plasma and missile fire emanating from the behemoth. The midrange armed freighters didn't do much better, and even our capital ships were getting slammed.

The *Liberator*, already wounded, didn't have a chance. The *Deathclaw*'s plasma and particle beam cannons made short work of the ship's engines, leaving it a wreck, hanging dead ahead of the Zhen ship. The *Deathclaw* fired a full salvo of missiles into the *Liberator*, explosions rocking the ship, plasma rupturing outward in several places as the fusion reactor went haywire.

Many of the crew were likely still alive, but it didn't matter for long. The damned Zhen just plowed their ship right through the *Liberator*. The smaller ship disintegrated, hundreds of men and women dying as the ship simply broke apart, splintering into millions of pieces.

"We can't beat that thing," Kiri whispered.

My eyes went to the alien device on my console. "Not on our own, we can't," I said. "It's time." I grabbed the device and pushed the button. "You were right," I said. "We need you. We're at—"

Before I'd even finished speaking, there was a bright flash of light that blinded us all momentarily. When it ended, the Kinj ship hung directly over the battle.

WE ARE COME, a voice said over the comms. It didn't sound

the same as what I'd heard before; that had been a gentle voice, almost motherly. This was a chorus of voices speaking in unison, with a deep, resonant tone underlying the words. And that tone was anger. VENGEANCE IS OURS.

"Kark it," I said. "I knew this would happen."

Kiri whistled. "Who the fuck is that?"

From the Kinj ship, beams of a coherent energy type I'd never seen before lanced out into the dark, hitting the thrusters of Zhen ships one after the other. There was no obvious damage, but as each was hit, their engines died, leaving the ships drifting on their previous courses.

YOU KILLED US ALL, the voice continued. WE BROUGHT YOU CIVILIZATION. WE BROUGHT YOU PEACE. WE BROUGHT YOU THE STARS. AND IN RETURN YOU BROUGHT US DEATH. NOW YOU WILL PAY WHAT IS OWED.

A single point of light flew out from the Kinj ship, scattering into hundreds of tiny points of light as it sailed through the void. The lights spread out and settled themselves on the surface of a Zhen cruiser. As soon as they did, the comms came alive with the sounds of Zhen voices.

"They're eating through the hull!"

"Shoot them, damn you!"

"We are! It has no effect!"

"Try to—" The voice dissolved into roars of pain that went on and on and on. The roars dwindled to growls and moans, and to pitiful wails, before silence reigned again.

The lights moved on, and there was nothing where the ship had been. Kiri frantically tapped at controls and checked her scans. "They destroyed it all," she said. "There's nothing left."

"Correction," Midnight said. "There is a rapidly expanding cloud of atoms where the ship was."

"Gods of my ancestors," I said. "She used me." I glanced at the Kinj box mounted to my console. "She's been tracking me, but she wanted me to let her know when we were at Zhen:da. It wanted me to call it in—I think maybe the records of the Kinj ship were damaged. It knew what it wanted to do to the Zhen but not where to find them. Once it had my signal, it jumped in."

"You knew it wanted vengeance," Kiri said.

"Yes. But I didn't think it would be this bad." I aimed comms for the Kinj ship. "Kinj vessel, this is Tajen Hunt. Stop what you're doing. You've done enough. I repeat, you've done enough. We needed to survive the fight; we did not come here for vengeance. Stop now."

THERE WILL BE NO END, the reply came. THE ZHEN BOUGHT THEIR FATE. The swarm of lights landed on another ship, and once more our comms filled with the screams of dying Zhen.

"Shut it off!" I said.

"I'm trying. The Kinj overrode our systems. It's broadcasting straight to our NeuroNets."

I got back on comms. "Kinj vessel, I need to speak with you!" There was no response. The lights finished their destruction of the second ship and moved toward another Zhen ship.

"That's the *Adamant*," Kiri said.

On impulse, I hit my thrusters, placing myself in the way of the motes of light. I half expected them to either ignore me or even attack me, but they stopped, hanging in space. MOVE, came the voice from the ship.

"Scan those things," I murmured before clicking over to the comms channel. "No," I said. "We wanted you to help us survive, not to commit genocide."

YOUR DESIRES ARE IRRELEVANT. THE KINJ MUST BE AVENGED.

"Why?"

THEY WERE DESTROYED. VENGEANCE IS—

I cut the voice off. "That's bullshit, and you know it! You exhibited an ability to think, when we met before. Think about this now. What is the point of killing the Zhen? It won't bring back the Kinj. It won't erase what was done to them."

KINJ LAW IS CLEAR. DEATH BEGETS DEATH. The drones,

or whatever the lights were, moved around my ship as if it was a rock in a stream, headed for the *Adamant*.

"Midnight, what can you tell me about those lights?"

A schematic appeared between Kiri and me. "Despite their appearance, they are physical objects. Drones, you might call them. We can target them."

"Kiri?"

"Yeah?"

"I'm going to do something stupid."

"Wouldn't be the first time. But what the hell – you do you."

I tried not to laugh, but it bubbled out of me, anyway. I pulled the ship around to face the cloud of drones. "Lock on to them," I said, sobering.

CHAPTER TWENTY-TWO

Liam

"Medic!" I yelled, running toward Hitchens. I hit the ground beside him moments before a medic slid into place. "He got lucky," she said. "Armor took most of it. Help me get this off him."

We removed his armored vest, allowing the medic to rip open his shirt, uncovering the wound. She'd been right; the armor had taken just enough of the blast to save his life – without it, the vicious burn on his chest would have been a hole straight through his heart. The medic grabbed a nanite pack and placed it over the wound, activating it with her NeuroNet. The block of gray matter dissolved, forming a patch over the wound. The outer shell hardened to cover and protect the wound as the inner parts sank into the flesh and began knitting it together.

I looked to the medic. "Can he be moved?"

"In a moment," she said. She injected Hitchens with something, and he groaned. "Anyone get the reg'stry on tha' ship?" he asked.

"Ha ha, very funny," I said. "Don't fucking scare me like that, kid."

"Sorry, sir." He tried to sit up, but his eyes widened in pain and he sank back.

"You'll need a few minutes," the medic said. "Let the nanites get started properly, then we can move you. The pain blocker should start working any second now."

"Yeah, it doesn't hurt as much now," Hitchens said.

Injala joined me, crouching beside me. She gave Hitchens a nod. "Brave lad." Turning to me, she said, "I have made contact with my agents."

"What the *kark* happened to them?"

"They were unable to meet our rendezvous, but they have slipped the net. They are preparing a diversion to pull some of these attackers off of us. Once that is done, they will be here soon to help us."

"Help us what?" I asked. "We're pretty pinned down here."

"They can get us into the palace," she said.

"From here?"

She made the Kelvaki equivalent of a shrug. "They say so."

I shook my head, "Well, hells, everything else has gone badly today, what's one more thing?"

"It might be a good thing?"

"I'm not that lucky. Whatever we gain, we'll lose—"

A section of the courtyard opened. My eyes went wide and I reached for my gun, but as I brought it around, a small hologram appeared above the hole, with a series of Kelvaki glyphs. I didn't take my eyes or my sights off of it, but said to Injala, "I don't know that word."

"It isn't one," she said. "It's the call sign for the head of my cell here." She spoke, but the words were Tradd, a language I didn't speak. A moment later, a Tradd head rose out of the hatchway and chittered to her. I belatedly activated my Tradd translation matrix. "—lost three of our cell. We're sorry to be so late." The Tradd's eyes went to Hitchens. "Did you lose that one?"

"No," Injala said. "But we don't have time for discussion. Let's move."

"Of course. Come down."

Injala looked to me; I signaled I was ready, and she smoothly moved to the hatch and dropped through it. A moment later, her voice came to me on comms. "Clear. We've got multiple routes to the palace."

I turned to our medic and pointed after Injala. "Alyssa, get Hitchens down that hole."

"Yes, sir." She took his arm and began to lever him up.

Hitchens protested as he got to his feet. "I can still shoot, sir!"

"And I may need you to, later. Right now, I need you to get in that hole, soldier. That's an order."

"Yes, sir," he grumbled, allowing Alyssa to lead him away.

I grabbed my rifle and brought it to my shoulder, sighting the opening in the wall. "Team C, converge on my location. Get below. Form up by teams and stand by."

"Sir!" The twenty-one members of Ma'Bhayi's team flowed almost like water across the courtyard and down into the hole. Once they were down, I said, "Team B, let's go!" Finally, I called for Burhan's team. "Burhan, start moving your team."

"Negative, sir. We just got a load of reinforcements dropped on our doorstep. You go ahead. We'll hold them here."

"Burhan, you don't have the manpower to hold this position forever."

"Shit, sir. We don't have to hold it forever, we just need to give you time to get to the target." She paused, and I could hear several small munitions going off. "We'll get the job done."

"Don't make me give you posthumous medals, Burhan."

"Wouldn't dream of it. I want to see your face when you see I did the impossible. Now with all due respect, get your ass moving, sir. We've got work to do and you're distracting me."

I couldn't help but like the woman; I could tell from her voice that as hard as her job had just become, she was enjoying the hell out of it. "I'm out," I said, and moved to the courtyard, slipping into the hatchway.

A Tradd commando team stood under the hatch, and if you're confused by that image, think how I felt. The Tradd were known to be sycophantic supporters of the Zhen, and I had never seen one even holding a weapon, much less brandishing it like they knew what to do with it. I moved to Injala, who was standing just behind them. "Who the hell are these guys?"

She smirked. "They are the Tradd Resistance."

"There's no such thing as the Tradd Resistance."

One of the Tradd said, "That's what you thought, *glakhim*."

The word didn't translate, and I cocked my head at Injala. "Did he just insult me?" I'd never, in my entire life, been insulted by a Tradd – and I'd had more than enough reason to be. I'd treated most of the Tradd I'd known with the same dismissive attitude most humans did.

"It doesn't translate perfectly," she said. "One might say it means 'excessively tall thing'."

I turned back to the Tradd, who at five feet tall was among the largest Tradd I'd ever seen. "The Zhen are taller."

"But humans don't kill us where we stand if insulted."

"Good point," I said. I turned back to Injala. "These guys are your agents?"

She smiled, an affectation picked up from humans, but she was careful not to reveal her sharp teeth. "I have humans, Tradd, Tchakk, even Zhen on my payroll."

"Any Zhen:ko?"

The Tradd snorted, but Injala merely said, "No, something always seemed wrong about them. Now we know why." She glanced up. "Are the rest of your team coming?"

"No, they're holding the rear for as long as they can. They'll fall back here if they have to."

She spoke to the Tradd leader too softly for me to hear. He signaled assent to whatever she said, then commanded some of his people to stay to help 'the excessively tall ones'. "We should split our people up," she said.

"Right. Ma'Bhayi, Dillon – I want a fireteam from each of you to go with me. Then you'll each take a route. You have a control device?"

Ma'Bhayi patted her bag, and Dillon pointed to one of his men, who was carrying the device.

"Right. If either of you get there, use it."

"Will it only work on Zornaav?"

I shrugged. "I asked the Tabrans about that. They're not sure how it'll affect other Zhen:ko. It might do some good, but the majority of their nanites would have to be from Zornaav's original supply, so it's unlikely they'll do a lot. Worth a shot if you have to, though." I looked around. "Any questions? All right, move out. Hopefully we see you on the other side of this."

★   ★   ★

I watched the two teams depart with their guides, then looked to our guide. The little Tradd adjusted his harness, then slid his gun into a holster on his haunches. "Let's go," he said, moving forward, his four legs moving quickly to keep pace with our longer strides.

The tunnels weren't very straight, and there were a lot of turns. I got completely turned around to the point where, if not for my implant, I'd have been completely unable to find my way out. "What's your name?" I asked the Tradd.

"Humans rarely ask our names," he said, "or much of anything else about us. I am Lenta."

I considered that for a moment. He wasn't wrong. Humans had long had a weird relationship with the Tradd. I wouldn't make any blanket statements, but I had never known a human claim friendship with a Tradd. I certainly had never known a Tradd as anything other than a functionary of a Zhen. "It is possible," I said, "that in our own struggles, we've failed to see we had partners. I'm Liam."

"We know who you are, Liam Kincaid. Your face has been on the news channels for some time. There is a rather large bounty on your head. When Injala contacted me, I had to think seriously on whether I would help you, or turn you in."

My eyes widened in alarm, but I noticed Injala's ears quivering, a sure sign he was joking. "Guess I can't blame you," I said. "So you guys have a resistance?"

His long neck undulated in the Tradd equivalent of a nod. "Yes," he said.

"What have you accomplished?" The moment I said it, I wished I could take it back. Lenta said nothing but his gait suddenly changed, his neck held in an awkwardly still position. I reminded myself that there was a bounty on my head, and that Tradd had a wicked spike in their jaw that would hurt if he used it on me.

After a moment, he returned to a normal gait. "We have survived," he said, "for all the millennia since our world was conquered. And we aided your own movement."

"Wait, what?"

"Did you not wonder how Tajen Hunt's broadcast made it to every Imperial world?"

"I did, actually. We figured the Zhen just weren't as good as our hackers."

He made a dismissive snort. "Kiri Hunt and her team are good," he said, revealing to me how good their information was, "but they are not better than the cadre of technicians working for the Zhen:ko. We had our own technicians embedded in their workgroups. They introduced errors into the software that allowed your broadcasts more time."

"Wouldn't the Zhen:ko have caught that and done something?"

"Yes. They did. Some programmers died as a result. It was regrettable...but necessary."

"Zhen programmers."

There was a beat, then, "No."

I stopped, and he stopped beside me. I'm not sure what clued me in, but I was suddenly certain he'd paid a price for that help. "You lost someone important to you."

A moment later, he repeated, "It was necessary." He moved on, and I followed. After a minute or two of silence, he said, "We are not as quick to act as your species. Nor as hardy." He glanced my way. "We have acted only when necessary, and only when safe. Your own actions caused us to alter our methods. Lives were lost."

"I'm sorry."

He waved one hand at me. "The past is past," he said. "And it's not all bad. Without the pressure of your actions, we would not have moved so quickly, or engaged in such risk. And we would not be so close to freeing ourselves."

"We've always just assumed you liked being the Zhen's—" I stopped myself before saying 'lapdogs', and substituted "—clients."

"You were going to say lapdogs," he said. At my chagrined expression, his body seemed to shiver slightly. "Don't worry. We have spent a very long time cultivating that image of ourselves. And," he said as we moved through a corridor junction, "it is true for much of our population. Our resistance is small, but our agents are very well placed.

We have been able to delay shipments to the Zhen on Earth and other worlds, slow ship repairs, even sabotage ships from time to time. But even to most of our people, the Resistance is a footnote in history, thought long-extinguished."

"How many of you are there?"

"I don't know," he said. "We operate in cells."

"Smart," I said. "We did the same on Earth."

"Yes. Funny how you all think you invented the concept." At my expression, he said, "You did not think your movement was the first human rebellion, did you?"

"I...I think we did, actually."

"Foolish. There have been several such movements over the last eight hundred years since the Rescue, as they call it. Most died quickly. It reinforced our own decision to work slowly."

Lenta, I could see, was enjoying bursting my little fantasy. And I couldn't really blame him. Humans had spent nearly a thousand years regarding his kind as clueless dupes of the Zhen, and here he was informing me that while my own people had tried to rebel several times and been smashed to bits by the Zhen Empire, his had been running a resistance movement right under the noses of their 'masters' for thousands of years now.

We reached a shallow ramp that rose to a blank spot in the tunnel's ceiling. One of the Tradd loped up the ramp and placed his – or her, Tradd didn't go in for sexual dimorphism – hand on a device on the wall, causing the ceiling to slide back. The other Tradd joined him and streamed out of the resulting exit. My own squads followed. As Lenta, Injala, and I joined our people on the surface, I said, "We appear to have much to learn about your people. I hope we get the chance."

"I am sure you will," he said, sniffing at the air, "but only if— *Duck.*"

I dropped to a crouch just in time to feel and hear the crackling ozone of a plasma burst fly over my head. I glanced around, getting my bearings.

We were inside the palace walls, in a wide stone plaza about two hundred meters wide and one hundred fifty meters deep. There were large plascrete planters filled with trees from the many worlds of the Empire dotting the square, and it was behind these that my people were huddling as Zhen soldiers fired on us from the barricade blocking the entrance into the palace.

"Nice," I snarled. "I thought we'd come out on the other side of this."

"Patience," Lenta said. "Your Team B is almost in position. We must draw the Zhen's attention so they can get in place."

"Hope you're right," I said. "Collins, Esposito! I want those shooters taken out. You got the fancy sniper rifles, let's see if you can use 'em."

Both signaled their assent, and I saw Collins sight in and fire. "One!" she called. "Bet you a week's pay I do more damage."

"Classy," Esposito replied, and I heard a shot from his position. "How about we just get through this alive?"

"All right, grandpa," she said.

"Hitchens, you still with us?" I asked on comms.

"Here, sir. And more or less in one piece. Nanites stitched me back up."

"Don't be a dead hero, Ryan. I promised Tajen I'd get you back alive."

"No dead heroes on this mission, sir. Got it. Maybe take your own advice, though."

"Good man. I will. Now, if you're done nursemaiding your CO, how about you get on the comms and let the other teams know our status? Tell 'em I said to hurry their asses up before we hog all the glory."

"Yes, sir!"

CHAPTER TWENTY-THREE

Katherine

When we got back into orbit, we found the Marauders had killed another carrier but then had lost two of the three ships equipped with the Death Lance weapons, including the flagship. Nikara had survived, but she'd had to flee to another ship, which was now fighting for its life against the remaining carriers and their fighter wings.

"Demon and Beggar flights," I snapped, "converge on the *Bark my Schlonky, Fork Boy* and pull those Zhen off of her. *Bark My Schlonky*, you're done – disengage from the fight and get out of here. The rest of you, keep hammering those fighters!"

Nikara's voice came back immediately. "I did not hand over operational command of this armada," she snarled. "You passed up your chance to take power. Do not presume to do it now."

I took breath to answer, but Andra broke in on the frequency before I could speak. "Nikara, old friend, your ship is falling apart. Is the Death Lance still working?"

There was a pause before she answered. "The captain informs me we might get one shot out of it, but it would cripple the ship. We've been too badly hit."

"Then do me a favor – shut the fuck up, and get out of here. The reforms die if you do."

Despite the sounds of debris pinging off my ship, I could hear Nikara breathing hard, trying to control her emotions. Finally, her voice came over the comms, gravelly but flecked with steel. "You have operational command. The *Bark* will leave the engagement."

I sighed with relief. "I'm getting too old for this," I said.

"Perhaps you should stop flying combat missions and leave the fighting to the AI," Dagger said.

"Where would be the fun in that?" I asked. "Besides, our literature is filled with stories where we do that. It never seems to go well."

"Do the AIs decide war is stupid and stop fighting?"

"Sometimes. Mostly, though, they decide humans are stupid and start killing us all."

A beat, then: "That seems to indicate a rather pessimistic tendency in your species."

I banked the ship, cutting my thrust and reorienting on a heading for the lead Zhen carrier. To Dagger, I replied, "You're probably right, but then we've grown up in a world controlled by the Zhen. You'd be pessimistic too."

"I'm based on the Tabran scans of your mind. I'm *already* pessimistic."

"All right then. What do you think our chances are against the *Aktan* there?"

"I'd estimate an eighty-seven percent chance of being blasted into many small pieces."

I thought a moment. "I can beat those odds," I said.

"I don't see how that's possible," Dagger said.

"I am forced to concur with Dagger," Simmons said.

"That's because neither of you is an expert in Zhen military ship classes." I grinned as I activated the comms channel. "Knives, let's hit the *Aktan*," I said. "Knife one, two, follow me inside. Four and six, cover us by giving the turrets hell."

Even over comms, I could hear Andra's confusion. "What do you mean, follow you inside?"

"The docking bays on *Shikasa*-class carriers are connected by service corridors to move ships and matériel around," I said. "We're going to fly the maze."

"You've got a death wish," Andra said.

"I can handle it. You telling me the Marauders' best pilots can't do it?"

I heard her take a deep breath before she said, "If you get me killed, I'm going to make you regret it."

"Seems fair," I said, and set my course for the docking bays.

Simmons looked worriedly at me. "This is a risky maneuver," he said.

I shrugged. "Of course it is. But *Shikasa*-class ships are too well-armored. There's no way we're going to get through that without the Death Lance beams. But if we head inside, we can blow that Imperial from the inside. Besides, I know the layout – it's not that bad. Tajen could do it."

"You yourself have repeatedly said that you are not as good a pilot as Tajen."

I felt irritated with him for saying it, but he was right. I'd said that too many times over the past few years. I was always doing that – setting myself up to be Tajen's second, to back him up but never stand on my own. He'd called me on it last year, but here I was still doing it.

"Yeah, I have said that," I said. "I guess it's time I proved myself wrong." I lined up the ship's nose with the first of the *Aktan*'s docking bays, took a deep breath, and slammed the ship to full thrust.

I'd expected to get more nervous as I got closer to the docking bay, but the truth was I got more calm. "Ready weapons. Once we're in, weapons free. Target infrastructure first, ships second. Dagger handles weapons, Simmons defenses, I'm on flight."

Simmons and Dagger acknowledged the order. Dagger didn't speak, but the icons signifying weapons readiness appeared in my vision.

As we flashed through the forcefield that kept the docking bays filled with atmosphere, the ship shuddered – those fields aren't meant to be passed through at speed, and they knocked us around a little. I corrected and cut throttle, yanking the flight controls back and slewing the ship around to starboard. As we slid across the deck, barely missing a wall and then leaping toward the ship's bow, Dagger let weapons fly, and plasma bolts leaped toward the fuel storage in the forward part of the bay. Just seconds before the bolts hit, we flashed past them and made a hard left turn into the service corridor. "Nicely timed, Dagger."

"Of course it was," he replied. Out of the corner of my eye I saw Simmons grin at me; I wanted to return it, but if I did, we'd probably end up flattened on something.

Ahead, a line of soldiers had formed, firing heavy ordinance at us. Well, it was heavy in terms of foot soldiers, but against a starship's shields they were just nuisances. We blasted past them, Dagger taking some potshots at them with the tailgun even as the main weapons fired at ships and matériel scattered across the bay's decking.

As we flashed over a bomber prepping for launch, Dagger dropped a mine and fired at the bomber using the railgun. Just as we reached the opening for the service corridor to the next bay, the mine and tailgun both got lucky hits. The bomber's fusion core went up, taking out a huge chunk of the bay. The downside was that we got slammed from behind by the shockwave. I fought to retain control of our flight. "Everyone okay back there?" I said over comms.

Andra's voice came from knife one, not far behind us. "Ship's got some new scars, but I'm fine," she said. "Not sure about knife two, he got the brunt of that shockwave."

"I'm fine," knife two responded, "but I'm not with you anymore – got blown right out the bay's main entrance. You'll have to watch your own backs now."

"Join four and six," Andra replied.

The corridor dipped suddenly, and only a last-second correction kept us from scraping the entire top of our ship against the corridor's ceiling. "This is the long leg," I said. "Once we get to the forward portside bay, we'll fuck it up and then go through one more tunnel. Andra, head out the next bay's main entrance. We'll hit the last one on our own. Dagger – arm all mines left in the launchers. When we hit the last bay, drop everything we've got in them as we head back out to open space."

Dagger said nothing, but I saw in the corner of my eye the indicators for the mines flipping to ARMED.

We broke through the corridor into the bay. Dagger immediately began firing on the bay's infrastructure, causing docking structures to collapse on soldiers and ships alike. Almost immediately, I swerved around a fuel depot and raced into the connecting corridor between this bay and the next. Behind me, one of Andra's gunners hit the depot on her way out the main entrance, and the shockwave gave me an extra push down the corridor, threatening to destabilize my flight.

"Hold it together, girl," I muttered.

"Excuse me?" Dagger said, his tone dripping with disdain.

"Sorry, Dagger. Force of habit." As I said the last word, we burst into the final docking bay. Dagger began firing before we'd even cleared the corridor. We rocketed through the space, dropping our mines and firing at everything. I whooped as we shot through the forcefield and into open space – and immediately lost all control as the shockwave from the mines we'd dropped and the resulting explosion raced out behind us, slamming my ship so hard my hands were knocked from the controls and we began tumbling.

"Dammit!" I cried, grabbing at the controls. I fought to bring us under control, managing just in time to fire the dorsal thrusters and get us out of the way of a piece of onrushing debris. "Status on the *Aktan*?"

"All four docking bays have been rendered useless," Dagger said. "I am monitoring a series of internal explosions and cascading failures. I believe the *Aktan* is out of the fight, though not destroyed."

"Good enough," I said. "Simmons, any word on where we're needed next?"

"The *Sudden but Deep* reports that a series of heavy attack ships are headed for Terran orbital control," he said. "They are currently too busy preventing the Zhen forces from firing on the surface to be of aid to the orbital."

"Can't they put the orbital under their shield?"

"Not without exposing a large portion of the planetary surface."

I sighed. "All right. All ships – anyone who can, head for the orbital control station and protect it." I shut off comms and asked Dagger for an intercept course. I brought us around to match the course he laid out and engaged thrust.

There were eight ships on my scopes, each approaching the station from a different vector. I quickly assigned targets to the ships who'd come to help – not as many as I'd hoped for, but we'd get the job done.

With Andra on my wing, I zeroed in on my target and locked

weapons. "Weapons free," I said, and Dagger immediately fired missiles and plasma bolts at the Zhen heavy attack ship just ahead of us.

The target's shields held. "Andra, focus fire on this spot," I said. "Dagger, keep firing – but not missiles."

"Very well." The ship's plasma cannons fired over and over, resting every few seconds to let the guns cool. Andra didn't have an AI, but only a limited subroutine to handle firing. Dagger was able to work with that subroutine so that neither ship stopped firing at the same time, giving the Zhen's shields no time to recharge.

"Their shield is about to collapse," Simmons said, his eyes never leaving his displays.

"Dagger, the moment that shield is down, fire a missile right up his tailpipe."

"I assume by your use of 'tailpipe' you mean the main thruster housing?"

"Yes. The thrusters, Dagger. Slam a missile right up there."

The shields flashed and were gone, our plasma blasts hitting the ship itself. Little bits of liquified metal flew off the ship as our weapons chewed at the hull, but it was the missile sailing right into the ship's thruster core that caused it to bloom into an expanding field of metal and gas.

The computer immediately switched targeting priority to the next ship, and I pulled back slightly. "Andra, take point on this one," I said.

"Glad to," came the reply, and Andra's ship, more bulbous and older than my own, slid into place ahead of me as I drifted to the side to cover her.

We began firing as before, but new threats appeared on the scopes. "Incoming Zhen interceptors," Simmons said.

"Point defense cannons online," Dagger said. "Rear turret is ready to defend as well."

"Good work," I said, and switched back to Andra. "Got incoming bogies, Andra. I'm gonna get 'em off us. You keep hammering that idiot."

"Will do. Careful out there. You still owe me a dinner."

"I remember," I said, feeling my face heat. "Do not say a word," I growled at both Simmons and Dagger.

I locked on the closest interceptor and peeled away from Andra, reorienting the ship and heading for my new target.

There were three interceptors approaching. Dagger took out the first one with missiles when we were still at extreme range, thanks to its shields being not much more than a suggestion by now.

The second ship might have lasted longer if the pilot hadn't made a critical error and pushed his engines past their breaking point. One second he was bearing down on us, the next he was an expanding cloud of superheated plasma.

Dagger began firing as soon as we got within range of the third ship. I started randomly shifting the ship's motions, moving to the side and up and down even as we approached the enemy, in an attempt to throw off their targeting computer. While they were still a ways off, I flipped the ship's orientation and began a braking maneuver – I didn't want them to get ahead while I tried to shed velocity. This was risky, of course – while my secondary guns could still fire on them, my primaries were fixed forward, meaning I was trading some firepower for enough velocity to stay on their tails and bring the big guns back into play. And, of course, once they saw what I was doing, they were almost certain to change their course or acceleration. They changed both. The course change wasn't a problem; with Dagger's help I matched their vector – when I came out of this maneuver, I'd still be behind them, and of course they had to adjust their own speeds as well. The ship's gravitic nodes helped a little in adjusting my flight path, but it wasn't perfect, and my aim was going to be affected.

It was the change in speed that really screwed me. I had to scramble the nav system to figure out a new acceleration curve to continue to match their speeds, and I lost precious seconds waiting for the course corrections. "Can't you speed that up, Dagger?"

"I am currently managing two hundred and thirty-seven distinct subroutines," he replied. "Which of them do you think I should abandon? Damage control? Shield recharge? Engine power manage—"

"Shut down the one that keeps you talking," Simmons snapped. "If you spent half as many cycles on your work as you do coming up with pissy comments, you'd be ten times more efficient."

"Simmons, I didn't know you could *get* emotional," I said.

He looked to me, chagrined. "Apologies," he said. "Sometimes Tabran AI personality modeling is too good – they can get on my nerves."

"No need to apologize to *me*," I said. "Couldn't have said it better myself." I waited a beat, then said, "Of course, Dagger maintains this tub's life support."

"My apologies, Dagger," Simmons said. "I—"

"No need," Dagger interrupted. "I am quite familiar with the emotional failings of humanoid lifeforms and will manage."

"Damn, Dagger," I said.

Simmons said, "Translated, he said, 'I'm sorry too.'"

I snorted. "Well, how about you two help me go save some more pilots from the Zhen, hm?" By this time our acceleration had evened out and we were on the Zhen's tail, firing at the interceptor. It peeled away, and I pulled a high-G maneuver to stay on him. I felt the weight of my body pressing farther into the pilot's seat, and my flight suit tightened down on my arms and legs, forcing blood out of my extremities and into my core. My vision swam, darkness creeping in from the edges. I forced myself to breathe, straining myself to breathe every few seconds.

As the maneuver finished, we were still on the interceptor, and as Dagger fired, I snarled with satisfaction as the enemy's ship crumbled.

"Andra, interceptors handled. You okay?"

"Confirmed kills," Andra said. "Terran orbital control is safe."

"The *Sudden but Deep* is hailing us," Simmons said.

"Andra, stand by." I switched channels. "*Sudden but Deep*, this is Lawson."

"Captain, the Zhen have been routed. We do not see any more approaching. But there has been a development at Zhen:da, and we are needed. Please prepare for transport back to Zhen:da."

"Understood." I switched to the TacComm channel. "All ships, head for the *Sudden but Deep*. Terran command, I'm sorry, but we're needed elsewhere."

"*Dagger*, this is Terran orbital. We can handle things from here, Captain. Thank you."

The ships we'd brought headed for the Tabran ship. Those with extensive damage were directed to dock, and many docked temporarily to rearm themselves. As we cycled through the docking bay, getting our missile bays reloaded, I took a moment to breathe deeply and grabbed a stimulant from the ship's locker. I felt the weird ripple, just as before, and the launch alert sounded.

As we left the Tabran ship behind, I heard Tajen's voice on the system-wide band. "Katherine, tell your people – the Zhen are not our enemy anymore. Attack the alien ship with everything you've got!"

I looked at Simmons in shock. "Wait...what?"

CHAPTER TWENTY-FOUR

Tajen

As Midnight gave me a weapons lock, I fired the plasma cannons, sweeping target lock from each drone to another. The machines, powerful as they were, were unshielded, and shattered under the plasma fire.

STOP, the Kinj said.

"I can't do that," I said. I met Kiri's eyes, her hands brushing across her console as her eyes flicked back and forth for several seconds before they locked on me and she nodded. "Stop killing the Zhen and talk to me."

Suddenly I was in the Kinj AI core once more. "Oh, this trick," I said.

The AI's form coalesced in front of me. "Why are you protecting them? They are your enemy, as much as they are ours." The voice was just as I had heard before, a single feminine voice.

"You're singular. Why do you keep saying 'we'?"

"This ship is home to two thousand six hundred and thirty-four ships' intelligences. We fled the destruction of our masters under orders to avenge them."

"You tricked me to get that vengeance," I said. "You weren't stuck in that system for twenty-five millennia, were you?"

"No."

"Why lie to me?"

"We did not know then where Zhen:da was. We decided to maneuver you into bringing us the coordinates."

"Why didn't you just take it from my AI's navigation logs?"

"The AI managed to sequester that information. The logs were not in your brain's interface device."

"How did you lose it in the first place? Your people colonized the Zhen."

"That was many thousands of years ago. When the Zhen rose against us, their slaughter was methodical. They did not claim our worlds – they were too cold for them." As she spoke, her form became more and more human, until standing before me was my favorite teacher from my primary schooling. "And so they destroyed them. Before that, their AI fought ours. All references to their homeworld were destroyed, hiding it from us. Even the few Kinj who survived the massacre could not find Zhen:da. Is this not taught?"

"No. The Zhen erased you from their own records. Only some of them know who you were, why you were important. That's just one reason why this has to end. Most of the people you're killing don't even know what their ancestors did."

"That does not make them innocent," she said. "They have benefited from the destruction of my people."

"So have humans. Do you plan to destroy us too?"

"Humans did not destroy us. The benefits you received from the Zhen were not the same. You are not the same."

"We may not have been there and helped destroy you, but we have slipspace travel because you had it, and the Zhen took it from you. Nearly everything we have comes from the Zhen. Our ship designs are based on theirs. We've made changes for our different physiognomies, but the essential facts of the technology are the same. Our NeuroNets are based on Zhen designs – even the Kelvaki use those designs, and they don't even like the Zhen. Are you going to kill them too?

"Even without technology, we're not the same as the first humans in the Empire were." I said it on impulse, but the moment the words were out of my mouth, I knew them for truth. "Everything we are is a combination of what we inherited from our ancestors on Earth and what the Zhen gave us, taught us. And they're not all bad."

She scoffed. "They destroyed your world. They made you their servants and tried to make you grateful for it."

I spread my hands wide in a showy shrug. "I never said they were saints. They've made mistakes, and they're going to have to answer for them and make amends. But the fact remains, we are more like them than we'd have been if we'd never left Earth." My voice hardened. "But that's the real problem, isn't it? They didn't start this. You did. The Zhen, the peoples they've conquered, the people they've gone to war against? We're all your mistakes made manifest."

Her head whipped around to me, and the kindly face of my old teacher was replaced by the alien suggestion of a form. "Explain," she snapped.

"The Zhen didn't bootstrap themselves into space and then start colonizing other worlds," I said. "They learned what they became at the feet of the Kinj."

The female voice gave way to the many voices we'd heard in the real world. WE BROUGHT THEM PEACE.

"How do you figure that?"

THEY WERE A WARRING PLANET OF FACTIONS. TRIBAL WARFARE HAD ALMOST WIPED THEM OUT MULTIPLE TIMES. WE BROUGHT AN END. WE MADE THE ZHEN:KO THEIR LEADERS AND TAUGHT THEM HOW TO LEAD.

I blinked several times as I tried to make sense of what the voices had said. "You...made the Zhen:ko their leaders?"

THEY WERE A DYING CASTE, SHUNNED FOR THEIR DIFFERENCE. WE MADE THEM OUR VOICE, THE INTERMEDIARY BETWEEN THE ZHEN MASSES AND THE KINJ.

I shook my head, not sure whether I should laugh or cry. "You *fools*. You took a caste that had been trod upon and mistreated, and gave them the keys to the planet? Don't you know what they did?"

THEY RULED.

"Yeah, they ruled. Just like you did, with anger, with cruelty."

THE KINJ RULED PLANETS. ONE CANNOT RULE A PLANET WITH KINDNESS.

"Did you ever try?" I asked, deadpan. The voices made no response.

"You taught the Zhen too well. Once the Zhen:ko had become their planet's leaders, it was simple for them to turn on you. In a sense, the Kinj destroyed themselves by teaching the Zhen to conquer. You made them who they are."

YOU ARE TRYING TO CONFUSE US. WE ARE NOT CONFUSED. THE ZHEN AND ALL THEY HAVE INFECTED MUST DIE IN PAYMENT FOR THE KINJ LIVES THEY STOLE.

"Then you're going to have to kill me too. And every people they've ever touched. Every human, every Tradd, every Tchakk, Kelvaki, and Tabran in the galaxy."

CORRECT.

And with that chilling word, I was back in the cockpit. "Shit," I said, looking bleakly at Kiri. "We've got a problem."

CHAPTER TWENTY-FIVE

Liam

Crouched behind a planter, I concentrated on not panicking. Glory, my ass.

It wasn't just that this wasn't an ideal situation – I'd fought in many battles in my time, and a lot of them were incredibly bad times, but this one took the cake.

We were hiding behind plascrete boxes maybe a meter high while Zhen soldiers fired on us from a fortified position. "Hitchens, I need a drone!"

"Launched, sir!"

I found the drone in my contact list and connected to it. There was a slight feeling of disorientation as my body fought to remember it wasn't actually moving and airborne. I could see through the drone's sensors.

There were five problems we needed to get past. The first was a simple metal barricade across the entrance to the palace building. There were four Zhen behind it, each armed with plasma rifles and backed up by more Zhen I could see deeper inside. That was easily dealt with – take out the gunners at the door, knock down the barricade, and storm the inside. Close-quarters fighting isn't the Zhen's strong suit; they need room to move those long arms of theirs. We'd have an advantage there – a small one, but life rarely gives you the overwhelming advantage in my experience.

The rest of the problems were four fortified gunnery stations, placed in two ranks, one after the other. Each one mounted a heavy plasma cannon, capable of killing a man in one hit and mounted with 180-degree firing arcs. And right now all of them were firing, pinning us in place. I took a moment to look around and saw there were Zhen behind us, just outside the palace walls, but they weren't moving forward.

We were in a killing ground.

"We need to move," I said. I activated my comms implant. "Hitchens, have we got any armed drones?"

"One, sir. The other teams have the others."

"Send it up and switch me to it."

"Got it." A few seconds later, he said, "Switching now," and my vision jumped to the left. I locked in on the four Zhen at the barricade and fired, the drone's auto-targeting protocols automatically firing and moving the drone to hit all of them in short order.

I set the drone to attack the first two gunner stations next. It lowered itself to the level of the firing port and sent several bolts of plasma fire into the nest.

Unfortunately, that was the last thing it did. The other gunner fired at the drone, hitting it and knocking it right out of the air. My vision swam and then blacked out as the drone skittered across the plaza, coming hard up against the palace wall. I disconnected from it and swore when I saw it on the ground, sparking.

Moments later, reinforcements arrived. They renewed the fire, and under their cover, another Zhen climbed into the gunner nest and began firing, his gun suddenly looking like a metallic middle finger from the gods.

As if the universe couldn't resist piling a little more on, my comms chirped. "Kincaid, go."

The voice was clearly Zhen. "Mr. Kincaid, listen, you've got Zhen air support incoming. Your people need to get out of that plaza."

"Who the fuck is this?"

"A friend." The comms went silent. In the distance, I could hear aircraft incoming. "Shit," I muttered. Raising my voice, I looked to Lenta. "We need to get out of the plaza. Where the hell are the other teams?"

"They should have been here by—"

My comms blasted my ears with the emergency signal, followed by the sounds of gunfire and yelling. "Liam, this is Dillon." I winced at the volume – he was clearly still underground, and the echoes were deafening. "We met up with Ma'Bhayi's team, but we ran into an ambush. We're locked down! You need to go on without us. We'll try to— Shit! Wong, get on that—" The message dissolved into static.

I looked at Lenta. "Is there any other way in?"

"Not from this position, no," he said. His head rose on his long neck, peeking above the planter to check out the situation for a moment. "We must retreat," he said. "There are too many Zhen behind the ones at the door."

"We can't," I said. "This mission has to succeed. Today."

"There is nothing we can—"

"Fuck this," I heard Hitchens say, and my gaze snapped to him, two large plascrete planting boxes over, as he rose to his feet.

"Hitchens, stand down!" I shouted. "Wait for orders!"

"No time, sir!" he called.

His rifle to his shoulder, he advanced on the right gunner nest, firing at the nest and the Zhen in the doorway. He was trying to flank the heavy gun, but the Zhen in the doorway could still fire at him from the position they occupied. I said, "Covering fire!" I needn't have bothered; my troops knew their jobs, and they'd begun firing almost as soon as he'd risen.

Moments after he stood, he was hit by a rifle blast, the plasma bolt burning through his armor and into his flesh before dissipating. He gritted his teeth and kept moving, never letting up on his fire. He managed to get to a relatively safe position where the turrets couldn't get to him and paused long enough to refresh his rifle's power pack. Our covering fire kept the Zhen manning the doorway from leaning out and hitting him.

He fumbled something off his belt and slapped it on the base of the gun in the nest, then scrambled back several paces, ducked, and covered his head. The demolition charge he'd placed went off, ruining the gun and sending the Zhen who'd been operating it scrambling away from the gun screaming.

"One down," he gasped, "two to go."

"Negative, Lieutenant," I said, stressing his rank. "Get back to safety. We'll get someone else in there."

"Sorry, sir. I hate to – *ow* – disobey a command, but there's no way anyone else will get this close, and you know it. I can do it."

I was about to order him back when Injala spoke from behind me. "Would you ask any other of your soldiers to retreat, when you know it must be done?"

"Damn you," I muttered to her. "All right, Hitchens. Get the job done."

"Yes, *sir*," he said, rising to a runner's starting position, bouncing on his toes, and then shot across the open space between the first two turrets. The Zhen soldiers and the other turrets fired on him, but he was moving too fast and they couldn't get a bead – until a rifleman's bolt hit him in the side, knocking him off balance.

He stumbled, but managed to stay upright, and got across and out of the second turret's firing arc. Seconds after, the gun exploded as a rocket hit it. I turned and saw Esposito ducking back down. "Why didn't you do that before?" I asked him.

"I didn't have the shot before he drew their attention."

I was annoyed with myself for even having asked. I got back on comms. "Hitchens, you good?" I asked.

"I'm good," he said.

I could hear the strain in his voice; he was clearly trying to hide his pain. "Ryan, hold tight. Collins, you're closest. If we cover you, can you get in there?"

"I think so, sir."

"Do it."

"Belay that!" snapped Hitchens. "Sir, apologies, but you'd just be ordering her to her death."

"Fuck you, Ryan," Collins said.

"I know how good you are, Elsa," he said, "but I can see shit from here you guys can't. If you stand up, you're dead – the third gunner has you dead to rights."

"Ryan, can you get to him?" I asked.

"I think so. Once I deal with number three. Four's the one with a bead on your position. When I'm ready, you can pin him down while I sprint over."

"Understood. What's your play here?"

"I've got two more demo charges. Keep the riflemen and the gunners occupied while I move."

"Will do."

At his signal, we began covering him. Rather than stand and run for it, Ryan crawled toward the third station, trying to keep behind the smaller planters in that section of the courtyard. When he was only a few meters from the gun, one of the riflemen saw him and began firing at him. Our cover fire didn't do much to deter him, and Hitchens was forced to crawl back into the shelter of a plascrete box.

"Ryan, you okay?" I asked.

"I'm alive. Can't get to that gun, but I have an idea." I saw him pull the demo charge from his belt and arm it, then he raised himself on his left elbow and drew back his arm, aiming to throw the charge at the gun.

I saw it happening, and I tried to cover, but I couldn't stop it. As his arm drew back, the Zhen rifleman who'd already seen him fired. The plasma hit Hitchens's elbow, burning through his arm in seconds and dropping his sundered forearm to the ground beside him.

"No," I whispered. I rose to go to him, but Injala held me back. As I struggled with her, I saw Ryan get to his knees, holding his severed right forearm in his left hand. The demolition charge still clenched in his right hand's fingers, he threw it at the gun, sending the detonation signal just as the arm hit the gun's shield. The explosion killed the gunner, destroyed the gun, and knocked Hitchens onto his back with the shockwave.

"Hitchens, stay down!" I snapped, pulling myself out of Injala's grasp.

He didn't listen. As I headed for him, firing at the Zhen riflemen, he rose to his feet, holding his rifle in his off hand, the remains of his right arm hanging uselessly at his side, and advanced on the riflemen, firing from the hip and stalking toward them.

I'm not sure what happened to the Zhen, but seeing a lone human missing half an arm firing at them must have surprised them, because they paused just long enough to give the rest of my men time to get into a better firing position. Several soldiers sent plasma fire directly into the cannon on the last gunnery station, forcing the gunner back as the metal shield began to warp and heat up from the repeated hits.

As good as we were having it, Ryan's luck had run out. He took a hit to his leg that didn't knock him down, but it slowed him, and finally he was hit in the same spot where he'd earlier lost his armor. That hit was the one that took him down, where he lay, motionless, on the plascrete.

At first I thought the scream of rage was mine, but then I realized it was coming from a few meters to my right. A soldier named Jenkins jumped to his feet and started running for the doorway, screaming the whole way, firing with one hand as he grabbed plasma grenades from his belt with the other and slung two of them into the doorway.

He almost made it, but just before the grenades exploded, a last fusillade of plasma fire speared out of the doorway, hitting him at point-blank and burning into his chest and head. The scream cut off abruptly as Jenkins stood on his feet for one impossible second before toppling over, dead.

The rest of my squad surged for the doorway along with Injala and the Tradd, taking it in a flurry of gunfire. I barely noticed, as I was rushing for Hitchens, Seeker beside me.

He was still alive, though barely conscious. As my medic arrived, Hitchens's eyes found me. "Did we do it?"

"We did," I said. "I mean, I'm not gonna lie to you, you're pretty fucked-up right now."

"You idiot," Seeker said, but there was admiration in her voice. I opened my mouth to speak but was interrupted by the medic.

"Sir, we need to move him inside before that air support gets here."

I helped the medic get Hitchens inside. Once he was inside and the doorway closed, I got on the comms to command. "Zhang, this is Kincaid," I said. "We're in the palace, but most of our forces are pinned down. I'm moving on with what I've got left."

"Understood."

"If I don't make it, tell Tajen I tried my best. It won't help, but maybe you can make him laugh if you add that I'm really gonna miss his—"

"Liam."

"I was going to say 'his chili'."

"Right," she said, her tone making it clear she thought I was full of crap. Which, to be fair, I was. She clicked off.

I turned and saw Lenta and Injala staring at me. "What?" I asked.

Lenta turned to Injala. "Humans are very strange."

Her ears quivered. "Indeed they are," she said. "But they do make life interesting."

Lenta made a noncommittal sound.

I rose and surveyed who I had left. The lieutenant Ma'Bhayi had left with me was marshaling her remaining soldiers and setting up a defensive formation facing both the doorway and the interior of the palace. Of my original team, Hitchens was down for the duration and Jenkins was dead, but that left me four soldiers, including Injala and Seeker, plus Lenta and four Tradd soldiers. It'd have to do.

I caught the eye of the lieutenant and beckoned her over. As she trotted up, I asked her, "What's your name?"

"Bowes, sir."

"All right, Bowes. You're in charge here. Keep the medics and our wounded safe. If Ma'Bhayi and Dillon get free of their ambush, send Dillon's team after us and keep Ma'Bhayi's here."

"Understood." She turned to her second and continued where she'd left off.

"All right. Command team, on me." Injala and Seeker were already beside me, the latter staring at Hitchens, and we were joined quickly by Esposito and Collins, the only remaining grunts of my team. I looked deeper into the palace corridors. "This isn't going to be easy," I said. "We need to get to the One, and there are a lot of Zhen between us."

"We can bypass many of them," Lenta said. "We need only get to a servants' door and we can enter the back passages of the palace, used

by the Tradd to move about." He looked me up and down. "You will
have to duck, I am afraid."

"You don't sound *too* upset about it."

"I am not," he said, matter-of-factly, and frankly I am to this day not
sure if he was making a joke or just stating a fact. In either case, I had to
do considerably more than duck to get through the passage, which was
so low it required me and most of my crew to crouch down to about
half of our usual height to move through it.

At one point while moving through the servants' passages, we came
across a Tradd servant going about his business. He said something in
what seemed to me to be an indignant tone, which Lenta answered
quickly and with a soothing motion of his arms. The other Tradd's
long neck shivered and extended out toward me. They said something I
didn't understand, speaking very slowly and deliberately, before moving
on, squeezing past us and ambling down the hall even more slowly than
they had been.

"What'd they say?" I asked.

"She was concerned about what we were doing," he said. "I told her
who we are and our mission here."

"You what?"

"Relax," he said. "She is one of our agents."

"But what'd she say to me?"

"She said, 'Do not fail us.'"

"No pressure," I said.

"The pressure will be considerable," Lenta replied.

"Yeah, that was sarcasm."

"Ah. The refuge of your people when emotions become too
difficult."

I couldn't help but chuckle at that. "You make a good point." I
looked up and frowned. "Why haven't they set off the alarms?" I asked.

"They have."

"I don't hear anything."

"Audible alarms would disturb the palace, and so are forbidden. The
alarms are sent out via NeuroNet, and only to authorized persons."

"Clever. Anyone not aware of that might blithely amble through the palace thinking they've made it in without tripping alarms and get slammed by the guards when they least expect it."

"That too, yes."

We climbed several levels and then went back down. Finally, Lenta signaled a halt. "This is when things get cubed," he said.

"Cubed?"

His head shifted to the right in an unfamiliar gesture. "Difficult and potentially dangerous, with an unhealthily large percentage of random chances to go wrong?"

"Ah. *Dicey*."

"Dicey. Thank you." He gestured to the doorway opposite us. "This is the nearest entrance to the throne room. There are guards." He gestured, and a data packet flowed to me, along with a connection. I accepted it and got an instant view of the guards. They were ranked in three rows of seven in front of the sealed chamber, with the Zhen:ko standing in the rear, towering over the others. To either side of the ranked guards, two turrets scanned the corridor outside the throne room.

"Holy shit, that's a lot of Zhen to fight through with only eight fighters," I said. "Anyone got grenades?"

Seeker said, "We don't need grenades, boss. I got this."

"What are you going to do?"

"Kiri and I have been working up some ways to use the NeuroNets against the guards. They're all signed into the palace's version of TacComm, so we can use that network against 'em. You want 'em dead, or just knocked out?"

"You can do that?" I turned to glare at her. "Why didn't you do that earlier?"

She shrugged. "Most of the soldiers weren't hooked into the same network. I only got a couple of them. The rest were on a more secure network, but I've been working on that while we moved. I think I've got it licked, now."

"You think?"

She frowned. "I do. But I don't like to promise when I don't know I can deliver on it. Last time I did that, me and Kiri ended up tied to chairs and almost got killed."

"I remember," I said. "But they've got a Zhen:ko out there. Can you get him too?"

"I hope so," she said, "but be ready to take him out if I don't. I can't tell if he's on the network or not."

"I'd bet he isn't."

She pursed her lips a moment, then looked at Injala. "You want to hack the turrets?"

"With pleasure," Injala sad. "Send me the code."

"You got it." Seeker turned back to me. "Still need to know – kill 'em or knock 'em out?"

"Knock 'em out," I said. "We're not here to kill anyone unless we have to."

"Got it." She flicked her fingers around for a few seconds, setting up programs on an interface I couldn't see. She looked up at me. "Ready when you are, boss-man."

I returned my attention to the overlay showing the guard position. "Do it."

"Loading."

Nothing changed in my view of the corridor for several seconds. I tried to calm myself, but I knew that one way or another I was about to go into action, and that meant it was time to get jittery again. "I'm going to sleep forever when this is over," I said to nobody in particular.

"I have the turrets," Injala said to Seeker. "Standing by."

"Loaded," Seeker said. "And...executing."

Through the feed, I saw all the guards but the Zhen:ko stiffen and then fall over like puppets whose strings had been cut. As they fell, the turrets both turned toward the Zhen:ko.

At that moment, Lenta opened the door and led the way out. I followed, coming out of the servants' tunnels down and across the corridor from the throne room door. My gun was up and pointed at the

:*ko* as we approached. "Drop it!" I said. I could hear the high-pitched whine that told me the turrets had primed for firing.

The Zhen:ko dropped his weapon. "Liam Kincaid," he growled. "Of course it is you."

"I'm sorry, have we met?"

He merely bared his teeth. I turned to ask Lenta a question when the Zhen:ko leaped toward me, or at least, he tried to. Both turrets fired nearly immediately. The combined fire took him down, dead before he even hit the floor.

I nudged him with my boot. "Poor stupid shit." I looked at the sealed door, then asked Lenta, "We sure the One is in there?"

"Affirmative," he said.

"Seeker. Door."

"On it," she said, kneeling before the door and opening the access hatch on the controls. "This thing isn't on the network, so I'm going to have to hack it hardwire."

"Is that safe?"

She looked up at me and shrugged. "Not really."

I regarded her for a moment, weighing what I should say, before settling on, "Good luck." I turned to the others. "Set up a perimeter in case they send more guards. Be sure you don't get in the turrets' way." I glanced down. "And clear these guys out of the way. How long'll they stay down, Seeker?"

She shrugged. "Couple of hours, I think. I flooded their bodies with narcotics from their med implants and shut down their senses."

"Dirty trick," I said.

"Eh. Better than dead."

"True. Door."

"I'm working on it. Course, it'd go faster if nobody was wasting my time and taking half my attention."

"All right, all right." I stopped talking and watched her work for a minute. "But just so you remember, we could have more Zhen on our butts any second."

She glared at me.

"All right, I'll shut up."

A few seconds later, she said, "I'm in. Say the word and the door opens." She rose from her crouch beside the door and got out of the firing path that would open with the doors.

I gestured to the others, who formed up and readied their gear. The high-pitched whine of plasma rifles priming filled the air. "Be ready for anything," I said. "Open it."

As the two halves of the blast door slid apart and into the walls, I raised my rifle to my shoulder, ready to fire on the guards.

Only there weren't any.

From the open doorway, the chamber stretched one hundred meters to the throne, where a lone Zhen:ko sat, calm in her resplendent robes. To either side of her were three Tradd, each holding a plasma rifle on her. There were no guards.

Her voice echoed through the chamber. "You may approach, Liam Kincaid."

"Seeker, give me a scan," I said.

A few moments later, Seeker said, "Anti-virus protocols confirm there's nothing interfering with our vision. Everything is what it looks like."

I was confused. We'd fought our way here, but to find nobody in our way was insanity. "Injala?"

"No idea," she said.

"Everyone inside. Seeker, lock it back up behind us. Lenta, with me," I said. I walked toward the One, slowly, keeping my gun on her as I did. Even though Seeker had confirmed we were alone, I didn't want to bank on it. Behind me, I heard Collins giving orders to the others.

As I got closer, I saw that the One – Zornaav – wasn't quite as calm as she'd appeared from the doorway. From time to time she glanced nervously at the Tradd holding their weapons on her. I gestured to them and said to Lenta, "Yours, I assume?"

"Yes." He spoke to them in Tradd, then said, "I would have told you, but I never received confirmation from them."

"This room blocks all communications from outside," Zornaav said drily. "A design flaw I had not anticipated being a problem until now."

"Seeker, did she get a transmission out?"

"Nope!"

I approached the throne. Zornaav watched me like a predator suddenly unsure of her place in the hierarchy. "Good afternoon, madam," I said.

Her crest vibrated in the rhythms associated with agitation and anger. "Killing me will not win your world back," she said. "It will only accelerate my plans."

I faked a kind smile. "Oh, we're not here to kill you," I said, pulling the Tabran device from my pack. I turned it on, and in my vision, a targeting graphic settled on Zornaav. TABRAN NANITES CONFIRMED appeared in the air between us. "No, the Empire would just put another on the throne. Normally, we'd maybe consider that – it's always possible the new emperor could be reasoned with."

"But?"

"But you've got that pesky little hivemind. It took us a while to figure out how you could use that, but we got there. And that's just not something we can allow. So I brought this," I said, brandishing the device.

"And what, pray tell, does that do?"

"Oh," I said, nonchalantly. "It interfaces with Tabran nanites – and controls them." I activated the device.

Zornaav stiffened, but there was no other sign it was doing anything other than my device flashing WORKING in my vision, along with the control interface I'd been trained on by Rememberer. I could see the nanites within her as a cloud of azure light, spread throughout her body, concentrated in a few spots. I flexed my fingers and *reached* for the nanites, my gestures mimicked by the device.

And then Zornaav stood. The rifles of the Tradd primed, but she made no move except to point at me. "You have miscalculated," she purred. "I am no longer the only source of Tabran nanites on Zhen:da.

The Zhen:ko are *all* infected by the Tabran swarm that bonded with me. I am not just the center of the web. *I am the web itself.*"

As she spoke the words, the interface's visual spread, and I cursed to myself. Whereas before I had seen the Tabran nanites within Zornaav, now I was aware of them, well, everywhere.

There were thousands of Zhen:ko, and nearly all of them had some of Zornaav's nanites within them. In some it was just small clusters monitoring what they saw, heard, felt – in others it was more extensive, allowing Zornaav to take control of individuals within her web.

And now, through the nanites in her system, I had access to all of it, each Zhen:ko in the web linked through it to the One and to me.

I shook my head and got to work. The difficulty of what I was attempting had ramped up. I had to keep it locked on to the nanite swarm within Zornaav, but also on the offshoots of that swarm, dispersed across the vast distances of the Empire, linked by technologies I didn't understand. And now instead of one target, I had *thousands*.

This was going to be harder than I'd thought.

"You brought this on yourself," I said, and through the device, I reached out for her nanites.

CHAPTER TWENTY-SIX

Tajen

The Kinj drones began to turn back toward me. Midnight began firing again as I slammed the thrusters to full and tried to evade them.

"Shields are holding," Midnight said.

"Kiri, get me the *Adamant*."

"On comms."

"*Adamant*, this is Tajen Hunt on the *Midnight*," I said. "Are you still down?"

"Our engines are coming back online," he said. "Where did that ship come from?"

"It's a remnant from the Kinj," I said.

His voice took on a didactic tone. "The Kinj Heresy is—"

"Very real," I snapped. "In fact, it's trying to kill us all." I swooped around a drone, keeping my nose pointed at it as the ship swept by, sending my ship into a loop around the drone as I poured plasma fire into it. "It's my fault they're here – I didn't know what they planned."

"I am not sure whether I believe that or not," he said.

"Well, consider that my trying to stop them from killing *you* resulted in them trying to kill *me*," I said in an aggrieved tone. "And it's not going to be much longer before they start firing on *my* people, so maybe we could cut this bullshit out and work together?"

"I see your point. I—" He paused for a moment. "I am intercepting reports from Loyalist ships – the Zhen:ko have all gone silent, and are not responding to their crews."

"Liam made it to the One."

"Apparently. I will attempt to rally the Zhen to our side. Jinasek out."

"Get me TacComm," I said.

"You're on," Kiri replied.

"All human ships: if they haven't already, the alien ship is going to start firing on all of us. Defend yourself. Stop targeting the Zhen and target that ship."

"Zhang here," came a reply. "Why don't we let the aliens deal with the Zhen? We can run."

"Not for days, we can't," I said. "We used the inhibitor, remember? Besides, they're not going to give us that long. And the Zhen aren't our enemy – not all of them. The Empire as a whole, yes. The rank and file, no."

"The rank and file are the ones with their boots on our necks, most of the time."

I looked to Kiri with a question in my eyes, and she nodded – this was all still on TacComm, being broadcast to every human and Kelvaki ship in the Zhen:da System. "Admiral, that's true, of course. And I've killed my share of Zhen soldiers and then some in this war. But there has to come a time when the war is put aside, either because we won, or because a bigger fight is here. And this is the bigger fight.

"If we do nothing, that ship is going to kill every Zhen, every human, every Kelvaki, Tradd, Tchakk, and Tabran in orbit. And then they're going to sterilize the planet below us. When they're done there, they'll go for Terra, and then Elkari, Fiktosh, Imiri, Jiraad, and every other world in the Empire, and more Zhen, more humans, more Tradd and Tchakk are going to die there. And then they'll move on to Kelvaki space, and maybe even the Tabrans. They want to destroy everything the Zhen have ever touched – and that includes Earth and our families.

"This isn't just a fight for the Zhen. This is a fight for all the people of the Empire, willing or not, and for the rest of the galaxy too. Or we're all dead."

"Okay, I'm sold. And judging by the comms I'm getting, so are the rest of the human fleet."

"The Kelvaki are with you," came Dierka's voice from his command ship.

"The Marauders are always up for a fight," said the Marauder commander on-station.

Midnight spoke up. "I have relayed your speech to the *Sudden but Deep*. They are finishing the fight and will be here as soon as possible."

"Good," the admiral said. "Now we're all agreed on what we need to do, any ideas how we're going to do it?"

"Actually...yes." I quickly sketched out my plan.

"That plan assumes the Zhen ships will declare an armistice and fight beside us."

"Yep."

"Is that likely?"

"I'm not sure they have any real choice. Just be careful once it's over."

"Understood."

Kiri said, "I've got Jinasek on comms."

"Put him on." At her signal, I asked, "What's the word, Commander?"

"Something is happening with the Zhen:ko. Some are silent, others are screaming. I assume this is something to do with Liam's mission."

I shrugged. "Probably. The Tabrans didn't seem to know what would happen to them."

"Their crews have placed them in their med-bays for now – they are with us."

"All right," I said. "Let's dance."

"I'm reading more Zhen ships coming online," Kiri said. "Looks like they're targeting the Kinj."

"All ships, take out those drones," I sent out over the comms.

When I'd fired on them earlier, the drones had been pretty easy pickings. Now that the Kinj saw me as a target rather than an ally, they were anything but.

"Dammit, stand still!" I muttered, trying to keep on a drone's tail while Midnight fired on it. Finally, the shot connected, shattering the drone. Unfortunately, it was only one of hundreds.

"Kiri, Midnight – any chance you can ID a control node for these things?"

"Working on it," Kiri said. "Their transmission isn't on any frequency or wavelength I'm familiar with, though. Right now Midnight's giving me a look at the scans during your conversation with the Kinj to see if we can isolate their carrier."

"While firing my weapons?"

Midnight replicated a disdainful sniff. "I am a multi-cored AI capable of running a ship thousands of times more complicated than this one. I could fly, too, if you like."

"No thank you!" I said. "I do the flying around here."

"Very well."

I saw an incoming drone and quickly fired the dorsal thrusters. The movement taxed the inertial dampers and sent us flying up against the restraints. Kiri yelped in surprise, then took another look at her board. "Midnight, I'm noticing some similarities in environmental factors between Tajen's last conversation and the one he had with the Kinj previously. Can you run a check for me, see if I have it?"

A few seconds later, Midnight said, "That looks like it."

Kiri thanked Midnight, her hands flying over her board and in the air above it as she manipulated controls only she could see. Finally she grabbed at something and 'tossed' it to my workspace, making it visible to me.

What unfolded before me was a schematic of the Kinj ship. Kiri pulled her hands apart, and the ship 'exploded', the outer layers peeling away until a small node appeared. "Get us in there," she said, "and take that out. It'll knock their drone control out."

"How do we know there aren't any redundancies?"

"There are," Midnight said. "I've sent similar targeting schematics to several other ships and assigned them the other nodes."

"All right then." I mentally flicked a switch, then said, "Zhang, keep 'em busy. We'll take care of your drone problem."

"Understood!" she called, and before the channel went silent, I heard her snapping orders to her crew. I grinned manically at Kiri. "Ready for a fun ride?"

"Are we likely to die?"

"We generally have been ever since we left home." I glanced at her and, like me, she was trying very hard not to laugh. Despite ourselves, we were both having fun. "Let's kick their asses," I said.

"Will there be cannons shooting at us, drones chasing us, and an ancient alien ship out to kill us and everyone we've ever known?"

"Yep."

She turned to her console and raised her hands to the controls. "Bring it on."

CHAPTER TWENTY-SEVEN

Liam

At first everything went fine, exactly as I'd been promised. I reached out through the Tabran device and made contact with the nanites, and transmitted the command codes I'd been given. I felt control of them pass to me for a moment. But then Zornaav screamed, a sound full of rage and hate and despair all at once, and suddenly I was struggling.

Until now we'd assumed that the Tabran swarm called Keeper of Broken Promises had been suborned by Zornaav, that the swarm was controlled by her. Sunset's theory was that something had gone wrong in the swarm, robbing Keeper of its volition.

We were wrong.

Now that I was in there, I could feel the gestalt nature of the One. Keeper might have been compromised; I'm not an expert on basic computers, much less on sentient nanite swarms. But it wasn't subordinate to Zornaav's will. The two were perfectly in sync with each other – and Keeper was far better at exploring my hardware than I was theirs.

I could feel them, crawling along the pathways of my nervous system, exploring the hardware of my implants from the NeuroNet itself all the way down to my—

Oh, no.

No.

We'd all assumed that Keeper of Broken Promises had been somehow overpowered by the strength of Zornaav's will. The truth was far worse. Keeper wasn't a prisoner; it was a full and willing participant in Zornaav's actions.

Zornaav hadn't just spread her nanites to the rest of the Zhen:ko to turn them into unwitting spies. Zornaav and Keeper had used their nanites to overwrite the command structure of *all* the nanites in the Zhen:ko, linking them to Zornaav's own system using hybrid designs Keeper had helped her build.

Zornaav's body held transmitters that linked her in real time to transmitters she'd had built all throughout the Empire, linking her to every Zhen:ko in existence, overwriting their nanites' operating systems with her own. In their bodies, similar transmission and receiver systems had been built. They were made when a Zhen:ko came of age, allowing her to override their minds and take control of them whenever she wished.

But the worst part of it was the glimpse I got of Zornaav herself. The woman was ancient, from a time long before I'd been born. I knew, from Tajen's conversations with her during the war's early battles, that she was twisted, that she believed the Zhen, and therefore she as their leader, were better than all other species.

But she was so much worse than that.

I don't know if something went wrong when Keeper tried to join with her, or if her insanity had always been there and had infected Keeper. It didn't really matter; the two of them had joined so thoroughly that there was no longer a Zornaav, no longer a Tabran called Keeper. There was only the One.

She was a creature of pure hate and malice, so in love with power that she would see the universe burn before she allowed it to slip from her control. And she had made herself effectively immortal, able to flee this body and travel along her web to another, taking over that Zhen:ko forever, killing the original owner of the body.

An ancient poem Tajen had recited to me one night in our cabin, after he'd spent the day going through an archive of Old Earth literature that had been discovered etched on crystalline discs, came to my mind unbidden: "And what rough beast, its hour come round at last/Slouches towards Bethlehem to be born?" Tajen had said it was a question about the future, asked in a time of war. He'd fallen in love with the poem the moment he'd read it.

We didn't need to ask the question anymore. Here was the beast, ready to take over everything. The One was beginning to spread beyond the Zhen:ko, to suborn the Zhen:la, the 'ordinary' green-skinned Zhen that made up the majority of the Empire, bringing them into her web as well. Those linkages weren't as significant; they didn't have the control implants, and thus she didn't have any ability to control them, but she had even more access to their experiences than we'd believed the intelligence services had.

In a very real sense, every Zhen in the Empire – and, I realized, quite a few humans – could be her eyes and ears whenever she wanted. And I could see that she planned to make them her puppets as well, once this war was won.

If we didn't stop her, she'd take over every living thing she could.

I felt her reaching for my NeuroNet, directing my nanites to create the same structures in my brain that she'd created in the Zhen:ko. I wouldn't just be her eyes and ears, like most Zhen, but a full proxy, as the Zhen:ko were.

I tried to fight, to wrest control back, but I was paralyzed. I dimly felt my knees impact on the floor, followed by my face. I rolled onto my side, looking at her, and I could see, as if through a thick fog, the One's grin as she leaned toward me. One of the Tradd stepped forward and shoved the muzzle of his rifle into her face, forcing her back. She leaned back, but her triumph never left her face. She'd won, and she knew it. Nothing else mattered.

Someone turned me over, and cool hands brushed against my forehead. Seeker spoke, and I heard her in my mind as much as through my ears. "Liam, let me in. I can help you. I'm the hacker, remember?"

I 'felt' her reaching for me through the link between her Tabran device and my own. I accepted the connection, and instantly the pressure of Zornaav's intrusion was lessened, at least a little.

Soon others joined, and I could feel them through the link between our devices. Injala was there, and Seeker, and even Hitchens, his mind fierce and bright even as his body was fighting to survive.

The four of us were linked in ways I'd never experienced before, forming our own gestalt. Communication was swift and wordless, intent immediately and perfectly understood by all of us. Hitchens and I pushed back against the One, holding her data probes away through the digital equivalent of brute force, forming a shield of bright blue energy between us.

While we did that, Injala explored the connections between the One and the rest of the Empire. Seeker, using what Injala found, built us a firewall, coding it from sheer instinct and skill to keep the One from finding help in the other Zhen:ko.

Even as the firewall took form, we all knew it wouldn't last long enough. We were doomed; four of us against all the Zhen:ko in Zornaav's web, all fighting with her will, and with the help of a symbiotic living computer hundreds, if not thousands, of years ahead of our understanding.

The oppressive force that was the One loomed over us in the impromptu virtuality in which we found ourselves. She looked like a younger, more vibrant version of herself, but larger than any Zhen I'd ever seen. Her claws glowed an angry red color, the malevolent glow flashing with sparks as she raked her claws across our shield again and again. The Tabran part of her, appearing as tendrils of silver light, reached from her back and slammed against the firewall, looking for a weakness to exploit to get through it and back to the rest of the Web.

Seeker frantically rebuilt the firewall even as the Tabran broke into it, but it was a losing battle and we all knew it. Hitchens and I rebuilt our shield, which was going to last even less time.

"We can't remove the nanites," Injala said. The computers linking us allowed us to speak more or less at leisure, nanoseconds stretching into minutes in our perception, but the hard deadline of how long we could last against the One was fast approaching.

"No shit," I snapped.

"But we can end this."

"Not really looking to die right now, Injala."

"Of course not. We can end *her*."

"I don't understand."

"All it takes is a virus," she said. "The devices the Tabrans gave us have the tech we need. We only have to get it into the One's tech. If we can do that, it will distribute itself across her web, infecting every single Zhen:ko system she is connected to. It will destroy all the nanites."

"What would it do the Zhen:ko hosts?"

"I don't know," she said.

"I do," Seeker said. "I looked at the code on the way here. These things were designed in a time of war, when the original Tabrans were fighting for survival of their species. Anyone who'd been taken over by the nanites was considered dead already. 'Our' Tabrans didn't have time to refine it. They just made the tech smaller. It'll destroy the nanites, all right, but in a pretty explosive way. Some of them might live, but most of the adult Zhen:ko, the ones with all those extra implants in them? They'll be killed."

"Shit."

"Yeah."

"I do not understand your hesitance," Injala said. "They're your enemy, why do you care?"

"Zornaav is the enemy," I said. "The rest of them are victims."

"That may be, but right now it is the Zhen:ko or all of the Empire descends into war, and my people too."

"I don't know that I have the right to condemn an entire people," I said.

"Of course you don't," Injala said. "But I'm not sure you have a choice."

Seeker gestured, and lights spun from her palm, taking form as a gun, just like the pistol I carried in the real world. She offered it to me. "This will set the virus in motion," she said. "All you do is shoot her."

"Easy enough," I said.

But of course it wasn't. Injala was right; I didn't have the right to condemn the Zhen:ko, but I also didn't have a choice. "On my mark, drop the shield," I said.

"Ready," Hitchens said.

"Now!" I called, and the shield vanished. Even as it did, my finger tightened on the trigger, sending a huge pulse of bright white fire into the form of the One.

At first she didn't even seem to notice the shot. She swung her claws, and I dove out of the way, barely managing to avoid the metaphorical hit that would have probably fried my brain, had she connected.

A moment later, and she looked down at herself, confused. "What is this?" she asked. A second later, a scream tore from her throat. When it ended, she rounded on me. "No! I will not die here!" She reached for me, and dammit, I didn't move fast enough.

Her claws grabbed on to my head, and liquid fire raced through my veins. I felt her, invading my NeuroNet, sliding along my neural pathways, her rage and hate seeking to build a home in me before her body gave out.

I tried to stop her, but I was a leaf in the hurricane of her power and hatred. I could feel Seeker and the others trying to get through the storm to my side, but she batted them aside with a thought, knocking them right out of the shared virtuality. She raced against time, ordering my nanites to build a home for her in my body.

I wrenched my consciousness back from the virtuality, reaching for my gun in the holster at my side, but it wasn't there. So I did the only thing I could, and reached for the only weapon I had left.

I reached for my husband.

CHAPTER TWENTY-EIGHT

Tajen

We'd taken out the drone control nodes, but the ship itself was still a problem. "I'm concerned," I said, bringing the ship around and heading for the Kinj.

Kiri's eyes flashed over her displays, looking for the problem. "What?"

"I think you might have inherited my stupid love of danger."

"Oh. That. Yeah, no shit."

I dodged a piece of debris flying off a Zhen ship and shook my head. "Got us a plan yet?" Midnight continued firing at drones as we passed them, but since they were dead in space, it was more preventative – in case the Kinj had repair drones – than it was useful in the moment.

"I thought you were the planner."

"Right now I'm the guy flying the ship. Midnight's firing the weapons. That leaves you making the plans."

Her eyes wide, she gestured at her board. "I'm keeping the ship in one piece!" she said.

"And making battle plans. Find me a weakness on that ship we can use to take it out."

"I'm scanning," she said, with an air that told me she'd been doing it all along. "This'll be fun. I think I might have something, but I need a closer scan here." She flicked a location on the ship to me.

I glanced at it and cursed. "That's not going to be easy."

"Nobody ever promised it would easy," she said. "Just fun."

"We need to have a talk later about your idea of fun," I said. On the comms, I said, "Flight, I'm sending a probe for a closer look. Cover me."

"Roger that."

"Midnight, you have flight control."

I launched a probe from the ship's drone bay and took control of it, sending it flying toward the Kinj ship. I kept one eye on the readouts the probe was giving us of the ship's structure and energy output.

"Are you sure we can get through those shields?" I asked.

"Yes," Midnight said. "My scans indicate the shields are calibrated to stop plasma weapons and fast-moving missiles, but will allow us through if we are going slow enough."

"How slow is that?" The answer flashed into my visual field. I quickly pulsed the retro thrusters on the probe, matching its speed to the target, and passed through the shield.

As the probe passed through, I realized the Kinj ship wasn't quite as solid as it looked from outside. There were empty spaces within the superstructure, places I could fly Midnight into – with a little care.

Well, maybe a lot of care, I realized as I entered one of those spaces. The ship had turrets inside, as well. They picked up the probe and began firing, but the small size of the probe, its speed, and the electronic countermeasures it carried to prevent weapons lock all did the trick, and we got through the area without getting hit.

As the probe closed on Kiri's target, she focused the scans on it. "How long do you need?" I asked her.

"About a minute."

I shook my head. "A minute is a long time out here, Kiri. I'll do my best." As the probe scanned the structure ahead, I moved the probe around to Kiri's specifications, ensuring we got a full scan.

The space we were in was more open than those we'd come through, a sort of 'eye in the storm' of the Kinj vessel. It was a large half sphere mounted to the underside of the ship. The curved surface was a hive of openings, through which could be seen some kind of energy flowing along an intricate series of conduits. "What the hell is that for?"

"It appears to be an energy regulation structure for the ship's reactor,"

Midnight said. "The energy you see is similar to high-energy plasma, and is in a highly excited state."

"No turrets in here," I said.

"No, they'd be too dangerous," Kiri said. "If a stray shot hit that structure, the whole thing would go up."

"There's our plan," I said. "Mark the target."

"How do we get our ships through the turrets?"

I thought for a moment. "Let's try something else first." I moved the probe as far away from the structure as I could, then sent it at full thrust toward the inverted dome of the power regulator. I aimed directly for one of the openings, slamming the probe through it and into the structure.

Nothing happened except that the probe fried the moment it hit the plasma, doing no damage at all.

"It was too small," Kiri said. "Probably got destroyed by the heat before it got close enough. It's like a small sun in there."

"Will our firepower do any better against that?"

"It should," Kiri said. "Especially if we combine missile strikes with energy weapons."

"Confirmed," Midnight added.

"All right," I said. "But we need to clear the way first. We'll send in the smallest ships to clear the turrets, then bring in some of the bombers to take out the regulator. Midnight, draft an order of battle."

"Done. Give me TacComm."

"You're on."

"All fighters," I said. "We're sending you new orders. First wave, we go in ten seconds. Capital ships, give us cover." I cut the feed, and said to Midnight, "Send the orders."

"Done."

Five seconds later, Kiri said, "All ships acknowledged. First wave reports ready."

"All ships…go!"

As one, we accelerated toward the Kinj, coming in from various vectors to make it harder for the Kinj to fire on us. The larger ships, mostly Zhen vessels, fired on the Kinj to give us cover, keeping its attention fixed on them.

As we began to close on the Kinj, the Tabran vessel appeared in the system, with the Marauders tucked under it. Almost immediately, the Marauder ships scattered, and I saw some of them headed for the Zhen.

I quickly got on the comms. "Katherine, tell your people – the Zhen are not our enemy anymore. Attack the alien ship with everything you've got!"

Her face appeared in my view. "Tajen, confirm your last message. Code Takeshi."

"Confirmed, Katherine. Liam's still dealing with Zornaav, but the Zhen in orbit are on our side. That alien ship is the true threat. Code Baker."

"Code accepted," she said with a wry expression. "We'll play it your way, but I'm going to insist on a full explanation later."

"You'll have it. For now, hammer that ship." I cut the feed and rolled the ship to avoid an incoming plasma blast. "I think we might have pissed it off," I said.

"I'm getting that feeling," Kiri said.

As we entered the killing field within the Kinj's superstructure, the fighters in my wing scattered, each picking a target and taking it out. We were all good enough that we could avoid getting in each other's way, but the unpredictability of the turret fire was a bit of a problem. Even as I slewed my ship around a turret, pouring fire at it, another's fire raked across my shields, shaking my ship and making my own maneuvers harder.

I gritted my teeth and kept going, eventually reaching the 'eye' around the ship's energy regulator. I began to turn the ship, headed back to the turrets for another pass, when I felt something brushing against my mind via my NeuroNet. "Liam?" I said.

Kiri's eyes snapped toward me. "Tajen, what's wrong?"

"I…I feel Liam reaching for me."

"Is he okay?"

"I don't...I don't think so. I need to help him. So we need to get this done."

We made another pass at the remaining turrets on the way out, more ships joining me. "Bombers, GO!" I shouted into the comms, making Kiri wince beside me. "Sorry," I muttered.

The bombers began their run. Even though there were no turrets to fire on them, I and the rest of my wing followed them in.

"Incoming Kinj drones," Kiri said. "They must have repaired a node."

The drones made straight for the bombers. I angled in, accelerating and locking on to the drones. Midnight fired, most shots hitting their marks.

The bombers largely ignored the drones, leaving them to the fighters, and went straight for the kill. As they all fired, they immediately moved to exit. One of the bombers misjudged his maneuver and slammed into the larger ship's structure, causing the bomber to lose integrity; the reactor went up as a miniature sun before the reaction petered out seconds later. I grimaced at the loss of life, but there was nothing we could do.

I led the ships out from the Kinj structure at a frankly ludicrous speed, given the space. Kiri shouted warnings and pointed to hull structures she thought we'd hit, and I did my best to ignore her and concentrate on flying. I didn't even spare the amount of attention it would have taken to stop her; I didn't have that kind of time. Besides, this whole time, Liam's request for connection hadn't stopped, and I was desperate to get us clear so I could answer it.

About halfway from the regulator to the exit from the Kinj ship's innards, there was a bright flash of light behind us. "Midnight, what was that?"

"The energy regulator has blown up," Midnight reported, and I could tell she was broadcasting her reply to all our ships. "A chain reaction is now building in the Kinj vessel. Recommended minimum safe distance is one thousand five hundred kilometers. More would be advised."

I increased speed even more, as the space was more open now, and the ships around me did the same. We cleared the Kinj ship and burned at full throttle for the safe line.

WE WILL BE AVENGED, said the Kinj voices. WE ARE NOT—

The Kinj vessel exploded as the sun in its center blew. The gigantic vessel was erased from the universe in a bright flash of pure white light and heat. Midnight's radiation warning flashed, and I glanced at the indicator in alarm, but relaxed when I saw the radiation was being handled by our shields. Others weren't so lucky, and many would end up in hospital undergoing radiation treatment – but that wasn't a problem for this moment.

"Kiri, you're in charge," I said. "Liam needs me."

"What?" She looked panicked. "I'm an engineer, not—"

"Don't do that," I said. "Midnight's an AI. She's more than capable of flying the ship, but you need to take command of the Alliance pilots. You can do this."

"But—"

I stopped listening to her and accepted the connection from Liam.

And suddenly I was in a world of pain.

I found myself in a virtuality, standing in a blasted land of gray. Ahead of me, Liam knelt, screaming, as a huge Zhen towered over him, tentacles of some kind of energy pulsing from the Zhen's body into his.

Other tendrils ran from Liam to somewhere else, somewhere I couldn't see right now, the forms vague and hazy, as if something were hiding them from my view.

I ran forward, dropping to my knees and throwing my arms around my husband, his back against my chest, my arms wrapping around him. Even in this ad hoc virtuality, his presence felt utterly real. "I'm here," I said into his ear. "I'm with you."

His hand found mine, and as we clasped hands, he opened to me completely, connecting our NeuroNets.

"What took you so long?" he asked.

"Sorry," I said. "I had to blow up an alien ship before it killed us all."

"So, typical day," he said, ever the jokester. "Time for part two." He gave me full access to his NeuroNet, on a level we'd never tried before, and I saw immediately what the One was doing – cut off from the rest of her web, she was trying to create a new home within Liam's neural system, directing his nanites to build the data structures she needed within his body, making him an extension of her existing web.

Like hell.

I'm not a hacker, but I didn't need to be. Now that Liam had given me full access to his systems, I saw everything that had transpired before I joined the link.

Most of the advantages I'd given myself by hacking my own NeuroNet, back at the beginning of the war, were gone, made obsolete by updates the Zhen had made to their own systems. But I still had a frankly ridiculously high-level access. I didn't use it often, because honestly I barely know what I'm doing when it comes to virtuality technology, but I knew enough for what I wanted to do now.

I reached for Seeker, reestablished the link and brought her back into the virtuality, where she wasted no time, but began to help Liam fight the nanites on the program level.

Liam hadn't brought me in to help in that fight. He didn't need me to hack, but to help him withstand what Zornaav was doing, to give him the strength and stability to keep him in one piece while he and Seeker fought the battle. Because he was losing, fading into the background of his own mind as Zornaav poured more of herself and her Tabran symbiote into his NeuroNet. Without help, she'd overwhelm him and eventually replace him in his own mind.

There was no way I'd allow that.

To fight back against the pressure she was putting him under, I sent all that Liam and I had been to each other into the link, reminding him what we were to each other. I reminded him of our first meeting, of how ridiculous he'd looked, upside down with his legs sticking out of an access hatch in my ship, of my indignation when I'd first seen a stranger messing with my ship's wiring, and then my indrawn breath when he'd pulled himself out of the hatch and I'd realized how attractive he was.

I showed him our stolen moments during our flight from Zhen:da, the arguments we'd gotten into during our search for Earth, and the revelation that he'd been interested in me too. I showed him our wedding, and our home on the shores of Loch Lomond, thousands of miles away from the desert city of Landing. I showed him our arguments when I'd tried to walk away from the fight against the Zhen Occupation, when I'd retreated into myself. I showed him the anger I'd felt at his trying to pull me back to it, but also the love I'd felt that he would keep trying even as I made him suffer for it. And then I showed him the chagrin I'd felt when I'd realized he'd been right all along, and the gratitude that he'd never given up on me.

Most of all, I showed him my need for him, and for the life we had yet to live.

I reached for Injala, who had been our friend since this mess began, and brought her into the link as well. And then Hitchens, our little project, the boy who had become a soldier and nearly died in service. Somehow the word must have gotten out, because soon others were joining, all linked through the Tabran anti-nanite devices to our little struggle.

Katherine suddenly stood beside Liam and me as she joined the link. She immediately dropped beside us and folded us into her arms. "Sorry I'm late," she said. "We had some trouble getting the system up." As one, Liam and I opened ourselves to her, the three of us now linked together in ways physical and spiritual, the three humans who had started this war, now become the three who would end it, universe willing.

And then I felt Rememberer of Unpleasant Truths in the link, his alien thought patterns reaching out still farther, linking hundreds of humans and Kelvaki, Tradd and Hun and Tchakk, Marauder and Earther and Zhen alike, into a gigantic web of minds standing in opposition to the One, with Liam, Katherine, and I as the focus through which this new web of light would do its will.

She stood firm, the Zhen/Tabran gestalt, and her voice raked across us like glass shards. "I will not be denied," she said. "I have stood for generations of your people, and I will be here long after you have gone to dust. Die, all of you. Die and make way for the future of the Empire."

The three of us didn't need to look at each other, but we did, and then, as one, we turned to her.

The three of us gathered the power of the web we felt, the desires and hopes for an end to terror and war and death, for freedom and for self-determination, for peace, that rang through the web the Tabrans had built. We gathered it all up and poured it into the One, the sheer power of billions of voices rising up to protest her actions, her desires, her rapacious nature.

And she shattered. The Tabran swarm within her was overwhelmed by the virus Liam had introduced, and her attacks on us were turned away by the billions of voices that were done with the Empire and its wars. The implants within her body, and within the Zhen:ko she'd suborned over her decades as an incarnate, detonated, all but wiping the Zhen:ko from the universe.

EPILOGUE

Tajen

I stepped out of our cabin and watched the Kelvaki shuttle land. When the doors opened, Dierka stepped out and stood in the sun while the security team fanned out to form a perimeter. His ears twitched in amusement, and he held a hand out to someone still in the shuttle.

As I joined them, Injala took the proffered hand and stepped out of the shuttle. I bowed to them both. "Ascendants," I said, "you are most welcome."

"Ah, *draka*, none of that *shrak*," Dierka said. "To the people of the mighty Kelvaki Assembly, I am the Ascendant, to be feted and admired, and maybe even feared. But to *you*, and to your kin, I am only Dierka." He leaned closer. "Though if I may give you some advice, you may perhaps be best served by continuing to use my wife's title."

"Nonsense," Injala said. She disentangled herself from her husband and took my arm. "It's been over a year since I last saw you," she said. "How are you and your family?"

"We're fine," I said. I led the two of them toward the cabin. "Everyone is healthy and happy."

"Where is your husband?" she asked.

"Liam's been held up in Landing," I said. "The Zhen ambassador wanted to discuss the best way to handle the security for the Liberation celebration tomorrow."

"Security is needed?"

"Well," I said, "it's only been five years since the Battle of Zhen:da. Things seem pretty settled, but since this is the first time the Zhen consul is coming to Earth, the ambassador wanted to be sure things were safe

– for everyone, he says, but of course he's probably most worried about the consul. Not everyone on Earth is ready to forgive the Occupation, yet."

"Why is the consul coming so soon?" Dierka asked.

"Jaata feels that we can't really heal from the war until the former Empire apologizes for the actions of Zornaav and the Zhen," I said. "I'm sure he's right, but I still wish he'd left more time. Both our republics are still new. It might have made sense to wait.

"The Zhen Republic," Dierka said. "It still takes getting used to. On Kelvak, we often find ourselves saying 'Empire' and then looking around to see if anyone noticed."

"We do the same around here," I said. We circled the cabin to the large deck Liam and I had built onto the back of the house. It was decorated with seating for at least thirty people, couches and chairs arranged to create discussion groups, but all of it easily moved. My husband and I had taken to having guests to the cabin so often that we'd built a guesthouse a few dozen yards away, but kept the deck as the central socializing space. We'd installed several forcefield generators to handle inclement weather, and we had other field generators that kept the tiny irritating insects that lived on the lake at bay. "You know," I said, gesturing to the guesthouse, "you're welcome to stay. We made sure the furniture can hold you."

Dierka laughed, that horrible sound, and I did my best not to wince at it. "No, my friend, my security officers would not hear of it. It was hard enough to get them to not send an entire platoon of soldiers down with me."

"Just the one squad in the shuttle, then?" I asked.

Injala's ears quivered with her amusement. "You noticed. My my, you are improving."

"It just occurred to me that in all the time we've spent together, I've never heard you laugh out loud."

"Unlike some," she said with a glance at her husband, "I am aware of how awful it sounds to humans."

I looked to Dierka, who pretended to have heard none of that.

Gesturing them toward seats, I poured some Kelvaki liquor for my guests and a whiskey for myself, and we sat to talk about the changes over the last five years.

Not all the Zhen:ko had been killed in the final strike against the One; she'd left a few of them out of her web for her own purposes, and of course the children had all survived. But while their tribe remained more or less viable, their political power had been broken. When the Talnera, the legislative body that had acted as elected advisers to the ruling council, had declared a Republic in place of the now-defunct Empire, it hadn't been a happy day for some, but most – after glimpsing the true madness of their leader through the Tabran web – had welcomed the change. The Talnera had wasted no time in pushing through some reforms they'd been itching for, but the rest had come much slower.

The Talnera was now the elected ruling body of the Republic, with one of their number elected to finite terms as the consul. They'd been very careful to build in term limits and ways to remove the consul if necessary.

The Tabrans had promised peace and signed a temporary treaty that would last for twenty years. They said they'd be sure to start negotiations on a new, more permanent treaty once they'd worked out a few internal issues, and we were scheduled to meet with them in ten years to begin those discussions.

The Kelvaki, of course, had signed a deal with Earth pretty much immediately upon the end of the war. Dierka had ascended to the throne a couple of years after that, when his uncle, the former Ascendant, had been unable to continue his duties.

We were interrupted by the arrival of Liam's shuttle. As he came through the house, I realized he had someone else with him, and I was delighted to find it was Katherine. I jumped up and gave my husband a hug, then folded Katherine into my arms for a long moment before pushing her back to get a good look at her.

"I see the frontier agrees with you!" I said.

"Well, I had to get out from under your shadow, and the edge of known space seemed like just barely far enough," she replied.

"Feh."

She flashed me a grin. ""Get me a drink?"

While I fixed her and Liam's drinks, she went to greet Dierka and Injala. Liam, who'd already greeted them, joined me at the bar. "I called Ben," he said. "He wanted me to tell you he'd love to come, but he's got a patient who just went into labor today, and he promised her he wouldn't leave until she gives birth. He'll join us tomorrow if he can."

Ben had done everything he could to continue providing medical care to both the Resistance and nonaligned citizens during the Occupation, and his steadfastness in treating everyone with the same standard of care – even Zhen, on occasion – had earned him a sterling reputation and a thriving practice.

"How did your meeting with the ambassador go?" I asked.

"Everything's fine," he said. "The Zhen just wanted to make sure we had the right security protocols set up. He was satisfied with what I showed him."

"Well of course he was. You're not in charge of EarthSec for nothing."

"Not anymore," he said.

I looked at him. "You mean...."

"Effective the day after tomorrow," he said.

I handed him his drink and gave him a long kiss. We clinked our glasses together, both of us smiling like idiots, and rejoined the others.

As I handed Katherine her glass, she said, "I'm pretty sure the Marauders will be changing their name soon. They're discussing a few options, but nothing's definite yet."

"Are they changing their operating mode too?"

"Already done," she said. "No more predation on Zhen ships – or Kelvaki or anybody else. They've been increasing mining and exploration aims. In fact, they're probably going to be changing a lot more soon. Now that the Hun homeworld is opened again, a lot of the Hun are thinking about returning. And there are a fair number of humans who are talking about migrating to Earth." She shrugged. "Some of them will stay, I'd bet, but nowhere near all of them. Living in space for so long changes you, and they may still be human, but their ways are not the same as ours anymore."

"As long as they stop preying on shipping, I don't see any real problems. Both Earth and Zhen:da would love to trade with them, I'm sure." I raised my glass to her. "So, is your mission there over?"

"Yep. I'm back on Earth now for the duration – at least, until Liam here finishes his term."

"My replacement is almost ready," Liam said. "Give him maybe a couple of near-catastrophic incidents to deal with." Almost immediately, he said, "I'm kidding!" Then he looked to Injala. "Unless you could arrange something? Not too bad, just a little damage?"

"I have something in mind," she said mildly.

"Wait. No. Don't do that."

She smiled, an affectation for her species. "All right," she said.

Liam turned wide eyes on me, communicating in the pseudo-telepathy we'd had since connecting our NeuroNets in the final battle. *Remind me not to play with her like that.*

I answered, *I'll do my best.*

"Hello," came a new voice, and we all turned to see Hitchens enter, his right arm long since regrown. With him came Seeker, and the way their hands were entwined made me happy. I looked to Liam with a smug grin.

"I see that," Seeker said. "Stop it."

Kiri arrived just after them, with Aleph, her hacker friend. I made sure everyone had a drink, then stood in front of them all. "My friends," I said, "I have an announcement.

"When Kiri and I met Katherine, Takeshi, Liam, and Ben back at the beginning, we knew we'd made friends, but we had no idea how far we'd all go in the years since. I'm proud to know all of you." I cleared my throat. "Which is why it's hard to say goodbye."

"What?" Kiri asked.

"A few months ago, I found some evidence in the archives of another colony ship," I said. "It went off in a different direction, almost diametrically opposite to the one the *Far Star* took. I'm going to go find it."

Liam and Katherine rose and stood beside me. "*We're* going to go find it," Liam said. "We've prepped a ship. We're leaving within the next month."

"Holy shit," Kiri said.

"I wanted to tell you," I said. "But I wasn't sure we were going to do it so soon – I had to wait until Liam was ready to resign."

Liam added, "Which I did, today, effective the day after tomorrow. From then on, Earth is in the hands of my former assistant and new head of security for the Solarian Republic, Ryan Hitchens." He gestured grandly toward Hitchens.

The young man turned almost as red as his hair. "Thank you, sir. I won't let you down."

"See that you don't," Liam said. "I expect there to still be a planet here when we get back."

Hitchens looked way too serious for it to be natural. "I'll do my best, sir."

We talked for the rest of the night, about Earth, and Zhen:da, and the changes to both. And we talked about the changes yet to come, as Earth and the others all walked together into this new galaxy we'd all created.

Kiri found me later. "I'll miss you," she said. "Wish I was coming with you."

"No, you don't," I said. "You're building a life here, and it's a good one."

"Yes, but I'm still sad to say goodbye."

"Hey," I said. "This isn't forever. Whether we find them or not, we'll be back. Do me a favor and keep this cabin going – I want a home to retire to when I'm ready."

"I will," she said. "I love it too much to stay away from it anyway."

When everyone but Katherine and Liam had left for the night, we three remained on the deck, looking out over the lake behind the house and watching the stars.

I leaned back and gazed upward. Somewhere in orbit, the final touches were being put on our ship. When it was ready, the three of us would head off into the black, leaving behind the familiar structures of known space, and seek out our lost brothers and sisters while expanding Earth's knowledge and reach.

As if reading my thoughts, Katherine said, "What do you think we'll find out there?"

"Maybe adventure," I said. "Excitement."

"Are we sure we want that?" Liam asked. "I mean, this place is nice. After the last few years, maybe a nice, boring retirement is a good idea."

We all looked at each other. I met both their eyes, and drawled, "Naaaah."

We all began to laugh, and we didn't stop all night.

AFTERWORD

As usual, there are people to thank.

My editor, Don D'Auria, helped make this book much better than the draft, and the team at Flame Tree Press have done an amazing job turning it into a physical object.

My wife, Elli, kept me sane during the writing of this book, and my daughter, Tegan, kept me alternately laughing and tearing my hair out, as teenagers do. My VP17 classmates, especially Beth Tanner, M.E. Garber, K.A. Anderson, E.D. Walker, John Wiswell, and Laurence Raphael Brothers, all contributed cheerleading and feedback, as did my meatspace friends Terry Meyer, Miles Cochran, Jim St. Claire, and many more I'm probably forgetting.

Ryan Hitchens' exploits in the climax are a slightly exaggerated retelling of an incident that happened to the late Senator Daniel Inouye, way back in WW2. I recommend you look it up if you want a real-world example of a complete badass in a time without nanite-based medicine and plasma weapons.

Wow. My first trilogy is done. It's kind of bittersweet, saying goodbye to Tajen, Liam, and the gang. But you noticed, I'm sure, that I left myself an option to return to them someday, if the need and desire are great. But there are more characters, and more worlds, coming from me.

I can't wait until you see them.